Necromancer

Graeme Ing

Necromancer

First Edition 2014

Cover by Erin at EDHGraphics
Interior art by Bradley Cavin

Edited by Lynnette and Michael at "Labelle's Writing on the
Wall - Editorial Services"

ISBN-13:   978-1500585723
ISBN-10:   1500585726

For my darling wife,
and her fascination for all things dead.

 ONE

The stench of undead in the street was palpable. A persistent breeze off the harbor carried the vile odor to where Hallum and I lurked in the shadows.

"I think they're that way, Maldren." He pointed to a narrow street that curved down toward the harbor.

Dogs barked in the distance and somewhere a man and woman argued, but otherwise the city lay silent and menacing. Vandals had decapitated the nearest street lantern, and the pale light from Lunas barely penetrated the chasmlike street, flanked on both sides by tall tenements.

There was one way to find the creatures. I drew a strand of magic from deep within me and shaped it into *Perception*, and then I pushed out the invisible field of magic in a cone ahead of us.

My mind twitched as I sensed my surroundings, much like a spider detects prey by the tugs on its web. Tiny sparks of energy rippled through my mind, some to the left, others to the right—simply the odd ghost sneaking through the buildings. A couple hundred feet down the street I sensed several larger distortions, like clods of dirt squatting in my mental web.

Tomb wights. At last, we'd found them.

I couldn't stop myself grinning as I squinted into the night.

"You sense them too?" I whispered.

A crease deformed Hallum's high brow. "Three, maybe more. We should return to the Guild and bring reinforcements."

"You're kidding. We can handle them."

He had ten solars' seniority on me, and at twenty-five, I was overdue making Master rank. He was being overcautious as always.

"Scared?" I said.

He snorted. "No, just wise. Those things will tear us apart, I'm telling you."

He raked his unkempt beard with his long fingernails.

"It's what we're here for. Let's go." I started down the street, but he pulled me back and took the lead.

"I don't like you, Maldren. You take unnecessary risks. We'll do this my way. Stay behind me."

Lak and all his demons! He always had to take charge. I had to get another partner. Meanwhile, I'd play nice.

I sighed. "Lead the way then."

We crept along the street, keeping close to the buildings on one side as we watched our feet on the uneven cobbles. Most of the tenement windows were dark, but a diffuse orange glow seeped around the drapes in some of them. High above, an open window clattered against its frame in the wind.

"I've never heard of tomb wights venturing up to street level," I said. "I want to know why."

"Who cares? We get rid of them before they cause a panic, then get back to our beds."

That was the problem with the Guild today. No sense of pride or curiosity. Just do the minimum amount of work. Hallum sounded like the damn Guildmaster. There was a mystery here and I intended to solve it.

Halfway through the bend in the street, we spotted two sinister shapes shuffling in the gloom ahead.

Hallum dived into a dark doorway, and I stepped after him. We peered out. The run-down tenements leaned precariously into the street as if seeking the comfort of their neighbors opposite, or if they too were straining to catch a glimpse of the hideous creatures.

Their resemblance to humans was vague. Shriveled skin and tattered muscle hung loosely from their heavy frames, revealing the line of every bone, many of which had been twisted and snapped. The bones had mended at awkward angles, fused together by gnarly knots of calcification. Bone spurs pierced their paper-thin flesh. Ragged hair covered their naked bodies except their baldpates, which they raised high into the air. Their constant sniffing and labored panting reminded me of dogs on a scent.

"Why are we hiding in this doorway?" I asked.

"I'm studying them. Once they're distracted we'll attack."

It looked to me like we already had the advantage. Once they caught our scent, all bets were off. We should act now. I stepped into the street.

The sniffing stopped, replaced by a gut-wrenching growl, and then the wights shuffled closer. My heart thumped. A gust of wind carried their stench, and I recoiled. It smelled like a corpse smothered in rotten cabbage and vomit left to fester in the heat of the day.

Hallum came up beside me, raised one arm, and threw a ball of blue fire that impacted one of them, searing through its chest. Molten flesh and sparks dribbled from the exit wound in its back onto the cobbles. It uttered a guttural roar, and then both of the creatures launched into a pounce, hurtling toward us on all fours like apes. Hallum edged backward.

Well, what had he expected?

"Not *Shadowfire*," I yelled. "Use *Deathwall*."

I resisted the urge to fall back with him, tensed, and sucked energy from my gut. Magical fire surged through my veins. Fists clenched, I let loose a blast of shimmering particles. The magic splashed over both wights, and they flared purple before crashing motionless to the cobbles on their backs, their bones cracking. After pulling my knife from its sheath, I set upon the one at my feet and severed its foul head. I kicked it across the cobbles, enjoying the hollow, thumping noise it made before coming to rest against a wall. A dog howled from an adjacent street.

"Get the other one," I said, and Hallum mirrored my actions.

Two more wights rounded the corner at the intersection ahead. We had this. No problem. Like most undead, they didn't see well, but they had good noses. Pity they didn't realize how bad their own body odor was.

A door opened in the building ahead on our left and light spilled out onto the cobbles, silhouetting a brute of a man. He stepped out, hefting an ax. All his weight seemed to be in his chest and shoulders.

"What's all the ruckus going on out 'ere?" he cried.

The wights angled toward him with low growls.

"Go back inside," I said.

"Necromancers!" He spat in my direction. "What foul mischief are you up to?"

How rude. But I got that reaction a lot. People should have been more grateful when I was saving their behinds.

"Watch out," Hallum yelled.

One of the creatures bounded onto the angled roof of a dormer window that overhung the street. Aged tiles slid and crashed to the ground. It sprang again, pushed off the wall, and landed beside the man. Talonlike fingernails flashed in the lantern light, and the wight raked the man's forearm, shredding it. The man's shriek echoed from building to building down the street and into the sleeping metropolis. Blood pulsed from the open wounds, cascading off the man's useless fingers and onto the ground. The wight yanked the man's arm, ripping it free at the elbow. I cringed at the sound of tearing muscles and popping cartilage. Blood gushed from the stump, drenching everything. The creature lurched back a step and gnawed on the lifeless arm.

Oh, that's nasty. Behind me, Hallum retched onto the cobbles. Really? And he considered himself my boss?

The burly man in the doorway had guts, I'd give him that.

He whirled and sliced his ax into the creature's torso. The blade crunched into ribs and stuck. He let go and stumbled back through his open door, crumpling to the floor at the foot of a woman, who took up where his scream had finished.

Other doors opened and neighbors stepped out, holding aloft lanterns and assorted weapons.

This was turning into a debacle, and the Guildmaster hated a mess.

"Everybody, back inside," I shouted. "Bolt your doors. Stay there until morning."

While a dozen or more stood about in their nightclothes, discussing events noisily, a group of four men ignored my advice and advanced upon the fourth tomb wight.

"They're tougher than you think," I said. "Let the professionals handle it."

Well, one of us was, anyway. I looked back at Hallum, wiping drool from his mouth with the sleeve of his Guild robe. I shook my head. No matter. I knew exactly what to do. I only had to survive this to have a good case for promotion to Master.

I closed the gap with the injured tomb wight. With the ax still buried in its chest, it continued chomping on the severed arm. *Gross.* I held out my fist, thumb uppermost, and dispatched a bolt of blinding blue light at its ugly face. The crackling energy forked at the last moment and stabbed deep into both its eye sockets, burrowing into its head space. You can't kill undead that way, but it sure upsets them. Its knees gave way and it crashed to the ground. I stomped on its chest and hacked its head off.

I paused to wipe the sweat from my brow and catch my breath. This was fun. What had Hallum been worried about? I jogged to catch up with the foolhardy mob.

Sure enough, two of them lay in bloody pools when I arrived, one of them little more than a child. I clenched a fist. Damn the men. I had warned them. A lanky, gray-haired man stood abreast the wight that they had managed to bring down. The old man had some good moves as he pounded and stabbed it repeatedly, dodging its thrashing claws. It growled and snapped its jaws repeatedly. The other neighbor was clearly trained militia. His sword was coated with the gray ichor of wight blood as he hacked at its head. It took several attempts before the creature fell still. Dead for the second time.

The man pointed his sword at my belly, its blade unwavering.

"Take your perverted experiments elsewhere. We don't want your kind here."

So now it was all my fault? My shoulders drooped. People thought so little of my Guild. I wanted to explain that I was on their side, but there was no sense in arguing, so I rejoined Hallum.

"We should go before they mob us," he whispered, eyeing the gathering crowds.

"We can't leave those creatures lying in the street."

"We go. That's an order."

I scowled at him. He was wrong. A core Guild duty was to protect citizens from the undead among them. I didn't want children discovering such disgusting corpses in the stark light of day.

Neighbors continued to flood into the street, giving the wight corpses a wide berth. The crowd talked in hushed voices and glanced frequently in our direction.

Hallum might have been right about the mob, but we had to get rid of the creatures, and I still wanted to find out why they'd come up out of the undercity.

I pulled at the neck of my robe and shirt. Sweat beaded on my arms. The night had become unseasonably warm.

Someone cried out, and I turned to see the gray-haired man limping away from a sewer grate. Steam rose from between the bars of every grate along the street, like a line of geysers a hundred feet apart. What in Belaya's name was going on?

I hurried to the nearest one, raising my hands to shield my face against the searing heat rising from below. Vapor shrouded my vision, and even shaking my robe failed to clear the air. The stench of excrement made me gag, and the incessant bubbling of boiling water was loud and obvious. The sewers never got so hot, not even in the balmiest summer.

People shrieked and hopped about on bare feet like lizards on hot dirt. The melting soles of my boots stuck to the stone cobbles and made a slurping noise as I edged away from the grate.

Ten gold Malks said fear of the heat had driven the wights above ground, so what else was at work here? My *Perception* was tingling like crazy, so I projected it wide, up and down the street. Something immense tore at it, fragmenting it, tossing my magic aside like a child's toy. What could do such a thing? A frightening source of power rippled toward me. Kristach, it was using my own spell to find me. I stumbled under its might and canceled my spell. My pulse raced and I peered into every shadow.

Without warning, a building exploded into a fireball, lighting up the night. Bricks showered the street, followed by a rolling cloud of dust, from which hundreds of wooden fragments erupted and bounced onto the cobbles and surrounding buildings. Sheared timbers as thick as my torso flew about like kindling.

I dropped prone and one of them flew end over end inches from my face. It careened through a window, raining shards of glass onto the street. A cacophony of screams, rending wood, and bouncing debris assaulted my ears. *Lak and all his demons!* I flattened myself against the ground. My hands and cheeks singed against the hot cobbles. I squirmed and tried to shake the prickling pain from my fingers.

Flames soared a hundred feet into the air. They tore through the now-derelict building and flowed across adjacent rooftops like liquid, igniting them. The crowd scattered, diving for cover or fleeing into their homes. I squinted into the inferno and my eyebrows smoldered. The garish red and orange glow pulsed menacingly against the dark night, hiding the stars.

Is this how I'll die, cowering in a gutter?

The clamor of distant bells announced that the fire carts had been alerted. They might be too little, too late. Smoke billowed along the narrow street. I studied it. Though a light breeze blew the sewer steam in one direction, the smoke moved against it, curling and swirling. It wrapped itself into tight threads that wriggled and writhed like the tentacles of a mammoth sea monster.

"There's something...primordial out there," I said.

Hallum crawled up beside me and shot me a quizzical look.

"You think the wights caused that explosion?" he yelled above the roar of another building erupting into flame. "More likely we've stumbled upon an illegal alchemy stash. Everfire or lightsticks. Either way, this isn't a Guild matter. Let's get out of here."

"Not yet." I coughed against the acrid smoke. "There's more to this. Help me with *Dispel*."

I drew on the raw energy in my core, but what was I aiming at? I zapped a beam of searing white toward the burning buildings. Vortices of smoke twirled around the beam. Hallum's spell followed a second later. Our joint spells bounced back at us like a tidal wave rolling ashore. The force threw us both head over heels. My brain was on fire.

"See?" I screamed at him.

"See what? Double *Dispel* did nothing. For Belaya's sake, let's get out of here before the whole street explodes. We'll alert the Black and Reds and they can take over."

I shook my head. "We've got to find out what's behind this. Don't you sense that...immense feeling of malevolence somewhere within the fire?"

He grabbed my sleeve and tugged me away. "The wights are dead. The fire will dispose of them. We're leaving."

He was wrong. Something new, something sinister, hid beneath the flames and smoke. Never had I felt such power. Hallum was missing all the signs.

The air was no longer full of flying debris, so I leaped up and sprinted into the center of the street, away from the roof tiles crashing around us. Rivers of sweat stung my eyes. I held my sleeve across my nose and mouth. Thick smoke reduced my vision, yet cries and screams echoed between the close, overhanging buildings. I caught glimpses of people stumbling in all directions, ghostlike in the smoke. Three men stood coughing and choking. A rope of inky smoke slithered among them and coiled tightly about their bodies like a snake. There was nothing natural about its movement.

Instinctively, I reached for my magic, but doing so sent waves of pain through my body, thumping inside my skull. Having my own *Dispel* thrown back at me had hurt. A lot.

The men jerked and spasmed, tearing frantically at the insubstantial noose around their necks. I locked gaze with a weasel-looking man with matted hair. Madness burned in his eyes. He sucked in a deep breath and smoke leaped into his mouth. He uttered a low snarl and plunged a knife into the heart of the man next to him. His victim, a skinny, older man, crumpled to the ground, laughing maniacally as the blood gushed out of him.

Despite the heat, my body turned chill and goose bumps rose on my arms. I teetered backward.

A bulbous-nosed man with ridiculously large ears stumbled into the man with the knife. He clenched and relaxed his fists repeatedly. Big Ears roared and lunged at Weasel Man and they wrestled for the knife. They pushed and punched. Big Ears feigned a stumble and instead bit deep into his opponent's arm. Weasel Man howled. The knife clattered to the ground and they continued to pound each other with fists.

"Hallum," I croaked. "Get over here, now."

The world had gone insane. I spun around, fearing every shape in the smoke. One of them loomed before me. I drew my own knife and stared at it, astounded that it didn't shake. I tensed to stab my imminent attacker, but it was Hallum who stepped out of the smoke. Blood soaked his Guild robe and speckled his face. His chest heaved with every breath and his eyes were skittish. Had the smoke gotten to him too?

"Is that your blood or someone else's?" I raised my blade and backed away.

I toppled over a body, finding myself sprawled next to the prone, weasel-faced man. He twitched, uttered a half laugh, half choking noise, and white froth dribbled down his chin. His hands gripped a knife protruding from his belly. Blood bubbled up and soaked his shirt. *Oh Gods!* He wasn't trying to remove it. He was pushing it deeper, twisting it.

Hallum towered over me. "Give me your hand."

Blood dripped from his blade onto his fingers.

I shook my head and rolled aside. "Get away from me."

"Then die with these other fools." He vanished into the swirling smoke.

Let him run. I preferred working alone, anyway. I got to my feet but remained crouched, peering in every direction.

A gust of wind thinned the smoke. It brought clarity of vision, but not of sanity. Sweat poured off me. People ran from the spreading fire and down the street. Others stopped to help fallen family or to retrieve valuables from their homes. Many more lay dead or fighting. Like a puppeteer, inky tendrils of smoke maintained a grip on them.

I heard breaking glass and a woman's scream. She climbed out of a second-floor window onto a ledge and clung to the frame. Her nightgown and long, blonde hair billowed in the breeze. Fire raged on her roof, and a hand pawed at her from the darkness inside the room. A telltale wisp of smoke threaded its way through her open front door and up the stairs.

"My husband's gone mad. Please help."

So young. She wore the bronze ring of a newlywed. I hurried below her and held up my arms. The smoke probed insistently at my lips and nostrils. I shook my head against it.

"Jump."

She hesitated, whimpering. A hand snatched her leg. She kicked it away and scrambled further along the narrow ledge. The wooden casement began to tear from the wall.

"Now!"

She glanced at me then the ground below, but only clung tighter. A man appeared at the window, his teeth bared. Four scratches on his cheek oozed red. White drool speckled his trimmed beard. He clawed at her. She scrunched her eyes shut and wailed.

With a crack, the casement tore free, and she plummeted into my arms. We tumbled to the ground and the smoke surrounded us like a pack of wild animals.

I rolled to my feet, helped her up, and dragged her down the street, holding my breath as long as I could. She coughed and choked, resisting my pull. Murder flared in her eyes. I slapped her.

"Trust me. Hold your breath and stay with me." I yanked her forward.

I shouldn't have spoken. Smoke surged down my throat and I gagged.

Rage ignited inside me. I wanted to tear out her rabid eyes. My arm squeezed hers until she cried out, and I knew that I could break it with a twist, could snap her entire frail body. My gaze fixed on her pale, sweat-soaked throat. It invited me to choke the life from her, watch her struggle and finally go limp. My pulse quickened. Anger flooded my veins. Then my hands were around her throat, squeezing, crushing. She coughed and drooled thick, white saliva. Her blue eyes locked with mine but she put up no resistance. A smile twitched on her lips as my thumbs dug deeper. Ah, the sweet moment of superiority. How would it feel to kill? Delicious. It washed the tight pain from my head.

Something flickered deep within me. *This was wrong.*

I heaved and retched, blowing the noxious smoke from my throat, reaching and reaching until my lungs seared. Blessed clarity at last. Hastily, I molded a *Cleansing Shield* from my store of magic. It spread through my body, into hers and chilled the air around us. Our breath froze. The inky smoke fell as dust, and I sucked in the refreshing, frigid air. My hands fell away and the woman stumbled, coughing.

I was spent, with nothing to show for it but saving one solitary life. What else could I have done, damn it? I kicked a smoldering timber down the street. The smoke edged its way back toward us.

"Do as I tell you this time." I grabbed her wrist and half ran, half stumbled across the uneven cobbles, away from the raging inferno and heat, away from the madness. She didn't fight me.

We turned the corner into Lampwick Street, dodging two kalag-drawn fire carts and a torrent of Black and Reds and street workers. A growing swell of onlookers headed toward the fire. Damn the herd mentality. I had brought us halfway to Broad Street before the woman finally collapsed, panting and gasping.

"No more," she said. In the light of a street lantern, her gaze took in my robe. "You're a necromancer?"

I simply nodded while sucking in deep breaths.

She crawled away. "You've brought the curse of death to our homes."

She spat on my sweat- and smoke-stained robe, then leaped up and fled.

Thanks. *Thanks for saving my life, nice mister necromancer. Thanks for holding back the flood of undead threatening to take back the city.* You're welcome, lady.

 TWO

The next morning, I loitered in Maramir Plaza. Solas had risen over the harbor, washing the city in a harsh orange light. People glanced warily at the wisps of gray smoke spiraling into the cloudless sky. Fire was a constant worry in the cramped streets of Malkandrah. The late-season air remained chill, and I devoured my second, piping-hot sabata.

Maramir formed the largest open space east of the river. Here, Rat and Gold Canals intersected, chock-full of barges shipping slag from the mines, and Canal Street met Broad Street, the city's major artery.

The pungent aromas of spicy stew, cheeses, and street-weed masked the stagnant canal stench. Ranting orators clustered on the steps of the plaza's namesake, the statue of Maramir. He held a dramatic pose, warhammer raised aloft, and his stone face frozen mid battle cry. I chuckled. It tickled me that one of the city's most revered heroes stood speckled in bird shit.

The Guild lurked in the northeast corner of the plaza, an ostentatious, five-story building fronted by statues of Iathic demigods. Such a pompous institution. I was proud of my profession, just not the Guild that managed it.

Of dozens of guilds throughout the city, only two others were more populous—the Longshoremen and the

Mercantile—though mine was certainly the least liked. I watched the crowds give the Guild building a wide berth, many muttering prayers and averting their eyes as they passed. They treated me the same way. My shoulders drooped. I loved the city and its people. If only they would reciprocate. They wouldn't as long as the Guild operated by fear and awe.

I strode inside, and paused to allow my eyes to adjust to the dim interior, and my lungs to the musty air. Citizens crept through the hall, reluctantly seeking the Guild's advice. For all that they hated us they still wanted our help. They bumped into each other, craning their necks to peer at the spirit paintings adorning the ceiling.

At the rear of the cavernous hall, I marched into a shadowy passage shaped liked a fanged maw, and framed by a pair of rearing dracoliches. This place was one farcical thing after another, designed top to bottom to intimidate. Dust tickled my nose. I coughed, my throat still sore from last night.

The Prime Guildmaster kept me waiting in a stuffy, poorly lit antechamber. It reminded me of times I had spent on cold stone benches outside the masters' offices, awaiting my punishment for disrupting a class. The door to his study lay open a crack.

"Don't presume to lecture me, Imarian," the Guildmaster croaked from inside the room. "Three times the Council has rejected my *polite* requests for membership."

The Guildmaster hawked and coughed, making me cringe. He sounded like a wight. I had no idea whom this Imarian was.

"Give them time, Fortak," Imarian said. "They haven't forgiven the Guild for driving the Elik Magi away—"

"They can't hold me responsible for that. I allied with you so that you could bring reason."

Interesting. I leaned forward. The mysterious Magi had vanished a hundred solars ago.

"They remain confident that the Elik Magi will one day return," Imarian said. "I'm sorry, but you have only my vote and three others on the Council."

"I...the Guild is the only source of magic in the city now," the Guildmaster yelled. He coughed and wheezed. "Hold up your end of the bargain, Imarian. I must get on the Council before the Crown Prince's silly coronation. That's vital to our main plan."

I blew out my held breath. What were they up to? I'd always thought the Guildmaster was part of the High Council. I chuckled quietly. I didn't blame them for not wanting the old fool.

The door opened wide. I sat up straight. A tall, middle-aged man with an expensive-looking cane strode out. Emerald streaks in his immaculately combed hair marked him as aristocracy. He glanced at me as he would a servant, and hurried by without a word.

My thoughts raced. I could see the Prime Guildmaster needing a Duke for that boring political stuff, but clearly they were plotting something else. Did the other masters know? The coronation was, what, a sixday from now?

The Guildmaster exited his study. With a scowl, he swept down the hallway in the opposite direction. What was I, just part of the furniture?

"Hurry along, boy," he said.

I fell in behind him, breathing a heady mix of musk, rot, and stale wine in his wake. The silver runes on his robe writhed into one symbol after another.

"I have a busy morning. What is it you want?" He set an incredible pace for his advanced age.

"To report on last night's events," I said.

"Lord Prime."

"Pardon?"

"Address me as 'Lord Prime.'" He grunted a sigh. "Leave the report with my clerk."

"This is important enough that I tell you in person."

We emerged onto a balcony that circled the base of the dome, high above the Guild common area. He marched to the stone rail, turned, and looked at me for the first time. As apprentices we had speculated that he was several centuries old, and every time I saw his pasty, shriveled skin, I believed that. He had a commanding presence at six feet tall, but he had barely an inch over me. I resisted the urge to slouch against the rail and kept my back straight.

"Hallum already related the disaster." He dabbed at his weeping eyes with a crusty handkerchief.

"Then I'm glad you understand the portent of—"

"You were only supposed to dispatch a pair of rogue wights."

"There were four."

He blinked. "In any case, how did you end up burning down a city block? Hallum told me you refused to heed his advice."

That much had burned? I shuffled to my other foot.

"Something else was wrong. He didn't want to stay and find out—"

"Because he knows how to follow orders, something you've never mastered, have you, boy? You were supposed to destroy the wights, that is all." His sunken, bloodshot eyes bored into me.

I looked away. "We did, but some other entity was there. This was no common fire. Did he tell you he fled like a girl? I would never run."

I'd escorted the woman to safety.

"'My Lord Prime,'" he shouted. "You must refer to me as such."

A dozen conversations in the common area below us fell silent. The dome echoed his words as if teaching me a lesson. I glanced over the rail and curious faces looked up at me.

"I'm sorry." I wasn't. Goading him was far too much fun.

The Guildmaster coughed violently. It sounded like damp fever. I half expected his lungs to plop onto the floor. He made a final hawking sound and then stared at me, brow furrowed deep.

"You have such little respect for authority," he said in a normal voice. "You were an excellent apprentice, one of our finest, but I never understood why you stubbornly refused to do as you were told. The Guild has many fine traditions and protocols."

I glanced at my feet, feigning deference to hide the rolling of my eyes.

"How do you expect the citizens to respect us if we can't even complete a simple task? We mustn't appear weak. They must fear us, stand in awe of us. The more they cower from stories of creatures and restless spirits in the night, the more they need us and what our great tradition represents."

I met his gaze. A fine speech. I'd heard it before, but it shouldn't be about fear. Stodgy rules and procedures got in the way of us genuinely helping people, working alongside them. That's why they hated us.

"My Lord Prime." I knew better than to push my luck. "Please believe me. The cause of that fire wasn't alchemy as Hallum said. Something awful set that street alight, and I'm certain it was responsible for driving the wights aboveground too. I recommend we dispatch a team of Shadow Probers, and I volunteer. I want to find the source of that magic."

"No. You will not get involved." He sighed. "I have something else planned for you. You will learn that disobeying carries consequences."

I opened my mouth but he made a shushing sound. Then he leaned over the balustrade, pointed to someone in the crowd, and beckoned them with a skeletal-like finger. Master Begara hurried across the floor and passed beneath us.

I shuffled and chewed my lip. There was nothing I could say. It wasn't fair. No matter what I did, he'd never promote me to Master.

I looked out across the dome, reading the faded words of the Guild charter painted around its interior. While I waited, I reread the words opposite: *Bring no harm to the living.*

Footsteps echoed along the hallway, one heavy and one light, hurrying to keep up. I turned and peered into the darkness.

"You need to learn responsibility," the Guildmaster muttered. "So I'm going to give you some."

My head snapped back to meet his gaze. Was that the

beginning of a smirk on his thin, cracked lips?

Master Begara stepped into the flickering lantern light, accompanied by a girl. I blinked twice. She was a tiny chit, barely five feet tall, maybe fifteen solars old. Mousy hair draped over her shoulders and the raised collar of a pale blue shirt. Her skirt was clean, well made and reached fashionably to her ankles.

Begara dipped his head to the Guildmaster. "Good morning, Fortak."

The girl remained a pace behind Begara, and her large eyes flicked between him and me. I scratched my nose. She rubbed her own and looked at me, puzzled.

"Thank you," the Guildmaster said, and the man left.

I watched the girl's face when the Guildmaster turned into the light. Her gaze swept across his haggard features and her expression demonstrated some of that awe that the old man had been prattling on about. Where was this going?

"This is Ayla," he said. "Your new apprentice."

Something caught in my throat and I coughed. This was a cruel joke. There hadn't been a female in the Guild since my mother.

"Give her preliminary training before she starts with the other apprentices next semester."

Kristach. The gnarly old goat.

"I don't need an apprentice. Er...Lord Prime. Besides, I'm not prepared—"

"Really?" He smoothed his bushy eyebrows. "And I thought you were prepared for every situation. I thought you knew best. Knew better than your masters from what I'm told."

I opened my mouth, then snapped it shut, clenching my fists instead. I glared at the girl and she looked at me quizzically.

"Show me," he said. "Show me you have what it takes to be a master. Train your first apprentice."

"But she's a girl. She'll just get in the way, mess things up, faint and shriek. She's—"

"Your mother is turning in her crypt to hear you speak. You, of all people, cannot judge so." He slapped his hand on the balustrade. "Train her. This is not the foolish democracy of Kyria. My word is law."

He whirled about, whipping the girl and me with his robe, and then stormed off.

Lak and all his demons!

I blew out the breath I'd been holding, scowled at the girl again, and hurried into the gloomy passage. The morning had been a total disaster and I needed fresh air. I descended the back staircase three steps at a time.

"Wait," she called.

At the bottom, I increased my pace, huffing as I marched through the warren of back hallways until I emerged from the dracolich-guarded mouth into the public hall. People stared as I raced across the chamber. I stepped into the daylight and took a deep breath.

The glare of Solas forced me to squint. While I'd been wasting time in the gloomy innards of the Guild, the day had improved. The sky was the rich shade of evergreen trees, speckled with tiny clouds high in the atmosphere. Gulls and blackwings circled above Maramir Plaza, dive-bombing for scraps and then sweeping up to perch on the crest of ramshackle tenement buildings. None occupied the steep gables and dome of the Guild. Even the birds avoided us.

A twanging, clicking sound overhead heralded the approach of a sky carriage. Few people bothered to look up, but I stretched my neck to watch the egg-shaped gondola ride its cable down from the heights of Kand Hill, and then rumble away to the northwest.

"You can't lose me that easily," Ayla said from behind me.

Impressive, but I had no intention of babysitting a girl, even a clever one. I exited the plaza along Canal Street and headed toward one of my favorite lunch spots. I could ditch her there. Since my mother, no female had been approved for Guild membership. Why now? I rubbed my nose. The girl had shown no surprise upon hearing the Guildmaster's instructions, which meant she'd known before I had. I kicked a dead rat into the canal. So who was she?

"Why are you being so cruel? You don't even know me."

I whipped around to find her right on my heels.

"How old are you? Sixteen?"

"Eighteen." She stood straighter.

I scrutinized her but she didn't flinch.

"What in the name of the Gods are you doing hanging around the Guild?"

"I want to be a necromancer." The tip of her tongue poked from the corner of her mouth. It wasn't a childish gesture but an odd mannerism nonetheless.

"Right. Do you even know what one is?"

Her eyes narrowed. "I'm not a simpleton."

"It's dirty and dangerous. Can't you aspire to be something more normal, like...I don't know, like—"

"A whore?" Her thin eyebrows rose and she tried to stare me down. "You men are all the same. I want to be a necromancer. I can learn it just as well as any boy, as well as you. You're not much older than I am."

"I was going to say seamstress or midwife. Whore is your word, not mine. Calm down."

People were looking. I felt stupid arguing with a girl and I wished she'd stop using the n-word. I glared at her but she wouldn't back down.

"You've got guts," I said. "But you made a mistake. Your disguise has holes, my lady."

"What're you saying?"

I sighed. "Rich people don't join guilds. Isn't it beneath you? I've never heard of an aristo getting her hands dirty with the undead. But I get it. You're pretending to come from an Eastside slum, except you aren't pulling it off. For one, you're too haughty."

Her expression softened, but fire still burned in her eyes. "No, I'm not."

"Go back to your rich papa and momma and tell them all about your exciting jaunt across the river, where you got to mingle with the peasants. Impress your brothers and friends with your daring tale of visiting the Guild. Oh how they'll ooh and aah. It's all been a bit of fun. No harm done."

Her shoulders sagged. "How do you know I'm not from the slums?"

I tugged my right ear. She gasped and fingered the jeweled gold loop piercing her own smooth earlobe. I tapped my chest below my throat, and her fingers flew to the chain that hung around her neck, its pendant hidden beneath her shirt.

"And your hair is tinged with green," I added. "You didn't scrub it enough."

"Kristach."

I chuckled and turned away. "I'm going for lunch. Hurry home before dark. I'm sure a Black and Red can escort you, my lady."

"Stop calling me that. The Guildmaster said I was your apprentice. You can't abandon me. You have to do what he says."

I kept walking. Surely Fortak wasn't in on the charade, trying to trick me? Impossible. He'd never get involved in something so trivial, even for a big joke at my expense. Something wasn't right, but my stomach had taken control of my brain. I slipped into Petooli's, chasing the wafting aroma of roasted orjak and southern spices.

"I'm your apprentice," she said.

I glanced back. She struggled against the iron grip of the Uk bouncer. She took this far too seriously.

"Go home," I said.

I doubted she'd stand out in the street too long. I'd take a leisurely lunch alone and then head home for a nap.

I loved Malkandrah. It was the most magnificent metropolis ever built. Rainclouds had rolled in during my lunch but the downpour had graciously waited until I reached my apartment above an inn. I lived halfway up Kand Hill, close to the Artisan District. It was a hike from the Guild but I preferred the separation.

I climbed the steep, rickety staircase to my fourth-floor garret and settled into my favorite chair by the window. It was an uncomfortable seat, but I felt more connected to the city when I could stare out at it.

I pulled the stopper on my beer bottle and gazed across the sagging tiled roof of the tenement across the road. Beyond stood rows and rows of buildings lining the hillside. Rain pelted the window, running in dirty rivulets onto the rotten sill. So peaceful now that I had gotten rid of that irritating girl. I gulped my beer.

A knock at the door startled me.

"Are you in there? You've a visitor," Mother B. said.

"Come in."

She squeezed into the room sideways, huffing and puffing, pressing her enormous bosom against the door. I'd never figured out how she heaved her rotund self up and down the stairs, and why such exercise didn't reduce her weight. Sweat glistened on her scarlet face.

"You could have sent him up." I patted the bed beside my chair.

She slumped down and its frame creaked and groaned. "This place will be the death of me."

I grinned. She was the best landlady I'd ever had, the only one who never judged me. My glance swept to the open door and dim hallway.

"So who's the visitor?"

The girl from the Guild stepped into my room.

I gripped the arms of my chair and sucked in a breath. What was she doing here?

She looked like a drowned rat. She scrubbed her hair with a soaked towel and pulled at her skirt to stop it from clinging to her legs. Her glare said it all, but I had no sympathy.

"I told you to go home."

"You ran away and left me in the street."

"No, I went for lunch. You should have gone home to papa."

She folded her arms across her chest. "I'm your apprentice."

"No, you're not." I sighed. "The Guildmaster's playing a cruel practical joke on me. You're collateral damage."

She continued to drip water on the floorboards. I became conscious of Mother B. watching our exchange, her eyes wide.

"I'll arrange a carriage to take you home, my lady," I said, and waved one arm imperiously.

"My name is Ayla, and I'm not going home." She clenched her jaw.

What was it with this girl?

"The Guildmaster warned me you were stubborn," she said.

Had he now? Well that undermined me from the get-go.

"He was very explicit that I was to be your apprentice." Her voice softened. "I want to be your apprentice."

"Why can't she be your apprentice?" Mother B. asked. "The company would be good for you." She winked at the girl.

I waved my finger at her and raised my eyebrows. I wouldn't have them ganging up on me.

"But it's not my business." She scrambled to her feet with a groan. "I'll send up hot stew."

Ayla squeezed into the corner to let her by. The door shut behind the huge woman but the girl and I continued to glare at each other until we no longer heard the stairs creak. Ayla laid a dry towel on the bed and sat on it. Her gaze settled on the jumbled pile of books on my tiny shelf.

I exhaled noisily. "Go home or I'll find out who your father is and summon him to fetch you."

She snapped her head toward me. "Don't. Please. I left home for a reason and I'm not going back."

"Don't be ridiculous. The east city is not safe for the daughter of an aristocrat. You—"

"I can take care of myself. I found you here, didn't I?" She sneezed and blew her nose on a soaked handkerchief.

I rubbed my jaw. I liked her tenacity and it intrigued me that she thought she wanted to be a necromancer. *Don't get involved, Maldren.* I don't like partners and an apprentice had to be worse. I had a mystery to solve. What in Lak's name had caused that street fire? She'd only get in the way.

"I think it's brave what you do," she said before I could speak. She pushed her disheveled, damp hair behind her ears.

I blinked twice. "It's dangerous. I don't think anyone's called me brave before. Corpse-lover, filthy necro, death bringer, shadow scum, and worse. Brave, not that I recall."

She chuckled. "You're funny."

I'd been trying to scare her off. Clearly I needed a better plan.

"Thanks. That's another new one." I leaned forward. "Look, you think you want this but you don't, trust me. You'll be hated, spat at, derided, ostracized, and beaten up. That's just from the living. The dead will torture you, try to rip you apart, trick you, scramble your mind, or possess you. Did I mention that it was dangerous?"

"Yet you do it." Her deep brown eyes studied me. "You haven't asked me why."

I jerked my head in her direction and reclined in the chair, sipping my beer. It never hurt to listen.

"When my mother died, I didn't understand how she could leave me. She hadn't even said good-bye. No one answered my questions, not even Father."

She smoothed her hair and then her shirt.

"The only person to help me was a necromancer. He…contacted her, and we…"

Her eyes filled with tears and she dabbed them with her handkerchief. She cleared her throat but her voice wavered.

"We talked. Mother and I. She explained everything, told me it wasn't my fault, that I hadn't done anything wrong. I only found peace because of that kind, patient necromancer."

I knew that I should feel like a real shit, but I had a gut feeling she was playing me.

"Please teach me. This is my big chance. Don't reject me."

"It's not up to me. It doesn't work like that. You either have latent magic or you don't. It can't be taught."

"Oh. Do I have it? Can you tell?" She searched my face.

I put down my beer, fashioned a *Perception* spell, and let it seep into the room.

"That tingles," she said.

So she was magic-sensitive, but that didn't mean she could wield it. In my mind, the invisible spell rippled across her and rotated around her body. The vortex increased its velocity, tugging at my magic, drawing it into her.

"I feel that," she whispered, eyes wide. "What's happening?"

She definitely had it. I dispatched tiny stabs of magic into the vortex and she glowed violet in my mind's eye. I'd expected yellow. What did violet mean? I rubbed my nose and nodded, largely to myself.

"You have a latent ability."

She leaped from the bed and stood before me as I sat in the chair.

"I knew it. So I can be your apprentice now? You'll teach me?"

Her soaked clothes clung to her, dripping water into a growing pool on the floor, while her gaze burrowed into my soul. Damn girl was like a cling spirit and would likely grow into a succubus.

Lak and all his demons! I'd regret this.

"All right," I muttered, holding my hands before me in case she tried to hug me or something. "I'll show you life as a necromancer. Just a trial, mind."

"Thank you. I won't let you down."

"Now go and fetch those stews Mother B. mentioned, and ask her to find you a room for a few nights. I'll pay."

She sneezed.

"Then, for Belaya's sake, take a hot bath before you catch damp fever. Let me enjoy my beer in peace."

I turned back to the window. Crazy girl. Still, all I had to do was drag her round some death-stench crypts, give her a few scares, and then I'd be rid of her. My plan couldn't fail.

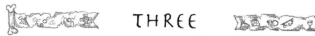 

THREE

I hesitated at the street corner. Hard to believe that so many buildings had stood here just last night. My stomach turned. Despite the warm day, I shivered, remembering neighbors slaughtering one another. My hands trembled. Had I really wanted to strangle that woman?

Ayla pushed in front of me, taking in every detail, sniffing the odor of smoldering wood.

The entire length of a city block had burned to a heap of smoldering timber and broken brick. A few buildings remained, scorched but intact. How they'd escaped the inferno was beyond me. Solemn work crews shoveled debris into carts, while their kalag ate from nosebags and shuffled their feet as if they sensed the morose mood. The overcast sky painted a tapestry of grays on the street, reminding me that even life and death wasn't black and white.

"What are we doing here?" Ayla whispered.

"Looking for clues. Like that." I pointed out a soot-stained shaft in the middle of the road, yawning wide like the entrance to the underworld. Its metal frame had melted and twisted and the wooden supports resembled flaking rods of charcoal.

A figure dressed in a brown tunic and hat caught my eye.

He stood partially hidden behind a mound of rubble, toward the end of the street where the wights had appeared. He didn't seem remotely interested in what was going on. The wide brim of his hat concealed his eyes, but I had no doubt he was watching us. Why?

Ayla had been talking, but I obviously wasn't listening.

"What?" I asked.

"I said what makes you think this fire wasn't an innocent mistake? An unwatched hearth fire or dropped lantern?"

"A street fire does not boil sewer water. Ever been in a sewer?"

She shook her head slowly and scrutinized the manhole. Of course she hadn't.

"Sewers are damp, wet places," I said.

"Not a place a fire would start."

"Exactly."

She stepped into the street. "We're not going to solve the mystery skulking here."

I snorted and slumped against the wall. There had to be more clues. My gaze roamed the street. The brown-clothed man had disappeared.

Ayla leaned precariously over the manhole shaft and peered down inside. Then she sat, swung her legs over, grabbed a hold of something I couldn't see, and headed down. In an instant she was out of sight.

I rushed forward. Damn, she was going to get into a heap of trouble down there. I hadn't seen that coming. Since when did spoiled rich girls like dark, dirty holes?

"It's not deep." Her voice was distant and echoing.

By the time I reached the top of the shaft there was no sign of her. Fifteen feet below, a large sewer pipe ran beneath the center of the street. The rungs of the ladder looked decidedly unstable, so I climbed down carefully then jumped into a thick sludge of debris, fecal matter, and soot that rose up to my ankles.

Ayla came out of the dark, sloshing through the filth. Dirt and other unmentionables speckled her shirt and beige skirt.

"There's a wider tunnel a short ways behind me." She grinned. "This is so exciting."

"You know you're filthy and you've got spiderwebs in your hair?"

She poked the tip of her tongue from the corner of her mouth, which I figured meant she was deep in thought.

"I think I'll live," she said. "Spiders don't scare me, so I wish you'd stop trying to."

"Yes, my lady."

"Stop that!" Her eyes flashed in the shadows. "So what're we looking for, *Master*?"

The sewer sloped downhill toward the distant harbor. Shafts of light poured in from the street above at regular intervals as far as I could see in both directions.

"The fire started that way. Hopefully some clue remains." I headed downhill.

The curved ceiling was low and forced me to stoop, though Ayla walked upright, ignoring the webs and roots that brushed her hair. We splashed forward, kicking up sludge that caked onto our legs and my robe. The horrendous stench of burned shit seared our nostrils. Ayla gagged often, but I had no desire to tease her. I'd have puked myself if I hadn't learned the trick of breathing through my mouth.

It was eerie not to hear the constant pitter-patter and squeaking of rats, though I stepped on plenty of their frazzled corpses. Ayla squished one underfoot and its guts burst out. I couldn't pass up such a great opportunity to scare her, so I trickled magic into the corpse, quietly, invisibly. The rat screeched and scrambled to its feet. Its eyes pulsed scarlet. Ayla cried out and leaped back against the brick wall. It bared its teeth and limped away, dragging the string of its innards.

"But it was dead," she said and stared after it.

I was animating it with my magic—no trace of the creature's soul remained—but I wasn't going to tell her that. Just for effect, I cast a tiny *Cleansing Shield*, turning the air chill. She shivered, eyes wide, and I fought hard not to laugh aloud.

We trudged onward, and each time we stepped into a shaft

of light beneath an open manhole, the sounds of muted conversations and the dragging of shovels drifted down. The going became difficult as we clambered over splintered timbers and smashed bricks.

"Do necromancers spend a lot of time in smelly sewers?" she asked.

"Usually crypts and catacombs. I warned you it was a dirty job."

I scraped a clump of algae from the wall and flicked it at her. She leaped aside.

"Yuk! Stop that." She sniffed. "But sometimes you help people by talking to their dead loved ones?"

"I thought you knew all about necromancers?"

"I do. You guide people's souls when they die, so they can rest, and protect their mausoleums from body snatchers and undead."

I nodded. "Those are the easy jobs. Our main purpose is to keep the city safe."

The stone-lined sewer distorted my chuckle into an evil cackle. Our shadows stretched menacingly before us.

"Horrendous beings lurk in The Gray," I whispered. "They voraciously strive to eat or corrupt the living. If people knew what we kept at bay, they'd never sleep at night."

She peered up and down the sewer and shivered. My plan was moving along nicely.

As we progressed, the walls showed signs of greater damage, many of them cracked and crumbling or smoothened as if they had been in a furnace.

"It's not going to catch fire again, is it?" she whispered.

"I think we're safe enough. Let me know if you get too hot."

She snorted.

Just beyond the light beaming down from the next shaft, we stumbled upon a body burned beyond all recognition, its limbs arranged in impossible directions.

A faint, luminescent miasma swirled out of the blackened body. It wafted with the breeze that ran along the sewer, then darted back on itself, knotting and looping, forking to form an expanding web of transparent threads. We became bathed in its pale blue light.

Ayla gasped and pressed against the wall. I noticed the reflections of blue and white in her darting eyes.

The non-corporeal tendrils rocketed toward her, their tips probing her arms, entwining them. Then the strands spread across her torso and she twitched under their touch. The web expanded, the writhing threads thickening like vines. They coiled around her thighs and zoomed under her skirt.

"What is this? What are they doing?" she asked, surprisingly calm.

I realized my mouth was open, so I snapped it shut. It took magic to entice these things, and I'd never heard of them seeking out the living like that. Why her?

Green flashes sparked along the strands, flooding the sewer in rippling patterns of blue and green. Geysers of luminescence erupted from the ground beneath the corpse to fill the tunnel.

Her eyes sparkled and she beamed with delight, waving her arms and watching the glowing threads strive to keep up.

Hmm, enough of this. We weren't here to have fun.

I trickled a gentle *Dispel* into the air, then stamped my foot, splashing sewer water everywhere. The threads detangled from Ayla and dived back into the corpse, fizzing and twirling. When they were gone, the darkness pushed in.

Her smile faded and she blinked several times. "Were they ghosts?"

Not a bad guess. "Cling spirits. You'll know a ghost if you see it. These are the residual life energy when you strip away the soul. A life shadow, if you like. They tend to hang around after the soul has moved on."

"So pretty."

They were, but I wasn't about to admit that, or that I was jealous that they had sought her out. Instead, I walked forward until, fifty feet later, the way was blocked by a mound of earth and heaped bricks. A brackish pool of sewage had formed, knee deep, backing up until it spilled into smaller side pipes no wider than my hand.

"Guess this is as far as we go." Ayla flicked ash from her hair. "I'm not complaining, but I do need a bath."

I pushed and probed the blockage. There had to be a clue, some kind of trail. Sewers didn't just explode and set fire to the neighborhood. Maybe Hallum had been right about the alchemy stash. Maybe the smugglers had been using the sewers. I placed one hand against the blackened wall. Something hot enough to boil water had passed through here last night.

Running water echoed far below in the depths, and I dipped my head toward the overflow pipes, pinching my nose against the stink of sewage. If I couldn't get past the blockage, maybe I could get below it. I drew energy from my core and fabricated a tiny ball of purple magic between my fingers. It rotated slowly, sparking and flickering. I tossed it into the pipe and the magic ball fell in silence.

"What are you doing?" Ayla asked.

"Shh." I closed my eyes.

Five breaths. Ten. Then my *Probe* spell burst and the magical echo washed through my mind. I tensed against the flood of tastes and smells: sulfur, water, copper, urine, shit. There! The same primordial power I'd sensed two nights ago. Hallum was wrong and I'd been right. Whatever magic had destroyed the street was way down there. Or had been.

I turned to Ayla. "The trail is cold here, but we can pick it up in the deep sewers."

"How deep?"

"Right down to the Gold River at least."

She shook her head. "What's that? Are we going there now?" Her eyes sparkled.

Did this girl never give up? I was tired of babysitting her.

"Enough for today," I said. "Bath time."

I waded out of the disgusting pool and peeled the sticky, dirty hem of my robe from my calves.

"You've been there before, right?" she asked.

"Sure."

"That's all right then."

"Last time I was lucky to make it out alive."

"W-what do you mean?"

I sloshed back uphill, not caring how much smelly sludge I kicked up.

I needed to see Phyxia.

That evening, I left Ayla with Mother B. and joined a throng of people meandering down Kand Hill. My destination was the Lantern District, a happening nightlife area that clustered around the base of a steep rock outcrop standing where the River Malik flowed into the harbor. Its heights twinkled with the multicolored hues of street lanterns and faery lights strung along its narrow walkways and winding stairs. An unlikely collection of houses and structures covered the rock, clinging precariously from its near-vertical sides. At its base, the crowds poured into the tunnels that honeycombed the interior, like an army of bugs returning to the hive.

Inside the rough-hewn caverns, I stopped to buy fresh roasted jit-nuts, Asibrian cheese, and a bottle of brandy—an expensive import, of course. Phyxia had sophisticated tastes. Lantern smoke collected in the arched tunnel like a dark storm cloud. It reminded me of the burning street, except that it bore a sweet, floral scent.

I started up the main stairway that spiraled lazily upward, crammed on both sides with stores carved into the rock. Goods and wares overflowed onto the steps, laid out for everyone to see: rugs, clothing, pottery, trinkets, canes. An endless supply of grubby urchins milled about, thrusting items into the hands of passersby. None dared to hinder me as I swept past. Let them cross themselves or mutter a prayer behind my back.

The curve of the stair gave me an opportunity to glance back. On the bottom step stood the man I was certain had been tailing me since home, a short, wiry man who hid his head beneath a wide-brimmed hat. I bristled. He tried to conceal himself behind an elderly man with a young tart on his arm. It wasn't the same man from the ruined street, but they dressed alike. Some form of silly uniform? I didn't recognize it.

All right, let the game begin.

Having gotten a good head start up the stair, I turned into a side tunnel. *Got to be quick.* I hurtled deep into the rock then up a narrow staircase. A labyrinth of tunnels and alleys opened up before me. *Should I hide and wait for him to tire and leave?* He probably wouldn't. I raced from one tunnel to the next, ducking my head in places, moving higher into the residential areas above the stores. His boot steps echoed behind me.

I sucked in breaths, not daring to stop. Had he taken a shortcut? There was no way I would lead him to Phyxia's door. I took a sharp left, left again and headed down, determined to find another way up. He wouldn't expect that. My aching legs screamed at me.

Blessed cool air washed over me, and I emerged onto a tiny walkway perched on the rim of the rock. It was a long way down. Sightseers edged away from me. My heart pounded and I panted like a dog. I'd lost him!

He stepped out of a low archway opposite, his large hat now strapped to his back. How had he gotten ahead of me? He was good. We faced each other, me sucking in air and he looking as if he had barely exerted himself. His sheathed rapier was obvious beneath his long coat. He wanted me to see it. He wasn't Guild, so whom had I crossed now?

The sightseers stepped between us, oblivious to our standoff. I seized the moment to race back into the tunnels. Behind me, I heard angry shouts and the sound of a struggle, and it gave me a moment to turn a hard right, sprint along a narrow tunnel, and upend a stack of baskets. They bounced down the hallway and my pursuer's curses echoed in the tight space.

I arrived at the base of a dimly lit set of stairs, which looked more like a ladder. I clutched my chest, fearful that my heart would pound its way out. I hesitated long enough to fish a silver Mikk from my purse and then I heaved myself up, both the handrail and I groaning. At the top I wobbled into an open courtyard, panting and wheezing. The only light came from Lunas high in the sky. A gigantic, wide-armed man with his belly hanging over his belt buckle guarded the single exit tunnel. *Thank Belaya!*

He cracked his knuckles—deafening in this isolated spot.

"Targ," I spluttered. "Behind me...tail."

I flicked the silver coin his way, and his huge bearlike hand reached out and caught it. Without a word he stepped aside. I pressed against the stitch in my side and pushed myself on, into the tunnel.

At the sound of a sickening crunch, I glanced back to see Targ launch himself at my pursuer, who barely had time to draw his rapier before Targ's belly crashed into him, smashing his back against the wall. Bones cracked and the man uttered a prolonged groan. I winced. Rumor had it that Targ was half-Uk. I could believe that. He made a great gatekeeper for those like Phyxia who hated uninvited guests.

Good game. I always played to win.

I exited the tunnel and negotiated a labyrinth of narrow alleys, until I arrived at a wooden door bathed in the flickering blue glow of everfire. My legs wobbled like jelly, so I perched on a low wall and breathed deep until my thumping heart settled.

What in Belaya's name had Hallum and I stumbled upon? Was he being followed too? Where did Ayla fit in? Her appearance seemed far from a coincidence. Phyxia always had answers.

I pushed on her door. It clicked open and I slipped inside.

Shadows filled the low hallway. The door shut behind me, and the uneven floor creaked as I crept cautiously forward. The hallway sloped downward from the door. I pictured her hovel sliding off the cliff and plummeting into the streets far below. Somehow, the dozens of similar shacks stacked on top of each other held them all in place. A house of cards. I carried my groceries into the main room.

A petite woman, five feet tall at best, stared out an open

window, her back to me. I watched her for a long moment. She wore nothing but a flimsy, almost see-through chemise, even though the room was icy cold. I shivered under my heavy clothing and watched my breath steam in the air. Her chemise clung to her every luscious curve.

My stomach fluttered. Did she enjoy teasing me?

"You brought me jit-nuts," she said in a quiet, distracted voice.

She turned and stepped into the warm glow of a pair of floor candles. The stench of umber wax hung heavy in the air. A smile spread across her narrow lips, which parted sensually.

"You're always so thoughtful, sishka," she said.

Her pale hair glistened like silver, cascading from two partings that formed at the base of two horns on her head. Not the brazen red horns of a lazoul, but feminine and short, speckled with green fur. How I longed to caress them, but dared not and knew I never would.

"And brandy," she added, as I pulled the bottle from my sack. "Sit and let us share."

She perched on the edge of a hard wooden chair, allowing me to sink into the more comfortable couch.

One didn't rush Phyxia. I was anxious for answers but knew she would tell things in her own good time. It was a ritual. I fidgeted and forced myself not to sigh.

To calm my jangling nerves, I poured the roasted nuts into a bowl, set out the pungent cheese that I had bought, and uncorked the brandy.

Her fine-boned, childlike hands snaked into the bowl and she crunched the fire-hardened nuts. At intervals her slim ears twitched, accompanied by an eye tic that could be mistaken for winking. I adored her quirks. Her presence relaxed me, made me feel safe.

"Have I ever steered you wrong?" she asked. "Misguided you?"

I paused, brandy glass halfway to my mouth. An ominous start.

"Why, are you about to?" I said.

Her eyes laughed, mesmerizing me with whirlpools of blue and hazel and brown.

"No. Not in all the time I've known you," I said.

"Remember that."

A shiver ran through me, not entirely from the chill air.

A smile quivered on her lips. "Ask your question."

I sighed. "I'm at a loss on how to advance in the Guild. Fortak wants everyone to fear us. It shouldn't be about that. The Guild is doing it all wrong. Am I being arrogant?"

I took a sip and swirled the warming liquid around my mouth.

Her ears twitched. "Humans judge too easily. Such matters require the perspective of decades. Don't concern yourself with such trifles. Be who you are. History will judge, not your peers."

I dipped a jit-nut into the soft and creamy Asibrian cheese, and savored the exotic burst of earthy, herb flavors. She talked about decades like I would a few lunars or solars. How many aeons old was she? Had she really lived through the Age of Chaos?

"When will you tire of this discussion?" she asked. "He is old and you are young. The future is yours, not his."

I helped myself to more cheese.

"Your question?" she asked.

"I've got a problem."

She chuckled, a melodic sound. "Only one?"

"Funny. This is outside my purlieu. The dead I can handle, the living not so much. This chit of a girl just became my apprentice."

"You could use the company."

Why did everyone think they could run my life better than I?

"I don't need a girl tagging along. It isn't play, what I do."

"She could watch your back. Another set of eyes and ears could come in handy."

"But—"

"You have a rare talent, sishka. It's your duty to pass it on.

There are few who care for your trade as you do." She gazed at the worn rug at our feet. "The world has become darker, the Iathic light long faded."

The floor candles seemed to dim. Her glance swept the room as if only now she grasped the reality of her decrepit surroundings. Why did she continue this masquerade? I loved her as a mentor—actually, I just loved her—but what was a being like her doing here, talking to a mere journeyman?

I shook my head for clarity and gulped my brandy, letting it burn my throat.

"You've never suggested that I take an apprentice before. Is there something you're not telling me, like I'm heading for a sticky end?" I laughed.

Her ears twitched and a smile spread across her petite face. She remained silent.

"Um, this is when you scoff and assure me that I'm being silly." I gestured for her to interject. "No? Great. I think I'd spend more time watching *her* back. Unless she's some Gods almighty necromancer like my dearest mother."

I threw my hands above my head and exhaled hard.

"Cut the crap." Her eyes spun like a demonic vortex and her horns flashed red. "I don't like this sarcastic streak that you culture. Stop hiding behind it and give the girl a chance."

"I'll think about it."

As quickly as her anger had risen, it faded, and she smiled. I refilled her glass with the expensive amber liquid, and slid another wedge of creamy cheese onto my tongue.

"Could you harm a friend?" she asked. "If much depended on it?"

Chewing gave me time to think about that. "Could you?"

"Yes." No hesitation in her voice.

"Why? Am I going to have to? Is this something to do with the girl?"

"Choices are all we have, all that we can depend on."

I gripped the arm of the couch. Talking to Phyxia was hard work. She was a fabulous mentor but had a way of making me feel inadequate. Is that what "the perspective of decades" does to you? Where was she going with this?

She raised her hand, fingers outstretched. "Ask what you came here for. Don't be shy."

I studied her immaculate manicure, a detail very much at odds with her decaying surroundings. My gaze drifted to her breasts, rising and falling beneath her chemise. We never had a chance, the two of us. Continuing upward, my eyes met hers. Color wafted around her irises like inks in water, as serene as I had ever seen them. The edge of her lip curled up. So inviting. Heat burned in my cheeks.

"Say it, sishka." Her whisper was barely audible.

Did she mean my longing or my question? I chose the easy road.

"Something monstrous, something…ancient is loose in the city. Everyone dismisses it, but you believe, don't you?"

A beatific smile lit up her face. Greens and blues tumbled in her eyes.

"There we are," she said. "Why couldn't you have started with that?"

Women! I could have started with that but she'd have steered me onto other things. I gritted my teeth.

She sipped her brandy, staring at me all the while.

"What is it?" I asked. "This entity."

She shrugged.

"It's important, isn't it? I'm right to seek it out?"

"Don't ask a question you already know the answer to. Choices, sishka."

"It's going to strike again. I know it is. How do I find it?"

"I cannot say."

"Cannot, or will not?" I slammed my hand on the arm of the couch. "Damn it! You're the only one I can talk to. Don't be so coy. What if it burns the whole city down?"

A tiny frown furrowed her otherwise perfectly youthful skin.

"You know what I am," she said. "There are matters in which I cannot intervene."

"I need something solid. Anything. Even a hint.

Who…what is it? Why did it burn a meaningless street to the ground? Why did it stop? What will it do next?"

She sighed and her frozen breath hung in the air.

"I'm sorry, sishka. I can only help those who cannot help themselves."

I brought my glass to my mouth and savored the brandy. Who can say what a creature like her can see of the future.

"I'm sorry I pushed you," I said. "Forgive me. That was incredibly rude."

"You're passionate about your convictions, but be careful. Others have been damned for doing likewise. Remember the legend of Caradan."

Why mention that old ghost? I drained my drink.

She crunched noisily on jit-nuts. Then she stood, a movement of effortless grace, and glided back to the open window.

I blew out my breath. My visit had been for nothing, just a handful of cryptic phrases. I leaned back in the couch, neck muscles clenched. All right, so she wasn't always relaxing— sometimes she could be damn infuriating.

But always right. What was she trying to tell me? I slapped my forehead with my palm. *Think, Maldren. What's she hinting at?*

FOUR

The next morning, I slouched alone on the south side of Canal Street, and squinted against Solas hanging low in the sky, framed between two buildings. A ragtag market was setting up on my side of the canal that ran down the center of the wide street. In half an hour the place would be crawling with people.

My head throbbed from last night's brandy. I drank it only with Phyxia and somehow I always ended up doing most of the drinking. If only I'd thought to grab a mug of mulip this morning.

The only clues I'd found at the burned-out street were the hints from my *Probe* spell. The cause of the fire still eluded me, and what evil magic lay behind that malevolent smoke? I rubbed my nose. To reach Gold River I'd need a bargee guide, and that had never been a fun experience. I squinted across the canal at one of their favorite taverns.

I'd been in The Downpipe a couple of times, not enough to have friends there. The two-story building stood sandwiched between two tenements, its bowed roof threatening to collapse, though I'd been saying "any day now" for five solars. Grimy moss clung to its facade, taking hold in the eroded point work, and when it rained, the whole wall oozed and dribbled water.

Frankly, the whole thing looked like it belonged in the sewer.

I cracked my neck to one side. This wasn't going to be easy. It was as good a morning as any to get beaten up, I supposed.

After checking on my knife concealed in my boot, I climbed the steep, stone bridge that crossed Rat Canal. From the top of its high arch I could see through the narrow streets to the harbor, six blocks away. From the corner of my eye, I spotted one of those damn spies slink into the shadows of an alley. I'd need to deal with them sooner or later.

I stepped inside The Downpipe and paused until my eyes adjusted to the gloomy interior. There were more people than I'd hoped for. Unkempt men with scruffy clothing sat in groups of three or four at circular tables piled high with empty beer flagons. A dozen faces turned to me. Two dozen eyes narrowed, and the muttering began.

The barkeep was a rotund, dog-faced man with a receding hairline. His eyes steered me to an empty table, so I sat, my skin itching without a wall at my back. At least I could watch both front and rear doors. I was glad not to have Ayla in tow. This was no place for a woman. Who was I kidding? It was no place for a necromancer.

A scrawny barmaid ambled over, her hair draped to one side in an attempt to cover an obvious scar on her cheek. I was glad that she walked proud, though, since even the scar didn't detract from her natural beauty. She placed a mug of short beer in front of me, palmed my coin, and scurried away. After the brandy from last night, my stomach lurched at the prospect of more alcohol, so I simply sipped, head lowered, my ears straining hard to catch each hushed conversation in the room. If only they would stop whispering about wretched necromancers for a single moment, then maybe I could learn something useful.

It was tough to remain calm while overhearing every detail of their plans to get me. After I had sipped half my beer, and most of the bargees had drunk a couple of pints each, I finally caught interesting snippets from a far table.

"…said it got so hot that it were boiling…"

"…died on Gold River. It be true what…"

A rowdy group at the adjacent table drowned out the rest of the conversation but clearly I'd come to the right place. Time to get it over with. Careful to keep my hands in plain sight, I picked my way around the tables toward the far group of three bargees. They stood in unison, chairs scraping on the wooden floor. Beady eyes stared at me from above beards dripping with beer froth. Muscles rippled on their forearms. A one-eyed man cracked his knuckles and stepped forward, and then I was surrounded by a horde of determined men from several tables.

Kristach, this was going to hurt.

"We don't want your kind here," One-eye growled. "You're souring our beer."

He jabbed a finger into my chest. His cabbage-beer breath made my stomach turn.

"I'm not looking for trouble, just information. I'll pay for a guide."

"What kind of information?"

"Throw 'im outta here, Pank," another said, brushing matted hair back over his shoulders.

I maintained eye contact with the man inches from my face. By the Gods he was ugly, and part of me wanted to tell him so. Not my best idea.

"I want to know what you and your friends were saying about Gold River."

"Snooping, were ye?" One-eye asked, spraying my face with spit.

I refused to flinch.

"Break 'is arms and throw 'im in the canal," a whiny, nasal voice said.

"The fire," I said. "A few nights ago. It's linked to your boiling river. I'm trying to find out what happened."

"Never known a necromancer be of any bloody use."

"Tell 'im nothin', Pank."

One-eye jabbed me again. His other hand snatched up a beer flagon.

"Word on the street is you corpse scum caused that fire."

"That's not true. We—"

"My brother was running Gold that night. Died of 'is burns. Yer come to 'elp 'is widow pay 'er bills?"

He swung the flagon at my head. I dodged and it smashed against my shoulder, drenching me. His fist was like a sledgehammer against my stomach and I doubled over, blowing out all my breath. I half turned before a stick cracked on the inside of my knee, knocking out my left leg. I crashed to the floor, sending a chair flying. *You asked for this, Maldren, you fool.*

The mob closed in. Their dirks remained in their scabbards, but I imagined their fists would do more damage. I made no attempt to go for my own knife or else they would kill me. There was a risk that they might in any case. I tried to roll away under the table but One-eye stamped on the same leg, and kicked me in the kidneys. Pain lanced through me.

"Oh, come on," I cried, hand clutching my side. "I'll pay for information. No need to break bones."

One-eye reached down, grabbed the front of my robe, and dragged me to my feet. I groped desperately for something to hold on to.

"Should've brought yer skeleton army," he said, causing his friends to guffaw.

He smashed his head into my nose. Blood spurted all over us. The metallic taste was disgusting. The room spun around me, and for a moment One-eye had two eyes. He released his grip on my robe as if flicking away a spider, and I crumpled onto the floor again.

"Aren't you going to cast a curse on us?" someone shouted.

"He's too craven to fight back."

I moaned and blew blood from my nose.

"I told you, I'm trying to help. Just listen, will you?"

"I've heard about enough from you." He kicked me in the side again.

I wouldn't take any more. *Lak curse them all!*

I grabbed One-eye's boot and yanked him off balance. He

careened into the bargee beside him, and I twisted his ankle as they both went down. Then I slithered under the table and pushed up on it with my back, walking it forward until its edge smashed two of them in the face.

Can't go down without a fight, but my odds were worse than a virgin in a bikka den.

I managed to swing a punch at a man with a deep scar along one cheek, before I crashed to the floor under five bargees, all of them punching and kneeing me. Every part of me ached. My eyes swelled and my vision tunneled.

"Stop! Let him go," a familiar female voice shrieked above the din of their jeering.

The assault on my body let up. As if from a great distance, I heard murmurs of surprise and the sound of the mob parting.

"Leave my father alone. If you cripple him, how am I going to feed Annie, Mysha, and Nolin, the poor children?"

Ayla. What was she doing here?

I pushed myself up on one elbow, gripped my nose with thumb and finger, and blew out the blood. It hurt, really hurt. She stood in the middle of the taproom, wearing a light blue dress, her hands on her hips, eyes welling with tears.

"All right, lads," the barkeep said in a bass voice. "That's enough. Tidy the place up."

And that was that. The men moved away, muttering apologies to Ayla. She winked at me. I wanted to roll my eyes but they hurt too much. She put her arm around me, and helped me limp into the street, where I collapsed on a bollard, tentatively stretching my limbs, wincing and moaning.

I must have passed out because when I opened my eyes I lay on my back on the seat of a carriage. Every bump and rattle across the cobbles sent stabs of pain to new places in my body that I hadn't realized were hurting. Something touched my swollen eye and I jerked away.

"Be still," Ayla said, moving into my field of view. She dabbed my face with her handkerchief.

"It's a good thing that I followed you. Didn't you think to dress down? Your Guild robe is far too noticeable."

"I'm not ashamed of who I am."

"No, just stubborn. I hope the beating was worth it."

I shrugged. Pain lanced down my side and I cried out.

"I would have gotten what I needed if you hadn't stormed in."

"Yeah, it looked like you had everything under control. Men. Is this how you negotiate?"

My mouth was bloody and swollen, but I managed a half smile.

"Something like that."

Ayla's berating continued until she helped me up the stairs to my room.

"You need to rest for a couple of days," she said, helping me into my chair by the window.

"Not while there's the danger of another fire."

She sipped a glass of juice. "Maybe it really was an accident. What makes you think it will happen again?"

"I can't describe what I felt that night. Something unnatural is going on, something from The Gray, or if we're really unlucky, The Deep."

I'd been stupid in the way I'd approached the bargees. I squirmed, and pain shot through my body. A girl had saved me! Warmth flushed my cheeks.

I scratched at the stubble on my chin and glanced out the window. The sky had turned gray. A quiet seemed to have settled over the usually bustling city.

"Trust me, we haven't seen the last of it."

"You could talk to the Guildmaster again." She watched me sip my beer through a straw and giggled. How humiliating.

"No." I glared at her with my good eye. "He's not going to listen."

Phyxia had held something back, I was certain of it. I gripped the arms of the chair to get up.

"On no, you don't." She stood in my way. "I bet you've got bruises all over. You can't see properly and your face is a mess."

What had I done to deserve a mothering slip of a girl?

"Thanks for the compliments," I said. "I don't have time to sit here and feel sorry for myself. We need to get to the deep sewers and see what's going on."

"Well you messed up hiring a bargee, didn't you? Rest until tomorrow."

"It's barely lunch—"

"Tomorrow."

We stared each other down, which wasn't a fair contest because I barely had one good eye.

"You're enjoying this," I said.

She blew out her breath. "Not really. Now drink that medicine that Mother B. gave you."

Her nagging made my ears hurt. "Yes, my lady."

She scowled and headed toward the door, and then paused with her hand on the latch.

"Have you seen my necklace? I took it off when I was in here the other day, trying to dry my hair."

I shrugged, and regretted the movement. "No. Maybe Mother B. found it."

After Ayla left and shut the door, I slipped my hand into a pocket and fingered her necklace. I could use it to find her father. Surely the man had been searching all over. All it would take is one messenger and I was certain he would be right here, thanking me for protecting her. Then I'd be free of her nagging. I looked out over the rooftops, trying to relax my aching body. After replaying her performance in The Downpipe it was no longer clear who was looking after whom. She was a spunky girl for sure. I left the necklace in my pocket and closed my eyes.

Lord Caradan gulped his beer, drew the back of his hand across his mouth, and tossed the tankard onto the rug by the roaring fire. Guild paperwork littered his desk next to a bookshelf crammed with dusty volumes. He crossed his cramped office to a coat stand by the door and dressed meticulously in his night-black robe, arranging the sleeve cuffs and collar just so. A chill wind gusted through the open tower window. Thick clouds chewed at the bright disc of Lunas in the sky.

A storm was building. A perfect night for vengeance.

Master Eclias slipped into the room. The man bore a sullen, determined face. The red glow of firelight flickered in his eyes.

"Is everyone prepared?" Caradan asked.

"Are you certain there's no other way?"

"The time for diplomacy has passed. Remind the men that our actions this night may damn their souls. Have them leave the tower if they have no stomach for this."

Eclias stood tall. "Yes, it's time we destroyed the Elik Magi. You handpicked your men. Every one of them is willing to face damnation at your side."

Caradan glanced around the room, and then exited into the dim hallway, Eclias at his heels. The two men walked in silence to the curved staircase that wound up and down around the inner perimeter of the tower. The first rumble of thunder rolled across the heavens.

On the floor above, they joined six grim-faced men, each dressed in pristine black robes flecked with silver and purple. A pair of spluttering wall torches painted grotesque shadows across the walls and ceiling. Caradan jerked his head at Master Petay, and then nodded at the closed door around which the men had gathered. Petay held up two fingers.

So be it. These two would have the honor of dying first.

Caradan marched to the door, threw it open, and strode into the reception room beyond. Within, two of his wife's Elik Magi reclined on couches before a fire that bathed the room in a demonic red glow. It emphasized the violet irises of the two sorcerers as they turned in surprise to face Caradan. The Magi were dressed in plain, comfortable clothing rather than the regalia of their order. They lacked the discipline of his Guild, his love for ritual. Caradan grunted.

His men filed into the room, causing both Magi to stand, their bodies tensed, expressions puzzled.

A blinding flash of lightning preceded the deafening

thunder and lit the night outside the window. It was time to demonstrate his power.

Caradan sucked power from his gut. His men did likewise, and the room seethed with magic that was palpable, almost visible. Wisps of gray appeared from thin air, transparent yet all too real, and in a single breath the wisps coalesced into creatures that vaguely resembled men. Their edges were indistinct, constantly shifting. The creatures' torsos revealed massive wounds, huge rends from which spewed organs and guts, while snapped bones hung by torn flesh and muscle. Claws ripped from the creatures' fingers and fangs dislodged teeth.

Seven such revenants hung in midair, gurgling and shrieking as if in pain. The Elik Magi stumbled backward and the creatures fell upon them.

Caradan observed every detail. Half-formed spells erupted from the Magi as they tried to erect protection shields. Their screams were cut short as claws and fangs shredded their throats. Blood splattered over every surface. Caradan didn't blink when the hot liquid drenched his face and dribbled down his cheeks. He stood tall and puffed out his chest.

Gobbets of flesh flew in all directions. Bones crunched. Mangled organs splattered against the walls, leaving blood trails as they slid to the floor. None of his own men flinched. The warmth of pride coursed through Caradan's veins.

The Magi lay on the floor, half disassembled but still twitching.

Caradan paraded once around the macabre scene and then dispelled the revenants with a wave of his hand. A toothy grin spread wide on his face.

The night had only just begun.

I jerked awake. Pain sliced through my bruised sides. My eyes darted around the room, now black as the night outside. Damn Phyxia for mentioning the Caradan legend. I ran my fingers through my sweat-soaked hair and shivered. Necromancers did not have nightmares.

Stiff, I squirmed in my chair by the window. What had been in Mother B.'s potion to put me out all afternoon? The swelling had gone down in most of my body except my nose, and my head no longer throbbed. My grumbling stomach reminded me that I'd missed supper.

I tiptoed onto the landing, careful not to wake Ayla in the room opposite mine. I didn't need her fussing over me again. I crept down the stairs and through the sleeping inn to the communal bathroom at the rear. Metal cauldrons stood in front of a hearth, and I poured hot water into the nearest copper tub, mixing generous handfuls of soap flakes. Once immersed in the hot water, the tension departed my aching limbs. I lay back and closed my eyes, glad to have the room to myself. I needed a guide to take me to Gold River, but I didn't think my body could stand more bargee beatings.

An hour later, the cold water drove me out of the bath. My shaving blade trembled in my aching arms, so I left the stubble on my face and combed my hair. Yellow and purple blotches covered me head to toe. I dressed in the clean robe I had brought down with me, and went next door to fix a midnight snack. I felt human again.

Back in my room, I stood at the window and watched the sunrise. A knock on the door disturbed my calm reverie. Would that girl never leave me alone?

"Come in, Ayla."

The door opened and a gray-haired man stepped inside. Silver and purple runes lined the sleeves and collar of his black robe, and several garish rings adorned his left hand. Thick eyebrows threatened to overgrow his eyes, and a beaklike nose dominated his face.

I instinctively stood straighter, then winced at the stabbing pain.

"Master Begara, what brings you out here? Please, sit."

No one from the Guild had ever visited me at home. What did this mean?

Master Begara perched on the edge of the still-made bed. I

had been far from his ideal student so I was eager to learn the reason for his visit.

He seemed to study the bruises on my face and calves. "Maldren, what in Lak's name happened to you? I'd heard you had a run-in with the Prime Guildmaster, but I trust this is not his doing."

"No, no, of course not. You know me, always getting into trouble."

"Indeed, I remember." He twirled his rings with the fingers of his other hand. "When are you going to stop irritating him?"

"I'm not trying to. I want him to give me the promotion I deserve."

He peered into the corners of the room. I grimaced. My room needed tidying.

"Ordinarily I'd tell you to follow his orders." He lowered his voice. "But this time I think you're right to be suspicious."

Interesting. I double blinked.

"Have you heard of Babbas?" he asked.

An old man with a crooked back and even more crooked sensibilities. Bargee by trade; thief, con man, and pimp by preference. Who hadn't heard of him? The Guild had used him on occasion but he was as unreliable as the weather.

"Of course," I said.

"Yesterday he was seen with a Guild journeyman."

"Who?"

"More importantly, why?" Begara raised one eyebrow.

I rubbed my nose and winced. "It sounds to me as if someone *is* investigating the source of that fire."

Someone who knew it had come from the sewers. Was Hallum part of this?

A smile spread across Begara's face. He stood. "Time I got back."

"Stay for breakfast? I'm grateful for your visit."

His smile faded. "I was never here. Understood?"

I nodded and he left the room, closing the door quietly. I returned my gaze to the city outside. This day was fast becoming interesting.

 FIVE

My plans to sneak out after breakfast to find Babbas went horribly wrong when Ayla snitched on me to Mother B., who insisted I stay home and rest another day. Only by letting Ayla join me had I escaped. The utter shame of it all.

The tall, ramshackle tenements and warehouses of the Waterfront District offered shelter from the biting wind coming off the harbor, but made the narrow streets gloomy and oppressive. Most stood three or four stories high, leaning out over the cobbled street. The air was heavy with a pungent miasma: lantern oil, candle wax, cooked meat, fresh dung, and a salty sea mist. Dogs barked, people argued, livestock grunted, and from the distance came the muted but unmistakable clash of steel upon steel.

Ayla and I turned aside from Moor Street into Pie Alley. Without cobbles, the surface was muddy, and more than once my bad leg slipped and I stumbled. The stench of decay and rat poison filled the cramped space, and I longed for a breeze. A mangy cat yowled and fled, almost tripping Ayla. She scanned the shadows, scrutinizing every detail, grimacing at piles of dead rats.

"You said we were going on a boat. The harbor's the other

direction."

I limped around the corner and gestured to the tiny canal running at a tangent to Pie Alley. Narrow enough to jump over, its soiled, trash-laden water flowed lazily past. It smelled unwholesome but free of sewage.

"On that?" She sniffed.

"Patience."

She kicked a pebble and it plopped into the water.

I led her along a narrow walkway between the canal and the windowless rear of a building, until an iron gate barred the way, its lock rusted closed. To one side, a set of worn, moss-covered steps descended beside the building we had been following.

"You should go back," I said.

Her steely glare said it all.

I led the way, wincing with each step of my bruised leg. Ayla moved up beside me, seemingly intrigued by the diffuse, sourceless light that held back the darkness at the bottom. A narrow passage ran beneath the canal, following its course downstream. Rushing water roared from somewhere ahead, and the faint glow provided enough light for us to navigate between stacks of bric-a-brac arranged to either side along the tunnel. It was the most unlikely collection of toys, statuettes, pottery, broken furniture, and discarded items I had ever seen.

"What is all this?" Ayla shouted above the din of the water.

"It's mine, that's what it is," a scratchy voice said from inside a doorway. The unseen man cackled.

Ayla stepped inside and I followed. She scanned the bizarre chamber that resembled the inside of a huge stone barrel, and gasped. From high on the curved right wall, the black water of the canal fell six feet and plunged through a grate in the floor, creating a spray that soaked the room, leaving every surface slick and glistening. Algae and moss invaded the circular walls and furniture. An assortment of broken objects surrounded the grate, pushed aside from the cascade that thundered into the depths below.

In the driest part of the room, beside a table laden with half-gnawed bones, upturned beer flagons, and a spluttering lantern, Babbas rolled back and forth in a rocking chair. His beard resembled a shrub of thistles on the moors, yet his head was completely bald, devoid of eyebrows. Beer dribbled down his stained shirt. He turned his rheumy eyes on Ayla.

"What d'we have here? Such a sweet thing. Come to barter yer body for me 'elp?" He grabbed his crotch and his gaze devoured her.

"Try it, grandpa," she said, "and I'll make it so you have nothing to squeeze down there."

Now I didn't feel so bad about bringing her.

He uttered a deep belly laugh. "A feisty one. Shame. I prefer 'em demure and afeared."

His chair groaned as he pushed himself to his feet. Unable to straighten his crooked back, he snatched a flagon from the table and crossed the room, getting drenched by the waterfall in the process. He jammed the flagon into my bruised ribs. I winced and stepped back. His eyes twinkled and a crooked grin spread across his gnarly face. Now he'd think me weak.

"Second corpse-licker in as many days," he muttered. "Babbas can retire early, perhaps."

Another bass laugh.

Everything I'd heard about him was true, then. Best get this over with.

"Three gold Malks to guide us to Gold River and back. I want to see where the bargees died. Pay my respects."

"How touching." He made a hawking sound and spat at my feet. "Five."

"Three."

He stared at me long and hard but I met his gaze, studying his milk-white eyes.

"Five. You be too weak to make it down there without Babbas."

"Three now. Two when we return."

I handed him three coins. He cackled and turned toward another passageway that I hadn't seen earlier.

"Let's be going." He clutched the beer flagon to his chest. He had no other equipment or weapons that I could see.

"Do you trust him?" Ayla whispered.

I shook my head and gestured for her to go next.

The passage sloped down into the darkness and turned a corner, cutting off most of the light and thundering roar of the water. We negotiated a short set of stairs, following the grunts and wheezes of Babbas. Ayla bumped into him at the bottom, squealed, and then squeezed back beside me. I wasn't keen on being down here with him, either.

Babbas chuckled and winked at her.

I barely made out a table in the near darkness, upon which stood a series of flagon-shaped objects covered by a blanket.

Ayla stood on tiptoe and cupped her hand to my ear. "I'm not going to carry extra beer for him," she whispered.

Babbas's hand snaked under the blanket and he pulled out a small cage the size of a lantern. Inside, a fist-size red beetle bounced around, banging against the bars, its wings a blur. An angry droning noise accompanied its futile attempts at flight, and its abdomen glowed, bathing us in soft, red light. Those things always reminded me of a brothel.

"What's that?" Ayla peered closer, jerking away when the beetle flew at her, rattling the cage.

"Glow beetle," I said.

Babbas belched, and with his beer flagon clasped in one hand, he held the cage aloft and crossed the room to another set of steps. Down we went, one staircase after another. The beetle settled, and its drone lessened to a hypnotic humming. Babbas ignored all side turns and passageways and then suddenly decided to take a turn to the right.

Was he playing with us? How did bargees remember which passage went where?

More steps down, these covered in algae and slick. We exited into a sewer and sloshed onward, splashing excrement all over our clothing. I breathed through my mouth. Ayla took a small vial from her pocket and dabbed its contents liberally on her dress and under her nose. We walked on in a haze of perfume, and I breathed deep of the fragrance.

The sound of running water grew louder once more,

becoming a deafening roar when we turned a corner and emerged at the lip of a vertical shaft, fifteen feet across. A cascade of water plummeted from above to form a frothing maelstrom of water, forty feet below. A narrow rope bridge led to a ledge on the far side.

You've got to be kidding me.

"One at a time," Babbas said.

The bridge bucked and bounced with his every step. I studied the frayed and sodden rope stays rubbing against the wall. Lovely. Babbas stopped midway to take a long swallow of beer. The beetle buzzed furiously as the spray drenched it.

Ayla turned to me, one eyebrow raised. I shrugged.

When Babbas had reached the other side, I sent Ayla over while I held the bridge to dampen its movement. I nonchalantly sauntered across. All right, so I limped and tried not to look down.

"I had no idea so much was below the streets," Ayla said as we trudged along a new, drier tunnel.

"Malkandrah is ancient," I said. "Each city built on the ruins of the previous. See these glyphs?" Faint carvings were barely visible on the gray wall tiles. "We're down to the level of the ancient Iathic metropolis now."

"What's down here?"

"Sewers. Tunnels. Tombs. Smuggler hideaways and ruined temples, and who knows how many secret lairs lost to time."

She flicked rat droppings from her boots. "And shit."

I laughed.

"And the bargees know every passage?" she asked.

"Yep," Babbas said from the front, his shadow rippling along the uneven walls as if we shared the tight tunnel with a wraith.

I shook my head. "He's exaggerating. Maybe the uppermost levels and sewers. Enough to ship illicit goods under everyone's noses, and—"

"—and to guide idiots the likes of you." He frowned, which looked odd since he had no eyebrows.

The tunnel turned to the right in a long, graceful arc. It was dry and smelled of musk and dirt. I sneezed and wished that Ayla would spray some more of her perfume.

"I bet none of the bargees know what lies below, in the deep," I said.

"What does?" she whispered, eyes wide.

Babbas uttered a haunting moan that echoed into the distance. "Nasty things that eat little girls."

"Shut up," she said.

I nudged her. "I bet he's more afraid than you are."

The bargee wheeled about, bathing us in red light from the glow beetle.

"Oh, Babbas knows, all right. Stuff best left alone. Stuff you lot—" He waved his flagon toward me. "—keep dredging up with yer tristak shadow hexes. Damn you all to Lak!"

"Oh, shut it."

"I'm done with ye and yer bossy mouth, boy." He shoved us against the wall and stomped back the way we had come.

I sighed and rattled my purse. "Stop behaving like a kalag. No Gold River, no gold coin."

We faced off for several moments, during which he chugged from his flagon, and then he came back, huffing and mumbling. He kicked aside a dead rat, and yanked on a tree root dangling from a crack in the ceiling. Part of the stonework broke loose and a mildewed skeleton dropped down, its bones held together by leathery tendons and patches of mummified flesh. It hung itself on another root and dangled, grinning at us. Babbas cried out, slipped, and landed on his butt, where he cowered, hands raised in front of his face.

I laughed, and the tunnels laughed back, mocking me. Ayla remained quiet, studying the skeleton, which exhibited teeth marks and the patina of age. Did nothing frighten this girl?

"Get up," I said to Babbas. "We've been down here two hours. How far's the river?"

"Not far," he replied, voice wavering. "You lead for a bit."

Ayla caught my eye and grinned.

I winked back at her and readjusted my robe, brushing away the dust. Yes, I should control this sorrowful outfit.

We emerged into a semicircular tunnel, forty feet across and with a ceiling twelve feet above the full-fledged river that flowed along it, inches below the narrow landing upon which we stood.

"Gold River," Babbas said with a sweeping wave of an arm, as if opening the door to a treasure vault.

The water was ruddy brown in color and laden with mud and silt. A metallic stench stung my nostrils, which I found a teeny bit preferable to the reek of sewage. The river flowed swiftly and silently, scraping the sludge and moss from the tunnel walls.

A low, flat barge lay tied to a bollard on the far side, at the foot of worn steps leading up to another passageway. Huh. We were on the wrong side of the river. No way I would swim in that. Babbas could do it.

"It's brown, not gold," Ayla said, hands on hips. The wide tunnel echoed her words.

Babbas and I stared at her. What had she expected, a river of liquid gold?

If I hadn't seen the melted manholes in the street, I'd never have believed this chill river could get hot enough to boil. I rubbed my nose. My plan had a flaw—if I searched long enough, I was bound to come face-to-face with whomever, or whatever, had caused the fire, but then what? I'd been so caught up in the search, I hadn't thought through my endgame. I cast *Perception* so that I wouldn't miss anything.

"Take us to the section that boiled the other night," I said.

Babbas fished a sludge-covered rope from the water. When he pulled, I saw that it ran under the surface to the boat. He gave a sharp tug and the rope slipped the special knot on the bollard across the water, allowing the barge to float free. He hauled it over against the persistent current, then placed one foot in the barge and held it against the side.

Ayla's hand slipped into mine. My stomach fluttered at her warm and soft touch. She stepped gracefully into the boat, using me for support, and then pulled me after her. I rocked the boat enough for me to tumble into the middle, and she kept a firm grip on my hand. Babbas kicked off from the side and sat. The river swept us away. He painstakingly coiled the rope, and then picked up a short pole and punted from a sitting position. The barge leaned precariously with each thrust. He slowed us to a stop and then propelled us upstream, grunting with each push on the pole.

"This is great," Ayla said, her gaze flicking everywhere.

I pried my hand from hers and shot her a long, hard stare. She wasn't supposed to be enjoying it.

"Are we going to find more skeletons?" she asked. "Moving ones?"

"Undead. They're called undead. Skeletons aren't usually a threat." I left the follow-up unspoken, glad that she didn't pursue it.

"Can you teach me some spells?"

"No. You're nowhere near ready for that."

"Yes, I am."

"You're not. I say when you are. But since you asked: lesson one—"

"Great!" She sat up straight and leaned forward.

"I'm known as the teacher. *You* are known as the apprentice. *My* job is to set the rules. *Your* job is to stop arguing and do what I say. End of lesson one."

She glared at me, pouting like a child. It was an unattractive gesture for the daughter of an aristo.

The tiled ceiling slid by endlessly above our heads. There were few cracks and no root damage. The glow beetle cast deformed, shadowy copies of us across the curved walls. History had forgotten the reason why Gold River had been constructed. The only thing we really knew was that its color came from slag flowing from the copper mines.

Soon, black soot replaced the brown silt on the walls. Burned rats lay on the side paths, entombed in a sludge of ash. The blackness seemed determined to absorb the beetle glow. My grip on the gunwales tightened. There was no doubt that whatever had burned the street had been here too. Why the sewers? Were they being used to move around the city unseen?

The only sounds were the drip-drip of water and the splashing of the pole into the murky water. The effort of pushing us against the current had covered Babbas in sweat. We didn't pass or meet a single other boat or human. So much for my mental picture of waterways crowded with boats trading illicit cargo.

Something tickled my *Perception*, so I pushed my spell out further. There! The same magic residue I had felt from the *Probe*. Its faint presence permeated everything, even the water. We'd come to the right place, but I needed a stronger clue.

A landing stage appeared out of the darkness, and Babbas steered us effortlessly up to it. I glanced at his hunched form as he wrapped the rope securely around a charred pole. How did bargees remember where they left all the boats?

"There's sumfing you should see."

"What?"

"You're the expert," he said. "Babbas is just the idiot, remember? Down the stairs, first chamber on yer right."

"You're not coming?" I narrowed my eyes.

"I'll wait 'ere."

"But you're our guide."

"Bargee guide. I stay with the barge. Go do yer business."

I joined Ayla on the charred landing. A dozen steps led down to a narrow hallway running in both directions. Dried stains of bronze ran like snakes down the steps, evidence of previous floods, but the stonework bore no evidence of fire damage. Inches of brown sludge coated the floor, and algae clung tenaciously to the smooth walls.

We descended and I peered into the darkness. Why had he brought us here? All I could hear was our breathing. I struck a lightstick against the wall and a fierce red light erupted at its tip, illuminating the hallway.

"It's silly that a necromancer doesn't have a light spell," Ayla whispered.

I scowled at her. "It's not the nature of necromantic magic. Apparently Elik Magi could manipulate light."

"How do you know? No one's seen one in forever."

"Their magic was different to ours. They manipulated the elements directly and their magic had no effect on the dead. In any case, shush."

Something wasn't right about this place.

I held the lightstick low and scrutinized the rubble at my feet. A section of the ceiling had given way. A hot wind blew from the gaping hole above me, ruffling my hair. Far ahead on the right, a crumbling archway provided access into a dark chamber.

What could possibly be in there that Babbas wanted me to see? I increased the sensitivity on my *Perception* and pushed it stealthily forward. Sharp, staccato jabs rippled back through my spell, a sensation I'd never felt before. Not good. Whatever was in there had a strong aura.

My arm tingled without warning, as if something invisible had passed through it. I twirled my index finger and cast *Shadowsee*.

A spectral, undulating rope of ectoplasm became visible, writhing in midair next to me. Nothing physical held it aloft. It snaked ahead of me and arced directly into the suspicious room. Behind me, the translucent umbilical cord pierced Ayla's chest and stretched far into the hallway beyond the steps.

Lak and all his demons!

I laid a gentle hand on Ayla's shoulder and channeled my *Shadowsee* through her so she could see it too.

She leaped aside, clutching her breast, but the thing had left no mark. "Gods. What's that? It's not real, is it?"

"It's a shadow link. What it's connected to is very real. And mean." I jerked my head toward the chamber.

"And what is it connected to?" She stared at the wriggling cord.

"A grak."

"What's—?"

"Later. Stay back."

Why had Babbas brought me to a grak's lair? Graks didn't start fires or destroy streets. I chewed my bottom lip. How had he even known about it? Master Begara's advice in class had been pretty specific regarding the grak: "Turn and run."

I took a deep breath and wriggled my shoulders. I could beat it. The tomb wights had been easy.

I pushed Ayla back toward the stairs. She glared at me.

"This is dangerous," I whispered. "I know what I'm doing."

Did I? I handed her the lightstick and crept forward, nudging loose stones with my boot to clear the way, never taking my eyes from the archway. The room was filled with heaps of rubble. The spectral rope snaked behind a huge fragment of a fallen buttress lodged against one wall.

Come out, come out, wherever you are.

I drew a sizable ball of magic from my core and blasted a massive *Dispel* into the room, bathing the entire area in a purple flash.

The grak leaped onto the ceiling, sending rubble clattering in all directions. It scuttled toward me, upside down, hundreds of barbs along its ten legs clinging to the bare stone ceiling. A razor-ridged carapace protected an abdomen the size of a barrel, yet the thing stretched eight feet in length, counting its forked, bony tail and oversize head. Two spheres of flylike eyes reflected a distorted version of my look of horror. Saw-toothed pincers clacked repeatedly and its antennae quivered, probing the air in front of it.

I stumbled backward, my heart thumping in my ears.

Kristach. I'd hoped it'd be smaller.

"Run for the boat," I yelled, following my own advice as the creature chased me from the room.

Once she saw it, Ayla screamed loud enough to wake the dead, then slipped on the rubble and landed on her butt.

I grabbed her wrist and yanked her up. She broke from my grip, flew around the corner, and thumped up the steps toward the barge. "Cast off, cast off."

A heartbeat behind her, I limped up the stairs and skidded to a halt, kicking up a cloud of ash from the landing.

Babbas and the barge had gone.

 SIX

"He left us behind," Ayla said, peering up and down the shadowy river tunnel.

"The tristak son of a bikka!"

The grak crunched over the rubble at the bottom of the steps. I whirled about, scanning the dock for an escape. We were trapped.

The creature crouched low, its spectral cord flailing behind it, and then it sprung off with all ten legs. I planted my feet firmly as it flew up the stairs toward us. Kristach!

Magic seethed within me and I launched a bolt of red fire from my fingers. My *Necrotic Ray* scorched one of its legs, causing it to shrivel and rot away. Amid a stench of decaying flesh, the creature fell back down the stairs.

"Gods, it's gross." Ayla glanced down at it. "Things like that live down here?"

Worse, honey, much worse.

The grak righted itself and raised up on its hind legs, watching us, its antennae plucking the air. Ayla jabbed the lightstick toward it but it didn't seem bothered by the blazing light or the sparks dripping from the end. The grak hissed and clacked its huge pincers. Ayla stepped back and her foot crunched through a rotten board, sending her lurching toward the frigid river. She grabbed the wall to save herself. The lightstick fell onto the landing between us.

The grak leaped again, this time running up the walls. Its pincers opened wide, revealing rows of barbs.

I'd made a crucial error in judgment by disturbing the grak. I stepped back. There was nothing between me and the river now.

I shot another *Necrotic Ray* at its head, and grunted with the mental exertion of the magic burning through me. The creature rolled aside and the ray hit another of its legs, which turned black and fell off. The creature continued upward, filling the landing in front of us.

Belaya preserve us. This thing was huge.

My whole body tensed, still hurting after my beating in the bargee taproom. I drew on my magic, siphoning it through my body, my arms tingling. Blue energy arced from my fingertips, lighting up the whole tunnel in a blinding blue flash. Lightning flickered across the grak's body. Its legs and antennae quivered in a frenzy. Its shrieking wail deafened me and I winced.

Ayla sprung forward, brandishing a hunk of wood. She stood at the grak's flank and struck it again and again on its head until the wood splintered and broke. The creature retreated, scampering back down the steps, only to regroup and sit atop a giant chunk of rubble. I threw another lance of magic at it to show who was boss. It snatched up a broken tile and deflected the beam.

"What are you doing?" I asked Ayla.

"Helping. I'm not standing by uselessly while you have all the fun."

"That's exactly what I want you to do."

This was tough enough without looking out for her too.

"How can it do that?" she asked, peering around the corner. "How can a giant bug use tools like that?"

The grak snatched a rock with one of its feet and hurled it at me. It repeated the motion, flinging a flurry of masonry up the stairs. I jerked my arms up to protect my face. Rocks pummeled my sore body until I collapsed to my knees, quivering in agony. *Mustn't cry out. Not in front of the girl.* I bit my tongue and tasted blood.

The lightning should have dropped it. This was embarrassing enough without Ayla watching me getting my ass kicked. And what in Lak's name was she doing now?

Ayla darted across the landing, dodging the missiles. She snatched up fallen chunks and hurled them back. The rocks crack-cracked as the grak batted them aside with its tile shield. Its own bombardment ceased.

She growled. "I know this is a test. Give me more time. I'll find a way."

A test? What?

"Get back and keep quiet," I said.

I slipped my Ashtar dagger from its sheath and inched forward to the top of the stairs. A hundred glistening eyes stared up at me. Its pincers sawed back and forth. When its maw opened, green goo dribbled out, lubricating the saws. It rocked side to side.

I tensed and gripped my knife so hard that my hand began to shake.

It sprang, every vicious barb on its legs extended, its tail arched over like a scorpion. Ayla moved too late and it slammed her aside, smashing her against the wall. I was slow to sidestep, and razor barbs shredded my robe. Pain exploded along my side. I gritted my teeth and stabbed my dagger deep into its head, which crunched and squelched. Limbs thrashed all around me, threatening to disembowel me, but I pushed the knife through the back of its head cavity and into its abdomen, my arm up to the elbow in its hot, slimy innards.

Ayla picked up a six-inch splinter of wood and threw herself on the creature's back, driving the stake into an eye. The eyeball exploded, drenching me in ichor.

Disgusting! I scraped the stuff from my face, blinking hard.

Finally, the grak's legs gave way and it belly flopped. I twisted my knife one last time and withdrew it, flicking the goo from my arm. Ayla rolled off, leaving the stake embedded in its head. She clasped her bleeding arm and glanced at the corpse, her nose scrunched.

"I was expecting ghosts and skeletons," she said. "Stuff from graveyards."

"Yeah, well some real nasty things live down here, and there are deeper, darker places than this."

Maybe people wouldn't hate necromancers so much if they knew what we protected them from.

Her eyes grew as wide as plates as she studied the corpse. Her body trembled.

"This thing is real," she muttered.

"You think? What do—?" I sucked in a breath. "Are you kidding me that you thought this was a test?" I screamed.

"Like a rite of initiation, or something."

I leaned against the wall, one hand clasped to my bloody side. I panted heavily.

"You saw this thing. It nearly killed us both. You thought this was make-believe?"

She nodded but fire burned in her eyes. "How was I to know? You could've conjured it all to see how I'd react. I wasn't scared of it, you know."

"Well you should have been. Kristach, Ayla." I shook her by the shoulders. "I told you necromancy was dangerous. There aren't going to be any tests down here in the real world. That's for the classroom."

She jerked herself free and stepped aside to dab her arm with a handkerchief.

"We'll have to disinfect that when we get back," I said.

My insides screamed at me and a dull ache covered me from head to foot. I cautiously probed beneath the shreds of my robe. No serious harm done, but damn, it hurt.

I retrieved my dagger, wiped it on my ruined robe, and replaced it carefully in its sheath. The gem set into its hilt pulsed bright yellow, whereas previously it had been dull and lifeless. I shuddered to consider that the grak's depraved soul lay trapped within the gem. The knife had been a gift from Phyxia. I treasured it but its power over life and death gave me the creeps.

I watched the river sweeping by. Babbas would never have found the grak himself and lived. Someone had told him to bring us here. Someone who wanted me dead. I wiped the sweat from my brow. What did I know that put my life in danger? What had Phyxia been trying to tell me? I stamped my foot. Infuriating woman.

I had enough magic left to replenish my *Perception* and *Shadowsee*. The creature's spectral cord remained, flickering and barely visible.

Ayla reached for it and her hand passed right through it. "If it's dead, why is this still here?"

"The grak was being controlled by a spell. Like a puppet show. This is a clue to who cast it. We need to follow it before it fades."

I picked up the lightstick, ushered her down the steps, and followed the ghostly rope along the hallway.

"What if there's another one?" she asked.

Then we were dead. I had insufficient magic to go through that again.

"Hurry," I said. "The connection spell will fade quickly."

The hallway was dry and free of rubble, but every step jarred my aching body. I cursed not being able to move faster, but clenched my teeth and manned up. The spectral cord no longer writhed, but simply floated in midair. We wound our way around corner after corner and up several flights of ancient stairs. My limp grew more pronounced and I panted with the exertion.

"Where did that thing come from?" Ayla asked. She'd slid under my right arm to offer some support. "An egg? Tell me that wasn't a baby one."

"You don't want to know."

The grak's cord was barely visible now. I nearly missed it when it angled sharply to the right into a narrow pipe that spiraled downward. Water dribbled down the center. I slipped and fell, then slithered and slid down the steep pipe on my butt. Hardly dignified but it worked. Ayla followed, landing beside me.

I hoped that she had forgotten her question. I didn't want to lie, but neither did I want to tell her what a grak really was— the soul of a person imprisoned inside any one of a number of foul and disgusting creatures, to do the bidding of its controller until insanity and depravity took over.

"It's gone," she muttered.

I recovered my breath and got to my feet. Great. Deeper in the undercity than I'd care for, and the trail had gone cold.

"Hear that?" she whispered.

I held my breath and strained my ears. A voice.

"This way," she said, taking a step into the hallway we'd tumbled into.

I put my finger to my lips. "Sound carries a long way underground. Be quiet or they'll hear us too."

The lightstick had all but burned itself out. I handed it to Ayla behind me, so that I masked most of the light as we advanced. The tunnel turned and emerged into a hall. Glow beetle light flickered from within, so I took the lightstick and crushed it underfoot until it went out with a flash of sparks. We crept inside the hall and crouched in the inky shadows.

Two lines of pillars ran the length of the room to a distant exit. Each pillar propped up a giant, seven-feet-tall skeleton. Cobwebs and dust covered them from head to toe. There was no end of bones and skeletons in the undercity. Big deal.

Two men stood in the center of the hall, a glow beetle cage on the floor between them. They resembled demonic conspirators in the eerie red glow. One man looked about my age, dressed in a Guild robe. I'd seen him around but never learned his name. The other was Babbas. My fists clenched. I'd turn him into a grak, if I only knew the spell.

"I told you everything," Babbas said. "Now pay up."

"Liar. You warned him," the other necromancer said.

"Did not. Babbas followed your instructions."

"The grak was supposed to kill *him*, you fool, not the other way round."

The man wore a journeyman robe. My conversation with

Begara came flooding back. What fool had taught a journeyman how to control a grak? What in Lak's name was going on?

"Maybe they killed each other," Babbas said, hand held out. He cast a crooked, menacing shadow on the wall.

"You'd better hope so." The journeyman plopped a purse into Babbas's eager hands. Coins chinked. "I'm not going back there to find out. Get the light. We're leaving."

He strode into the hallway at the far end of the hall. Babbas picked up the beetle cage and scurried after him. The chamber around Ayla and I grew dim.

Ayla stood on tiptoe before one of the giant skeletons, peering up into its rib cage. What was she gawking at? I grabbed her by the sleeve and set off after the two men. We'd gotten halfway through the long chamber when a shimmer of magic prickled my skin.

The giant skeletons tore themselves free of the pillars, creating a horrendous grinding and scraping sound that echoed around the chamber. Webs and dust flew in all directions as their bones clacked and rattled, stretching as if from a long slumber.

A second ambush. *You fool, Maldren!*

I ran for the nearest wall. "Ayla, over here."

"I didn't touch them."

"I know. They're sentinels."

The monstrous skeletons crowded toward us, gray shapes in the encroaching darkness. Only the barest glimpse of light remained from the receding men. I counted a dozen of them clawing the air, before they'd surrounded us with our backs to the wall. I groped at my belt for another lightstick.

My gut was empty of magic. Kristach, we were in for another beating.

"We can't just stand here." Ayla stepped forward and kicked the leg out from under one of them. The huge bone clattered across the floor and the skeleton clung to its neighbor, hopping on one leg. She stepped among them into the gloom.

Bony hands grabbed hold of my torso. I dodged a punch and stuck my hand into the nearest rib cage. Ancient bones are light. I lifted him off the ground, him still kicking and punching, and I flung him against another. The pair of them tumbled to the ground in a pile of legs, arms, and ribs. That wouldn't stop them for long.

The last of the light vanished, plunging us into utter blackness. Bones rattled and clacked in front of my face. Something kicked me and pain shot up my leg. I stumbled back against the wall.

The unlit lightstick fell from my hand.

Ayla shrieked some sort of battle cry. Bones clattered on the stone floor in the same direction as her cry. Damn it, I couldn't see anything!

"Come and get it," she yelled. "Who wants broken bones next?"

An ominous thump echoed in the chamber.

"Maldren, help."

Lak and all his demons!

I took a punch to the gut and doubled over. Since I was halfway there, I dropped to the ground and groped for the damn stick.

"Are you all right? Keep talking so I can find you."

My fingers closed around the tar-wrapped cylinder and I struck it against the floor. Red light blazed, illuminating the entire chamber. Six skeletons loomed above me, while four more pummeled Ayla. The two I had smashed had finally figured out whose bones were whose and were reassembling before my eyes. Nasty, tenacious things, sentinels.

I snatched up one of their thighbones, scrambled to my feet, and headed toward Ayla, swinging my club wildly. She had managed to snap one of their arms off, and she smashed at its ribs as she sheltered her head with her other arm. I whirled like a dervish and careened into the mob, my thigh club knocking three heads from their shoulders. Skulls thudded as they hit the ground. I fought my way toward her, biting back against the cramping in every muscle.

"You should have let me handle it," I said.

"I'm not useless, and I'm not scared."

A skeletal hand gripped my arm. I pulled it free, shoved his sternum and he fell back into another. They stuck together, broken ribs interlocked. Four more stepped forward.

I didn't have time for these games. The journeyman was getting away. I owed Babbas a kick in the nuts too.

I dredged deep within, gathering up every dribble of power, every trickle of magic. My head pounded. Pins and needles doubled me over. I needed one last spell. I gritted my teeth and scrunched my eyes closed.

"Cover your eyes," I said and threw my club to the ground.

I clapped my hands together and could see the blazing light I had created through my eyelids. The skeletons exploded. Bone shards rattled against the walls and rained down on us. Then there was total silence. Despite Ayla's bravado, we'd have lost. *Bones to Dust* was an effective but messy spell. It also tended to splash magic over a great distance. The journeyman would know I was here now, as would every creature within half a league.

"They look shattered," Ayla said, deadpan, but winked at me. She brushed off hundreds of tiny bone fragments and fingered her bruises, wincing.

I rolled my eyes. Despite the beating, I believed that she had enjoyed the fight.

"Follow me." I hurried toward the far exit as fast as my limp would allow.

A long tunnel curved to the right, bisected by smaller ones. They'd likely head for the river so I trusted my direction sense and stuck to the major passage. It turned to the left, and we thumped down a set of dusty stairs. Boot prints were everywhere but that didn't mean anything. At the foot of the stairs, we splashed into filthy sewer water, sending rats scurrying into a myriad of holes.

I headed left. It seemed right. We sloshed forward.

"It's so hot," she said.

It was. We hadn't rested since finding the grak. Sweat

poured down my face and inside my clothes. Steam rose from the water at our feet. I stopped.

"We should go back," I said. "Now."

"Wait. I hear them."

I did too. I'd recognize Babbas's deep, whiny voice anywhere. Something splashed into deep water.

"They're getting away in the boat." Ayla hurtled onward.

"Come back. Let them go."

She disappeared around the corner and I limped after her. The walls were slick and warm. She yelped, and then a wall of rats screeched and scrambled toward me. I stepped to one side and they flowed over my boots, trampling and climbing over each other in their effort to escape. I couldn't believe I'd just yielded to rats. Rats were smart. *I should run with them.*

I hurried after Ayla, crashing into her back where she stood on a wooden landing stage. The boat was already in the middle of the river, Babbas punting furiously for the far side. Steam filled the tunnel, and the boat swirled in and out of view as if into a fog bank. Condensation ran in rivulets down the walls of the semicircular river tunnel, and the water in the sewer behind us had begun to bubble. I finally registered a distant rumble that had risen to a roar. The men in the boat glanced upstream.

"Row, row," the journeyman said. He dipped his hands in the river to paddle, and then jerked them out again with a cry.

"Run," I said to Ayla and shoved her roughly back into the sewer. "Run as if Lak was at your heels."

He was.

The roar became deafening. Before we turned the corner, I glanced back to see an inferno engulf the boat. The men hadn't even had time to scream. The firestorm consumed the entire river tunnel, scorching the stonework as it rushed by, heading downriver. I shielded my face from the searing heat and limped after Ayla.

SEVEN

I caught snippets of distant, unidentified noises, and a close, whispered voice. I exhaled slowly and stretched my stiff muscles from my neck down to my toes. Oh, what a wonderful, relaxed state.

"Aren't you ever going to wake up?" Ayla asked.

"No. I'm enjoying my body not aching. If I get up, something will just make me hurt again."

"Funny." She shook me.

I opened my eyes. She stepped away from where I lay on my bed. How long had she been there?

The enticing aroma of hot mint drew my gaze to the mug sitting on the small table by the window. Beside it stood a plate heaped with honey cakes.

"It's past lunchtime. You must be starving." She frowned and tucked her bangs behind her ear. "You've been dead to the world since we got back from Gold River yesterday."

I snorted at her choice of words, cracked my neck, and got out of bed. I was still dressed in my dirty, bloody clothes. I scanned the room.

"If you're looking for your robe, I gave it to Mother B. last night," Ayla said. "She made a lot of huffing noises and declared it beyond repair."

I had others stashed in the corner. My body was sore and I had to favor one leg, but the limp was less pronounced, and my eye no longer throbbed. I dropped into my chair by the window and sipped the hot mulip. Something pulled tightly against my side, and I lifted my shirt to see clean bandages wrapped around my middle, where the grak had clawed me. Ayla's right arm was bandaged from elbow to wrist. I drank again and jerked my head toward her arm.

"Mother B.," she said and sat on the bed. The room wasn't large enough for a second chair.

"I helped with yours." Her face flushed red. She wrinkled her nose. "You need a bath."

I could tell from her damp but neatly brushed hair and clean clothes that she'd already taken one. Dried blood and grak ichor caked my arms. I picked out minute slivers of bleached bone from my hair. The last thing I remembered was us breaking out of a sewer grate beneath one of the wharves in the harbor. I stuffed a whole cake into my mouth. *Mmm, still warm.*

"Was there another fire last night?" I mumbled, spraying crumbs.

She shook her head.

No way was it a coincidence that the fire thing had been down there with us, but had it intended to kill me, or Babbas and the journeyman? All of us? Unfortunately, my star witnesses that someone in the Guild was trying to kill me were flakes of ash long washed out to sea. Now I had to start over, look for new clues. I blew out my breath.

"What do we do now?" Ayla said.

"It's the Day of Solace," I said. "I'm having dinner with Phyxia tonight, and no, you're not invited."

I started on another cake.

"I think I deserve a decent meal after yesterday." She prodded her bandaged forearm and winced.

"Sorry, it's a regular ritual. Just the two of us."

She shot me a dagger look. "Then I'll stay here and finish

your book on elementary power usage."

There was a gap in the haphazard rows of dusty books on my bookshelf.

"You stole my book while I was sleeping?"

"I borrowed it." She scowled. "I'll teach myself."

"You can't. It doesn't work that way. That's why you need the Guild. Besides, you're not ready to learn yet."

"According to you I'll never be ready. Stop treating me like a child. I can help if your ego will let me. If you're going to dinner, I'm reading the book." She stood. "If you want a peaceful afternoon, submit."

We stared each other down. Definitely the daughter of an aristocrat. Had I been so feisty as an apprentice? Yeah, I'd been a nightmare. I sipped my drink. She'd thought the grak a test. She had guts. More than I'd credited her with. I knew a dozen male apprentices who'd have run and kept going right out of the city. She wasn't the soft, whimpering aristo I'd expected.

"Sit down. Remember when I warned you how dangerous this job is? And that was before someone tried to kill me."

"You don't know that they are. Maybe that bug creature—"

"—grak—"

"—was a mistake. Maybe that hideous hunched man got scared."

"Someone in the Guild was controlling the grak," I said. "And don't forget the skeleton ambush."

She smoothed her skirt and flicked aside an ant. "Maybe he didn't know it was you. Maybe the skeletons—"

"Stop trying to justify it all. Whatever the reasons, you could have gotten killed. Stuff like that tends to happen when I'm around."

She shook her head. "I'm not going home. I'm not giving up."

"Then go back to the Guildmaster and get yourself assigned to someone else. Someone in better favor. Someone who will teach you."

She scowled and tipped her head to one side.

"Don't look at me like that. I didn't ask for an apprentice. Hanging around with me isn't the best start to your career, trust me."

She smiled sweetly. "But being with you is more fun. I like you, and I know you'll be a great teacher."

Gods, not the wide, pleading eyes again.

She winked mischievously. "Since you've failed to scare me off, give me a chance? Oh, you didn't think you were being obvious about it?"

I blew out my breath. "All right. Study that book and tomorrow I'll teach you basic power sensitivity. Now leave me in peace, woman."

She gave an "I win" smile, leaped up, and left the room.

Midafternoon, I slipped out and wandered down the hill to the Guild. There, I cornered Master Begara as he exited a classroom, and I actually startled the old man.

"We need to talk." I raised my voice above the din of his departing students. "Please."

He stepped back into the classroom and I followed. It wasn't a large room. Six rows of benches faced a chalkboard and a teacher's desk stood on a raised platform. Graffiti had been carved into the seats, some of it mine. The basement classroom had no windows, only bowls of everfire suspended by chains from the ceiling.

Begara sat at the desk. His face bore a guarded expression. I closed the heavy wooden door.

"You were right," I said. "There was a Guild journeyman in the sewers with Babbas. I saw them both down there."

"Did you identify him?"

"I wish I had because he tried to kill me."

Begara frowned. "What do you mean?"

"I paid Babbas to guide me, but he delivered me into the clutches of a grak."

Begara blinked rapidly. His fingers tightened on the edge of the desk.

"The thing was no match for me." I smirked. "I followed the thread and guess who was controlling it? The journeyman."

Begara gasped. "There must be some mistake."

Why did everyone insist that this wasn't a plot to kill me?

"We need to see For—the Prime Guildmaster," I said. "Immediately."

"No." He paced in front of the board. "We shouldn't bother him. He must have authorized the man to be down there."

"Are you suggesting he told the journeyman to kill me?"

"Of course not." He chewed his fingernail. "The idiot had to be acting alone."

"Well he won't again. He and Babbas are dead."

Begara recoiled and his eyebrows shot up.

"There was another fire and it killed them both."

"Leave this with me." He glanced nervously toward the door. "Have you spoken with anyone else?"

I shook my head.

His gaze darted around the room, seeming to rest everywhere. He avoided looking at me directly.

"Stop poking around," he said. "I don't want you getting into further danger."

"I appreciate that, Master, but I can look after myself." I turned and opened the door.

Behind me, he cleared his throat. "Coming to me was the right thing to do. Keep it between us. There's a good lad."

I stepped into the empty hallway and closed the door. Maybe he was right not to escalate this. Fortak would blame me. It wasn't until I was halfway home that I realized he hadn't showed surprise when I'd mentioned the fire.

Mymar's was my favorite restaurant. It wasn't the best in the city, but Mymar's was special. Since Phyxia first took me, we'd been dining there almost every Solace Day since. That was the only reason. It wasn't like I hung out in the Plaza District. Snobs, the lot of them.

A roar of applause and laughter filled the night air of Theater Street as I hurried up the thick, luxurious carpet from my carriage to the lobby of the Sylarian embassy. I didn't know how Mymar had negotiated situating his restaurant on the top floor of the embassy, but both the view and the food made it a popular nightspot. Even dressed in my best outfit and new robe, I paled against the brightly hued clothing of the rich, and the endless twinkling of their jewelry in the faery lights suspended above the wide walkway. Baskets of sweet-smelling feresens filled ornate tubs on both sides. I tried to melt into the few shadows at hand.

Begara had been of little help, and I hoped Phyxia would have clearer advice than last time.

Inside the embassy, a tall, dark-skinned Sylarian strode effortlessly toward me. His hazel eyes shone in the bright overhead lights. With a low bow, he directed me to the lifting carriage. Sylarians didn't seem to mind necromancers for one reason or another. Another plus in Mymar's favor.

I stepped into the lifting carriage, joining a poshly dressed elderly couple. Blue and green streaks contrasted the gray of the man's hair. With a scowl, he led his companion back out into the lobby, leaving me with the Sylarian lift operator.

The doors closed, gears grinded into movement, and the lobby fell away below us. We rattled our way up the core of the building. At the fifth floor, the lift carriage jerked to a stop and the doors opened to reveal the welcoming, tastefully decorated entrance to Mymar's.

The restaurant host wasn't so welcoming. Not a Sylarian. His patronizing smile faded and he studied me as one would a kalag at market. He must have been new here.

"This is a private establishment." He moved forward to intercept me.

Was he afraid I'd summon wights to eat his dinner guests? I crowded into his personal space and he cringed.

"I'm here at the invitation of Ambassador Cach'el'soprine."

His eyes widened and met mine for the first time. "The ambassador is—"

"I know the way." I pushed past him.

Diners gawked at me as I paraded through the room, and there was a symphony of the clink of silverware hitting china. Conversations turned to muttering. I made certain to hold my head high and meet everyone's gaze. I belonged as much as any of them. It was my city too. Chill air hit me as I emerged onto the rooftop terrace, at the top of a staircase inlaid with a carpet of the deepest blue.

Lunas appeared larger than life, rising from the ocean beyond the harbor. The pinpoints of stars above paled against the glitter of Malkandrah laid out below. Phyxia sat with her back to me at a table overlooking the river, but I recognized her by the cute bonnet she wore to conceal her horns. As always, she had claimed a table close to one of several bronze bowls filled with burning oil. I smiled. She remembered how cold I got. The intense heat soothed my aching muscles, and I slid into the chair beside her.

"Oh, sishka, your life would be easier if you'd dress to blend in." She traced her fingers along the runes of my robe.

I studied her expression—those sensuous lips that formed a half smile, half smirk; her deep, intelligent yet mesmerizing eyes, their color drifting from blue to green and back. I sloshed brandy into my glass, took a quick swallow, and let its fire etch my throat.

"I'm not ashamed of who I am."

Her tiny hand brushed mine, and delightful tingles ran up my arm, quickening my pulse. My whole body relaxed, forgetting the beatings and abuse of the past couple of days. She held her glass up to Lunas and observed the swirling, amber liquid in its glow. Then she chinked my glass and sipped.

Once the waiter had taken our order, I lowered my voice and told her everything about my foray down to Gold River. A chill gust swept across the rooftop and I shivered. Phyxia stared out into the city. I knew better than to rush her so I poured more brandy. Her tall ears twitched. There was something comical about the way they stuck up on either side of her bonnet.

"You're doing just as you should," she said. "Follow the trail. Make the right choices."

"How can I do that when I have no idea what I'm looking for? Why won't you—?"

The waiter appeared beside us. I shut my mouth with a clack of teeth, and sat stiffly in the chair while he laid steaming plates and lidded pots before us. He bowed low to Phyxia and pointedly ignored me. How rude. I muttered a fake curse. His face flushed and he scampered away.

The aroma of her fish entrée teased my nostrils. I breathed deep of lemon and brae-grass. She picked up a dainty china jug and dribbled a pungent sauce onto the glazed, jit-nut-encrusted filet on her plate. I set aside the copper lid from my bowl to reveal a simmering, lurid yellow, pulta hotpot. I took a spoonful and rolled the delicate flavors across my tongue.

Choices, she'd talked about back at her hovel. What if I made the wrong ones? I nibbled my lip.

"I'm stuck," I mumbled. "I get that you prefer me to solve things by myself, but this isn't the time for that. People are dying. I'll probably be next. Why are you withholding advice when I need it most?"

I took another bite of tender pulta.

She swallowed and sipped her drink. "The nature of events means that I cannot—must not—help you. It is the way of my kind, sishka. You have always respected that."

I sighed. "I do, but allies are hard to find right now."

Her thin lips curled into a smile, and a jet of blue chased green around her gorgeous eyes. I blinked and turned back to my meal.

"You have Ayla," she said. "No sarcastic remarks today? Perhaps you already see her worth?"

What did she know about Ayla? I shook my head. Phyxia had an otherworldly gift for augury.

She glanced at me. "No matter what you believe, always believe in her."

That made no sense. Why did everything she said feel

scripted?

"Perhaps you should seek your mother's advice," she said.

I washed down my pulta with the brandy. It burned and settled uneasily in my stomach. Really? She was bringing that up now?

"When was the last time—?"

"No." My fork clattered against my plate.

The people at the next table looked at me. I scowled them into submission.

"Nothing will bring me kneeling before her grave. I'll never forgive her."

Phyxia crunched on jit-nuts. Her ears twitched, the way they do when I imagined her laughing inside.

"You're so like her," she said. "Always trying to prove yourself. Such ambition. How much fun you'll be when you're older and wiser."

Her gaze shifted over my shoulder and her smile faltered. Behind her, a woman pointed and gasped, her hands flying to her mouth.

I swiveled in my chair and my heart skipped.

EIGHT

A swathe of fire slashed through the city on the far side of the river, a flickering wound of oranges and reds. It illuminated a carpet of inky smoke that boiled out into the surrounding streets. I imagined a tear in the fabric of the world, as if Lak himself had chosen to rip a gateway from his own fiery demesne into ours.

"Another tenement fire?" a man asked. "Wretched peasants need to be more careful. Sheer clumsiness to let another fire burn free."

"It will clean out the slums at least," a woman said. Her partner laughed.

My hands balled into fists. Even halfway across the city, screams carried on the wind. My mind flitted back to that first street—burning timbers careening in all directions, crashing roof tiles, the smoke snaring its victims, driving them to acts of depravity.

My goblet slipped from my grasp and shattered on the tile floor. I shook the horrific image from my mind.

In the distance, a fiery column erupted high into the sky, illuminating a round, stone tower, out of place among the tenement buildings.

"That's my street." I leaped from my chair. "Phyxia, please. Tell me how to stop it."

Our eyes locked. Was that fear I saw? I turned toward the stairs but she grabbed my arm. Yellow flecks whirled ever faster in her irises.

"If you put a defenseless person between a wight and a ghoul," she said, "why do the creatures attack each other and not their victim? Why?"

I blinked. What? That was no help whatsoever. I pulled away and bolted for the stairs.

My stomach turned over and over. I swallowed hard.

Mother B.

Ayla!

What was I doing, dining with Phyxia? The fire creature had struck again and Ayla was defenseless against it. My pulse raced. I'd let her down.

After hurtling down five flights, I stumbled into the cold night air, gasping for breath. Where were the damn carriages when you needed them? I raced toward the river, clawing at the stitch in my side. A block later, I collapsed against the pole of a street lantern, my lungs ready to explode as I sucked in air. Sweat beaded on my skin. I was going to get there too late.

A man dismounted from his heleg in front of a tavern.

"Emergency," I gasped, snatching the reins and thrusting three Malks into his hand. "I'll send it home, I promise."

The beast snorted and backed away, its wide, black eyes rolling in their sockets. It took me several attempts to get into the saddle, but finally I yanked the heleg around and drove it down the cobbled street. Behind me, the man shouted for the Black and Reds. Steering my mount proved difficult. The tristak thing didn't like me one bit, and I had to cling on for dear life against it trying to throw me at every turn. Did I stink of death?

At the end of a wide avenue, I bullied the creature ever faster across City Bridge. The river ran black and cold beneath. On the east side of the river, the heleg put up a bold fight, spinning around and arching its back, kicking the air behind it.

My moves weren't elegant but I stayed on, and that seemed to have impressed the beast enough that it whisked me down Broad Street without further shenanigans.

At the foot of Kand Hill, it skidded to a halt as people poured around us, fleeing toward the river, crying and shrieking. The heleg's coat was slick with sweat and its breath steamed into the night air. It whinnied and jostled. I led it to a trough, dismounted, and patted its nose. He'd done his part.

The last stragglers emerged from narrow streets and lanes that wound up the hill. Street lanterns shone through a haze of thin smoke, and the air was heavy with the stink of ash and charcoal. A sickly orange glow reflected in windows in the streets above me, and beyond roared a wall of flame. Tortured screams in the distance. The clanging of fire cart bells.

My heart raced. Could I go back into that madness? I took a deep breath and set my teeth. I had to.

The heleg fled, its hooves clattering on the cobbles. Alone, I started up the steep street. After the first turn, I lost sight of the river. The smoke grew thicker until it was like walking through an ocean fog, stumbling from one dulled street lantern to the next. Locked stores and tenements loomed on both sides. My hands trembled as I homed in on the screams and the crashes of fighting and smashing glass.

One block below my home street, I turned a corner and a blast of heat almost knocked me over. The smoke swirled into inky tendrils that probed every doorway and alley. The smoke was alive. Who or what controlled it? Wasn't incinerating its victims enough?

I siphoned energy from my core and molded a *Cleansing Shield*, encasing myself in a buffer of frozen air.

In a corner store window, I spotted the ghostly reflection of two men clubbing each other with burning timbers. An old woman seized a shard of glass and held it aloft, twisting and turning it in front of her face as if contemplating what to do with it. The circling smoke seemed to egg her on. My hands trembled. *Move, Maldren!*

By slipping into a narrow alley I hoped to come to Mother

B.'s inn by an easier route. Round Tower Street was close. Or what remained of it.

I shouldn't have deserted Ayla tonight.

A house's burning frame tumbled into its neighbor with a crash, cascading rubble and burning embers into the alley. Without hesitating, I ran through, trusting my shield to hold back the heat. My foot caught a broken brick, and I tumbled into the gutter of an adjacent street.

A man lurched around a corner, coat sleeve pulled over his mouth. His clothes were singed and covered in streaks of soot, but I recognized him as the stableman at the inn. He spotted me and backed against the wall. Then he tried to edge past me, his eyes full of fear. Fear, but not madness.

"Pilk," I yelled, and moved to intercept him. "It's me, Maldren."

The blade of his knife flashed in the firelight.

"I'm not mad." I showed him my empty hands. "The smoke hasn't got me. Did they get to safety?"

He squirmed past, his gaze flicking between me and the blazing inferno at the top of the road.

"Mother B., Ayla?" I asked. "Where are they?"

Tentacles of choking smoke pushed at my magic shield's invisible barrier, like roots searching for moisture. When they failed to reach me, they snaked toward Pilk. He squealed and made a break for it, sprinting away downhill.

"Mother died before I could get to her," he said over his shoulder, sobbing.

My legs sagged and I crumpled to the ground.

"The girl?" I shouted. "What about the girl?"

"She fell from a burning window." He turned the corner out of sight.

I rolled over into the wet gutter and pounded the ground with my fists.

I'd failed everyone, abandoned these people that I shared a home with. I could have helped them. Saved them. While fine brandy had burned my throat, Mother B. had died a horrible death to the flames, and as the liquor had descended into my stomach, Ayla had plunged from her bedroom window.

Damn it, I had no way of knowing when and where fire would strike. I should've been here but it wasn't my fault. But it was my choice what to do next.

I jerked upright, aware of the searing heat on my face from the blazing buildings. Fire leaped from rooftop to rooftop, rolling like a juggernaut down the hill. Back on my feet, I yelled defiantly against the deafening roar of the flames, the crashing of timbers and falling masonry.

"The dying stops here."

At my command, ice traveled my veins, bleeding from my body to replenish and expand my shield. Even as I shivered, a cauldron of power boiled in my gut. There would be no rest until I'd exhausted every spell I had against whatever primeval force powered this destruction.

At the very edge of the inferno, I stepped over burning rubble and charred corpses. A curious blue fire enveloped the dead. It shimmered and wavered in the wind and then zipped skyward, leaving a faint trail, quick to fade.

I sucked deep of the power within me. Every part of me hummed and tingled. Never before had I manipulated so much power at once. Magic arced and crackled from my hands to the metal posts of nearby street lanterns.

I hurled my fury at the fires surrounding me, discharging freezing lightning into the adjacent buildings, extinguishing them in an instant. Steam and ash surged into the road, but the street ahead—my street—still raged in the heart of the inferno.

The fire shrieked and whistled as if in pain, and the flames leaped high into the air until the sky burned. Like a vision from The Deep itself, the aerial firestorm broiled and swirled, flexing its muscles, pulsing and spitting. Surely now the demons of Lak would rise from the abyss. The fiery wall towered over me like water brimming a dam.

It roared, it screamed. It was alive, I was certain of that now.

"You want a piece of me?" I screeched. "Then come and get it."

A torrent of heat poured out of the sky, flowing down the road and reigniting everything around me. My eyebrows burned. I caught the stench of my smoldering hair. The fire creature was all around me: in the sky, the buildings, in the very air pressing down, making my lungs burn. I sensed a presence as old as time itself. What was this thing?

I cast *Death's Spark*, with such intensity that I cried out in pain. My lightning rocketed into the sky, sparking blue until it exploded in the heart of the firestorm above me.

Thunder boomed across the city.

Gobbets of fire rained down. The burning wasteland around me offered no cover. No one lived to see my struggle. A ball of flame plummeted from the sky, exploding in a nearby abandoned cart, the flames like a plague of insects devouring an animal.

Raw, limitless power overran my *Perception*, shattering it. I had no chance so I ran.

Orange phantoms swirled out of the smoke and circled me as I sprinted along the burning street. Their hair was alight, and their faces seared and blistering. I snapped my eyes closed and muttered a protection spell, but they continued inside my head, wailing and whirling. Thousands of voices.

End our suffering. Free our souls.

The anguish! My head felt ready to burst.

Release us.

"I can't. Get out of my head."

I ran on blindly, waving my arms, swatting at ghosts, dodging fireballs detonating around me. I hurtled toward the river, fully intent on plunging into its icy depths. A sudden back draft grabbed me with a deafening whoosh, jerking me off my feet and smashing me into a street lantern. I clung to the pole with both arms. Boxes and barrels, debris and straw blew by me, sucked back toward the fire. A yowling cat flew past my head.

Then the sky went dark. Total silence. The air pressure equalized and I crumpled to the ground. The heat had gone, the firestorm extinguished supernaturally. Only burning embers remained, billowing smoke into the night.

The creature had chosen to withdraw. Why?

I lay motionless, my arms still wrapped around the metal pole. The only sound was the thumping of my heart. A breeze blew in from the river, and with it a chill fog. Ayla swirled out of the gloom, her clothes shredded and blackened, her eyes hollow, lifeless. She seemed to float upon the fog that billowed along the ground.

"I'm so sorry." I moaned. "I'm too late."

My head dropped to the cold cobbles.

She glided forward. Was the girl going to cling to me in death as she had in life?

"Go." I waved my arm feebly. "Be at peace. I'm not your master now."

"What're you talking about?"

"Don't make me dispel you. It'll hurt. Both of us." I groaned. My gut ached.

Ayla's ghost snorted. *They can do that?* She knelt and wrapped her arms tightly around me. Her body warmth seeped into me.

"I'm not dead," she said. "I made it. We both made it."

She clung to me and wouldn't let go. Thank Belaya! I squeezed her tight and pressed my head into her lavender-scented hair.

I awoke to the aroma of mulip, fresh and minty. I savored the moment, relaxed on my bed, eyes closed. The world rocked gently. Had I gotten drunk the night before? Was that why I couldn't remember returning to my room? I pitied whoever had carried my dead weight up the steep back stairs. My eyes jerked open and I sat up, cracking my head on the wooden frame of a bunk above me. The room was totally unfamiliar.

"Careful," Ayla said. "Didn't you get banged up enough last night?"

She lay cold, damp cloths on my arms and legs. They soothed the heat rashes on my skin and reduced the inflammation.

"That feels so good," I murmured.

I studied her concerned expression as she perched on a chair by my bedside. No longer black with soot, her skin was pink and clean beneath her disheveled clothes. She pushed a steaming mug into my hand.

"You mumbled all night long about freeing spirits," she said. "More than once you cried out for Mother B."

My shoulders sank. Of course this wasn't my room. It didn't exist anymore. The whole inn, the whole street...gone.

"I'm sorry I wasn't there. I'm sorry I was across the river when it happened. I should—"

Her shushing sounds cut me off. "Don't blame yourself."

Morning light streamed in through a circular window at one end of the room, and through cracks in the ceiling boards. At the other end, a sturdy door stood open. It didn't reach the floor—there was a six-inch step at the bottom. The whole room rolled side to side, accompanied by the occasional splash of water. The enticing smell of toasting sabatas wafted through the door.

"Why are we on a boat?" I asked.

Ayla dabbed at my burned arm. It was covered with scratches and flaking skin but I'd gotten off lightly.

"After I found you last night, you babbled on and on about getting to water."

There was a gaping hole in my memory. Her hugging me beneath the street lantern was my last recollection. I shook my head and then groaned at the throbbing in my skull.

"I tried several inns," she said, "but you kept pushing me away and mumbling about boats. Don't you remember?"

"Where are we?"

"Boattown. I figured that's what you meant, but you were rambling. I didn't know where else to go."

"Whose boat is this?"

She shrugged. "He seemed nice enough and the rent was cheap. This is a good place to hide."

Boattown was a superb place to lie low, among pirates,

thieves, and lowlifes running from the law, but how had she gotten in? It was a miracle the boat owner hadn't slit our throats and tossed us into the harbor. I imagined her walking into the heart of the floating slum, in the middle of the night, propping up a necromancer. Tongues would be wagging this morning, but she'd done good.

She stroked my arm. "Thank you for coming back for me."

I lost myself in the depth of her chestnut eyes. My heart thumped and warmth spread through me.

"Go up on deck and get some air," she said, removing the now-warm cloths from my limbs. "I'll join you in a moment." She stood and headed for the door.

I crawled out of the bunk, one hand holding my head, and stepped into a walkway containing half a dozen identical cabins. The door at the end opened into a galley, but I climbed a nearby ladder into what had once been a mess hall. It was now a mere shell with gaping holes in every wall. Beyond lay a spacious rear deck.

Solas was halfway to the zenith, and I tipped my head to soak up his warm rays. Our boat was packed among a flotilla. Some were broken merchant vessels like ours, others were huge hulks, or open and narrow. All had been lashed together with rope and planks. The wooden mass bobbed and undulated like a bed of moss upon a pond. Our boat lay close to the clear water of the harbor. Dozens of ramshackle boats had been moored between us and the rows of warehouses and silos on the shore. This was one place that fire creature would never venture.

Ayla joined me, balancing a tray laden with steaming mugs and delicious-smelling sabatas. I snatched one and bit into its flaky pastry, blowing hard against the hot meat and vegetables inside.

"This is really good."

She frowned. "You didn't think I could cook?"

"To be honest, no. Didn't you have maids and servants to—"

Her eyes flared. "Why do you hate aristocracy so much?"

I was on dangerous ground, ironic since I wasn't on ground at all.

"It's good," I said. "Thank you."

She nibbled daintily on one end of her sabata.

"Mother B. was the only person who ever looked after me and cooked for me," I said. "My mother..."

I glanced at the trash-laden water sloshing between the boats.

A violent trembling seized Ayla, as if she'd been holding it back but could do so no longer.

"Everything burst into flames," she muttered. "There was screaming...breaking glass...people leaped from windows. It all happened so fast."

"I thought you had leaped too. Pilk said you had."

She shook her head.

"I was downstairs. People ran in every direction." She picked at her breakfast. "It was total mayhem. So many bodies. Then the smoke came. It...it..."

"I know," I murmured. "I've seen it."

Her eyes brimmed with tears.

"It was horrible. The smoke was alive. People started..."

A single tear raced down her face, over her lips and chin. I had an urge to wipe it away, but stayed my hand.

"There were...fights. Someone grabbed my arm. Mother B. pushed me clear. Oh Gods, the man's eyes."

She dropped her forgotten sabata and her whole body shook.

"He had an ax. He...he...and she...so much blood."

"I know, I know."

I wrapped my arms around her and she buried her head into my chest, sobbing. I didn't know what to do or say, so I simply held her. I understood her anguish. Undead in the sewers were one thing, watching friends and neighbors die was another.

No one should witness the horrors of that writhing smoke. The Guild should be keeping people safe from such horrors. Why wasn't Fortak organizing them to seek and destroy this thing?

I patted Ayla's back. She should be living a life of luxury with her aristocrat parents, safe from all this. I remembered the burning souls from last night, how they had wailed to be released from their torment. Even death was no escape. I looked across the city, where wisps of gray smoke spiraled into the clear green sky, like a tombstone marking a grave.

 NINE

I squeezed through the ridiculously narrow alley that led to Phyxia's door. High, ramshackle walls of wood and tin restricted the daylight. I ground my teeth. This time I needed answers, not evasion. The fire had taken my home and friends. It had gotten personal.

The door to her hovel was ajar. My pulse quickened, and I carefully pushed my *Perception* into the three rooms of her abode. Nothing dead lurked within. No grak, no skeletons, but that didn't mean someone wasn't inside. I pushed the door and it swung effortlessly open, gently bumping the wall. The hallway was empty. Daylight streamed into the pantry at its end, likely coming from the window in her living room.

"Phyxia?"

I tiptoed down the hall, avoiding the loose boards that always squeaked. The door to her bedroom was closed. Items looked out of place in the pantry, and cupboard doors gaped open. The tap-tap of loose tin sheeting on the roof broke the eerie silence.

"Hello?" I said.

The hairs on my neck stood erect as I entered the living room, my fists clenched and every muscle tensed to react.

Drapes billowed at the window. Hanging paper charms twirled silently in the breeze. The pages of an open book riffled on a side table, beside a bowl of jit-nuts.

The uneven floor creaked behind me.

I launched myself toward the couch. A massive club smashed into the floor where I had previously stood. Off balance, I thudded into the back of the couch, which tipped, sending me shoulder-first into the wall. I cried out and crumpled into a heap on the floor. Rolling my shoulder, and nursing my bad leg, I crawled to one end of the couch. Splinters of wood lay scattered around the hole gouged in the floorboards.

Something moved in front of the open window and a forbidding shadow loomed over me, like a giant with a hunched back. I scrambled away from the couch, shaking pins and needles from my left arm. With my other I drew my Ashtar dagger. The intruder's belly wobbled with each stride, and all I could distinguish from his silhouette was a mussed haircut and crooked nose. I circled around the couch.

"Targ," I said. Had he gone insane?

He lowered his club, leaned forward, and scrutinized me. "I mistook you for another one."

"Another what?" I sheathed my knife.

"Spy. I think they've taken 'er."

"Phyxia? Who has? Taken her where?"

"Let's find out." He lumbered out of the room.

This made no sense. I doubted any spy or agent could capture Phyxia.

"Where're we going?" I asked his back, as I followed him out of her shack. "Talk to me."

Somehow he made it along the narrow alley, squeezed sideways and sucking in his belly, huffing all the way through. A sky carriage rumbled above our heads, decelerating toward the cable station on the summit, barely fifty feet above us.

"I captured one," he said, descending two stairs at a time. "You're going to help interrogate him."

"Where's Phyxia?"

He wouldn't answer my questions, so I followed him through the hollow labyrinth of the Lantern District until we arrived at one of many doors along a curved hallway tunneled into the rock. He pulled an iron key from his belt. It rattled in the lock and he pushed the heavy door open, motioning for me to precede him. I paused, peering into the darkness. Targ had always protected Phyxia. I had to trust him.

I stepped inside. All I could see in the gloom were shapes resembling barrels and crates. The door shut behind Targ, plunging us into total darkness. Someone else was in here, breathing heavily. Chains rattled. The scratching of a firestarter rasped beside me. There was a pause, and then soft lantern light bathed the room.

A man slumped against a barrel, heavy chains binding his legs and arms to a ring set in the wall. Dried blood crusted his swollen, purple-blotched face, and his right eye was bloodshot and half-closed. A gash oozed above his lip. His brown coat was torn and smeared with more blood.

"Looks like you started without me," I said to Targ, and sat on a wooden box facing the prisoner. It was hard to picture him before his beating, but he didn't look familiar.

The man's head rose slowly. He glanced at my clothing and then his one good eye met mine. He sneered. A bold move given our relative situations.

Targ crossed the room in two strides, grabbed a wad of the man's hair, and smashed his head against the barrel. The prisoner groaned and fresh blood trickled from his nose.

"Going to talk now or must I pull you apart bit by bit?"

I had no doubt that Targ would. It was like I had wandered into a thieves' den or gang hideout, and I pictured the stories I had heard, some of which made the undead look like playmates. Did I have the stomach for it? Definitely. No one messes with Phyxia.

The prisoner actually laughed. "I won't tell you anything."

Targ's maul of a fist smashed into the man's face. Nose bones cracked.

"Ha," the prisoner said and spat blood at Targ, who drew

his fist back for another punch.

"Wait," I said. "You brought me here for a reason."

Using magic to torture this man went against everything I stood for, but if I didn't intercede then Targ would turn this room into an abattoir. The man would take his secrets to the grave, and I hadn't yet mastered *Séance* with unwilling spirits. I shuddered, masking it by stretching.

Some theater first. Maybe I could delay the inevitable. I pulled gently from my energy core. My gut still ached from flinging everything I had against the fire creature the night before. I projected a *Cleansing Shield*, for no other purpose than to chill the room. Our breath steamed before us. Both men shivered. The lantern dimmed. A simple *Signs from the Grave* spell brought dozens of beetles and centipedes scurrying out of the woodwork, crawling over the prisoner's legs and up his body. He watched them with wide eyes.

"I'm summoning something from your worst nightmares."

I spoke in a deep, hollow voice. Master Semplis had often done so with great effect. I leaned forward and held out my hands palm down as if pulling something from the ground.

"It will burn your mind from the inside, steal your memories, and spill your consciousness. Speak now while I can still dispel it."

The man's tongue snatched a three-inch-long centipede from his face. He bit it in two and spat the ends at me.

"You think I'm scared of bugs, boy? I'm not afraid of your fake bogey monsters. Go back to mummy and let the real men play." He squinted at Targ through swollen eyes.

Kristach son of a bikka. All right, he deserved it all.

Enough of trick spells. I released summoning magic into the air, keeping a tight grip on my spell. The last thing I needed was something truly nasty showing an interest. I spent extra energy to cultivate a false show of strength. The more powerful spirits rarely hunted by day. What I wanted was a lochtar.

And there she was.

She hovered around the portal I had opened to The Gray,

watching me, sizing me up. Her form shifted between a wisplike ball of shadow energy and a woman with alabaster skin and red, unblinking eyes. Her clothing was devoid of color. She sniffed hungrily like a hound, seeming to taste the prisoner's life force. Her eyes flared and she materialized in the room, translucent and shimmering but at the same time menacing and real.

Targ stumbled behind me, his breathing fast and heavy.

Our prisoner smirked and spat more blood. "More parlor magic?"

"Where's Phyxia?" I asked. "The woman in the house you were spying on."

He attempted to stare me down.

"Last chance. Where are you holding her?"

"Go jump in The Deep."

I twitched my finger and the lochtar extended a spectral hand, reaching effortlessly through his skin and deep into his chest. His whole body arched and shook, rattling the chains. The metal manacles tore into his skin, rubbing it raw, and he bit hard on his lip. I could only imagine what the lochtar was doing to his insides. It looked like she was rifling through his organs.

"She was already gone." He screamed and tilted his head toward the ceiling. "I didn't see her. I don't know where she is."

I reined the lochtar back, relieved that she obeyed. Her hand withdrew, clean and unbloodied. No wound showed on the man's chest.

"How many of you are there?" Targ asked. "What do you want with her?"

"I'm only following orders." His breathing was sharp and ragged. His gaze flicked between the lochtar and me. Every time she drifted near, he winced, sucking on his bloody lip.

"Whose orders?" I asked.

He said nothing, staring at the lochtar's pale face inches from his. She smiled, one moment gracious and beautiful with white hair tumbling over her eyes, and then she turned into a rabid, drooling corpse, hissing in his ear.

"The Duke," he said, voice trembling. "Get it away from me."

"Which Duke?"

"Imarian. Duke Imarian."

Interesting. I tried to recall the Duke's conversation with Fortak at the Guild. *Kristach, I should have paid greater attention.*

"Why is this Duke holding her prisoner? He could have invited her for dinner."

He shook his head rapidly. "That's all I know."

He was lying.

I gave a psychic nod to the lochtar, and she cupped her hands to the side of his head, pushing her fingers into his skull. His head jerked back and he screamed. His eyes bulged and his mouth filled with frothy saliva. I had to look away. The screaming went on and on. I wanted to cover my ears.

"Guild…" he mumbled. "The Guild…"

I tore the lochtar away. She spun and hissed at me so I blasted her with a wall of energy. It hurt to maintain it, but eventually she backed down. She was in my world, at my bidding. I wore the pants.

"What about the Guild?" I asked.

The prisoner's head lolled forward, almost to his lap, and he whimpered.

"Louder," Targ said and shoved the prisoner against the barrel.

"The Guildmaster wanted her," he said. "Not the Duke. Make that thing stop."

The room spun. I swallowed repeatedly. What were Imarian and Fortak up to?

"Only if you tell me everything," I said, and slapped the box I sat upon.

"The Covenant. They called it the Covenant." His voice wavered and he stared warily at the spectral figure floating before him. "I don't know what that is, Belaya be my witness."

"What else?"

I prodded the lochtar, and her crooked, rotten hands

reached for him. A wicked grin spread across her previously beatific face.

"All right, all right," he said. "They're blackmailing the High Council. I know nothing else. I just work for the Duke. I follow orders. I swear."

Blood and drool dribbled from his mouth, and his fingers twitched. Veins pulsed on his forehead. I'd broken him. I wasn't proud of that.

I cast *Dispel* on the lochtar and my spell dragged her toward the portal. At first she resisted, then she smiled at me like a loving mother and winked out of existence.

"I'm glad I'm on your side," Targ said. "Let's finish him."

"Don't you think we've done enough? He's a pawn, nothing more."

I stood. Bile rose in my throat. I needed fresh air.

"He'll report back," Targ said.

"Fine. I'm already on the hit list, and you're no use to them." I hesitated at the door. "The lochtar has his scent. I think he'll be a good boy now."

My head spun. What in Lak's name was going on? My predictable world had been turned on end. I needed alcohol. The Bloated Fish, just outside the Lantern District, was as good a bar as any.

A young serving girl thumped a tankard on the pitted, cracked table in front of me and hurried away. I didn't register her face or anything else about her. Instead, I slid further into the shadows of my booth and took a big gulp of beer. The din of a dozen lunchtime conversations faded away. I made creatures by tracing the marks and scratches on the table—a grak here and a lochtar there.

They'd taken Phyxia even if the spy had no knowledge of it. There was no way he could have lied, not at the end. What did the Guildmaster want with her? She'd never mentioned him, never cared about the Guild at all. I clenched my fists. How dare they treat her like that?

I took another swallow, enjoying the bitter, hoppy taste.

What was this Covenant? Nobody could blackmail the Council. As a member himself, how did this Duke Imarian get mixed up in all this? He and Fortak had said something about the Guild regaining a seat on the Council. What did that have to do with Phyxia? Who knew what higher power she worked for, but it certainly wasn't the Council. I ran my fingers through my hair. Politics were beyond me.

The man's screams echoed in my head, and his tortured convulsions played across my vision. I shuddered, downed my beer, and banged the tankard on the table. *Bring no harm to the living.* I felt dirty for unleashing that thing on him. Who'd been the bigger sadist, Targ or me?

Sick. Sick and dirty.

A petite hand took my tankard.

"Akra," I said. "Bring the damn bottle, girl."

She returned with an uncorked bottle and a glass. I mumbled an apology and gave a good tip. My hand shook as I poured the amber liquor into the glass and shot it back, throat burning. Another. I ran my finger along a deep scratch in the table. What had I stumbled into? How long had spies been following me? Nothing made sense, except that the fire creature at my apartment building was definitely not a coincidence. Friends had died.

I stuffed the cork back in the bottle and put my head in my hands. Getting drunk would only lead to a darker place.

Did Phyxia think I was dead after running from the restaurant into the fire? She couldn't be killed, and they'd regret it if they tried to torture her. I doubt they knew the extent of her powers. I didn't.

I blew out my breath and rubbed my temples. All I had were questions, not a single answer, and no one who could shed light on any of this.

It was lonely without her.

The day had turned unusually warm for so late in the solar,

almost as if mighty Solas was trying to raise my spirits. I lifted my head high and soaked up the warmth. At every street corner, I glanced over my shoulder. No tail that I could see. To be certain, I plunged into the web of tiny alleys that riddled the tenements and warehouses at the waterfront. It was easy to dart this way and that, cutting through the communal areas and small open plazas filled with clotheslines, crates, livestock coops, and other flotsam. Finally, I bounced down a half-rotten plank onto the makeshift wharves of Boattown.

Ayla was asleep in one of the cabins on our boat, clutching the book she had smuggled from my old room to her chest like a great treasure. I hadn't noticed, but she must have carried it from the fire at the inn. That spoke volumes of her determination to join the Guild. The only one of my books to survive. No matter, I rarely referenced them.

I tiptoed down the hallway to the tiny galley, and helped myself from a pitcher of amalan juice sitting on the table. I grabbed a hunk of hard-rind cheese and sat on the tiny bench seat. It was a large ship for the two of us, but had likely been jammed with over a dozen crew in its heyday. The berry juice was tart. I chewed the cheese, my nose flaring at its pungent smell. My fingers drummed the tabletop, tapping to the rhythm of the ship's hull groaning as it pushed against the adjacent boats.

I'd failed to kill the fire creature. Sure, I could pretend that I'd driven it away, sent it packing with its flaming tail between its legs, but why fool myself? It could have crushed me, incinerated me, but it had chosen to withdraw. What clue was I missing?

It was time to get Ayla to a safe place. This wasn't her fight, despite what Phyxia had said. I'd put it off for too long, but now I needed to find her father and tell him to collect her. She deserved the life she'd been born into, not this, not hiding on a damp, decrepit boat. I stuffed the rest of the cheese in my mouth and pulled her necklace from my pocket.

I lay it in my palm and studied it in the daylight streaming through the open hatch overhead. A crest had been engraved in blue on the gold pendant, that of a crown upon a stack of metal ingots. Her father probably owned copper mines east of the city. A list of noble houses and their crests played in my mind, and then the name came to me.

I thumped the table and the pitcher rolled off and bounced across the floor, splashing blue juice everywhere. I clenched my fist around the pendant, feeling it cut into my flesh.

Her father was Duke Imarian. Kristach!

Ayla rushed into the galley, looking me over and scanning the mess. She retrieved the pitcher from under the table. "What happened?"

I dangled the necklace before her. "You left this in my room. You know, the room I used to have before it burned to the ground."

"Why are you mad? I thought I'd lost it." She reached for the necklace.

I jerked it back. "I want the real story of why you ran away from home...Ayla Imarian. Nice touch about your mother and the necromancer, but there's more, isn't there?"

She double blinked. "How did you find out?"

Her eyes flicked to the necklace.

"I want to know the truth. Why does the daughter of a Duke run away?"

"Don't shout." A frown creased her brow and her chestnut eyes studied me. "I don't want to grow up the little princess my father expects. I'll die if I hang out at another ball dancing with moronic, sissy boys all hoping their daddies can marry us off so that they can go into business with my father. I want to be a necromancer. We've been through this already."

Having watched her stomp through sewers and smash skeletons, I couldn't imagine her prim and proper in a ball gown. Or dancing.

"Why me?" I asked. "Mentioning your daddy's name could have gotten you a more shining example of the Guild. I'm more of a pariah."

She shrugged but eyed me warily.

"The Guildmaster picked you, and I'm glad he did." She

looked down at her feet and her cheeks flushed. "I like you."

I narrowed my eyes. She was trying to distract me. My pulse raced. It was time to challenge her lies.

"He picked me, or you did?" I said.

Picked me for a sucker?

"He did, of course. I didn't have a choice. I didn't know anyone at—"

"What's your father's connection with the Guild?"

"I...I don't think he has one. Why all the questions?"

I stood. She bristled but stood her ground.

"So you ran away from home, wandered into the Guild, and just happened to get pally with the Prime Guildmaster? And your father had nothing to do with it?"

I grabbed her arm and gave her a shake.

She pulled away. "No. He has no idea."

"Well, I have an idea. Let me tell you what I think. Your father plotted with Fortak to get you into the Guild."

She flinched and her gaze flicked momentarily aside. Guilty as charged.

"As my apprentice you became the perfect spy—"

"Spy?"

"—reporting back on my every movement. When I left you at Petooli's you crossed half the city to find me at my garret." I leaned forward, and stabbed a finger at her. "How did you do that, huh? How did you know where I lived?"

"But—"

"Ah, but the Guild knows, and they told you." I paced the tiny room. "And what about in the sewers? You tried so hard to convince me that everything had an innocent explanation."

"This is stupid." She folded her arms across her chest. "I haven't spoken to anyone at the Guild since I left that day with you. I'm not a spy. That's silly. What's gotten into you?"

"I'm not done." My cheeks flushed hot and my fists clenched. "Out of the thousands of streets in the city, that fire thing burns down mine. You were there, yet somehow you escaped and everyone else died."

I slammed my hand on the table and she jumped.

"Then, conveniently, you manage to convince all the thugs and thieves of Boattown to rent us a boat. I bet that was easy considering you had all the resources of your father behind you."

I clenched my teeth and glared at her.

"Are you done?" Her eyes flared. "Because you haven't analyzed all the evidence, mister genius."

"Oh?"

"You say my father planned it all, yet any number of things in the past two days could have gotten me killed. The grak, the skeletons, the river, the fire. You think he wants his only daughter dead? You think the fire was intended for you? It's always about you, isn't it? Since I knew you were going to dinner last night, why didn't I just tell whomever it is you think I'm spying for? Maybe I should have told this fire creature of yours that you weren't at home."

Her small hands made fists, and her body trembled.

Oh, she was good, faking anger at me. Her speech had sounded rehearsed.

"Everyone has gone to The Deep since I met you," I said. "You're the perfect spy—flattering me, trying to get information from me in the guise of learning, following me like a lost puppy-"

"I'm not lost. I can take care of myself."

I stepped onto the ladder and climbed up to the outer deck.

"Then stay away from me," I called down to her. "I'm leaving and won't be back. Don't try to follow me."

"I won't."

With only the belongings I had on me, I stomped across the creaking plank to the adjacent boat, and then threaded my way from vessel to vessel until I reached the shore. I wanted to meet someone, anyone, if only to glare at them and swirl my Guild robe, but every deck was empty, the lowlifes hiding from the day. I strode up the final ramp to the wharf and hurried into the maze of city streets.

At Canal Street, I sighed noisily, turned around, and went back to see an acquaintance who lived on a boat near the grain silos.

"Jagga, you know the girl I came in with?"

He picked food out of his beard, a bushy expanse that threatened to overgrow his entire face. His weathered, scarred hands shook uncontrollably. I tried hard not to stare at the tic under his right eye.

"Aye. What of 'er?"

I stepped aboard. The single-cabined boat stank of booze.

"She have any visitors while I was away this morning? Did she leave?"

"Nay. Not that I saw."

I nodded. Nothing moved in Boattown without Jagga knowing. I placed three gold Malks in his palm and pushed his quivering fingers closed around the coins.

"Keep an eye on her for me. Make sure no one harms her."

It was time to pay Duke Imarian a visit.

 # TEN

The sky carriage swayed erratically with each gust of wind, and the incessant creaking of wood and pinging of the taut cable frayed my nerves. My teeth mimicked the grinding of the wheels on the cable above. Two hundred feet below, white-crested waves buffeted the boats in the harbor. Dark clouds threatened to engulf the sky, turning the green heavens into a muddy brown.

I slumped back on the bench. Ayla had taken me for a ride. How could I have been so blind?

The isle of Sal-Urat spread out in front of me. It had been two solars since my last visit among its palaces. The aristos had made a fool of me. It was payback time. As my carriage angled toward the western end of the island, the Bridge of the Goddess came into view, its perfectly paved road barely forty feet below me, but high above the entrance to the harbor. The largest ship afloat could sail through each of the four arches without topping its mast. Legend said that law would prevail in the North as long as the bridge stood true. So had it been for a millennia.

The carriage vibrated violently as it rattled across the last of the cable piers, and then descended steeply toward the station.

The Elik Magi had built the carriage system over a century ago. Did anyone know how to maintain it? If the cable broke, I faced a long fall into the frigid harbor.

The warm morning had been replaced by a biting wind. Once back on solid ground, I hurried through the wide avenues of the Mansion District, each impressive thoroughfare lined with mature trees and perennial flowers. Pink and orange blossoms fell like snow, carpeting everything in color.

Duke Imarian's house filled an entire city block. The gargantuan, sprawling mansion rose several floors above an encircling wall. It was humbling to consider the riches and political might on display here, but by the time I came across the gatehouse, my resolve was back.

I gritted my teeth. I was fed up of events happening to me. Now I would control *them*.

Two burly men stood inside the open gates. Dressed alike in green trousers and leather shirts, they also wore copper helmets emblazoned with the Duke's crest. Ostentatious fellow, this Duke. I could see why Ayla disliked him. The two guards ended their conversation at my approach, and tapped the handles of their long spears on the gravel driveway.

Whatever.

I swirled my long robe behind me, set my gaze on the house, and strode past. One of them muttered something to my back, but I kept going, maintaining an even crunch-crunch along the raked gravel. I smirked to myself. Being feared had its perks.

The house had two wings, one each side of an impressive central core from which rose three round towers festooned with wide windows, clearly not intended for defense. Irritated by the gravel, I cut across an immaculate lawn to the main entrance, six granite steps leading under a canopy supported by copper-plated columns. I bet he had a copper chamber pot too. The floor of the entrance foyer was a mosaic of polished marble. Glittering chandeliers hung high above.

"Welcome to Imarian Manor."

The short man who approached wore a green, satin robe

cinched at the waist with a copper sash. Highly original. He wore effeminate slippers, and his hairy legs contrasted bizarrely with his shaven face and bald, lumpy pate. He stopped six feet in front of me and clasped his hands.

"How may I assist? Do you have an appointment?"

"I must speak with the Duke urgently. I report to the Prime Guildmaster."

Not a lie. I didn't say I represented him.

The man bowed low. "His Lordship is busy and unable to receive at this moment. Shall I make an appointment for another day?"

I stepped forward. "He will receive *me*. Now."

He backed up and glanced nervously toward a door at the rear of the entrance hall. I heard muted, gruff voices within.

Now I got to have fun. I'd been hoping for a chance to be an ass.

"Don't insult the Guild by making me wait," I said, once again emulating Master Semplis.

There were no visible signs for many of my spells, and it was a simple matter to mold my energy into *Signs from the Grave*. Beetles and millipedes spewed out of my sleeves, tumbling onto my boots and crawling everywhere. Blood dripped from the hem of my robe, splattering on the polished tiles. The servant shrieked and retreated from the spreading plague of bugs. I followed him step for step, and as we passed a pair of waist-high pots, the plants wilted, their leaves curling and shriveling. Bare branches remained. I waved one arm imperiously, and exotic satin roses turned black and flaked into dust. *Oops, I'm sure they were rare and expensive.*

"I'm not here to harm the Duke. Take me to him."

His tight fists had turned his knuckles white. He opened his mouth to speak and then became distracted by a brown, furry spider the size of my hand, plip-plipping along the marble floor.

"All right, all right." His voice squeaked. "Make those things go away."

He fled toward a side door, dancing around the bugs as he

went. I ought to advise the Duke to hire staff with stronger stomachs. I canceled my magic and the bugs crawled away into the cracks and corners. I was cruel to torture a poor man only doing his job, but I had to see the Duke. Intimidating a manservant was easy, but cheap gimmicks wouldn't impress the Duke.

His reception room lay at the back of the house, overlooking a verdant garden of shrubs and color-coordinated flower beds. A tall, middle-aged man turned to face me. I recognized him immediately.

Did he remember me from outside Fortak's study?

His purple robe was accented by sparkling gem-encrusted rings and a necklace hanging low over his chest. His arms were loosely crossed, one hand smoothing his goatee.

The servant cleared his throat. "I'm sorry, your Lordship—"

"No more visitors." The Duke waved him away, staring at me all the while.

I stood tall and studied the room. Plush couches with bronze legs faced each other across a low, polished copper table set with a silver platter of decanters and shiny goblets. Nautically themed tapestries adorned the walls.

"My street agents said you had bravado," he said once the door had closed behind the servant. "What do you want before I have you arrested?"

Does arrogance follow power or vice versa?

"I know what you and Fortak are up to, and I intend to stop you."

Always start strong. Other than the existence of the Covenant, I had no idea, but he didn't know that. I hoped.

He raised a single eyebrow. "Indeed? You've upset him. He's been trying so hard to get rid of you."

I startled, and couldn't mask the movement. *Kristach! My own Guildmaster was trying to kill me?*

He laughed—a hollow, mocking sound. "You didn't know? I've never seen the old goat get so worked up. You've made a fool of him and that puts you in a really awkward position.

You're playing games beyond your abilities, boy."

He walked around the back of the couch, toward an end table stacked with books, their corners neatly aligned. I tried to read the spines but they sat at the wrong angle.

"And what is it that you think you know?" he asked. "Clearly you don't grasp the extent of your own naïveté. And stupidity."

He withdrew a loaded crossbow from behind the couch, leveled it at my chest, and tapped his finger on the trigger housing.

I jumped and my hands jerked defensively into the air above my head. My breathing quickened.

He moved out from behind the couch.

"You have no idea what is going on." His tone was even but his thin lips curled into a snarl. "Don't try anything silly, and no spells. I'd hate you to break your petty Guild oaths."

"I'm unarmed," I lied. Sweat trickled down my forehead.

"Did you even prepare before barging in here? You don't seem to have brought your own crossbow." He snorted. "Well, boy, I have a dilemma."

"What?"

"Do I kill you now, give your corpse to Fortak and get one up on him, or deliver you alive and allow him his choice of demons to rip you apart from the inside out." He moved his finger to the trigger. "Both tempting."

The crossbow didn't waver. I blinked the sweat from my eyes and tore my gaze from the glinting tip of the barbed bolt. Targ said that you could tell a man's intent from his eyes. The Duke's were focused on mine, unblinking. My skin crawled, expecting metal to rip through my body at any moment.

He was wrong. I had a plan. Of sorts.

"You won't do either," I said.

"Won't I, now?"

I breathed deep. Make-or-break time.

"I've got Ayla."

"No you don't. Fortak's looking after her."

If his men had recovered her from Boattown this morning

then I was dead. My heart pounded in my ears.

"Is that what he told you?" I pulled her necklace out of my shirt and dangled it in my trembling hand.

His eyes narrowed. "If you've harmed her…"

So I had a play after all.

"I haven't." I jerked my head toward the crossbow. "Please put that thing away and let's talk in a more civilized fashion. Why waste two comfortable-looking couches?"

"No." He took aim on my heart. "What do you want with my daughter? I swear if you've touched her, I'll tear you apart myself."

"You're the one putting her in harm's way. What kind of coward uses his own daughter to spy for him? Do you realize she'd been with me every single time someone tried to kill me? Is that all she is to you, a disposable asset? For Lak's sake, she's only a girl."

"Spy? What are you talking about? I'm her father. What kind of monster do you take me for?"

"One who signs a secret pact with the Guild, one who…"

What, Maldren? What are they up to? Here you go, running your mouth off before thinking it through.

He sized me up. What was he thinking? I'd surprised him twice now, easily, unless he was faking it. *Kristach, I'm not a politician or a strategist.* For a moment I'd hoped he would lower the crossbow, but I obviously hadn't pulled the right lever.

He sighed. "You're confused. You have no facts that I can see, only wild accusations and conspiracies. You can't touch me, and my daughter is innocent. Return her."

"So you deny introducing her to the Guildmaster and—?"

"Of course I do."

His gaze locked on her necklace in my hand.

"Ayla was upset and seeking a way to hurt me. She was a fool to approach the Guild, but Fortak promised to keep her safe until she returned to her senses."

The resolve returned to his eyes.

"But none of this is your business. Bring her back to me at once."

"He lied to you, Duke. He made her my apprentice. He gave her to me. Does that sound like he's keeping her safe?"

The crossbow dipped. That was the lever.

"Fortak is playing us both," I said. "If she isn't your spy then he has something else in mind for her. Duke…"

I took a step forward, keeping my hands in the air. The crossbow wavered but stayed down.

"She isn't ready to return home, but in time I can convince her. Until then, I will keep her safe."

What was I thinking, using her as leverage in a game I wasn't equipped to play? This was my chance to be rid of her and I'd just proclaimed myself her protector. I'd left her alone with all the ruffians in Boattown. Not a stellar start to my new role. Imarian was right. I was in over my head. *Lak and all his demons!*

"Here's my deal," the Duke said. "Bring Ayla home and I'll forget everything—your trespass, accusations, all of it. We can end this simply. Today."

"But it doesn't end there. Why does Fortak want me dead? And why have your men seized Phyxia?"

"I don't intend to explain myself to you, boy."

"Think of your daughter."

He strode to the window and stared out at the bushes blowing in the stiff breeze. After a moment he turned.

"Stop dragging her into this. She—"

"I didn't," I said. "Fortak did. Release Phyxia. It's the only way to get Ayla home. Trust me."

"Don't blackmail me." He brought the crossbow to bear, aiming across the couch at my head. "Fortak wants you dead for some reason. You're holding my daughter, and you demand my trust?"

I'd blown my advantage. *Keep his focus on the girl, Maldren.*

"Ayla would be dead without me. I'm the only one protecting her. You want your daughter, and I want Phyxia safe. We can help each other."

"I can't." He lay the crossbow on the couch. "I can't betray Fortak."

"Yes you can. For your daughter. He'd betray you in an instant."

"You of all people should know why I cannot," he said, barely audible. His shoulders sagged. "Fortak used a lochtar to bind me to silence."

I pictured the chained spy squirming and shrieking with the agony of the lochtar penetrating his body. I'd sunk to the same level of depravity as Fortak. My stomach flipped. I vowed to redeem myself for that cruel act.

"Give me anything," I said. "One little thing. I swear I'll protect Ayla."

He stared at me for a long moment.

"Caradan's Tower at dawn," he muttered, and turned back to the window. "Tell Ayla that I miss her very much."

The gate guards paid me no attention when I left the mansion. Maybe I should have stuffed a handful of the Duke's silver under my robe. The wind had died down, and Solas shone feebly through a light overcast layer. A fine but persistent rain soaked through my clothing, chilling my body. The bleak weather matched my mood, and I was glad for the deserted streets as I marched back to the Bridge of the Goddess. Blackwings and gulls circled above, cawing and diving to rooftop level. I turned away from the sky carriage station, tired of the ostentatiousness of the rich and their gimmicks. If Belaya had intended us to move through the air, she'd have turned us all into birds.

The rain fell harder, splashing on the cobbles and running along the wheel ruts, just as it dribbled from my hair down my face. I leaped into a regular carriage, its pair of helegs stamping and whinnying. Steam wafted from their backs.

"Temple Plaza," I directed the driver, and sat back, shaking the water from my head.

I wanted to check out Caradan's Tower in daylight. There was no way I would show at dawn unprepared, with the Duke expecting me. His words tumbled around my head. How much was truth? He hadn't shot me, so that was a start. He obviously cared for his daughter, but was likely playing both sides. I exhaled loudly. *Yeah, he'd tell Fortak everything.*

The mansions fell behind as the carriage whisked me across the bridge. The city stretched out before me, everyone going about their lives and business. If only I could be as innocent.

What did Fortak have against me? I'd only just found out about the Covenant, so why had he been trying to kill me? I was still missing something. What purpose did Phyxia serve to this Covenant that they would be so bold as to kidnap her? It was a reckless move given her ambassadorial status, but foolhardy given her powers. Why had she let them take her? Was it her pacifist nature or an augury?

My brain hurt. I rolled my head around, forcing myself to relax. Every bone in my neck cracked.

Lord Caradan climbed his tower to the floor above, where the doors to the great hall lay open. A warm glow spread out across the hallway floor like a welcoming mat. From within came the sounds of supper: cutlery scraping across plates, tankards bumping on the table, the gurgling of keg taps, belches, chatter, and laughter.

He led his men inside and exchanged greetings from more of his Guildsmen, and the half dozen Elik Magi eating alongside them. He hated that his wife insisted that her Magi live in his tower. With a wave of his hand, he dismissed the servants from the room, and they pulled the doors closed on their way out. The huge hearth was alight for the purpose of heating the skewers of meat and cauldrons set before it, but the high-ceilinged chamber was lit by bronze bowls set high on the walls, each filled with everfire. Caradan surveyed the empty gallery that circled the room on the floor above.

Thunder rolled across the sky, growing ever louder as the Gods gathered to witness the massacre.

At the prearranged signal, each of his men let loose their magic. The very air crackled and hummed. Caradan embraced the raw power that rippled through him. The room grew chill and unnaturally dark. Conversation halted, giving way to the squeal of chairs as the Magi leaped to their feet, drawing on their own power.

Caradan smirked. Now came the fun part.

He clicked his fingers and lochtars whirled from the darkness to circle the room, their fine white hair streaming behind them. Spells of every color zapped from the Elik Magis' fingers, and they wrapped shimmering fields around the vicious creatures. The lochtars dived at the sorcerers, their elegant, fine-boned faces transforming into chattering skulls with withered hair. Shrieks echoed around the hall.

"What are you doing?" one of the Magi cried out.

"Yolanda, come quick," another called.

Yes, where was his wife? Why did she not fight beside her men as he did?

An invisible wall of force swept Caradan off his feet, carried him through the air, and smashed him against the wall. Red sparks flickered across his vision. Jarring pain rippled across his back. He tumbled into a heap and rolled behind a row of beer kegs. The nearest exploded in a green fire, drenching him in warm ale. He peeked around the keg that hid him.

Derren, strongest of the Magi, stood in the center of the fight. His green force shield flared each time a lochtar drew near, bouncing it away stunned. Unable to harm the undead, he took aim on Master Petay who promptly erupted in a column of roaring white fire. Petay screamed and screamed, flailed his arms, and fell to the ground. The rug ignited under him.

Eclias faced another of the Elik sorcerers. Five feet apart, they flung magic with wild abandon, and a rainbow of colors flickered around them. They seemed equally matched until one of the Magi's blinding white rays burned a hole clear through Eclias's abdomen, and he stumbled. Blood and intestines spilled from the hole. Teeth clenched, he lurched forward and fell at the foot of the Magi. The latter dipped his head in remorse before turning away.

Caradan spat in disgust at their distaste for killing, obviously gutless compared to his own brave men.

Eclias, lying in a pool of his own blood, reached up and grabbed the Magi's shin. Necrotic magic pulsed from his fingers, causing a black rot to spread up the sorcerer's leg. It consumed the Magi, crumbling flesh and bone to powder. The Elik Magi wailed and attempted to blast off his own leg, but to no avail. A moment later, only a heap of gray dust remained. Eclias pitched forward, dead.

Caradan surveyed the scene with clenched teeth. Most of his men lay dead, their souls delivered to Lak. Half of the Elik Magi remained. Master Binar joined him behind the kegs, his body covered in blood, his clothes singed.

"It's time for the wraith," Caradan said.

Binar's eyes widened. "There has to be another—"

"No. We end it now."

They cast together, joining their magic in the forbidden spell. It didn't matter now. Their souls were damned. Might as well gain favor with Lak.

The darkness spread, extinguishing the flames in the hearth and dimming the everfire. The air became heavy and chill. Something stirred in the black corners of the room, not visible directly, only obvious when Caradan looked at it sideways. An unwholesome shrieking came out of nowhere and built to a crescendo. Men from both Guilds faltered and covered their ears. United for the first time in the battle, they inched toward the door.

In an instant the wraith was upon them, a writhing cloud of manifested anger and malice that tore around the huge chamber. Caradan set his teeth, unable to prevent the twitch under one eye as he endured the screaming pleas for mercy and screams of torment. The entity smothered every living thing, enveloping them like a black sheet, sucking them into The Deep, condemning them to an eternity in the clutch of the wraith.

Only Caradan and Binar remained, immune to their own spell. Binar cried like a baby, rocking himself back and forth. Caradan stared blankly at the wall. He'd had no choice but to sacrifice his own men to eradicate the Elik Magi and the threat they posed to his Guild.

I jerked upright, cracking my head against the wooden frame of the carriage. One hand flew to my dagger. Another jolt shook the carriage and the driver up front murmured an apology. I blew out my breath and slumped back into the seat, blinking hard to rid the macabre scenes from my inner vision. My face was drenched in cold sweat.

Why was Caradan in my head? How did these nightmares fit in with the jumbled pieces of my puzzle?

The rain had stopped, and a moment later so did the carriage. I stumbled out and paid the driver. Temple Plaza. I swore the entire population of Malkandrah could fit into it, even the dregs from Boattown. I could scream at the top of my voice and no one on the far side of the vast, fountained lawn would hear me. I was told twenty-seven temples lined the perimeter. I'd never bothered to count.

A cliff of alternating strata of red and gray rock dominated the southern end of the plaza, rising up to my right toward the highlands above the city. High on the cliff nestled the green and blue spires of Belaya's temple. I always imagined that it resembled the face of the goddess watching over her city, looking down on the other Gods that she dominated.

"My Goddess," I murmured, touching two fingers to my head, above my eyes.

I'd never believed that she cared enough to listen but thought of it as insurance.

Crowds wandered the plaza but I made a beeline for a quiet street that resembled a gorge between two gargantuan temples, their minarets piercing the sky. Basalt and granite walls towered over me, and I picked my way between cascades of rain water pouring from the fanged mouths of bikka gargoyles high above.

Eventually, I stood alone at an intersection behind the temples. Before me, a single wall ringed an entire city block, though it had been intended to keep things inside rather than keep trespassers out. The necropolis surrounding Caradan's Tower wasn't a place even necromancers dared to visit, long ago pronounced off-limits to thrill-seeking apprentices after many had failed to return. Ivy smothered the wall, and several branches and bushes had thrust their way between the stones, bowing the wall outward, shattering it in places. The whole thing looked as tenuous as my patience.

The twelve-feet-high wall prevented any glimpse inside, so I climbed a nearby pile of rubble and slipped easily through a hole in the wall.

The clouds chose that moment to engulf Solas, and a damp gray settled over the city.

 ELEVEN

I jumped down from the broken wall into a garden filled with a treacherous mix of roots and grass-covered boulders, with some sinkholes thrown in for good measure. Around me, slabs of gray poked up from the verdant carpet of weeds and grass. Some were rectangular, others rounded or cross-shaped.

I bent before the nearest and scrubbed away the dirt of ages, tracing the unreadable carved script with my fingers. Only Solas worshippers buried their dead a few feet below the surface. *Closer to him, I suppose. Give me a nice deep crypt or catacomb any day.*

The derelict Caradan's Tower lurched at an angle away from nearby Temple Plaza, as if cowering from the Gods. By counting windows, I judged it five floors high but it had once stood taller. After the bloody massacre of Caradan, a century before, a disaster had befallen the tower, causing it to sink partially into the ground. It didn't seem to want to be here any more than I did.

A balcony jutted out close to ground level, against which someone had erected a plank, granting access to the balcony and a dark and uninviting doorway. Red hawks perched in a line along the ivy-covered railing, and at first glance I mistook them for gargoyles. A handful took flight, settling into the trees where they studied me, turning their heads to one side.

The gray overcast pressed down, threatening to rain at any moment.

Fetid marshland surrounded the tower. Islands of turf, grass, and reeds speckled the marsh, and the water between them was green and stagnant. A cemetery had once stood at the base of the tower, but now only a handful of gravestones and mausoleums remained, half-sunken or toppled, strangled by vines and moss, and draped by a persistent mist. The sounds of the city were muted, as if the land inside the boundary wall existed in a world of its own.

Haunted, people said. I shrugged. Everything was haunted.

I could see why the Duke had brought me here. I'd choose this place to hide secrets too.

I perched atop a tombstone to think. Phyxia was right—I should visit Mother's tomb. It had been eight solars. I remembered little of my childhood, but yellow lilies had always sat in vases around our house. The sweet smell tickled my nose. Did her tomb lie as dilapidated and forgotten as the crooked, leaning ones around me? Even the gravestones were dying.

Phyxia would call that an augury.

I followed a trail of trampled grass through the swamp, taking short jumps from islet to islet. The ground squelched and gave way more than once, plunging me into bracken water up to my knees. It was a relief to step onto firmer ground. I craned my neck to study the tower looming above me. The hairs on my neck stood erect. I was being watched. My gaze scanned the windows, leaping from one dark slit to the next, but I saw nothing to validate my fears.

The plank propped against the balcony railing looked recent, and was solid underfoot as I crept up it. If Caradan's ghost lay within, he had no need for such a bridge, so something human had been this way. The Duke? How many people made up this Covenant and what did they do in such a depressing place?

Vague shapes stood in the shadows inside the door. I pushed out a gentle *Perception* and it tickled immediately. Skeletons. I detected several more deeper into the tower, and dozens on the floors above and below. Why so many? What did they guard? What did the Duke want me to see? I wasn't about to walk into another skeleton ambush. Sure, I could defeat the lot of them, but not yet, not until I knew what I was doing here.

I hurried back through the half-sunken necropolis, seeking the perceived safety of the trees. Something malevolent hung over the area, like nothing I had sensed in any crypt or deep place. I glanced behind me at the tower and replayed my nightmares, imagining the brutal war of magic that had taken place inside.

At dawn, the Duke had said. Very well. I would return then. I had a plan, and it involved my old tutor, Master Kolta.

From my vantage point high on the vaulted roofs of the Guildhouse, I watched Solas sink to a fiery death in the ocean, turning the water a hundred shades of burnished orange. The smell of fish and salt hung heavy in the air. I crouched below a chimneystack, having jammed my feet in between the jagged, broken tiles to prevent myself sliding off and plunging into the alley.

Knowing what I did now, I'd been a naive fool to walk into Begara's classroom that time. If Fortak caught me walking the hallways, it'd all be over.

A mubar monkey scampered over the ridge of the roof. When it saw me, it puffed its fur and hissed.

A tile dislodged under my boot and I tumbled sideways. I clawed desperately for a handhold, but succeeded only in tearing another tile loose. The tiles and I made an infernal din as we slid and clattered down the roof. The dark chasm of the alley approached at great speed. Hoping my apprentice memories held true, I rolled onto my stomach and slid feetfirst over the precipice.

My arms reached beneath the dark eaves and I came to an abrupt stop, jarring my wrists and popping one shoulder. There I hung, clutching one of the bikka-shaped gargoyles for dear life. That it hadn't snapped was amazing. Trying not to think about the four-story drop to the alley, I lowered myself onto a narrow windowsill.

I rapped on the dirty glass, then again, louder. The window opened, almost knocking me to my death.

"Master Kolta," I said. "It's Maldren. I need to see you."

He stuck out his head, twisted it upward, and surveyed me with his bug eyes. They always looked about to pop from his head.

"What in bloody Belaya's name are you doing? Get in here."

His head darted back inside and he extended his hand to assist me. I slipped, sending chunks of the rotten windowsill plunging into the darkness, but he yanked me inside and I tumbled onto the rug. He perched on the chair before his desk and gestured to the bed, within touching distance in his cramped quarters.

"Everyone's looking for you," he whispered, his gaze flicking to the closed door. "Fortak is bloody pissed, screaming at everyone."

I sat on the hard bed, nursing the ankle I had banged on the window frame.

"I don't have time to explain. Do you trust me, Master?"

He nodded vigorously, sniffed, and picked inside his nostril. "Of course I do. Lak, if he finds me talking to you…"

"I hate to get you involved but I need a favor."

"What do you need?" He studied the snot on the tip of his finger. "Need I tell you what he'll do to you?"

I blew out my breath. "I know. Believe me, I know. He already tried to kill me."

Kolta's mouth fell open. Absentmindedly, he flicked the booger onto the rug at our feet.

"I need *Walk the Bones*," I said.

"That's a Master-level spell."

"Which is why I need your help."

He sniffed and gyrated his nose. "What's this about? What have you gotten into?"

Just like old times. How I'd missed my tutor. Boogers and all.

At thirty-five, he was barely ten solars my senior, and a good reminder that not everyone in the Guild was a pompous ass. I trusted him but wasn't ready to tell him the full truth. I didn't even know what the truth was. Besides, he was a master of the Guild and I couldn't say with certainty that he wouldn't turn me in if I started ranting about conspiracies.

I told him as much as I dared about the fires, the grak, and visiting Duke Imarian, but avoided mentioning any connection to the Guildmaster. Kolta had a lot of questions and kept eyeing me suspiciously. I chewed my lip. He knew I was holding back. Finally, he agreed to help me gain access to the tower.

"One proviso, my boy."

He waggled a finger at me and I eyed it carefully, wary of him flicking boogers at me.

"I'm coming into the tower with you. No complaints. Fortak is not to be trifled with. You're going to need my protection."

Was I still his baby apprentice? He beamed, broke the seal on a pair of beers, and handed me one.

This was going to be fun. The two of us once more.

"Now what's this about your new apprentice?" he said. "A girl, no less?"

I grimaced. "I don't know what to make of her. She's not as useless as I'd expected and has a lot of spirit, but I'm worried she's a spy for her father."

"Messy business. How's her tuition coming along?"

I rubbed my nose. "I don't want to waste my time. Once I figure all this out, she'll be going home to her father."

Was she still in Boattown? I doubted it, since I'd told her that I wasn't coming back. Life would be easier if she'd tucked her tail between her legs and gone back to daddy. Maybe then the Duke would trust me.

Kolta tut-tutted. "You can't leave your apprentice in the dark, my boy. You've got to have a solid schedule of lessons, reading, and tests. How's she going to learn? You've got a responsibility now."

I must have put on my "do I have to?" face, because Kolta laughed. "You can't make Master without an apprentice."

He guzzled his beer.

I studied a dusty painting of Belaya explaining the final Test of Ascension to Lak, failure of which resulted in him being cast into The Deep. I'd assumed Fortak had been setting me up by assigning Ayla to me. What if he'd genuinely wanted to test me, force me to step up? Was him trying to kill me his final test for me? That was stupid. I shook my head. Too many questions, not enough answers.

We had dinner in Kolta's room and spent a wonderful evening reminiscing about the old days. I almost managed to forget my problems. Almost, but not entirely.

We left the Guild in the quiet dark of the early morning hours, he by the stairs and me via the treacherous, icy roof. Having slid down the last section of wall and bashed my knee on a sewer grate, I was glad to be in one piece when we met in an adjacent street. Our breath steamed in front of our faces and we pulled our robes tight. With no carriage in sight, we walked in silence through the gloomy streets washed with a harbor fog. Mercifully, it didn't rain.

"I've never seen you so bloody skittish," Kolta said, obviously noting my constant glances behind us.

"Half the city seems to be following me lately."

He chuckled. "You don't seem your usual cocky self."

I snorted. "People keep trying to kill me. Forgive the dent in my confidence."

He extended his arms in a peace offering.

"I'm not criticizing, just observing. I always liked your bravado. It made my lessons more…interesting." A grin filled his face. "Watching you go toe to toe with Semplis was priceless."

"Master Semplis is a stuck-up geriatric."

Kolta laughed again, an alien sound in the quiet night. "I miss those days. I miss you in my class."

We continued across the city deep in our own thoughts. We arrived at the crumbling wall surrounding Caradan's Tower just as the sky had turned a pale green, ahead of the dawn. No one else walked the gloomy alleys behind Temple Plaza. Two dogs barked in the distance. I blew on my frozen hands, and then led the way through the hole in the wall and into Caradan's domain.

Thick fog shrouded the meadow, threatening to gobble us up. Silhouettes of trees loomed like deformed giants. I didn't want to advertise our movements with a light source, so I insisted that we crept among the rocks and potholes, stifling our gasps as we stubbed our toes. All manner of creatures lurked in the shadows, pinging and rippling my *Perception*.

Upon reaching the necropolis, we hunkered down behind a large gravestone. The tower was barely visible in the gloom. Kolta nudged me, gesturing toward it. His eyes and teeth appeared bright in the near darkness.

"You're right," he whispered. "I sense a dozen sentinels in there."

Of course I was right.

"*Walk the Bones* will get us in." He looked around. "We'll need two skeletons."

"Where am I supposed to get them from?"

He patted the grass of the grave we knelt on. "Dig."

"You're kidding."

"This is your plan. I can't help it if you forgot the shovels." He jabbed his finger up one nostril and started his own form of digging.

Kristach. I yanked at clumps of grass and scooped up dirt with both hands. It was wet and muddy, and before long I was caked in it up to my elbows. Worms and spiders crawled all over me. I imagined myself a ghoul, hungrily tearing at the earth to reach a corpse. Crypts were much more civilized.

Kolta snorted. His hand flew to his mouth, but he giggled like a girl.

"What?" I stopped and flicked a wad of mud at him.

"Maldren, Maldren." His whole body quivered. "I'm sorry, it's painful to watch. My sides are going to burst."

He wrapped his hands about his belly and took a deep breath. I scowled at him.

"I have to commend your dedication," he said. "But you have so much to learn."

I clenched my teeth and sat back on my heels. "What? Then teach me."

Red wisps of magic snaked from his hands and into the small trench I had dug. The earth shook and squirmed. Beetles scurried away. The tip of a bone broke the surface. It kept rising, and then others poked up around it. As fast as I plucked them from the loose soil, others pushed up in their place. That was a spell I needed to learn. Eventually two piles of bones sat heaped in front of us. *Why are there so many damn tiny bones in the human body?*

"Ready for this?" Kolta whispered. "Last-minute regrets?"

I rolled my eyes. "Get on with it."

"We need to get this done fast, before ghouls come sniffing."

I peered into the darkness. There was nothing to see, but I could sense them at the distant edge of my *Perception*.

My flesh tingled at the touch of his spell. Every hair on my skin jerked erect and my nerves jangled. I lost all my senses simultaneously. I wanted to cry out but couldn't. With no sensory input, I hung in a limbo of nothingness. Something had gone wrong.

When my vision returned, a gargantuan spider stood before me, its furry legs twitching, ready to trample me. Kristach. I wanted to flee but nothing happened—I had no feeling in my limbs. I tried to shake my head but it wouldn't move. A woozy feeling of light-headedness persisted, as well as the unnerving sensation that I wasn't whole. My mind reeled.

Kolta had paralyzed me!

My perspective shifted. I rose into the air and the alien world began to make sense. What I'd thought were boulders resolved to mere clods of dirt. The spider shrank to normal size. My viewpoint had been a mere inch above the ground. I had no idea what was lifting me, but at least now I could turn my head. Below me, my body lay crumpled on top of the grave.

I saw the tombstone, trees, and the far-off wall, clear as day even in the darkness. My eyesight was different somehow, tinged pink. The feeling in my limbs returned, but they remained stiff, inflexible.

Kolta stepped into view and waved. My upward movement had stopped and he faced me at normal eye level. My own hand was light but rigid when I lifted it. A skeletal hand appeared before my face, finger bones joined with nothing but air. Slowly, I wiggled the fingers.

Lak and all his demons!

Kolta faked alarm. "Oh, no, a skeleton."

"Funny," I tried to say, but no words came out. I moved to hit him but he easily dodged my sluggish slap.

That wasn't fair. I could hear but not speak? And no ninja skeleton abilities?

Kolta winked, then his eyes rolled up into his head and he collapsed to the ground. What? At the sound of clacking bones, I stepped aside and watched the second pile of bones reassemble themselves, jostling and jumping over one another to connect to the right neighbor. The skull rose to sit atop them, and he faced me, grinning inanely, red glows filling his eye sockets. I hoped I had demonic eyes too.

I glanced down at my ribs and pelvis. Why hadn't he warned me this would happen? I thought we were going to control the skeletons, not become them. Our real bodies were hidden from the tower by the gravestone. We looked asleep. Lying on the wet grass would play havoc with my back. I hadn't seen any animals inside the wall, but I was more worried about the ghouls. I'd hate to come back and find they had gnawed on me. I attempted to bite my lip, but only succeeded in clacking my teeth together.

I jerked my head in the direction of the tower, but the

gesture turned into a slow, sideways motion of my skull that caught me off guard, and I fell against the tombstone. *Careful, Maldren. These are brittle bones. You'll break yourself.* My whole body felt wooden. It was like learning to walk all over again.

We shuffled side by side along the path and through the swamp, and I rapidly got the hang of being a skeleton. This would work great. Now where were those skeletons lurking inside the tower? I reached for my magic to cast *Perception*. No power coursed through my veins. Kristach, I didn't even have any.

I faltered. There was energy inside me, but it seemed distant, diffuse, and unapproachable. I turned to go back. Powerless, it made no sense to proceed.

Kolta grabbed my humerus. I searched his grinning face but there was nothing there to read. I tapped my ribs. *Do you understand, Master?*

He nodded and pointed back toward our bodies, and then he rapped his own ribs with his fist and pointed again.

Oh, that's how it works. My *Perception* was active, I could sense it, but centered on my real body. Unfortunate, but at least we'd know if something approached them.

My hand had gotten stuck in my rib cage. I glared at my misbehaving body. *Lak, are you playing jokes now? Not funny.* I worked my hand free but my middle finger snapped off and fell to the ground. Stupid, rebellious digit. Kolta clacked his teeth repeatedly. Was he laughing at me? He snapped off one of his own fingers, threw it into the swamp, and made a thumbs-up gesture.

We splashed onward through the swamp, not even bothering to jump between the islets, until we reached the base of the tower. With my new night vision it was easy to see the pair of skeletons inside the open balcony door. Their red, unblinking eyes glared back. Without hesitation, I climbed the plank, Kolta right behind me.

I pushed between the skeleton guards, careful to keep my limbs from entangling in theirs, and continued into a hallway. I heard them turn to track me. A second pair stepped aside to let us through. *Yes, I belong here, I'm a skellie too.*

This was such a smart plan of mine.

The inner hallway bisected the center of the tower. At either end, adjacent to the outer walls, narrow stairways led to other floors, up to my left and down to my right. A heavy wooden door stood open on the opposite side of the hallway.

Something whispered in the air. I turned, but we were alone. I hoped that we hadn't awoken Caradan's ghost. It felt wrong to trespass in what effectively was his tomb, but technically I wasn't. I was just along for the ride in a skeleton.

I advanced to the open door and froze. Magic flickered in my mind's eye, and creatures whirled about the great room beyond. Necromancers turned on sorcerers. Men died horrific deaths. Screams echoed through the tower. I stepped backward and shook my head to clear it, and the room became empty once more, except for dusty furniture. Kolta's presence beside me was reassuring. He gave no indication he had shared my vision.

More voices. Boots thumped on the plank outside.

I rapped Kolta's scapula and headed up the stairs at the end of the hallway, following the curve of the outer wall. We clacked and scrambled up the steep steps, around the curve, and out of sight of the hallway.

Several people spoke in low voices as they moved past the skeleton guards. Fortak's distinctive cough echoed through the tower.

I climbed another step and then stopped. This was silly. We were just another couple of skeletons so why were we skulking around the corner like a pair of naughty apprentices? Before I could start back down, a rattling of bones drew my attention to the floor above, so I continued up instead. At the top, two skeletons barred the way, brandishing iron bars as clubs. Their red eyes scrutinized me, and I stood perfectly still for a long moment. Was I supposed to make some kind of signal? Apparently satisfied, they headed away in opposite directions along a wooden landing. I felt invincible. This was so much fun.

The stairway to the next floor above had been bricked up, so we had no choice but to follow the other skeletons. We emerged onto a gallery that circled around the upper part of the great hall we had just visited, the one from my dream. A single door exited the gallery opposite us, but it too had been bricked up.

I surveyed the room below. A dozen chairs surrounded a huge wooden table, and the hide of some bizarre creature had been stretched and nailed to the longest wall. Moments ago, the fireplace had been dark and cold, but now flames roared between the stacked logs. The flickering orange contrasted oddly with the stark shafts of early daylight stabbing across the room from numerous arrow slits. The everfire bowls from my dream were dry and no longer burned.

I turned my attention to the men filing into the room. Fortak walked directly to a wooden throne at the head of the table nearest the hearth. He squirmed into the unpadded seat and coughed into his handkerchief. I was careful to act the uninterested guard, hoping no one would notice there were now four skeletons up here instead of two.

Duke Imarian and Master Begara entered. I leaned heavily on the gallery railing. No wonder Begara hadn't wanted me going to Fortak. Begara had been such a gentle soul. His history lessons had been the highlight of my studies. Damn, it had been his idea for me to seek out Babbas. Maybe he hadn't known that Fortak had meant for the bargee to trap me? How could he be a part of this despicable Covenant?

Then Phyxia glided into the room.

 TWELVE

I almost toppled over the railing. My finger bones crunched as I made a fist. She moved to a vacant chair of her own accord—no restraints, chains, or manacles, not a word or attempt to flee. She wore a diaphanous gown that would make a normal woman turn blue with cold. Her head was uncovered, and while I could usually tell her mood by the color of her horns, everything looked red in my supernatural eyesight. Had the sons-of-bikkas drugged her? As if sensing my urge to hurtle down the stairs and into the room, Kolta moved up beside me.

Two final men entered in a hurry, pausing only to close the door. Something about the first man screamed military, though he bore no weapons. His face was scarred and weathered, and his head was bald. The last man to arrive looked younger, athletic but well muscled, with ordinary travel clothes beneath his swirling gray cloak. He greeted the others in a heavily accented Wynarese, and he bore the distinctive red beard of the Northerners.

"Well?" Fortak asked.

"That boy...Maldren, survived your efforts," the Duke said.

"I know that." Fortak glared at Begara.

"You had no right to use my daughter to distract him. You promised—"

"I expected him to accept the challenge of training her and stop prying. That boy always disappoints."

"Inquisitive like his mother," Begara said.

"I can see that."

I glanced at Kolta but he ignored me, his glowing red eyes locked on the scene below. His skeletal hands gripped the railing tightly.

Fortak swiveled to face the Duke. "You told the Council that I...that the Guild is willing to help?"

The Duke nodded. "They didn't appear unduly concerned about the fires. Perhaps—"

"They have yet to feel the pain. Only then will they act."

I snapped to attention.

"Why should the Council worry about burning slums?" the bald man asked. "It plays right into their hands. A tighter grip on the weak. Put out the fires. Rebuild the streets. People are grateful."

Fortak looked thoughtful.

"They will care if the fires moved across the river into wealthier districts." He scowled at the Duke. "Lean on them. I want them scared with the coronation coming. By the time I save the city from burning to the ground, I want them running to me for guidance, fawning over me with accolades. Over *us*."

He cleared his throat, coughing phlegm into his handkerchief.

"It would impress them more," the Duke said, "if you came out of your hole and met with them, re-pledged your allegiance to the Crown Prince."

"I told you before," Fortak said in a calm, controlled voice. "I refuse to go down on one knee to placate the Council. I will teach them all a lesson, and then the new King will owe *me* a favor."

No one moved. No one spoke. All eyes stared at the Guildmaster. I couldn't believe the treason in his words. Cashing in on death and suffering for personal power was beyond even him. Wasn't it?

"It's no coincidence that we meet in this place," he said, as if delivering a lecture to students. "Prime Guildmaster Caradan once took the Guild on a bold new path. I'm sure he would approve of our cause. With his power we could achieve much greatness for Malkandrah."

Caradan again! I gritted my teeth. How did all these pieces fit together?

Fortak's eyes swept every part of the room as if he expected Caradan's ghost to be present and listening. When he looked up at the gallery, I turned away and joined the pacing guard skeletons. I imagined Fortak's stare on my back. Had he sensed our presence?

Kolta stood before me, and a horrible thought gripped me. What if Kolta was one of them, ordered to restrain me here? I froze. *Should I turn back to the stairs or would that be suspicious? Stop it, Maldren. You can trust your tutor. Kolta would never side with Fortak.*

"What about the boy?" the bald man asked.

"Find him. Double your spies, Imarian."

I risked a glance at the Duke, but his attention was focused on the men at the table. I rubbed my nose. Instead of skin, I scratched a series of small bones. *Oh yeah.* I'd forgotten. He clearly hadn't told Fortak about our meeting yesterday. Ayla was better leverage than I'd imagined.

Begara sighed. "We should wait for the Council. I'm not happy about further destruction. So many have died already."

"You are no longer with us?" the bald man asked.

"Yes, of course, but I think we've made our point. No more fires." Begara squirmed in his chair.

Fortak leaned across the table.

"Have you not been listening? We must up the ante, force them to act. Begara…" He reached out and patted the master's arm. "The future of our Guild, perhaps the city itself, rests upon our plan. If I must, I'll burn whole districts to the ground."

My jaw dropped, threatening to dislocate my lower

mandible.

He wasn't trying to stop the fire creature. He was controlling it.

I teetered dizzily and steadied myself on the wall. Now it all made sense. I stared down at them, my skeleton eyes and the firelight tingeing the group red, like some demonic gathering. I had studied under two of these men. What pact with Lak had they inked to unleash such atrocities upon our poor city, to slaughter innocents, to murder my friends? *Begara, how could you?*

Skeletal hands gripped the railing beside my own. I recognized the missing finger and looked into Kolta's glowing eyes. Damn these skeletal forms that I could not read his emotions. His hand covered mine and tapped it gently. I was not alone. What was going through his head? Did he understand Fortak's confession?

"Are you certain you can retain your grip on that thing?" The Wynarian spoke for the first time.

"It will do my bidding," Fortak said.

"Don't be a fool, Fortak," Phyxia said, clear and loud.

My gaze snapped to her petite form. Her face was tranquil and regal, yet her ears had flattened somewhat. If only I could see the color patterns in her eyes.

"Few men have displayed the arrogance to believe they can harness an elemental and treat it like a pet. All have died. You are no better than they."

Fortak steepled his hands before his nose. "Half my life I have studied their kind. Countless nights toiling over long-forgotten summoning spells. My plan is comprehensive, Ambassador. It answers to me."

"It answers to no one. Your goals are merely aligned. You think you will simply dispel it when its work is done?"

"I drew it into the world and I will send it away, while the entire city watches and proclaims me their savior."

I shook my head in disbelief.

Phyxia chuckled. "The power of an elemental is beyond even your grasp, Fortak. It will not slink into The Deep when you tire of it. In its wrath it will devour the city."

"Your augury is flawed if—"

"How dare you!" Her voice echoed around the chamber. Both Begara and the Duke startled.

My mind twitched violently, tuning her out. Danger tugged at my consciousness. My *Perception* bucked and rippled angrily. Something was among us. Where? I scanned the gallery and the room below, and then I caught a whiff of decay. A tombstone flickered into view, hovering before me, and two decrepit, slavering creatures clawing from the earth.

Ghouls had found our bodies.

"—will not usurp my authority," Fortak said. "I masterminded this plan for the glory of the—"

"For the glory of yourself alone," Phyxia said.

Kolta's skeletal hand fastened on my shoulder and he steered me toward the stairs.

The stench of fresh dirt assaulted my nostrils. Razor-sharp claws caked with rotting flesh reached for our bodies. My *Perception* screamed at me. Two ghouls loomed over us.

"—the reason I came to you, Fortak, to contain the elemental."

I jerked free of Kolta's grasp and strained to peer over the railing. *The sounds, the smells, the panic in my head. Shut up.* I had to hear her out.

"Only I can bring this to fruition," she said. "I can protect you, and I can send it back when you succeed. Together we—"

Grave dirt filled my nostrils. I lay on the damp grass, coughing and choking up soil and bugs.

The voices of Phyxia and the Guildmaster droned on, distant, unclear. A ghostly image of the great hall hovered before me, transparent against the swamp and trees bathed in the first rays of dawn.

Something lunged at me, grunting and growling in one hideous sound. I rolled against the tombstone and the misshapen creature pounced where I had lain, its hands raking the ground, flinging dirt everywhere. My head spun with the dual sensations of grass glistening with dew beneath me, and the hard stone of the gallery where a pile of bones now lay. It was being pulled in two directions. It hurt.

Desiccated flesh hung from the body of the ghoul, revealing glimpses of yellowed bone beneath its torn, paper-thin skin. Another lunged at Kolta, who had bolted upright while I had been lying in the dirt. Behind them, more ghouls clawed free of the ground.

Filthy creatures.

I siphoned power from my core and unleashed *Deathwall*, a blast wave that tumbled the ghouls into a heap. A decomposing hand, armed with talonlike fingernails, fastened around Kolta's ankle. He stamped on it and let loose a bolt of fire, setting several of them alight. The reek of burning flesh almost cost me last night's dinner.

Tombstones toppled under bulging mounds as dozens of ghouls pulled free from the soft earth.

"There might be hundreds of them," Kolta said as we stood back to back. "We can't fight them all."

It would be bloody but I believed that we could. However, I was fearful that members of the Covenant would emerge from the tower at any moment.

"Run," he yelled.

I stood and watched instead. The power leeching from him sizzled through my body. My hair crackled. He thumped one fist into his palm and a purple shock wave raced out in all directions. Every ghoul within twenty feet of us exploded, raining body parts. The remainder squealed and thrashed their limbs, scrambling and pushing each other in their attempt to burrow back into the earth. Kolta's magic barreled them off their feet, smashing them against gravestones or sending them splashing into the swamp.

I wanted that spell.

Kolta yanked me toward the outer wall. It felt good to own a real body again, running fast, heart beating, lungs gasping. He didn't let up the pace until we had scrambled back into the street and were sprinting toward Temple Plaza.

"How did you know about this?" he asked, panting. "What

else do you know?"

"Stop." I doubled over, sucking in air. I waited a long moment before straightening. I needed to look into his eyes. "Master, promise me you aren't a part of this."

Deep furrows appeared on his brow, and his face was the color of wine.

"I'm hurt that you think I would be. I can't believe what they're planning," he said. "What ungodly business has Begara gotten himself into?"

He shook his head and walked away. I followed, and we emerged into the plaza. The babble of conversation was welcome after the silence of the tower grounds and the primal screams of the ghouls. I breathed deep of the sweet nectar of feresens flowers that had been arranged in baskets and hung from the street lanterns.

"Will you help me?" I asked.

"Stop the Guildmaster? I don't think that's possible, my boy."

"You're going to do nothing?" Passersby stared and I realized I'd shouted.

"I need to find out who in the Guild is involved. This is very dangerous for you. For us. Don't tell anybody else, and for Belaya's sake, lay low."

I scratched my nose. It had become decidedly itchy since returning to human form.

"Do you know who those others were?"

"One of them used to be captain of the Black and Reds." He studied my face as we walked. "You seemed overly interested in the ambassador, the woman with the horns. I've never been introduced but you know her, don't you?"

I thought I had. I returned his gaze for a half dozen steps, and then I looked away.

"No. No, I don't know her."

With a mug of karra in one hand, I picked at a bread roll with my other. The abandoned remains of my cold breakfast lay in pieces on the table.

The midday rays of Solas glistened on the river. How many hours had I sat there in Petooli's staring down Canal Street? Less than I had spent wandering the city that morning. I remembered Master Kolta by my side at first. Bless him, he had tried so hard to engage me in conversation. He might have left, muttering, at the corner of Broad and Canal.

A white-sleeved arm pried the mug from my hand and replaced it with a steaming one. A bowl of vandesh was set before me, and its sharp aroma of peppers and spiced mushroom tickled my nose.

"Ye must eat, lad," Petooli said. I nodded without meeting his eye, and he left.

I belonged to an organization whose leader had slaughtered hundreds in the name of personal glory. How endemic was the rot? Who could I trust besides Kolta?

I sipped the sweet karra, wincing as it burned my mouth.

Everything I touched burned me.

Phyxia. She'd been everything to me. The times we had shared, the advice she'd given. Never again would my skin tingle at her touch. How I'd yearned for her to kiss me just once. Life was perfect in her company, a warm cocoon that I'd never had at home.

Phyxia, Ayla, Mother B., I'd lost them all. If Kolta was smart he'd stay away from me too. How many more pointless, horrific deaths could my conscience bear?

They'd called it an elemental. Ironically, it was from Begara's class that I'd first heard of this creature of legend. There were very few ways to destroy such a creature and I knew of none. A throbbing, dull pain seized my temples. I drank some karra, my hands trembling. Fortak had been right. I should never have gotten involved.

Children giggled in the street below, chasing rats back into the canal. I had once played those games. *Enjoy while you can, little ones, before you grow up and life burns you.*

I sucked in a deep breath and held it.

Enough.

If I couldn't defeat the elemental, there was at least one good deed I could perform—reuniting the Duke with his daughter. I put down my mug and spooned up the spicy, aromatic vandesh. The Duke had wanted me to witness that meeting. Was he getting cold feet? That was a stretch. He'd done it to get Ayla back. Had he told the truth about her not being a spy, or was his entire rhetoric an elaborate ruse to convince me? Had he formed a plausible defense to mask that she was a spy after all? The Duke played both sides, of that I was sure, but he'd know that if I caught him in a lie she'd be in danger.

I missed Ayla. My stomach tingled. Having her beside me had created a soft spot in my heart, absent now. Ayla wasn't a spy. She couldn't be. Her innocence warmed me more than the soup. I slurped it hungrily. I'd been mean to her. I sighed. The Duke had trusted me enough to betray his fellow conspirators. Now I had to honor that trust and protect Ayla.

On my walk back to Boattown, I tried to plan what to say to her, but still hadn't come up with anything by the time I threaded my way across the makeshift wharves, planks, and gangways toward our ship. I'd gotten halfway when she appeared on deck, raising her arm to block Solas's glare. Her head bobbed side to side, as if she were trying to figure out who I was. How many visitors was she expecting dressed in a Guild robe? She put her hands on her hips and glared when I climbed up beside her.

"The great necromancer couldn't survive without me?" Her nose wrinkled and she sniffed loudly. "You stink."

Her lavender scent washed over me, very welcoming after a morning groveling in the mud with ghouls.

I sighed. "It's been a rough morning. Can you shout at me now and get it over with?"

She tipped her head to one side and studied me, still scowling. "Go below and get cleaned up. Have you eaten?"

"Sort of."

"Then I'll brew mulip."

I followed her below. She turned forward to the galley and

I went aft to the tiny washroom and shut the door. There was no lock. She'd laid out several buckets of water, already filtered through the boat's charcoal tank. Cold, like her mood. Actually, she was being quite magnanimous considering how we'd parted.

I heard her slump against the outside of the closed door. I washed my clothes first, and then started on the blood and dirt caked on my body.

"I'm not a spy," she said at length. "You know that in your heart, don't you? I don't want to fight. I want to be your apprentice."

She was making up with me? I felt like such a piece of tristak.

"I know you're not." Why was I not apologizing? "I spoke to your father."

"You did what?" She thumped the door. "You had no right to do that."

She cursed and stomped away.

My clothes were soaked and I didn't have any spares. I'd lost them all in the fire. I wrapped a towel around me and sat on an upturned bucket, head in my hands. When she returned, she inched the door open and pushed in a steaming mug. A minty aroma filled the room.

"Hand me your clothes. They'll dry quicker outside."

"You just want to trap me in here."

"You deserve it."

I thrust them through the gap in the door into her waiting hand, and then she closed it. The mulip warmed away the chill, though Akra would have been better. I gulped it down and listened to her move about the boat. I missed her conversation, her endless questions.

Almost an hour went by before she cracked the door and pushed my folded clothes inside. A little damp, but I wasn't about to argue. She was being more than generous. I joined her in the galley, and we sat opposite each other at the tiny table.

"Why did you go to my father? You promised you wouldn't tell, promised that I wouldn't have to go home."

"I told him nothing."

"Then what did you talk about?"

What to tell her? That daddy was part of a plot to blackmail the High Council by burning down the city?

"He misses you." That was safe. "He wants you back."

"I'm not slinking home like a little girl. I want to be a necromancer. I want to be with you."

The sudden softness in her deep brown eyes surprised me. She flushed and looked away.

"At least write him a letter so he knows you're safe."

"Why should I?"

"Because he's your father."

I didn't like the man either, but at least he cared about her. I had no memory of my father and precious few of my mother.

"Because he worries about you. Because you might not get another chance if that thing comes after us."

She returned to the stove and refilled our mugs. I drank deeply.

"What are we going to do about that?" She traced one finger across the worn tabletop.

"Hide here until it's all over. I've had enough. We can't defeat it. It's impossible."

 THIRTEEN

"I was taught that nothing was impossible," Ayla said, a thin furrow creasing her forehead.

She was naive. I told her about the Covenant's plans and their secret meeting, being extra careful to omit any reference to her father.

"We'll find a way." She touched my hand.

My skin tingled and I wished the contact hadn't been so brief.

"I believe in you," she said. "I've seen you use your magic, and it's incredible. Maybe your masters can help?"

She leaned forward. Her jaw was set with determination.

"I only trust Kolta. Fighting ghouls and skeletons is easy. This is an elemental." I slammed my palm into my forehead. "I should have known that's what it was. How could I have been so stupid? But then why would have I suspected? These creatures go back to the birth of time, to when Belaya fashioned the world."

"You're not making any sense."

"It doesn't matter. It's pointless to continue. Fortak has half a century of magic to draw upon. He's probably invented more spells than I ever learned, and I shudder to think how much power Phyxia can bring to bear."

"Your mentor," she whispered.

"She betrayed me." My voice wavered. I bit back tears and my stomach cramped. Why was there no Akra on this Lak-be-damned boat?

"We've got no chance," I murmured.

"So you're going to give up? Just like that?"

I shrugged and lifted the mug to my lips.

"No, I don't believe that," she said. "Not you. This is our city. Its people aren't pawns for the Guildmaster and his...his Covenant to play with."

Ayla pointed in the direction of the shore, but I kept my gaze on her, the way her cheeks dimpled when she spoke.

"Go outside and look at all the streets," she said. "The buildings. All the poor families. They're terrified. They're innocent."

I fished a dead fly from my mulip.

She grabbed my arm. "Listen to me."

The hot drink splashed in my lap and I jumped up. "Hey!"

"You're so stubborn." She leaped to her feet. Her fist thumped my arm, and my mug bounced across the table, soaking the surface and the wall.

"These people need someone to protect them. They don't have magic like you. They're not rich like my father." Her hand still clutched my arm and she shook it violently. "Look me in the eye and tell me you'll sit and mope while little children burn to death."

"Stop being so melodramatic."

I swatted her arm away with my left hand, while my right grabbed her chin. I gave her head a shake and her hands dropped to her side. Her huge, brown eyes sucked me in, stifling the tirade I'd prepared. It wasn't her defiance that intrigued me, but her passion, her courage.

"I'm sorry," she murmured.

That was unexpected. How like Phyxia her mood swings were. For a fleeting moment I expected to see swirls of color in her eyes. I released my grip on her chin.

"No, you're right," I said. "It's me who should be apologizing."

We held each other's gaze for a long moment. I became conscious of my breathing matching the rise and fall of her breasts. I couldn't believe that I'd once thought her younger than her eighteen solars. She was quite a spunky woman. I liked that. She slipped both hands into mine, hers warm and soft. After staring at my lips for a long moment she pulled me into a hug, pressing her head into my shoulder. The heat of her body made me tingle all over. I breathed deep of the lavender scent of her hair.

"Thank you." I patted her back, not sure what she expected. "For reminding me who I am."

She didn't want to let go, so I pushed her away gently and we sat, entertaining our own thoughts for a moment.

"I can help if you teach me some magic," she said. "Why don't we start right now?"

She expected to be casting spells by supper, I could tell. Kolta was right. I needed to teach her.

"I'm exhausted. Tomorrow."

"Promise?"

I nodded and headed for my cabin.

We spent the entire next day in lessons and exercises, and I had to admit that it was fun to teach. She was an attentive student. Certainly she had her moments of being a spoiled brat, and patience definitely wasn't one of her virtues, but she worked hard and hung on my every instruction. How fast would I have learned as an apprentice if I'd been as studious?

We were still at it when Solas dived a golden death toward the ocean beyond the harbor. We sat on the narrow walkway that ran between the fore and stern decks of our boat. Though the harbor side walkway was blowy and without shelter, I preferred that we not draw attention from anyone in Boattown, or strangers looking out from the shore.

"How long do I have to do these stretching exercises?" she

asked. "Aren't we going to cast spells?"

"You won't be capable of spells for a long while. The first step is to get accustomed to, and develop, the core of energy within you." I tapped my gut with one fist.

She sighed. "I can barely feel it. I might even be imagining it."

"You have the latent power. It needs to be teased out."

That morning I'd run another check. She had a consistent, well-shaped aura, but I still couldn't understand why it was violet and not yellow.

"So how long before I can use it?"

If I told her the best part of a solar, she'd either freak or sulk.

"It varies with each student." That wasn't a lie. "Do these exercises as often as you can. Every day. You'll feel your core strengthen."

"So we're not going to do anything else?"

I chuckled, remembering my own frustration as a freshman apprentice.

"We have a lot of theory to cover, but not now. I'm tired just answering your questions. Enough for today."

She brought her knees up to her chest. "Thank you. I really do appreciate it. Um…" She chewed her lip.

"Just ask," I said. I had a fleeting vision of Phyxia saying the same thing the night I had brought her brandy and jit-nuts.

"Can you…? Would you help me talk to my mother?" She shot me a sideways glance.

"I can, but I shouldn't."

She sighed. "I know. We shouldn't disturb the dead."

"That's true, though I was thinking about you. You need to let go."

She nodded.

"I'm going out tonight," I said. "Stay inside. All sorts of unsavory characters haunt this place at night, both living and dead."

"Where are we going?"

I opened my mouth to speak, but her glare made me close

it with a clack of teeth.

"You promised to include me in everything, remember? You said I was safer where you can see me."

"I never promised, and that doesn't work if I'm in danger too."

"You told my father you'd look after me."

I glanced at a crack in the deck. Had I really said that or was she guessing? It was true, though. I grunted agreement.

She smiled. "Great. So where are we going?"

"Up on the moors." I jerked my head to the plateau high above the eastern city.

Her eyes sparkled.

I tugged Ayla up the last steep stretch of thistles and rocks. Ahead lay the dark, windswept moors, dotted with the sinister silhouettes of ancient ruins. We collapsed onto a boulder facing the city below, catching our breath and sweating from the climb.

Malkandrah appeared magical at night. The cloak of darkness masked the smoke, the smog, the slums, the chaotic tumbling tenements, and the filthy, smelly alleys. From up here, everything looked serene—a blanket of sparkling lights, a yellow warmth shimmering from tens of thousands of windows, and the threaded white lines of street lanterns.

The seemingly haphazard sprinkling of lights was as clear to read as any map. The densely packed but dimmest glows marked the sprawling slums of the Waterfront and Guildhall districts. To their right, red and green lamps wavered like a cluster of metronomes, betraying the multitude of vessels at anchor in the inky black expanse of the harbor. The black snake of the River Malik bisected the city, separating the poor from the rich. The brighter, more consistent lighting across the river made the richer districts obvious.

"What are we doing up here?" Ayla asked.

"A hunch."

Actually, something that Phyxia had said: *If you put a*

defenseless person between a wight and a ghoul, why do the creatures attack each other and not their victim? Nothing that woman said was by chance, and her words had been haunting me. Now I understood. Evil is chaotic. It attacks the greatest threat. Evil abhors evil.

"Care to let me in on it...Master?"

I was about to correct her that I was only a journeyman but stopped. The title was mine by rights. Besides, to her I was a master.

"One lore lesson coming up," I said.

She swiveled on the stone, hands in her lap, back straight, face attentive. I chuckled.

"Elementals gain power from a massive loss of life, the more traumatic the better. This fire creature has been gobbling up the souls of its victims. A water elemental might feast upon the crew of a ship wrecked at sea."

"Death attracts them, or creates them?"

"Neither. They're ancient beings, but they wax and wane in power over the aeons, which is why we rarely see them in our world. This one was summoned here."

"So every time it strikes, it gets stronger?" she asked.

"Exactly. The other night, while half my neighborhood burned, I sensed the trapped spirits." I looked at a pebble next to my boot. "It was leeching their life force."

She shivered and pulled her cloak tighter. "That's horrible. So why are we up here?"

I stood and turned my back on the city. "It'll be warmer if we walk."

We trampled into the moors, its thistles and heather brushing as high as our knees. I led us wide of the first ruin, its walls and shattered pillars overrun with weeds. A single, gnarled tree pushed up through the remains of its roof. A tingling in my *Perception* alerted me to a handful of wights lurking inside, probably looking to pick off stray dogs, children, or lovers come up for the view. The dreadful creatures got everywhere. I knew they sensed my aura—a wide sphere of necromantic magic that yelled "don't mess with me."

"There's rumored to be a soul wraith up here," I said.

"Is that as terrifying as it sounds?" she whispered.

"Worse. Wraiths are wretched things at the best of times. This one—"

"Eats souls?"

She chuckled and her teeth flashed white in the light of Lunas above us.

"There's no fooling you," I said.

"Well, it's not a clever name, is it?"

"True."

"So you think this wraith could devour the souls trapped in the elemental, and weaken it enough that it's forced to leave our world?"

I double blinked. Smart for a novice. I was right to insist she came along. Phyxia was smart too. The wight and the ghoul—evil fighting evil. This plan had to work.

I stopped, hands on hips. She took another step before halting, her brow furrowed.

"Now you've got it all figured out, you don't need me." I held back a laugh. "Off you go then. I'll head home for a warm brandy."

She gave me the evil eye.

"Sorry. You're doing good. Really."

After the third ruin, I veered south, picking my way carefully around the sinkholes and mine shafts that riddled the plateau. Now and then, the cranking sounds of mining lift engines drifted up from below, before being whisked away on the wind. Lunas had moved noticeably across the sky.

An earthen barrow loomed out of the fog that had drifted ashore. It stood six feet tall and fifteen feet long, covered with heather and thorny bushes. I'd seen more impressive burial mounds.

Moments later, I found a handful of stone steps descending into the ground to a slab of rock, marking an entrance that looked undisturbed by tomb raiders. That was the fake trapped entrance, of course, so I backed up two paces and yanked heather and weeds from the ground. Then I knelt and scraped away an inch of topsoil to reveal the real entrance slab.

We had a tough time lifting it. If only I'd thought to bring a crowbar. Finally, we edged our fingers under it and half lifted, half slid it aside. The hole was four feet deep and shored up with small rocks. A dark tunnel ran under the barrow.

I dropped down inside. Even doubled over, the tunnel was a tight squeeze. It reeked of damp earth and stale air. I struck a lightstick against a rock and squinted against its harsh red light. It sparked and sputtered in the dead air.

Ayla jumped down beside me. Why is it that everywhere we went, I had to crouch and she got to avoid a crick in her neck?

A stone-lined hallway ran about fifteen feet, sloping downward, ending at a vertical stone that sealed the tunnel. The floor was compacted soil and devoid of tracks. Nooks in both walls served as platforms for statues. Made of stone and patinaed copper, they were effigies of ancient Iathic deities, but resembled demons in the red glow of the lightstick.

I motioned for Ayla to stay put and advanced cautiously, scrutinizing every tiny hole in the wall, checking the floor for trips or pressure plates. Nothing. At the end of the hallway, I sensed the tickling aura of magic from beyond the stone. It didn't feel like death magic, but more like a curse. Beyond it lay an ominous presence—a dark blotch buckling the field of my *Perception*. Definitely tougher than a wight or ghoul. Maybe I could catch it by surprise.

I examined the solid slab that served as a door. I put all my weight behind sliding it, and the spring loading was obvious. The barest crack appeared at one edge of the slab, followed by a hiss and a cloud of yellow gas. I held my breath but the stale stench of decay made me choke. In seconds it had escaped into the hallway. I let the slab close.

I turned back to find Ayla playing with cling spirits. A half dozen luminescent threads had emerged from the walls and twirled themselves around her arms. As she moved, they snapped back only to return, probing her skin. What was it with her and those things?

"I can't help it," she said with a coy smile. "They came out of the floor. I didn't do anything."

I frowned. "You realize those are all that's left of the soul wraith's dinners?"

This place had to be crawling with them.

"Ew," she murmured.

Her hand flew to her mouth and she hurried to join me. The cling spirits retreated into the walls of the barrow.

"Why did you have to say that? I thought they were pretty."

I rolled my eyes. "This creature is not to be trifled with, so I need you to do what I say at all times."

"Yes, Master."

The dutiful apprentice stands before me at last.

I handed her the lightstick. "When I slide the stone back I need you to brace it. Use your whole body. It's damn heavy. Stay out here. Don't come in, no matter what. If I turn and run, let the stone go and run for your life."

"But you'll be trapped inside."

"I'll make it out the door, believe me. If I don't, well…just keep running. Got that?"

"I'm not going to—"

"This is serious. If this thing touches you, you're dead, like that." I snapped my fingers.

Her eyes were as wide as plates. She clasped her hands together, but I saw them tremble. Good. She should be afraid.

"Isn't there an alternative? Is this our only chance?"

I sighed. "I'm sorry that I don't have a safer plan." Well, any other plan at all, really. "As you reminded me, the stakes have gotten too high. I have to try this."

She touched my arm. "You'll run if you can't beat it? Promise?"

"Believe it, so you'd better be ahead of me."

I slid the stone open once more, got my weight behind it, and heaved it back halfway. Beyond, lay a square chamber fifteen feet across. Iathic runes had been etched into every inch of the slate tiles sunken into the walls. The only contents were a jumbled heap of wood, earth, cloth, and bones in the center. I shook my head. Crazy to build a barrow to survive the centuries but choose to inter the body in a cloth shroud atop a wooden altar. At least that was what I imagined it would have looked like.

I went over the plan in my mind: Step into the room, activate the curse—I'd deal with that later—the wraith would rise out of the corpse, there'd be a bloody battle to within an inch of my life, but I'd beat it down, capture it, then back to town for beer. I rubbed my nose.

Could I take down a soul wraith? Sure I could.

Ayla put her back to the stone and I inched away. It slid partway closed, her boots slipping on the earthen ground before she managed its weight.

Here goes.

I strode into the room and triggered a blast of magic that flickered through the chamber. An unseen force pushed at the center of my back, sending me stumbling forward. A restraining field. I tried to step toward Ayla but the magic was harder than rock.

Awkward.

The bones strewn about the floor collected themselves together with a hollow, rattling sound, pulling the ragged, rotten cloth with them. A cloud of dust and the stink of dry rot washed over me. The cowl of its robe fell across its skull, partly obscuring the baleful, blue orbs that pulsed in its eye sockets. A shadowy, transparent body coalesced around the bones. Non-corporeal talons slid silently from its finger bones, and two points of yellow light whirled around its head in a tight orbit, leaving a faint trail in the air. It throbbed with power.

Behind me, Ayla gasped.

Kristach! Pictures didn't do it justice.

 FOURTEEN

I resisted the sudden urge to vacate my bladder, swept out my Ashtar dagger, and released the soul of the grak from the hilt gem. Free of its prison, it sprayed out like a thin mist.

The wraith lunged at it with incredible speed, uttering a sucking sound so hideous and unnatural that the hairs on my neck stood erect. I shivered head to toe. There was a second sound, a haunting wail that grew louder with each of my rapid breaths. Was that Ayla? Ugh, it was the freed soul as the wraith devoured it.

I blundered back against the wall. I was wasting my distraction tactic. *Focus.*

I stabbed a blast of necrotic energy from my fingers. The wraith turned its blue-fire eyes upon me, but continued to absorb the last wisps of the grak soul. The wail had attenuated to a final gasp. What a way to die, but probably a relief to the poor person who'd had his life and memories transposed into the body of the grak. His pain and madness had finally come to an end.

I unleashed a *Death's Spark*, wrapping the wraith in crackling lightning that crawled over its bones. I might as well have stuck my tongue out, for all the good my spell did. I edged around the wall, probing at the restraining field by the entrance. Its strength was beyond my power. Now I was in a jam.

In a blur of motion, a ghostly tentacle ejected from the wraith and coiled tightly around my neck. Ice seared my head and shoulders. I stumbled around the room but the tentacle remained attached, now probing up my cheeks and into my nostrils. My skin crawled even while my brain told me nothing physical touched it.

Another tentacle darted across the chamber and into my chest. My heart thumped with an erratic rhythm, skipping beats, slowing, starving my body of blood. I crumpled to the ground and cracked my head on a slate wall tile. The room blurred and dimmed, except for two menacing blue orbs bearing down on me. I gasped for breath, my chest heaving. Every muscle cramped. A tingling pain gripped me. My vision tunneled and the world faded.

Someone screamed. Me, or Ayla?

Both ghostly tendrils shifted to latch on to my head. The pain was excruciating, as if they were inside my skull, squeezing my brain. They rifled around in my head, sending garbled flashes of my life ripping through my conscious mind. Silence seized my world. My vision returned, fuzzy and dark. I could hear again. My right eye went blind. My left arm spasmed violently. Then my chest. The shock startled my heart back into rhythm.

I hadn't expected any of this. I should have paid attention in class.

I was done for. All I could do was buy time for Ayla to escape. I strained to turn my head toward the entrance, fighting the urge to let go and give myself freely to the wraith. *No!*

A shadowy figure leaned against a rock, pounding on the magical barrier with one hand. Phyxia? I blinked the fog from my mind. Ayla. Why wasn't she running?

The intense pressure on my head ruptured my mind, and a monstrous maelstrom formed inside my skull, into which my life swirled. That screeching, wailing sound was me. I teetered on the edge of the abyss, body numb. *Get out of my head.*

Time seemed to jump. An instant later, Ayla lay on the floor in a fetal position. The stone slab had closed, but somehow she had gotten into the chamber. The wraith stood over her, yellow flashes whizzing insanely around its head. A spectral tentacle jabbed into her, and her back arched, her limbs thrashed. Her scream was deafening in the enclosed space.

Not her. She was supposed to run. *Run, Ayla!* What kind of protector was I? I willed myself to crawl to her but my body wouldn't comply. My mind reeled as it dipped lower into the menacing whirlpool inside me. Oblivion lay within. Nothingness. No hope to return. If I succumbed, Ayla would be next.

Blue light flickered in the chamber. Angry threads of luminescence erupted from the ground all around Ayla. Cling spirits writhed over her body, coiling around her limbs until they enveloped her. They began to constrict the wraith's spectral limbs, fizzing and sparking, yet the wraith simply shook them off. I stared, unblinking. I'd never seen cling spirits act aggressively.

I too would defend her. The creature had caught me off guard, but now I was ready. In truth, I was desperate. Magic surged through me, melting the wraith's icy grip. Purple fire sparked across my skin and crackled into the air. My spell coalesced into a wall, which I launched at the wraith. With a nerve-jangling screech, it stumbled backward.

I pulled myself up, every movement an unbearable chore. Cramps tore through my limbs. My knees buckled and I crashed back to the earthen floor.

In an instant the wraith was back at my side. Its skeletal claws slipped into my chest. Even though they were incorporeal, pain spasmed up and down my limbs. Lashes of agony tore through me. I became the chained-up spy when my lochtar had plunged her hands into him. My insides quivered and I imagined the wraith shoving my organs aside. Did I not have a soul for it to find?

Ribbons of color flashed across my vision. I snapped my eyes shut but the colored streamers persisted. I couldn't take much more.

Belaya, Lak, whichever of you laughs at me this moment, I confess defeat. Is that what you want to hear? I'm fallible. Happy now?

I channeled more energy and flung it blind into the chamber, sensing the magical backwash when it impacted the creature. The stabbing in my head ceased. I gasped for breath, clutched my chest, and peered tentatively through my eyelashes. One half of the room was bathed in a stark red from the lightstick, and the other a cool blue pulsing from the cling spirits enshrouding Ayla.

The wraith stooped, stunned, among the wooden debris of its ancient sarcophagus. Halfway between us glistened the blade of my dagger. The gem was dull, the soul long absorbed by the wraith. I leaned against the wall to pull myself to my feet, but my legs refused to walk. I'd never crawl that far. I had enough magic for one more spell. It had to be enough.

"Run."

Ayla stirred, said something I couldn't hear, and groped and pawed at the heavy stone door.

"Get up," I said. "Now."

I lunged for the knife. When I hit the ground, I dumped every last shred of my energy into a *Necrotic Ray* aimed at the wraith's face. The rags of its clothing erupted into flame, a red halo around the creature's blue eyes.

It shrieked and turned on me. *Not again. No more.* The depraved intent of the creature was palpable as it dominated my head, crushing my life essence into a corner, where I cowered, watching it tear through my thoughts. Everything I was lay on the brink of extinction. Why had I been so arrogant to think I could win this fight?

A curious, unknown stream of energy washed through me, seeming to come from behind, not from the wraith. What was this? No time to reason. Beggars can't be choosers. I tugged at it, grasping for one more thing to try. Power gushed into me like a river over a burst dam. My skin buzzed. The magic was raw but malleable. I siphoned it crudely through my body, no finesse, no control, then let it blast from my fingers. The magic broke over the wraith like a glowing blue wave. Much of the power missed its mark and splashed the chamber walls.

The creature tumbled from my skull like driftwood coming ashore in a storm. I reclaimed my head, grimacing against the surge of sensations and emotions.

The wraith knelt before me, bones splintered, its ghostly image winking in and out of existence. I thrust my Ashtar dagger so hard into its eye socket that I bruised my knuckles. Its bones tumbled into a heap amid smoldering rags.

In an instant, the river of power ceased. Silence dominated. I crumpled to the ground and the world went black.

My entire head throbbed and ached. Needles of pain stabbed me all over. I had no memory of why. Had I been fighting again? Lak himself by the feel of it. Warmth bathed my face, so I peered cautiously through narrowed eyes. I lay on my back with a square of blazing daylight above. Vertical walls of earth filled my peripheral vision.

Great, I'd woken in a grave in time to be buried. I expected to see Caradan's Tower looming above, but I saw only a sky of leaf green.

My jumbled memories made no sense—luminous blue strands, a girl, bright blue orbs, and a skeleton. Oh, and pain. Lots of that.

"Thank Belaya," said a female voice from out of sight. "I was terrified that thing had taken you, leaving your body an empty husk. I don't know what I'd have done if you'd never woken."

"I'm not sure that waking did me any favors, Phyxia." I raised a hand to my head. *Ouch.*

"I'm Ayla," she said firmly.

Yes, of course.

"The elemental was here?" I asked. That didn't sound right.

"The fire creature? No, the soul wraith."

It all came flooding back. "My dagger, where is it?"

"I put it back in its sheath on your belt."

I struggled to reach it. The hilt gem pulsed menacingly. I exhaled noisily. *Thank the Gods.* I hadn't fought the wraith in vain.

"Relax," she said. "You defeated it. It's just a pile of bones, though it's been creeping me out all night."

We were still in the barrow. I sat up, ever so carefully, and rested my back against the damp earthen wall. Above me lay the entrance, and I faced the hallway of statues. The ground looked disturbed, grooved.

"I tried to drag you out," she said, following my gaze, "but I couldn't lift you out of the hole."

She shivered, her lips blue, and she pulled her cloak tight.

The poor thing had stayed here with me all night. The lightstick must have gone out not long after I had, leaving her in pitch blackness. The nights can be freezing up here on the moors.

"I can walk." I winced as I stood. "It won't be the first time I've leaned on your shoulder. Let's go home and get some hot food."

I lay on the deck of our boat, soaking up the noon rays. The wind was calm, and the harbor reflected Solas like a mirror. Sailing vessels sat becalmed at anchor while smaller boats rowed between them. A small flotilla of boats had set off from the Market Pier. It was a gorgeous day, the sky a clear, pale green. Ayla's singing filtered up through gaps in the wooden boards, as she bathed in the tiny tub belowdecks.

My stomach full from a hot breakfast, I nursed an egg-beer. Perfect cure for hangovers and it worked as well on my headache. Even so, I was exhausted. Twice now, I had sucked every ounce of magic from my core. At least I knew what I was capable of. I gnawed my lip. It hadn't cut it in either fight. It hurt to realize that I was no longer a match for everything out there. Ghouls and wights were easy, but now I'd entered a world I hadn't prepared for.

There'd been a bizarre surge of power back in the barrow. Had Belaya or Lak chosen to respond to my plea? I chuckled. I'd go to temple every day if I thought that was likely to happen. If only I'd paid more attention to Master Semplis prattling on, instead of summoning impish germaines to annoy the old man. He'd probably talked about all sorts of energy sources. I closed my eyes and tried to recapture the feeling of the cool energy flowing into me, but couldn't. Learning more about it would be a game changer.

Last night had nearly ended in disaster, but the risk had paid off. I glanced at the dagger on my belt and shuddered to think of that creature so close to my skin. Was the soul wraith strong enough to weaken the elemental?

I shifted onto my side and stretched my back. Maybe I could lie right there for a few days. I downed the rest of my beer.

The cluster of boats had made good progress into the middle of the smooth-surfaced harbor. They maneuvered into a tight circle, having stopped well short of Sal-Mah, the royal isle. War galleys stood sentinel around its rocky shores. The little boats had been draped in purple linens, matching the robes of the priests and mourners aboard. There was no wind to carry their prayers to me, so I watched in silence as their ceremony unfolded, ending with the lowering of a purple-shrouded corpse, weighted with iron chains. It sank below the surface.

I rolled to my other side where warehouses fronted Boattown. Water burials were stupid, encouraged by an ignorant clergy that feared the undead. Draugr inhabited the harbor. I'd seen their dark silhouettes on Lunas-bright nights. If the corpse escaped their clutches, then the tides would drag the dead out to sea, and the Nikar would claim them. Bodies given freely to the waters were beyond my help. Savage practice—no better than the graves of Solas worshippers. Crypts and mausoleums were much more civilized, and I could protect them with wards, replenishing the magic often to defend the deceased.

I knew then what I had to do.

No matter how much I hated the idea, I couldn't push it from my mind. I tossed this way and that, and finally sat cross-legged and practiced calming mantras. My fingers drummed on the deck. I clenched them into fists and counted chimneystacks across the city, except that I kept losing count.

Kristach!

"Are you dressed down there?" I called to Ayla.

"Yes."

I climbed down the ladder and walked to her cabin. She looked up from her book—my book. Her hair was wet but brushed, and she had dressed in one of the new sets of clothes we had bought. It was a knee-length wool skirt, brown with flecks of gold. Into it, she had tucked a crisp, pearl-colored blouse. How can women present themselves so immaculately in such squalid conditions?

"We're going to visit my mother," I muttered, and dropped my gaze to a spider. *Yes. I'll go scurrying to mother.*

"But you said she was... Oh. All right."

This time I didn't want anything to do with the tristak bargees. It would have been quicker to descend via the Gilt Road sump. We'd have gotten cold and wet, but the breech boy would have zipped us straight down the vertical spill sewer. We didn't take that way because the bargees operated it.

Instead, it had taken us hours to get deep below the western flank of Kand Hill, away from the mines. I think Ayla sensed my irritation and kept silent, and the only sounds were our boots on stone and the incessant buzzing of the glow beetle in its cage. Unlike the sewers, the air down here was warm and still, making us cough on the dust we disturbed.

We emerged from a side tunnel onto a wide, stone staircase that looped back on itself down into the darkness. A stifling-hot wind blew up the central shaft, like a chimney from Lak's kitchen. Ayla kicked a pebble over the edge. We never heard from it again.

"Who built such a grand stairway?" she asked.

She fingered elaborate stone handrails carved to resemble serpents. Pictographs and runes adorned the walls as far down as we could see.

"This is the infamous Eastern Stair," I said as we descended.

"Infamous? Why, where does it go?"

"Down."

"Funny."

Our voices echoed, so we spoke in whispers. Ayla kept licking her lips as she peered around each corner.

"It goes into the very bowels of the earth," I said.

"Have you been to the bottom?"

I shook my head. "This section's barely two centuries old, but it merges with another, more impressive stair that predates the Iathic. Even the deep dwellers don't know who built it or why."

"We should go to the bottom," she said, her eyes huge. "See where it leads."

"Not today."

"You've never spoken about your mother. What was she like?"

I let out a huge sigh and kept moving downward. "I was young when she died."

When she abandoned me.

We made another circuit of the stairs.

"You said female necromancers were rare," Ayla said,

"She was one of the best."

"You should be very proud—"

"I don't want to talk about it."

Tunnels led into the darkness from many of the landings, and at the sixth landing I led us into a triangular-shaped hallway, its walls covered top to bottom with faded glyphs. We heard a primitive grunting in the distance. Ayla paused and tilted her head.

"Ghouls," I whispered.

"Are we going to fight them? Like the skeletons?"

"Why are you so bloodthirsty?"

I turned right down a set of shallow stairs grooved into a crisscross pattern, and then left at the bottom. Ten minutes later the tunnel came to an abrupt stop. Ayla faltered, but I showed her the optical illusion that masked an entrance in the left wall. Her eyes lit up. She joined me and we stepped inside.

The air stank of desiccated flesh, embalming chemicals, and moldering cloth. I breathed deep of the familiar smells. Niches lined the vaulted hallway, each filled with a vertically standing coffin. I held the beetle cage aloft. The wood was riddled with tiny worm and beetle holes, as well as ominous scratches and bite marks. Most of the coffins were intact, but some had collapsed, spewing bones and rags across the floor.

Ayla's glance swept around the crypt.

"Is this where your mother's grave is? I'd expected something more…"

The catacombs stretched away in every direction, hallway upon hallway stacked with coffins. Stone mausoleums stood in the open spaces. Some were simple slabs while others had been decorated with statues of creatures and deities. In places, the wall or ceiling had collapsed, and more than one sarcophagus had been smashed open. We walked the wide avenues in silence, sidestepping heaps of stone and bones. Webs draped in front of our faces. I accidentally kicked a bone, and the sound of it skittering along the ground made Ayla jump.

I shook my head. How dare people let these catacombs fall into such disrepair. So disrespectful to the dead, and to think I'd been poo-pooing water burials. The Guild should be taking care of this and hundreds across the city. How much had I learned as an apprentice, exploring these places to restore wards and protections? Didn't they make apprentices do that anymore? Disgraceful.

Ayla seemed oblivious to the ramifications of the damage, and instead poked her head into every gap or hole. I studied her as she moved from coffin to coffin, bending to get a better view of a skeleton in rags. I'd never met a girl like her. Had my mother been like this as an apprentice?

We emerged from the cobwebs and stepped out under a

magnificent dome. Ayla gasped and craned her neck to study the faded paintings and scripts covering the hemisphere. Not a single sound filtered down from the outside world. How many topsiders knew that such an elaborate and tranquil boneyard lay deep under their feet? How many cared?

The largest and most elaborate mausoleums stood under the dome. I dodged behind a tasteless obsidian edifice, and into the second row, to the simple porcelain slab marking my mother's tomb. There I knelt.

"This is it?" Ayla whispered, scanning the slab for an engraving, of which there was none. "Are you going to raise her, or whatever you call it?"

"A summons would be extremely rude. Imagine me dragging you from a toasty warm bed and throwing you in a tub full of ice. We're just going to chat."

"Then why did you lecture me about not speaking to my mother?"

I sighed. "Not now, Ayla."

"Can I help?"

I handed her the beetle cage. "Watch for ghouls."

It'd been a long time. I should have come more often. My stomach fluttered. Maybe I should leave? Another idea would come to me. No, I'd put this off for too long. Keeping my *Perception* focused outward into the crypt, I channeled energy into my hands and laid them on the cold stone. Careful to keep anger from tainting my magic, I cast a very gentle *Séance*. She'd probably ignore me. I hoped she'd ignore me.

A pale spectral form leeched from the stone and coalesced in the air. Her youthful face and shoulder-length hair was just as I remembered. In my mind it was a light brown, while her eyes were the brightest blue, yet the ghost before me was monochrome.

 **FIFTEEN**

I rocked back onto my heels and stared into my mother's soft eyes. A smile spread across her face. Beside me, Ayla scanned the crypt, oblivious to the ghost.

Maldren, what a wonderful surprise. How I've missed you. You've grown so much.

Her hands reached toward me, paused, and then withdrew.

It was wonderful to hear my mother's clear, singsong voice in my head.

Hello, Mother.

Thank the Gods I didn't have to actually speak with the huge lump in my throat. I swallowed hard.

I see you wear the robes.

I straightened my collar. *It's an honest profession, Mother. I know you would have forbidden me.*

She frowned. *How is that life treating you?*

You hate that I followed you into the Guild, don't you?

I wanted something better for you, to—

It was good enough for you. Did I not meet your impossible standards? Were you that disappointed in me?

Our gazes locked and I searched her face for the truth.

Of course not. You were young, and I worried about you.

You had a funny way of showing it. I needed you.

Her spectral body sighed, but no sound came out of her mouth.

I regret not being there for you. I only wanted to protect you. Let's not argue. We have much to catch up on, but I'm sure you came here for other reasons than to reminisce.

I need your help.

Said so grudgingly. She blinked slowly. *I thought as much. You wouldn't have come here simply to pay your dearest mother a social visit. Your life is so busy that you can't spare a few precious moments for me?*

I clenched my fists. *That's rich. You left me to fend for myself.*

Her eyes flashed. *If you're so independent, you don't need my help then, do you?* She crossed her arms and scowled.

I stood. Ayla jumped up and looked around, peering down each of the crypt's hallways.

I should have known you wouldn't help me.

She stamped her foot silently in midair. *Don't be a brat, Maldren. I raised you better.*

You never raised me at all. You put everyone else above me, your own son.

The city needed me. I had responsibilities, I—

I flung my hands into the air. *Why did you do it, Mother? You gave everything you had—your life, for Lak's sake—for the city. I needed you and you deprived me. I loved you, and then you weren't there anymore.*

My vision blurred, and I scrunched my face to stop from crying.

Ayla's eyes grew huge. "Is your mother here now? Why can't I see her?"

My mother inched forward. *I did what I had to. Life is full of hard choices. It's not fair to treat me like this. You'd better be kinder to her than you are me.*

Who?

She rolled her eyes. *Your woman.*

She's my apprentice.

Typical. You're so wrapped up in yourself that you're oblivious.

What do you mean?

She shook her head. *You don't know her at all, do you?*

I snapped my head around and studied Ayla. She flinched but met my stare, her eyes flicking between mine.

"What?" Ayla whispered. "What's happening?"

Don't be selfish, Maldren. Don't break her heart.

My mother's ghost rotated in midair to face Ayla, who startled and turned pale, looking up into my mother's face. A moment later, Ayla gulped and nodded.

What did you say to her, Mother?

Never you mind. Why are you still so angry with me?

Mother's eyes became dazzling white, and I found myself drawn into their depth. My *Séance* flowed in reverse, and there was nothing I could do to stop her from reading my thoughts. I shivered, remembering the soul wraith, but nothing messed with my mind. Only the hairs on my neck stood on end. Her eyes returned to normal.

You know that Phyxia was a good friend of mine? She smiled. *I'm glad she kept her word.*

She'd done no such thing. That was a subject I didn't want to talk about.

I'll help you, my mother said.

You will?

I sat back down. Ayla squatted beside me and slipped her hand into mine, giving it a gentle squeeze. She remained transfixed on the ghost hovering before us.

Talk to the masters, Mother said. *Tell them what is going on beneath their noses.*

I tried. I'm worried most of them are in on it. Begara is, for certain.

Her brow creased and her shoulders slumped. *Try harder. It's your responsibility.*

That's your idea of help? If I wait for them, nothing will get done. I have to do this.

Headstrong as ever. Then do it yourself. But stop blundering around. Learn your history. What links the Guildmaster and Caradan? Maybe you'll understand the choice I was forced to make. Don't look at me like that. If you want my help, you must help yourself. She began to fade. *Good-bye, Maldren.*

Her image swirled into a milky fog that was sucked back

into her grave slab.

Wait!

Her presence had gone. I grabbed the beetle cage and stood.

"Your mother was so beautiful."

"But not so helpful. Come on." I led the way back toward the catacomb entry hole. "What did she say to you anyway?"

"I'm not telling."

I picked up a fallen skull and tossed it back in its coffin. Typical of my mother to be more useful to Ayla than her son. I knew she wouldn't help me. What a wasted day.

We'd emerged from the undercity and were halfway back to Boattown when I developed an itching sensation on my back. I glanced behind, and sure enough one of those annoying spies was following us. How long had he been back there? I snatched Ayla's arm and turned a sharp right onto Curd Street. Through the window of the corner store, I glanced back and recognized his grim expression partially concealed beneath a wide-brimmed hat. He was still in the game, even after being tortured by Targ and the lochtar. Brave. Or stupid. Two rapiers hung from his belt. This could get ugly.

Once I was certain that he had taken the same turn as us, I pushed Ayla into a narrow alley and behind a pile of refuse.

"Stay hidden," I said, silencing her complaints with a wave of my hand.

I drew my dagger. The gem still pulsed yellow. By the time the spy arrived at the mouth of the alley, I had the dagger clearly visible, and blue lightning crackled from my other hand. For good effect, I chilled the air into an icy mist that collected at the spy's feet. He took a step back, and his hands dropped to rest on the hilts of his weapons.

"Are you that eager to meet the lochtar again?" I asked.

He jerked his hands away, and his gaze darted from side to side.

"I don't want trouble. I bear a message from his Lordship."

Cautiously, he slipped one hand into his coat, withdrew a folded piece of paper, and tossed it to the ground between us.

The mist swirled and settled.

"That's it. I'll leave you alone."

And he did, hurrying back the way we had come. I put away my dagger, dismissed the chilled fog, and retrieved the letter, right as Ayla came out of hiding.

"Who's it from?" She came close beside me. With one glance at the wax seal she turned away with a snort. "My father."

I broke the seal and read the few short lines, indeed signed by the Duke.

"He wants to meet us tonight, in secret."

"That sounds like him, all cloak and daggers."

She glanced at my dark robe and her gaze settled on my own dagger.

"See him without me," she said.

Her eyes pleaded with me, not like a child, but more like a woman determined to make her own way in the world. I respected her independence. We were not so different. I laid a hand softly on her shoulder.

"I won't make you see him, but just remember that he misses you. Stay on the boat, all right?"

She nodded.

I led us by a different route back to Boattown, keeping a closer eye out for tails. How had the man found us? Was I that easy to follow? I knew the streets of Eastside better than most. I scratched the stubble on my chin. The Duke wanted to meet in a small tavern, obviously picked so that he wouldn't be recognized. Another of Fortak's traps? I was still inclined to trust the Duke. He'd had numerous opportunities to find us in Boattown and steal Ayla back. With luck he'd be of greater help than my mother had been.

The Stout and Puke was definitely not a tavern to take your woman to. A block north of Canal Street, it nestled, or some would say it was squashed, between a gambling den and a brewery, with the result that its taproom was choked with gamblers day or night. Beer fresh from next door was hard to beat, and its owners weren't picky over their clientele.

A stench of fish wafted up from the harbor on a persistent breeze. Swords clashed somewhere in that direction, along with shouts and cheers. Dogs barked from a nearby house. I stood under a vandalized street lantern, watching men come and go from the tavern. The Duke's stated time for the meeting had long since passed, but he could wait. Aristos needed to learn not everyone jumps at their beck and call. If his spies or Guild members had indeed established an ambush, they'd stationed themselves long ago.

I slipped in tight behind a group of punters and followed them into the taproom. Copious lanterns did little to dispel the gloom in the large room. I coughed on a smoky haze so thick you could almost chew it. Loudmouthed drinkers jammed against every table, bench, and corner. Boys squeezed among the throng, clutching pitchers tightly to their chests, yet still the beer slopped in every direction. Sticky clumps of straw littered the floor.

Obviously, the Duke wouldn't be prancing about in his finest regalia, so I looked for his men, and caught the eye of a burly, bearded man perched on the back stair. He jerked his head in my direction and started up the stairs. By the time I had fought my way through the crowd and up the rickety steps, he was waiting, arms folded, at the end of a long hallway. He turned and entered the room behind him. Talkative fellow.

I followed him inside, and he closed the door and stood purposefully in front of it. The din of the taproom faded, as did the stink of beer and street-weed. Burning logs crackled in a small fireplace, before which had been set two worn but serviceable armchairs. The Duke relaxed in one of them, dressed in simple merchant robes and leathers, no ostentatious jewelry.

"Fix yourself a plate and join me." He gestured to a side table laden with a selection of food.

My stomach growled. Never one to turn down a meal, I helped myself to cheeses, orjak pâté, still-warm fruit bread, and sweetmeats. My fingers hovered over the jit-nuts and moved on. I'd never be able to eat them again. I poured Akra into a goblet and breathed deep of its complex caramel aroma. With a glance at the guard, who watched my every move, I took my food and drink and sat in the other chair, facing the Duke.

"Go for a beer," he said over his shoulder.

The guard left without a word, but the Duke remained silent for several minutes, allowing me the opportunity to spread gooey cheese on my bread and top it with pâté.

"What do you have for me?" I asked between bites. "I appreciate your previous tip. That was an intriguing meeting of your Covenant, or whatever you call yourselves."

He stroked his graying goatee.

"I won't ask how you evaded Fortak's stupid skeletons, but you've proven your abilities."

He waved his hand dismissively, as if done with that topic. He stared at the ragged rug before the fire.

"How's my daughter? I'd hoped she would come."

"She's safe. I told you I would look after her."

He searched my face, and then nodded. "I don't blame you for wanting a bargaining chit. Does she miss me at all?"

His weakness for Ayla crippled his negotiation skills. Good. I had a bona fide Duke under my thumb.

His lips parted as if he wanted to say more, but instead he raised his goblet and drank.

"How's Phyxia?" I asked, my voice breaking. I faked a cough. Kristach, I'd just revealed my own weakness, but I had to find out. "The ambassador?"

"That's the second time you've asked about her." He raised a single eyebrow.

"Your spies were thorough in finding her." Had I led them there?

"Her place was empty when they got there. Seems she had already met with Fortak of her own volition."

So it was true.

I stuffed a hunk of bread and pâté into my mouth and chewed hastily. Only the superb vintage kept me from chugging the Akra, so I sipped instead, washing it around my mouth to release the intense flavors. Even in a poor solar, Akra never failed to deliver. At least some things remain true.

The Duke set down his goblet. "To business. Fortak plans to release the elemental tomorrow morning, for another...demonstration."

Logs in the fire crackled and spat.

"Where?"

"Gilt Road. After the jewelers and artificers open up shop."

"That's going to be a bloodbath." I looked him in the eye. "Tell me, do you sleep at nights?"

His gaze flicked to the closed door, and he leaned in toward me.

"It was never meant to go this far. Fortak tricked me. He had Ayla."

"Tell the Council the truth," I said. "You have a seat there. Get an audience with the Crown Prince."

He shook his head. "After everything I've told the Council, they'll strip my title if they discovered my part in this."

Did he plan to reveal his entire hand to me? Political suicide.

"So you're pinning all your hopes on me sorting out this mess?"

"I've checked up on you...and the Guild. I have a good spy network." He smirked. "Easy to see why few in the Guild would go against Fortak. You, though..." He gestured with a hunk of cheese. "You aren't afraid of him, and that's important. You seem to have principles, and you're tenacious and resourceful."

All right, maybe he was a good negotiator after all. He could stroke my ego anytime he liked.

The Duke took a sip of Akra and savored it. "Trade and commerce I know, mining I dominate, but this magic business is going to ruin my reputation. The best I can hope for is that the Council gives in, Fortak gets the power he seeks, and this whole dirty secret gets forgotten. And I get Ayla back."

"You forgot the ending where I destroy the elemental and

save the day." I smiled. "Then I single you out as the mole who helped me defeat the Guildmaster at every turn, right?"

He sat back, his brow furrowed. Firelight flickered orange across his face. Having a grateful Duke could do wonders for my career.

"Thanks for the information," I said. "Help me defeat the Covenant and I'll bring Ayla home safe."

I couldn't tell him that she wouldn't stay home.

A knock on the door startled us both.

"Protect Ayla," he said. "Please."

"Enter," he said loud enough to be heard through the door.

The burly guard strode in, his beard glistening with beer. I glanced at the Duke. His expression was full of control and regality. I nodded to him and stood. An interesting meeting—I hadn't realized an aristo could be so anguished.

The next morning, Ayla and I left Boattown and headed for Gilt Road. I allowed extra time to lead us on an intricate path, as I had the day before, to be certain that no one followed us. I was conscious of the holes and scorch marks on my Guild robe, but I had no spares and that was the least of my problems. Not that it mattered—everyone looked at me with disdain anyway. Ayla, on the other hand, wore a tan skirt and blue blouse with matching cloak.

We sat at a street café on Gilt Road and ordered breakfast. I fidgeted in my chair. A pack of dogs ran past our table, barking and growling at random people. Merchants and artificers hurried by, eager to reach their stores and begin the day's business.

I wanted to cry out, order them to flee and empty the street, but I knew they wouldn't listen to me. A pair of Black and Reds loitered at the next intersection and I'd soon be arrested. It hurt to be condemned every time I tried to help.

Ayla's chair rocked awkwardly on the uneven cobbles. She inched it to one side and bit into her steaming sabata, chewing and swallowing fully before speaking.

"What else did he say?"

I gulped my karra, now barely lukewarm. She'd been quizzing me about her father all the way here.

"He misses you but accepts that you will visit him in your own time. I think he's pleased that I'm looking after you."

She chuckled, almost choking on her food. "Oh, is that how you explained it? More like I'm keeping you out of trouble."

"Speaking of which, I'd rather you weren't here."

She frowned. "We've been through this. After the barrow, I'm not letting you fight these creatures alone."

I rolled my eyes. "Yes, Mother."

I was glad to have her with me. It was lonely being the only one trying to stop the Covenant's disgusting plan. My finger drummed on the table. Inside, my stomach flipped and I fought back the rising nausea. Would my plan work? Could the soul wraith destroy the elemental?

She touched my forearm. Her fingers were warm and soft.

"I know you worry about me, but aren't I allowed to worry about you?"

Her brown eyes locked on mine. I hadn't noticed her blue eyeliner before, and she'd rouged her lips a little.

She winked. "I think you like protecting me. And I'm still waiting."

What was she on about now? I couldn't keep up with her erratic thoughts. I shrugged, tired of guessing.

"How did my father know about this morning? Stop holding back. What's his link to this Covenant?" Her gaze dropped to the table.

Kristach. This wasn't the time, but she had a right to know. My shoulders slumped and I scratched my forehead.

"He was tricked by Fortak." Could I leave it at that?

She heaved an enormous sigh and I wanted to draw her into a hug. Not here. Not in public.

"He could go to the High Council or tell the Crown Prince," she said.

Déjà vu from last night.

She snatched up her sabata and took a bite, meeting my gaze. "My father's tricking you. I don't trust him, and neither should you."

"He hasn't been wrong yet."

She waved her sabata in the air. "This is what he does. Don't you see? He plays every side to make sure he wins. The tristak son of a whore knows exactly what he's doing. That's why I hate him. Gods, he's despicable."

"Such language." I grinned. "You're blending in with us commoners much better."

Part of me wanted to be mad at her disrespect for her father, but I understood. I really did. I couldn't imagine running away from a life where you had everything, including servants to pamper you, to end up in the seedy end of town with me. Her inner strength continued to amaze me. Her seething made her whole body quiver, and her teeth were clenched tight. If I tried to console her I'd likely get my head bitten off.

"Look, forget about him," I said. "We need to concentrate on the elemental and saving lives."

She folded her arms but her eyes softened.

I tapped the dagger in my sheath for the fiftieth time that morning.

"I wish I knew some spells. I feel so useless. I can feel the magic inside me." She thumped her belly. "But what use is it? Isn't there something…anything you can teach me to do?"

"I would if it were possible, believe me. Just stay close and keep an eye out for flying debris. The smoke…"

She nodded and looked away.

It started with a distant shout, then a hissing sound as steam spewed from the sewer grates. More cries followed, and then a crowd surged around the corner further up Gilt Road.

 SIXTEEN

I leaped to my feet with Ayla right behind me, and we hurried up the street. The fleeing crowds surged around us, pushing us back the way we had come. Ayla's hand slipped into mine and I clasped it tight, trying to pull her through the stampede. Shouts turned to screams, and people turned on each other, slapping them aside, punching and shoving. Many tripped and became trampled underfoot.

A man spun me around and I looked into the terrified face of a silversmith, evident by the trademarks on his coat sleeves.

"Necromancer scum," he cried and spat.

Phlegm dribbled down my face. I wiped it from my eyes.

"Get him," another man shouted.

Two others tried to drag me down. A punch to my stomach missed its mark, and I lashed out, pushing him away. Ayla kicked him in the shin and he fell back, knocked to the ground by the panicked crowd.

"Leave him, Jurga." A third man pulled the artisan away. "We should storm their Guild and burn *it* down," he said as the men fled.

I wanted to snap back with a smart retort, but they were closer to the truth than they knew. Damn my profession.

The streets were near empty now, and the cries became muted as the crowd descended the hill and spread out into adjacent streets. From far away came the clanging of fire cart bells. We were likely already too late. I led Ayla up the steep street, and as we rounded a tight corner, a blast of heat washed over us. Both sides of the road were alight with a sickly orange glow. Flames roared from manholes, igniting a wagon and sending the kalag hitched to it wild, crying, and lowing in its futile effort to break free. Ayla started toward it.

"Leave it," I shouted above the roar of the inferno.

"We have to free it or—"

"I said no. Stay close."

I continued upward, panting with the exertion. Stragglers fled the other way, their arms filled with looted jewelry and huge, clanking bags of coins. To my left, a man stumbled from a building as the walls crashed around him, spewing timber and stone into the street. The cloud of dust settled. A bloody arm protruded from the rubble amid scattered jewels. The arm twitched once and became still. Ayla turned away, hands to her mouth.

The heat was intense, singeing my eyebrows and the hair on my arms. Windows exploded, and glass tinkled as it showered onto the cobbles about us. I'd been here before. I snapped up my *Cleansing Shield*, dragged Ayla inside it, and we both breathed deep of the frigid air.

Most buildings stood four floors tall with stores on the ground level. To my right, a roof buckled and collapsed, ejecting a man from a flaming window. He plummeted, arms flailing. His short cry ended in the horrible sound of crunching bones. Screams echoed from every direction as women and children appeared at windows, coughing and crying, clothes held to their mouths, searching for a way down.

"Help them," Ayla said.

Nausea gripped me. I couldn't help them all. Bodies already littered the road, many still burning.

"Damn you to The Deep, Fortak." My hands clenched into fists. How could he do this to our glorious city?

I turned to tell her that we couldn't save everyone, that hundreds would burn for each life we saved, but she was rushing toward a handful of people picking their way through the carnage. They had arms around each other, helping the wounded, dodging the fire billowing from every building. The worst of the fire lay behind them. Gods, I'd only reached the edge. So much for my gaining an advantage.

Then I spotted the oily smoke snaking along the ground, stalking them.

"Ayla, the smoke. Come back."

She glanced toward it but hurried onward to assist a limping old man. She yelled at the people to move faster but their pace barely increased. The smoke lapped at their legs and coiled upward.

"Leave the wounded." I hurried forward. "Hold your breath and run. Run or you'll all die."

Magic seethed in my core, but I kept it lidded. I needed every ounce of power for the elemental. Trapped victims wailed from every direction and I spun around. Who was I to pick who lived or died? It wasn't fair to make me choose.

The group coughed and choked, almost completely concealed within the black smoke. I caught glimpses of shadowy shapes as I scrambled over a mound of rubble, scraping my elbows and legs. I gritted my teeth.

A girl Ayla's age lurched away from the others toward a flaming manhole.

"No," I screamed, so loud that I tasted blood in my throat.

She flung her arms above her head, twirled like a dancer, and plunged into the hole. The last I saw of her was her flaming hair like a wick on a candle.

Enough of this! I had to protect Ayla.

I leaped over a pile of flaming wood, caught Ayla within my shield, and yanked her away. Her eyes were wide and feral. I slapped her twice and shook her, not stopping until her gaze finally focused on my face. She shivered in my shield's icy grip and I knew she'd be all right.

A fight had broken out between two men. One of them

snatched up a chunk of wood, oblivious to the bent nail that pierced his hand. He clubbed the other man, while blood poured from his own palm.

Ayla recoiled with a gasp, wrapped an arm around my waist, and steered us away.

One entire side of the street gave way with a crash. We ducked against the cascading hail of bricks and brushed the glowing embers from our clothes and hair. I tucked her loose bangs behind her ear and a tiny smile spread along her lips. When the cloud of ash and dust settled we were alone. Nothing else lived in the devastation.

I'd already wasted too much time with no saved lives to show for it. I pulled Ayla close, set my teeth, and marched into the inferno, trusting everything to my magic shield. Anger had weakened my control last time. I wouldn't make that mistake again.

We had gone less than a hundred feet, picking our way through the rubble, before my shield could no longer hold back the searing heat. A wasteland of burning buildings, bloody, burned corpses, bricks, and the broken remnants of people's homes lay around us. As last time, curious blue flames sizzled around the dead bodies, and then spiraled up into the air. A roar like a thousand bellows thundered around us, but the real mass of the elemental had yet to show itself.

This was insanity. What did I think I could do here? My pulse pounded.

Thick smoke tendrils prowled like demonic hounds. They picked up our scent and rippled across the ground toward us. I planted my feet wide, clapped my hands, and cast *Shadowfire*. The spell fizzed blue and turned the smoke into a powdery ash that drifted to the ground. More coils of smoke circled, and I imagined them sizing us up.

Magic tickled my feet. I glanced down to see minute threads of light emerging from the ground, only to dissolve and fade before they could strengthen. Ayla's face was scrunched in concentration. I opened my mouth to offer advice, then decided to leave her be. Cling spirits were her thing.

I drew my Ashtar dagger from its sheath, grasped it firmly in both hands, and then gathered most of the energy from my core. The time had come.

All right, elemental. Let's see what you make of this.

I shaped the magic into a massive *Dispel* and projected a dazzling sphere of energy. A visible shock wave blasted into the surrounding buildings, gushing through the gaping doors and windows. In an instant the flames were extinguished, heralded by an ominous whumping noise. The scorching heat and background roar ceased abruptly, replaced by the popping and cracking of the remaining embers. Steam billowed from the ruins, blowing ash everywhere. I coughed and spat and shook it from my hair.

That should get its attention. *Recognize me, elemental? I'm back.*

The gem in my dagger swirled yellow. My secret weapon was intact, imprisoned inside.

The ground trembled. A column of flame thundered out of a sooty manhole barely ten feet away. I pumped power into my *Cleansing Shield* an instant before a fireball burst over Ayla and me. The pillar of fire rocketed into the sky, and from half a dozen such holes, the sewers puked the elemental. The sky flashed every shade of red and orange, spewing fire across several city blocks.

Lak and all his demons!

The very heavens seemed ablaze—a boiling firestorm of whirling flame and superheated gas. Fragments of thousands of shrieking voices sounded on the wind: *Free us. Save us.*

Fingers of fire groped downward. I grabbed Ayla and dodged behind the heaped remains of a fallen building. Fire flashed out of the boiling clouds as if the creature was trying to snatch us.

"Belaya, Lady of Justice," Ayla cried.

I followed her gaze upward, to where a fiery vortex swirled in the sky like a chomping maw. I cowered, expecting the creature to slurp us up and devour us.

Once more, flickering threads of blue fizzed from the ground, running up Ayla's legs like tattoos. She placed her palms on the cobbles, intensifying the flow of the pulsing, shimmering wisps.

This was far worse than last time. If I had any sense, we'd be running like everyone else. The ovens of Lak had been unleashed upon the world. I couldn't help but think that by day's end, our city would be reduced to a desolate landscape of bloodied ash. What lunacy had inspired Fortak to unleash such a monster?

Blasts of superheated gas jetted from the flame storm above us, forcing us lower until we groveled like cowards in the slurry of charcoal, brick dust, and blood that ran in streams down the steep road.

Why had I put Ayla in jeopardy once again? I gawked at her attempts to keep the cling spirits from burrowing back into the ground. They had more sense than either of us. Her teeth were clenched and her eyes narrowed. For all her inexperience, she made a superior partner to Hallum.

I punched a fist into one palm. I was letting events control me again. It was time to test my theory. If I was wrong then we'd soon join the ash blowing in the wind. I scrambled and slithered to my feet. Leaving power in my shield, I drew everything I had from my gut and dispatched a barrage of lightning into the sky. It tore into the elemental, and the roar changed pitch. It screamed in frustration, and then flung a ball of fire as large as a house at us.

My legs wanted to run, my stomach wanted to heave, and my bladder wanted to burst. I wouldn't allow any of those things. Instead, I thrust the dagger into the air like a lightning conductor. I shrieked a battle cry. Melodramatic, but satisfying.

Right before the fireball hit me, I freed the soul wraith from my dagger.

The shock wave pummeled us. My dagger bounced and clattered away. There was no immolation, no searing pain, only a blast of icy air that neutralized the fireball. An amorphous cloud of blackness climbed the column of fire, chasing it into the sky. The dark cloud writhed and expanded as it consumed the flames. Lightning crackled through the firestorm.

Ayla pulled me to my feet and we stared as the wraith consumed the elemental, smothering it like a blanket. Fire and hot gas streamed into the wraith as it bled the elemental dry. Wails, murmurs, and sighs accompanied the streams.

Ayla took both my hands in hers and jumped up and down, beaming a pretty smile. "You did it. You did it."

While she bounced around me, spinning me, I stared at the sky. It was like peeking into the Fury of the Gods at the creation of the world. Red and orange swirled around blackness and vice versa, mixing and diluting each other.

She stopped. "What's happening?"

The wraith was unraveling. Fire engulfed it, smothering it. A horrific screech set my teeth on edge. Kristach.

"Do something," she cried. "Before it's too late."

"I'm drained. I've used it all." I dragged her away down the street.

She resisted. "We have to help the wraith."

I blinked twice. That would have been comical at any other time.

"It's gone. It's over. The plan failed. We have to go." I tugged her forward.

The wraith had shrunk to a mere smudge. A cauldron of fire once more filled the sky, spitting gobbets of flame that burst and splashed across the ruined houses, and turned to steam against my *Cleansing Shield.*

"Run," I yelled.

A large force thudded into my back, pushing every breath from my lungs and sending me flying through the air. I crashed shoulder-first against a collapsed wall and crumpled into a heap. When I tried to sit up, pain split my body in two and I flopped back down, cracking my head against a rock. My vision blurred to a ghastly sea of orange everywhere I looked.

Then the orange became blue. A web of blue sparks crawled over me, tingling and stinging like an army of ants. In the midst of it all, Ayla peered down at me, her sweat-soaked hair draped across her face. I blinked soot from my eyes. She shouted something but I heard nothing. A blinding blue aura shimmered about her, and once again a river of immense, cool energy flowed through me.

A ball of flame streaked down from the heavens, exploding behind her. She stumbled forward but remained upright. Her hair began to smolder. I grabbed greedily at the source of power and pushed out a renewed *Cleansing Shield*, screaming at the ice searing my veins. Frost dappled her hair, putting out the burning ends. Our breath froze as we doubled over, panting. My ears popped.

"Can't stay here," she cried and dragged me to my feet. Cling spirits writhed all over her, flickering and pulsing white and blue. It was like Belaya herself stood before me.

I glanced around us, dazed. Total destruction. I'd been transported to The Deep. That had to be it. I had no sense of my whereabouts until I looked downhill, and through the smoke caught glimpses of intact buildings stretching down to the river.

No trace of the soul wraith remained.

A crowd labored up the steep road, armed with picks and shovels, and behind them three pairs of kalag strained at their harnesses to drag heavily laden fire carts.

"Stay away," I yelled. "Go back."

The cart wheels had become stuck in the rubble, but the men continued to approach.

Ayla's cocoon of cling spirits was bright enough to cast shadows. I squinted at her through half-closed eyes. My body throbbed with power, so much power. I could still win. I had to win!

I flung my hands above my head and unleashed a barrage of *Death's Spark* and *Shadowfire*. Lightning and purple flares tore apart a fireball in midair, splashing it across the entire street. I stumbled. If I'd learned one thing, it was that my spells were no match for the might of the elemental, no matter how much power I wielded.

The men halted and brandished their picks.

"He's a necromancer."

"A blue demon fights by his side."

"This is all his doing. Filthy death bringer."

Not again.

The men cast rocks and bricks that bounced and crunched around us. A sharp stone hit me on the arm. I shook out the pins and needles. My dagger glinted nearby and I snatched it up. Fire erupted in a building adjacent to the men. The stone throwing ceased, but not before a sizable chunk hit Ayla squarely in the chest.

She crumpled to the ground. The web of cling spirits dissipated like phantoms after a *Dispel*. The river of energy ran dry. Cramps filled the void in my gut and my stomach heaved. Vomit splattered my legs and boots, adding a decomposing vegetable smell to the stench of burned flesh and acrid smoke.

I crawled to where Ayla lay. Her chest rose and fell erratically. I cleared debris from beneath her head and gently tapped her cheeks.

"Wake up. Ayla, wake up."

I gave her a shake. She groaned but remained unconscious.

"If you've hurt her…" I cried at the men.

Another fireball arced from the sky, exploding close to the fire crew. The kalags reared, tipping a cart sideways. The men flocked to right it while uttering a stream of curses and shouts. They hadn't even gotten the water flowing. The whole neighborhood burned and they had wasted time hurling stones. These were the idiots I was risking my life to save?

"Come on." I willed myself on, fighting the exhaustion that had seized me. I scooped Ayla into my arms and stumbled into what remained of an alley, now little more than a gap through the ruined buildings. I focused the dregs of my power into my shield, warding off the black smoke that followed, sniffing at my heels.

I hadn't remembered a moment of Ayla dragging me to Boattown, but this time I remembered every weary step that it took to carry her from the same situation.

I slept through the morning and past midday, and when I

finally rolled out of my bunk, a minor storm of ash blew from my singed robe, settling throughout my cabin. The bed resembled the burned-out street. My bones cracked and my muscles twinged in sympathy. I could see why the masters enjoyed sitting behind a teaching desk. That was what I needed, a cushy classroom in the bowels of the Guild. Saving the city hurt. A lot.

I limped out into the narrow hallway, pausing at Ayla's open door. Her back to me, she plunged her head into a bucket of water, then rubbed soap flakes into her hair. Ash dusted the floor, disturbed only by her footprints. Her shirt looked worse than my robe, equally as black with large scorch marks and holes. I'd severely underestimated her. I knew few men with her guts.

She noticed me leaning on the door frame, and jumped. She raked her fingers hastily through her hair.

"Don't stare at me. I'm a mess." Her cheeks reddened.

"Sorry." I stretched, regretted it instantly, and groaned.

"Can I finish up here, please?"

I turned away. "Of course. I'll make a start on lunch. Take your time."

When she eventually joined me in the galley, I had filled a couple of bowls with diced meat, cheese, and vegetables, and was shoveling wood into the stove's firebox. She moved to the table and ground coarse brown seeds with mint leaves. The air exploded with a fresh aroma.

"What's next?" she asked. "Now that your plan failed. I mean…it was a great plan, only…"

"We're on the right track." I rubbed my nose. "The soul wraith did more damage than I ever did. We just need ten more of them."

She grimaced and scooped the mulip ingredients into a pot I had boiling on the tiny stove.

"It was kicking the elemental's butt," she said. "I was certain we'd done it."

I scratched my jaw. I really ought to shave.

"Negative energy," I murmured.

"Hmm?" She placed a pan on the other hot plate, added a glob of fat, and rolled it around, letting it melt.

"The elemental is positive energy," I said. "Light and heat. The soul wraith is negative. Dark."

"They both consume souls. Aren't they the same?"

"It's complicated."

She dumped my chopped ingredients into the pan, and they sizzled. She faced me with a scowl. I guess I hadn't taught her anything, really. I'd been a lousy teacher, but I could fix that.

"All right, I'll explain. The elemental is physically in our world. It is real, comprised of positive energy. The wraith was non-corporeal, like a ghost, a projection into our world from The Gray. That's negative energy. Furthermore, the wraith destroys souls, whereas the elemental traps and feeds off them."

"I understand." Her tongue popped out the corner of her mouth. I'd grown to like that habit of hers.

"We need more negative energy," I said, "though only the Gods know how. I'm not stalking more soul wraiths even if I thought they'd make a difference."

Truth was, the creatures were rare. Having met one now, I wasn't unhappy about that.

"Talking of power, how were you doing that thing with the cling spirits?"

She shrugged. "They seem to like me. You're the necromancer. You tell me."

I squeezed onto the bench by the table, and eyed the mulip brewing on the stove. My fingers drummed on the wooden table.

"You were absorbing the power of cling spirits. I've never heard of anyone doing that before. More importantly, you were channeling it."

"What does that mean?"

"You were sharing power for me to use. Very few necromancers can do that. Common among the Elik Magi, apparently."

Her mouth made an O.

"You did it in the barrow too, and saved my life."

"I was so scared. The soul wraith was killing you."

We stared into each other's eyes for a long moment. The tempo of her breathing increased, and my gaze dropped to watch the rise and fall of her breasts under her thin, clean shirt. She flushed, and turned back to the stove.

She truly cared for me and that made my insides warm and fuzzy. It had been a long time since someone had worried about me getting hurt. I'd been hard on her. It wasn't her fault she'd been paired up with me, and yet she handled it with superior grace than I. I'd never liked working with a partner at the Guild—except Kolta—but I shouldn't take that out on her. She was strong, smart, and willing to get her hands dirty. What more could I want from an apprentice?

"I wish I knew how you did it," I murmured. "The cling spirits, I mean. If you could learn to control them that could give us an edge."

She handed me a steaming mug of mulip.

"I knew I could help somehow. Maybe I can teach you some things." She winked.

She already had, but I wouldn't admit it.

"You did good. Thanks for saving my life. Again."

The boat rocked as someone stepped aboard. Footsteps thumped on the overhead deck. I tensed and reached for my dagger, realizing that it lay in my bed at the end of the hallway. Boots appeared at the top of the wooden ladder. Had Fortak's men found us?

 SEVENTEEN

I pushed Ayla behind me and raised my fists, balancing on the balls of my feet. I could have used Targ right now. A dark shape jumped down the ladder and I rushed forward, shoving the intruder against the wall.

"What in bloody Lak's name are you doing?" Kolta yelled, cowering, his breathing labored.

"What are you doing here? Couldn't you have announced yourself?"

His eyebrows rose. "I didn't think you'd attack me. Do you mind?"

He pushed lightly against my chest. I was totally in his face, so I backed down and gestured to the bench.

"Getting a little jumpy, aren't we?" His eyes bulged from their sockets.

He scanned the scorch marks on my robe and the ash covering the floor.

"You've been up against the elemental again? I told you to lay low."

He tossed me a new and folded robe. "Thought you might need a spare. Looks like I was right."

I nodded and fingered the thick fabric.

He squeezed onto the bench. "Maldren, my boy, this is beyond serious. This thing is going to kill you. Leave the city, I implore you."

"No," Ayla and I said in unison.

"If I do, we won't have a city left. Who else is going to save us? The masters?" I snorted. "Certainly not the Council. I was there at the beginning, Master, and I plan to be there at the end."

Ayla handed him a mug of mulip. He thanked her and cupped it in both hands.

"On the subject of which," he said, "Fortak returned from a summons to the High Council."

"And?"

"And he's mad about something." He shook his head. "He struck Begara."

I rubbed my nose. "That means they didn't beg him for help. I wish they'd just give him his damn seat on the Council. At least then he'd dispel the elemental."

"It might not be that simple. You heard what Phyxia said."

I nodded. "He's playing with fire."

No one laughed.

I wish I'd heard everything that Phyxia had been saying when those wretched ghouls had so rudely interrupted.

"If he's lost control of it..." Kolta broke off, frowning.

Ayla delivered bowls of bread and stew to the table.

"Sorry to interrupt, but I'm starving. Can we eat?"

"There'll be more room on deck." I moved aft to the ladder, juggling bowl and mug.

The day was warm though Solas dodged in and out of the swift-moving clouds. Wisps of smoke rose from the slopes of Kand Hill. Crowds lined the nearby wharves, every person hauling several bags, sacks, or chests, no doubt hoping to find passage. It broke my heart to see my people flee.

We ate in silence, sitting cross-legged in a circle, and I found the gentle rolling of the boat and the sigh of straining ropes relaxing. The whole of Boattown undulated gently, and I let my gaze drift across the flotsam and rotting hulks. I needed another chat with the Duke, but I knew that he had risked a lot telling me what he had, if Fortak had truly threatened him with a lochtar. Fortak had a reputation for paranoia, so it wasn't a stretch that he had little trust in his own conspirators.

"I need to know more."

"What?" Ayla asked.

I glanced at her. I hadn't meant to voice my thoughts.

"Oh, I was thinking."

"Uh-oh." She smirked. "What trouble are we getting into now?"

"Out of the frying pan, into the fire." It was an apt cliché. "It's all or nothing for Fortak at this point. Now things get dangerous."

Kolta nodded and wolfed down his breakfast.

"Bring the fight out of the slums..." I said.

"What?" Ayla and Kolta asked.

"They'd said that," I murmured, then I snapped my fingers and sat bolt upright.

"Market Plaza."

Kolta choked and sprayed food everywhere.

A dark cloud swallowed Solas, and a gloom settled over the city. A gust of chill wind blasted the deck.

"What about it?" Ayla asked.

"The coronation is only four days away," I said.

Her spoon slipped out of her hand and clanged into her bowl, splashing gravy.

"Gods, no," she said, voice breaking.

"Thousands will die," I said. "Then Fortak will take command and be a hero."

Assuming he could get rid of the elemental when the time came.

"That's h-horrible," she said. "Damn my father for being involved in this."

"He made a mistake. That's all. He was only thinking of your safety."

"He's right," Kolta said. "Once the Guildmaster had you, your father was doomed."

Her shoulders slumped. She put a hand to her forehead, pushing aside her bangs. Her face lost all its color.

"I did this to him. If I hadn't gone to the Guild then he wouldn't be in this mess."

She resembled a small child right then. Just yesterday she'd been mad at him. Her relationship with her father mirrored mine with my mother. We wanted to be angry with them, but deep down our hearts burned with an undying love. I pulled Ayla to me and wrapped my arms around her. She pressed her face against my chest, despite the ash smeared over my robe. The warmth from her body spread into mine. I could imagine her pain. Kolta grinned. I scowled at him, cupped the back of her head with one hand, and stroked her hair with the other.

"He's helping us now," I whispered. "It's not your fault. You couldn't have predicted this."

She nodded but remained in my arms. Kolta wiggled his eyebrows. Eventually, Ayla pulled away and sat with both knees up to her stomach. Her embrace had given me a new strength.

"I'll make this right," I told her.

Her eyes flashed. "No, I'll right my father's wrong. Don't you dare push me away. We're in this together, remember?"

I held up one hand defensively. "All right. Together."

"Hmph." She scrutinized me for a long moment and then stood. "I need a bath. Don't plan anything without me."

She stacked the breakfast bowls and took them below. I hadn't finished but I wasn't going to argue.

"Women," Kolta muttered when she had descended. "Moods change in a moment. How do you put up with her?"

"She's strong and independent. She'll make a great necromancer."

"I doubt Fortak intends to keep her in the Guild. Her only value was leverage with the Duke. Don't get too comfy with her, my boy."

"She has the talent. When she passes the initiation tests, her membership can't be refused."

"Then she'll be only the fourth woman in history to do so.

Your mother was the last, but she was incredibly powerful." He shuddered. "Scarily so."

Kolta was scared of my mother? Interesting.

"Well, she spent enough time at the Guild," I said. "More time than with me."

Kolta tossed a piece of scrap wood. It splashed into the water between the adjacent boat and ours.

"She saved the city," he said. "Don't belittle such a selfless deed. I see her bravado and moral fiber in you. Her stubbornness too."

He chuckled, but not before I spotted his wistful gaze. Had something gone on between them, or something he'd have liked to? Questions for another time.

"I ought to be more like you, Master. You were my inspiration. I learned everything from you, not her."

I hadn't been an easy student. I knew that. Many of the masters gave up on me, labeled me a troublemaker, but not Kolta. He nurtured me and became my greatest mentor until Phyxia. I let out a huge sigh. Here I was, looking back to him for guidance. My gut spasmed as if stabbed. How could Phyxia have betrayed me? So like Mother.

"Make peace with your mother. There's much she would teach you. I know she's proud of you."

I was done talking. "I can't afford to reminisce. I appreciate you dropping by but you should probably go."

We stood and walked to the stern of the boat.

"It's time Ayla and I moved out of Boattown. She deserves better than a rotting boat surrounded by garbage and hiding outlaws."

He nodded. "Where will you go?"

"The owner of The Pumphouse owes me a favor."

He clapped a hand on my shoulder and then descended the plank to the next boat. It bowed and bounced under each step. It took him ages to scramble from vessel to vessel toward the shore. Solas emerged from the clouds and bathed the city in light.

Later that day, Ayla and I crossed the City Bridge into the Plaza District. The narrow streets, hemmed in by tenements, opened out into wide avenues. The stiff wind off the harbor brought only a whiff of salt, not the stench of fish offal or moldering grain that was a way of life in the eastern city. Boattown had added its own odor: rotten wood, seaweed, and garbage.

"The air smells fresher already," Ayla said, breathing deep.

"More what you're used to?"

She hefted her sack onto her other shoulder and hummed a melody. I'd not seen her so happy and relaxed for a long time. I snorted. Promise a woman a proper bed and take her shopping for new clothes, and life becomes easier all round.

There was another thing I'd noticed as we'd crossed from east to west. Back east, citizens hurried the streets and shied from any sign of smoke, even that of the thousands of chimneys they had lived below all their lives. On this side of the river, people held their heads high, dawdled and laughed in the streets.

If only they knew.

Preparations had already started for the coronation of the Crown Prince. Citizens climbed rickety ladders to hang banners and royal flags—huge sheets of linen that flapped noisily in the gusty wind, fighting against their rope ties. Almost every building had been decorated with bunches of purple feresens, and the Lamplighter Guild was out in force attaching baskets of the city's adopted flower to every street lantern. Ayla paused and inhaled the sweet aroma. The sound of instruments being tuned filtered out of music halls. It was comforting to see at least some people in high spirits, but the difference in morale between east and west was stark.

I led us down Wall Street, stupidly named since there was no evidence that a wall had ever stood there. We arrived at a modest inn tucked tightly among artisan storefronts. The Pumphouse. The taproom was well lit, clean, and airy, and almost devoid of customers. Something I'd never see on my side of the city.

I greeted the barkeep, Lupan, with a nod, and strode to the long bar. He picked at his teeth and scowled. "What d'you want, corpse-lover?"

"That's no way to treat the man who saved your inn. By rights I should be your partner, but I'll settle for lodging."

He leered at Ayla. "Yer whore'd better not be a screamer."

Heat surged into my cheeks and my heart pounded. I leaned forward. "How dare—"

"I'll be quiet as a mouse, m'lord," Ayla said in a very believable slum voice. She slipped her arm through mine, grinning all the while.

I fought hard not to chuckle. "*Two* garret rooms, first sixday free."

"I ain't givin' you rooms for free. They sell out fast, y'know."

I glanced around the empty taproom. "Of course they do."

He scraped his teeth for a long moment, then reached below the counter and brought out two tarnished keys.

"Now we're even," he said.

Halfway up the stairs, Ayla spluttered into laughter and gave her opinions on Lupan in the same lilting slum voice. I couldn't help but laugh with her. We climbed five floors. The final stair was narrow, but in better condition than that of Mother B.'s. I told Ayla to settle in and then come by my room.

Larger than my old garret, this room even had a desk. First things first. I dragged the desk chair over to the window and sat to study the view. All I needed was a beer, but I wouldn't get room service out of Lupan the way I had Mother B.

Across the river, warehouses crammed the banks from City Bridge to Heroes Bridge, after which the tenements of Eastside took over. I leaned out precariously until I could see Kand Hill far to my right. I shouldn't have done that. Two black scars gouged its slopes, as if Lak himself had clawed the landscape. A grim reminder of the stakes.

A shout from a bargee drew my attention to the river below. I watched two men maneuver a barge heaped full of mine slag. I hadn't realized The Pumphouse backed right onto the river.

My door clicked open and I turned as Ayla slipped inside and perched on the bed. She bounced once then lay down. I raised an eyebrow.

"Yours is softer than mine," she said. "What're we going to do? If you think coronation day is his plan, then we need one of our own."

I let out a long sigh and clenched the arms of the chair. Time to be a good little boy and do what Mother had said about researching Caradan. She couldn't have given me a larger clue if she'd shouted. Unfortunately, research meant returning to the Guild.

"What're you thinking?" Ayla asked.

Mother was right about another thing too.

"I'm going to try and get the other masters on my side."

"Can I come?"

"Not this time."

She opened her mouth, but I was sure it was my glare that made her shut it again.

Once more, I hung from the crumbling chimneystacks of the Guild roof like a mubar monkey. I stretched my back and legs. My body had taken far too many beatings in the past few days. If I defeated the elemental—*when* I defeated it—I planned to soak in a hot bath from dawn to dusk with a crate of beer in hand.

I clattered down the steep tiles and grabbed hold of the rotten frame surrounding a skylight. They were never locked, and within moments I was inside, hanging from my arms and dropping the eight feet to the floor with a thud. I was in. The trouble was, I couldn't get out the same way. I shrugged. No one said saving the city would be easy.

My eyes adjusted to the attic's dim light and I peered at the stacks of junk and old furniture piled haphazardly. Some of it was protected by drapes but most stood in disrepair, nibbled by the rats and monkeys. Stark daylight poured through the skylight, illuminating a trillion motes of dust swirling in midair, disturbed and angry at my intrusion. My nose and throat tickled in the dry, musty air and I coughed. A dozen pairs of tiny eyes glittered in the shadows, blinking, watching.

I tiptoed to a set of crooked stairs choked with dust and cobwebs. Despite my care, the ancient steps creaked and complained, determined to warn the Guild of this intruder. At the bottom, I put my ear to the door. Silence. If Kolta had forgotten to unlock it, I would get awfully hungry up here. I turned the handle and pulled. Nothing. I tugged.

Kristach.

I yanked hard. The door popped open, tearing a chunk of the doorjamb with it. The damage wasn't obvious as long as no one studied the door closely.

Since I knew every twist and turn of the Guild's leagues of hallways, it didn't take long to descend to the inhabited levels. I couldn't forget that Fortak would kill me if he found me here. I'd tried to hate the Guild and pretend that I didn't miss it, but that was a lie.

Grateful that most Guild members were in class, I risked the quickest route, along the wide third-floor corridor we called Centerway. Dozens of hallways ran left and right, interspaced with life-size statues of famous masters. Each hallway was labeled, named after one creature or another. Some of my best tricks and capers had taken place on Centerway and, yes, there were the melted bricks on the corner of Lazoul Lane. My butt tingled as I passed. The worst caning I'd ever received.

I turned right and froze. Fortak stood less than ten feet away.

He stopped, eyes wide. He started to speak but doubled over coughing instead.

I spun and fled, sprinting headlong down Centerway.

"Get back here."

No chance. I glanced over my shoulder. He hobbled after me, handkerchief to his mouth.

"Stop," he yelled. "We need to talk, clear up this misunderstanding. Halt, damn you."

I wouldn't fall for that. I snaked through the corridors. There was no way he could catch me.

"Seekers, find Maldren and bring him to me," was the last I heard before I hurtled down a long flight of stairs.

On the landing below, I careened into two students, knocking one down and sending their textbooks in all directions. I didn't care who saw me now. Already the Seekers would have alerted the cepi, who would locate me in moments. I jumped the handrail, plunging six feet to the ground floor, to avoid a group of journeyman who had gathered at the base of the stairs. They cheered and egged me on. I had two choices: outside or the library. Both would evade the cepi. I hesitated.

Two of the creatures emerged from a nearby wall, twittering as they spotted me. Batlike, their wings beat faster than the eye could see, so they resembled a hazy, blurring shape with tiny antennae and luminous green eyes. Two more materialized out of the floor.

Kristach. It had to be the library. I'd never get a second chance.

I raced headlong toward one of several stone stairwells descending into the underground of the Guild. People got in my way, but none tried to stop me. They leaped back as I hurtled past. A dozen cepi kept pace right behind me, and a growing thunder of boots sounded on the staircase above. The Seekers had tuned in to what the cepi were seeing and had joined the chase. I panted and wheezed as I picked my way through the underground warren, past classrooms, study halls, and storerooms.

Master Begara appeared from a doorway ahead. He cried out, and I sensed the surge of power as he readied a spell. I bounced off a wall into a side passage, gritting my teeth against the stitch in my side and the cramping in my muscles. A sinister screech cut through the chattering of the cepi. That was a lochtar on my tail. *Holy Belaya!*

I sucked in air and forced my failing body into a new burst of speed until finally the ancient, decorated arch of the catacombs came into view. I sprinted beneath the monstrous skull that formed its keystone and threw out my hands to stop myself plunging over the low wall ahead. I gripped its stone rail and watched the cepi and lochtar smash against the invisible barrier beneath the arch. Its magic sparked and they vanished on impact, amid a myriad of bright flashes. That had been too close. I was committed now, or perhaps I should be.

I allowed myself a few precious moments to catch my breath, and then trotted down the long ramp that spiraled around a fifty-feet-wide shaft that bored deep into the ground. Globes of everfire floated in midair up and down the shaft, but no necromantic magic functioned in the catacombs that held the library. That made no sense to me, but I'd probably skipped the lesson about why that was.

I hurried on, knowing that the Seekers and Begara wouldn't be far behind. The warded arch wouldn't stop them. After two complete circuits, the ramp opened out into the library—aisles and aisles of bookcases stretching back into the earth like the spokes of a wheel. Since no apprentices were allowed, only a handful of figures moved between the bookcases.

I snatched a catalog and glanced through it on my way down, until I knew exactly where to find the books on Caradan. About ten feet of shelf space had been dedicated to him, and I fidgeted, peering at the spines in the low light while snatching glimpses toward the ramp. The Seekers would be along any moment.

Which books? I didn't even know what I was looking for. I grabbed as many volumes as I could carry and hurried down another two turns of the ramp for good measure. Then I headed deep into the library, sitting with my back to the rough outer wall.

I picked up the first book and skimmed the pages. What had possessed someone to build a library with such poor lighting? I knew that I was supposed to take the books to the study tables, but sitting in the bright light would be suicidal. The book narrated Caradan's legend, but I knew the story, everyone did. Lately I'd grown to know it too well. I shivered and tried to shake the images of men dragged screaming into The Gray by the wraith and the lochtars.

The horrific events of that night in his tower had resulted in the Elik Magi abandoning the city forever. He'd driven out the people's greatest defenders. Pictures in the book portrayed Caradan as a grim, ugly man. The book also spoke of Caradan's fears that the Elik Magi had planned a similar coup, to destroy his Guild. Such politics made no sense. Malkandrah needed both sects of magic. How could either be a threat to the other?

I fidgeted and the hairs on my neck tingled. The library was deathly quiet, but the Seekers had to be getting closer. I couldn't afford to get trapped here, but I hadn't discovered anything yet.

What links the Guildmaster and Caradan?

I flicked open the next book and stared into the haunting face of a woman. Dressed in green, her hair was pure white and her eyes were a dazzling violet. After my initial shock, I appreciated her exotic beauty. Caradan's wife. He'd slaughtered her too. The text confirmed the events of my nightmares, that she'd been head of the Elik Magi. The two most powerful wielders of magic married to each other. I turned the page to see the violet-eyed woman and Phyxia posing together. I gasped. Phyxia seemed to know everyone, but now I was totally confused about the woman's allegiances.

Shadows descended the ramp a single turn above me. I grabbed my books, leaving behind the ones I had already perused, and hurried to the ramp. I loped down another two turns and again out to the periphery of the book stacks. Somehow, I'd have to find a way to get past the Seekers and up to the main level. That was bound to be guarded. This was going horribly wrong. I hadn't given any thought to getting out, but then I hadn't planned on being spotted. In hundreds of hallways and passages, what were the odds of running into

Fortak?

I picked up another book and thumbed through the dusty pages. My gaze fell on Fortak's name. Only ten solars ago he'd attempted to resurrect Caradan. Kristach. I raced through the chapter, squinting in the poor light. It was clear that Fortak had based his iron rule on methods developed by Caradan, and had arrived at the preposterous conclusion that he and Caradan together would be an unstoppable force.

I rubbed my tired eyes. Did the masters know of this? Is that what Fortak really planned?

Footsteps hurried down the ramp. I couldn't stop reading now. Fortak had attempted a *Resurrection* in Caradan's Tower. That was a taboo spell. I couldn't imagine such a battle of magic and wits between two of the most powerful necromancers of the past century. I shuddered. The book droned on for several pages about the law against resurrections. I skimmed them and then closed my eyes, fighting back the ache forming in my skull. Ayla had been right—I needed more rest.

Somebody grabbed my arm and yanked me to my feet. With a yelp, I stared into the face of Master Semplis. How had he sneaked up on me?

"What have you done? What's gotten into you?" he asked. "The Prime Guildmaster has alerted the entire Guild to find you."

He tugged me toward the ramp, but I wrapped an arm around a stone pillar and held my ground. He opened his mouth to shout our location.

"Master, wait. I can explain."

"Save it for the Guildmaster. Down here," he yelled.

Kristach. I was dead if I couldn't win him over. I prayed to every God I could name that he wasn't a part of the Covenant.

"Hear me out, I beg you. I know you'll understand."

He gave me a shake and shoved me back against the pillar. His strength surprised me, considering his age. Ridges of hardened skin formed semicircles below his drooping eyelids, one eye blue and the other green.

"Someone in the Guild is behind the elemental attacks," I said in a single breath, keeping an eye on the ramp.

"What elemental?"

"The creature burning down the city."

His eyes widened. "Who in the Guild?"

"The Guildmaster..." *No, he'd never believe that.* "...is, er...protecting their identity. I'm trying to find out who it is."

He moved in closer. His breath stank of strong wine. "Why would the Prime Guildmaster do that?"

"I don't know, Master. To avoid scandal?" Yes, Semplis was a great protector of the Guild.

"How are you involved?"

"I was there at the first fire. With Hallum. Ask Hallum."

Or was Hallum in on it? Kristach, I was seeing conspiracies everywhere.

Shadows played on the ramp wall. A crowd descended.

"I've been trying to report to a master. Begara wouldn't help." That was a bonus, dropping that traitor in it.

His face was an inch from mine now. "Why should I trust you?"

A group of five Seekers, armed with pain-sticks, came into view on the ramp.

"Because I'm telling you...begging you to investigate."

He reduced his grip on my arm, allowing me to slip behind the pillar. The Seekers were almost upon us. The buzz of their weapons gave me goose bumps.

"I'm trying to help the Guild," I whispered. "I want to do the right thing. Help me. Please."

"Did you find him?" Two of the Seekers hurried along the aisle of books toward us. "Did you find him?"

"Yes," Semplis said.

I slumped against the rear of the pillar, trembling, remembering what the Duke had said about Fortak's demons tearing me apart.

Semplis moved to intercept the Seekers.

"He was headed toward the deeper catacombs. Hurry."

 EIGHTEEN

Caradan peered out from behind the beer keg. Binar squirmed beside him, his panted breathing increasing with each shriek of the Elik Magi as the wraith hurtled among them.

"What have you done?" a female voice bellowed from the gallery above.

Caradan's wife leaned against the railing, dressed in a long mauve dress and headscarf that covered most of her white hair. Two of her Magi stood protectively beside her. Even at a distance, Caradan could see the fire in her violet eyes.

"What I should have done long ago, Yolanda," he replied.

He reached one arm toward her and lightning crackled and sparked from each finger. She and her men scattered along the gallery and the lightning hammered against the wall where they had stood, melting the surface and staining it black. All three of them retaliated with coordinated green rays. Caradan rolled into the open, propelled in part by the force of the impact behind him. Hot blood and gobbets of flesh rained down on him, and he frantically wiped and smeared the remains of Binar, his childhood friend, from his face and arms.

"Lak take you, woman. I won't let you destroy my Guild."

Caradan poured energy into the wraith that he had

summoned. The amorphous blackness grew, engulfing the room, seeming to exert a pressure on the air, even though it did not exist in the material world. Shadows animated and reached, clawlike, for the living. Magic flickered throughout the room as one by one, the surviving Magi destroyed the lochtar stalking them. The wraith ascended toward the gallery.

A smirk spread across Caradan's face.

"Stop this," Yolanda yelled. "Are you insane? I..."

She braced against the full fury of the wraith, weathering its primeval roar and the vortex that tugged at her. Her scarf tore free and disappeared into the black void. Her long, white hair flowed out in front of her face. With both hands, she blasted magic into the faceless might of the wraith.

"I seek no such thing," she said. "Enough. Let's talk this through."

She waved one hand and blinding light flared into every nook and cranny of the hall. The wraith screeched so loud that Caradan clapped his hands to his ears. A cauldron of light and dark seethed in midair, and then, in an instant, both disappeared.

Caradan bellowed in frustration. It wasn't fair that his wife had mastered both disciplines, necromancy and sorcery. That she was leader of the Elik Magi was bad enough. How could it be that her shadow magic surpassed even his? He slammed his bloody fist into the floor. Damn the tristak woman.

"I don't trust you. Call off your men," he said.

"End this now, I beg you."

She hurled a spell and it exploded on the ground before him—a warning shot. The floorboards hissed and smoked as acid melted them. He rolled away once more and leaped to his feet, his back against the wall. A four-feet-wide hole gaped before him.

He forced a smile. "You're right, my love. I shall end it."

Magic gathered and burned in his veins. It threatened to consume him. Capillaries in his skin burst under pressure, and blood oozed from every pore to mingle with Binar's blood. With a grunt, he unleashed the spell, launching it at the wooden rafters. It triggered silently, ripping a hole between worlds from which revenants poured, croaking and gurgling as they swarmed the room. The remaining Elik Magi went down beneath a torrent of the vile creatures. Caradan stood, hands on hips, his eyes sparkling as the sorcerers were torn limb from limb.

There, woman! It is done. I win.

Without warning, magic tickled him and ice spread through his body as if he were plunged into an ice bath. He knew this spell of hers—hated it. His arms twitched uncontrollably, and his legs gave out. His stomach heaved. There was a transitory sensation of him existing in two places at once. The hall flickered around him.

The next moment, he crashed into the nightstand in his bedroom three floors above. A full washbasin overturned, soaking him. He roared in frustration, tore the wet hair from his eyes, and rolled onto his side. Fresh air gusted in the open window and he shivered in the chill night air. Pins and needles racked his body. Otherwise the room was still and quiet—no magic, and no undead whirling above his head. Yolanda sat on the edge of the bed, calm and unfazed.

"How dare…" He smacked his numb lips. "…you coerce me with that spell."

"It didn't have to be this way," she said. "Wherever did you get this flight of fancy? I never intended harm to your Guild. Why didn't you talk to me first, man to wife?"

Caradan crawled to the bed and pulled himself upon it. She tore away the remnants of his robe and bundled it up to wipe the blood from his arms, neck, and face. Then she threw the bloody rag into the corner, an action he thought mirrored her contempt for his way of life. He chewed his lip. What game did she play now?

"Why damn yourself over such a thing? Your soul…you've thrown it away." She ran her fingers through the hair on his chest. "Let me help you. I can help you, but you have to trust me."

Caradan narrowed his eyes but let her draw him to her

bosom. There was yet a way to win. He patted the dagger at his belt.

The warmth of Yolanda's body burned my cheeks, and her hand stroking the back of my neck soothed me. I reached up and fingered her hair. My gaze settled on the destroyed nightstand under the window, and my bloody robe in the corner. White drapes billowed into the room. I barely noticed the chill as I lay in her arms.

Wait. This isn't right. What foul dream is this? This is Caradan's life, not mine. Wake up.

I pulled away and shuffled to the end of the bed.

"What's wrong?" a woman asked.

I gasped. It wasn't Yolanda who kneeled on the bed, but Phyxia. My pulse raced. That wasn't how it was. Caradan was married to Lady Yolanda.

Phyxia's silken, silver hair cascaded from her head between her slender, twitching ears, but her eyes were a lurid violet like Yolanda's. I blinked furiously and slapped myself in the face. It was a nightmare. If I knew that, why couldn't I wake?

"Let me help you." Her arms reached for me. "Your revenants can't reach us here."

I glanced around the room, searching for inspiration, something to end the perverted twist to my nightmare. What if I simply left? My legs didn't want to move. I pictured the words on the page, having just read them in the library. This night had not ended well.

Phyxia-Yolanda pulled the dress over her head. My breath caught and my heart thudded. I gawked at her perfect curves, flawless skin, and her hardened nipples. A fire burned in my shorts.

Lak and all his demons!

She crawled toward me across the bedcovers, her tongue moistening her lips. How I'd longed to kiss those lips. Had Phyxia known how much I'd loved her? Surely she'd known. I shivered and shook my head to clear it. No. This was Lady Yolanda, long dead. This was a dream. But if it were a dream, what harm could come from a single kiss? I could forgive her betrayal for one kiss. Or more, perhaps.

"Sishka," she murmured.

My heartbeat boomed in my ears, and I moved to meet her halfway. She smelled of feresens, and my nostrils drank deep. My hands quivered as they settled about her naked waist. I closed my eyes and our lips met, gently caressing each other. My body numbed from the heat of that single touch and the closeness of her body. It wasn't a deep kiss but it was everything I'd dreamed of, and for now that simple contact was enough.

Something jabbed into my thigh. The sheathed knife.

I leaped back, mourning the parting of our mouths. Metal chilled my hands, and I studied the wicked blade that I clenched tightly.

Wake up! I don't want to be in this ending.

"What are you waiting for, sishka?" she asked. "You know how this sordid, twisted tale ends. Finish it."

I stared, lost in her unblinking violet eyes, then I lurched forward, my knife aimed between those perfect breasts.

Someone was screaming.

My eyes snapped open. I realized that it was me. My breath came in rapid pants. I wasn't in the tower. I wasn't holding a knife. I was safe in the inn, in my bed. I sat up and rubbed my eyes. I'd expected to see blood everywhere, but predawn gray lit the room in monochrome shades.

Now I remembered. Semplis had misled the Seekers, and then helped me escape the library and the Guild. My breathing slowed, but I couldn't stop shivering even though the window was closed.

Who was putting these tristak nightmares into my head? Why? Was I that dense that I couldn't grasp their meaning?

My stomach lurched. I cast the blankets aside, leaped out onto the cold wooden floor, and rushed to the window. I hung my head out into the freezing air, sucked in deep breaths, and waited for the nausea to pass. Back at the washbowl beside the bed, I plunged my face into the water and washed the sweat away.

"What happened?" Ayla asked from the doorway.

I jumped, nearly knocking the washbowl off the table.

She slipped inside and clicked the door shut. Her gaze flicked around the room, hovered on my bed shorts, and then traveled up my bare chest. Her cheeks flushed.

"I heard you screaming," she said.

She wore a flimsy, one-piece chemise, cut low over her breasts and hanging loose to knee height. I gasped. My turn to stare. She had clipped her hair back. For a fleeting moment Phyxia was before me once more, lifting the dress over her head. Then I saw Phyxia sprawled on blood-soaked sheets with Caradan's knife thrust into her belly. I swallowed the rising bile.

"What?" Ayla asked.

I shook my head and looked out the window. "Nothing. A bad dream, that's all."

"You look like you've fought an army of demons. You're shivering."

She stepped forward, then leaned into me and draped her arms around my bare torso. I stiffened momentarily at her touch and then relaxed, letting her head settle against my chest. Her soft hands moved rapidly up and down my back, and her warmth was like a stove. I breathed deep of fresh lavender.

I wrapped my arms tentatively around her and settled into her unexpected embrace. She pushed tighter and murmured softly. Her touch grew lighter and more sensual as she trailed her fingers this way and that across my back. It was like magic tingling across my skin. Then she pushed away enough to look into my face. She placed her hands against my chest and held us a few inches apart. I wanted to pull her back.

"What nightmares could a necromancer possibly have?" She smiled, teeth white in the gray gloom.

"I was dreaming of Caradan." I shuddered.

Her smile vanished. "It makes me nervous to see you so scared."

Despite her petite size, the tantalizing glimpses through her thin garment reminded me that she was a woman, not a girl. Part of her bangs dropped over her cheek, so I gently tucked the loose hair behind her ear. My touch lingered on her cheek and she pressed against my hand, uttering a tiny murmur. Her head tilted back and her eyes flicked rapidly between my own. She slipped her arms around my neck and pulled my head down, her lips moving straight for mine.

She tasted like oranges. I squeezed her tight against me, her breasts pushing against my chest, our lips working a different kind of magic than I was used to, but no less potent. I teased her lips with my tongue and became totally lost in the hunger of her kisses. I stroked her hair and the tickle of static sent tingles through me.

Without warning, she pulled back. Such a beautiful smile. Another detail that I only now fully appreciated. Her fingers traced the light hair on my chest and it ignited a fire within me that burned like the elemental. My breathing quickened, and I tugged her toward the bed. She tensed and searched my face, her eyes dilated. I gave another gentle pull, but she broke free and retreated to the door.

"I…" she began.

In the first rays of Solas through my window, her chemise did nothing to hide her figure. How blind had I been to miss such a woman right under my nose?

She smiled bashfully and then slipped out of the room.

I collapsed onto the bed and stared at the closed door. I thought that was what she'd wanted. Her body had quivered with passion. What had I done wrong?

The water in my bath was cold, but I didn't care. It helped me forget the fire burning through Ayla's chemise and into my body. I'd come on too strong. I'd misread the signs. How could I have misread? She'd thrown herself at me. Had she just wanted to tease me?

I leaped up, splashing water everywhere, and dressed.

Lupan was nowhere to be found but I paid his cook to make me a breakfast tray. I carried it upstairs and rapped on Ayla's door.

"It's me," I said, and then added, "With breakfast."

The door snapped open and she grinned at me. Well at least she wasn't mad at me. She took the tray and placed it on her neatly made bed.

"Come on." She patted the bed beside her. "I'm starving. You take longer in the bath than I do."

She had dressed in a bright blue dress and looked very different out of her plain, commoner clothes. The dress was probably closer to what she'd wear in her own world. It was all too easy to forget her upbringing after all that we had been through together.

I eyed the plate of pulta hash and spread some on a hunk of warm bread. There was fruit and steaming karaa too. I caught her staring at me. *Now what? Another change in her mood?*

"You look so different without your Guild robe."

I glanced down, forgetting that I'd donned only my trousers and shirt.

"You seem more approachable like this. Don't get me wrong. You look very dashing in your regalia, but it feels more intimate when…" Her cheeks reddened. That seemed to happen a lot lately. "I'm a lousy apprentice, aren't I? I shouldn't be so informal with my teacher."

"You're not a typical apprentice, no."

She flinched. *Smooth, Maldren, real smooth.*

"But then these aren't typical times. I'm not excelling as the teacher. I haven't taught you much." I put down my fork. "Ah, to The Deep with master and apprentice and all that pompous trash. I like you, Ayla. A lot."

I cupped her chin gently in one hand. Her hair smelled of sweet yibar blossom. She'd cut it shorter and shaped the way it fell to her shoulders. The burned ends had gone too.

"I love how you styled your hair. The length suits you, and it looks darker, more like your eyes."

"You're so sweet for noticing," she whispered.

Such gorgeous chestnut eyes. *Lak, take my soul now!*

I slid my hand along her cheek and she leaned into it. I kissed her lightly, glad that she didn't recoil. Instead, she slipped her hands around my neck and deepened the kiss. My insides flipped. We were both breathing heavily when we drew apart. Her hands slipped down my torso to find and hold mine. Our fingers locked together, and I continued to lose myself in her eyes. Maybe I hadn't blown it between us, after all.

"I feel like I've been so mean to you," I whispered.

"The Guild is a man's world," she said. "I get that. You didn't want a female apprentice."

"I didn't want any apprentice."

"Then I hope I'm proving you wrong."

After planting a swift kiss on my lips, she pulled away.

"We should focus on the creature," she said. "Did you find out anything at the Guild?"

I grunted. "Caradan holds the secret." The pieces clicked into place even as I spoke. "We need something far more powerful than the soul wraith. There has never been a greater necromancer. For a hundred solars his ghost has been brooding and seething in his tower, defying even Lak's attempt to drag him into The Deep. Imagine his pent-up anger and bitterness."

Ayla recoiled.

"Everything I've heard, everything I've read…damn, even my dreams have been pulling me in his direction." I gulped down my karaa. "Evil abhors evil. We're going over there right now to summon him, persuade him to help us."

She stared at me with puffed-out cheeks. Then she exhaled and burst out laughing.

"What?" I scowled at her.

"You're adorable when you're so confident." Her eyes sparkled. "It's not going to be that easy, is it?"

"I don't do easy anymore."

She laughed again and I joined in.

We ate the now-cold food in silence for a few moments, and then she asked, "When we went after the soul wraith you said it was easier to interact with spirits at night, so why are we going during the day?"

"Time's running out. Besides, Caradan at night will make that soul wraith look like a puppy."

I put on my robe. In my mind, lochtars and revenants swirled around Caradan's great hall, viciously dispatching some of the best necromancers and sorcerers the city had known.

We returned the breakfast tray to Lupan. No sense in giving him an excuse to evict us. The taproom was empty except for two undernourished barmaids balancing dozens of dirty breakfast plates. We'd languished upstairs longer than I'd planned, not that I was complaining. Lupan stood up from behind the bar and held out a callused palm, into which I dropped a silver Mikk. His food was worth it. I glanced at the shelf of liquor bottles and considered one for the road. Maybe later, when we'd earned it.

"This came for you." He tossed a folded note onto the scratched and pitted bar.

I recognized the Duke's seal and snatched it up. Ayla shot me a sideways glance. I couldn't believe his spies had found us here. Did I have no secrets anymore? Only Kolta was supposed to know. I broke the seal. It was the same handwriting as before.

Dawn. Same place.

"When did this arrive?" I asked Lupan.

"Late last night. While yous were no doubt creaking me bed frames." He leered at Ayla.

She winked at him, causing him to frown. *Oh, she was good.*

"You didn't think to send a messenger up?" I snapped.

"And disturb yer fun?" He attempted to lay his hand on hers, but she slapped his and stepped away.

It was too late to argue, so I headed for the door. A carriage rattled its way up Wall Street from the south. I stepped into the road to flag it down.

"Temple Plaza's an easy walk," Ayla said.

"We need to meet your father first. Let's hope he's still waiting."

The carriage pulled up beside us and I opened the door, nudging Ayla's back with one hand.

She hesitated on the step and her eyes narrowed. "I thought we didn't have time for this?"

"Get in. Please."

I climbed up beside her and slammed the door. Then I gave the driver the address of an inn two blocks from *The* Stout and Puke. Ayla fumed, making a show of smoothing out her dress. I let her get it out of her system, speaking only when the carriage crossed the river.

"I'm not going to let him take you, I promise. You're my apprentice. I need you."

She eyed me suspiciously.

"It'll be helpful for him to see you safe and happy. We need him as an ally, remember that."

She nodded and watched the city go by outside the window as we moved into the more constricted and windy streets of the eastern city.

"I know, but can't we see him later, after going to the tower?"

"His news has always been important. Perhaps we won't have to pay Caradan a visit."

In less time than I'd expected, the carriage drew to a stop. We jumped out and I paid the driver, slipping him an extra coin along with the finger-on-finger gesture universally accepted as "stay quiet." He bobbed his head, shook the reins, and the carriage clattered off along the narrow cobbled street. I grabbed Ayla's hand and steered her into a side alley, leading her on the back-alley shuffle to The Stout and Puke.

At the door, she dragged her heels. "I'll wait out here until you're done."

I tugged her forward.

"It's too dangerous and I don't want you out of my sight. You're my apprentice, so you have to obey." I winked.

She rolled her eyes but followed me into the dark taproom. I separated our hands as we crossed the threshold. Necromancers don't hold hands.

The dregs of society were already congregating, weaving drunkenly among stable boys scattering fresh straw. True to the inn's name, the stench of old vomit mixed with that of stale beer. Arms reached out to paw at Ayla, but when they saw my robe they slunk away into dark corners. I stood tall. *Yes, you lecherous mob, the necromancer just stepped into your sleazy world.*

There was no sign of the Duke's men, or anyone else trying to catch my attention. The back stairs creaked and bowed as we ascended, and I didn't risk putting weight on the unsteady banister. The upstairs hallway was empty, so we strode past several doors that muffled ecstatic cries or snores, and I knocked on the rearmost door.

No answer. Kristach, he'd left.

I pushed it open and froze.

I tried to block Ayla's view but she slipped past me into the room. She gasped and her hands flew to her mouth. Then she doubled over in a crouch and threw up, spraying her breakfast all over her feet. I hurried inside and shut the door. Thank Belaya she hadn't screamed, but she uttered a low, haunting moan, at the same time clutching her abdomen and trembling.

Duke Imarian's corpse slumped in the same armchair as when we had last met. His head drooped at an impossible angle to one side. His throat was a ragged mess, slashed more than once, and I saw right through to the white of the spine. A crimson tide had soaked his shirt and pants before pooling on the rug. The grievous wound still dripped.

No one should discover his or her father like this. I shouldn't have insisted she come up.

I helped her into a side chair, turning it away from the carnage, and knelt beside her, one hand on her arm and the other stroking her hair. She wiped the tears brimming in her eyes, and then spat chunks of sick from her mouth. Not at all ladylike, but who cared right now. The poor thing.

"Why?" was all she managed.

"We should leave."

She pushed me away and stood. "No, I want to see him."

"That's not a good idea. Let me buy you a stiff drink."

"I'm not a baby." She slipped under my arm and past me.

I put my head in my hands and stayed put, giving her space.

"I *would* have gone home to see him," she murmured.

"I know. He was a good man."

I had nothing else. I'd become numb to death. Funerals only made me awkward and embarrassed to be the only one bored and not crying. Her initial reaction had been visceral and very normal. It saddened me that as a necromancer, in time the numbness would take her too.

"I'm sorry for the anguish I caused you, Father. Everything you did for me, and all I brought you was grief."

Tears flooded her eyes. She knelt on the dry boards and uttered a quiet prayer.

"I forgive you for taking Mother from me."

She stood and caught me watching her. I shrugged in what I hoped was my best "none of business" manner, and turned to the window. A folded note lay on the side table. I opened the window as a ruse, palmed the note, and quietly broke the seal as I watched two carts trying to pass in the busy road. The note bore a Guild seal, but I'd already guessed its author.

"Read it aloud," Ayla said, her tone as cold as steel.

I sighed and did so.

"'I warned you. Cease your meddling or I shall kill every ally, everyone you hold dear.'"

The last line I kept to myself.

The girl dies next.

She gave no reaction, simply wrestled her father's ring from his finger. Then she reverently lowered a lap blanket over his head and chest. Her eyes were slits, her nostrils flared and her breasts heaved with forced breathing. I half expected her eyes to whirl with fiery reds.

"Let's finish this," she said. "I'll kill Caradan…again…with my bare hands if he doesn't aid us. With his support, your Guildmaster will pay for this."

She threw open the door and stomped into the hallway, and I had to run to catch up. At the bottom of the stairs, a pair of sailors intercepted her, bushy bearded with close-cropped scalps seemingly competing for the most scars.

"What's the rush, missy?" the fatter man asked. "Yer can't be off duty so early."

His muscled arm snaked around her waist.

"Purdy dress," the other said, gawking at her cleavage.

She tore free and punched the man in the face. No girlie punch, either. Bones cracked and blood spurted.

"Get away from me," she said, "or I'll tear off this railing and neuter you both. And I suspect my master won't be as gentle."

I descended the stairs to join her, seemingly right on cue. My face itched to grin inanely, but that would have ruined the effect.

The men backed off, grumbling and averting their eyes from me, but Ayla didn't stay still. She shoved another man out of her path, sloshing his beer everywhere, and marched right up to the bar. The crowds parted like ghosts from a *Dispel*. I followed to see how far the fun would take us.

"Innkeep," she yelled until he came into view. "My father, the Duke Imarian, is dead in a room upstairs."

Murmurs rippled through the taproom and all eyes settled upon us.

"Return his body to the manor, and show it every respect. If it's not there by day's end, your new clientele will become a horde of Black and Reds. Clear?"

Kristach!

The innkeep opened his mouth but no sound came out. He tried again. "That's gonna cost me—"

"Collect your blood money when you deliver his body. Don't make me hold a grudge."

"All right, all right, little lady. I's an honest man. I'll do it, I'll do it."

"See that you do."

She swept out into the street like the ebbing of the tide. I hurried after her, not sure that I liked this new game of me leading from the rear. She whistled for a carriage and we jumped in.

"Temple Plaza," she told the driver.

"Are you sure you're up to this? We could delay and let your feelings catch up." I touched her hand. "I'm sorry you had to see that."

Her anger had turned to shivering, so I slipped my arm around her.

"You're magnificent when you're angry," I whispered, leaning closer. So like Phyxia. My hand settled gently on her knee.

She pushed me away. "You're sweet to me, but I want to stay angry."

I nodded. Saving the city had given way to vengeance. For both of us.

 NINETEEN

There was a theater on Curd Street famous for cheesy productions. The opening line from its most recent performance popped into my mind as we climbed through the broken wall that surrounded Caradan's Tower: "Oh woe, for I have a clammy feeling of impending doom!" I couldn't get the image of me stabbing Phyxia on the bed out of my mind. Distracted, I stumbled over a hole in the ground and fell flat on my face. Caradan had gotten inside my head. This trip would end badly.

I took a deep breath. *Get a grip. Fear is for the weak.*

I led Ayla to the line of trees and thick undergrowth, and we studied the tower across the half-sunken necropolis. The very air oozed malice.

"It looks so menacing," she whispered. "I'd expected something like Father's manor."

"It was originally built as a fortress."

"Why has it sunk into the ground?" She cocked her head back and forth, as if unable to believe what she was seeing. "It leans too."

"After the massacre, Caradan ran the Guild for over a decade. Then his curse caught up with him. Rumor has it something nasty crawled out of The Deep." I remembered what I'd read in the library. "He fought back so hard that the ground shook, and the tower sank into the swamp."

"I hope the Covenant is in there right now." She flexed her fists. "I'll avenge my father."

"I'd rather they weren't, so we can do what we came to do."

I cast *Perception*, pushing the boundary of the invisible sphere all the way to the tower, a hundred feet away.

Ayla spun to face me. "I felt that." She hopped from foot to foot. "That's your sensory aura thing, isn't it?"

"You won't learn *Perception* for some time, but you can share mine. It takes getting used to. Do you feel that tingling?"

She twitched. "It tickles in my head."

"Concentrate on the exact sensations, the tempo, the intensity, the ripples. That's what skeletons feel like."

She shuddered and scanned the swamp in front of us. "Where are they?"

"Inside that balcony door, guarding."

"I'm not afraid of them."

The memory of the last skeleton battle flooded back. No, she wasn't.

"There's four," she said as we splashed through the swamp, jumping from islet to islet. "A pair and then another, further back."

"Good."

She really was a fast learner.

"Are you going to blow them up again?"

Should I? *Bones to Dust* would alert everything in the tower, but I'd feel safer if Caradan knew we were coming. I didn't want to surprise him, for sure. He was certain to spell first and ask questions later.

We stepped onto dry land at the base of the tower and I peered up at the arrow slits. They resembled sinister, narrowed eyes watching us. The back of my neck itched. It was too quiet. Even the red hawks were nowhere to be seen. Getting trapped inside on Caradan's home ground wasn't my idea of fun.

Perhaps there was another way.

Ayla nudged me. "Are we doing this?"

Too late to back out now.

Our boots thumped on the plank, and then we stepped onto the slanting balcony and peered into the dim room beyond. My pulse roared in my ears. Going inside as a skeleton had been one thing, but now we had no such disguise.

Two skeletons jerked as if startled awake, swished their swords in front of them, and advanced. I let loose *Bones to Dust*. The skeletons disintegrated. A flurry of bone fragments whirled around the room like a tornado, bouncing off the walls and finally settling, to cover the floor in a white carpet that resembled snow. The clanging of their metal blades on the stone floor reverberated through the tower.

We knocked on the door. Time to find out who was home.

Ribs and finger bones crunched underfoot as we moved deeper inside. The interior hallway was gloomy and constrictive, quite different from last time. I put that down to the red-tinged vision I'd possessed as a skeleton. Ayla looked resolute, absentmindedly picking pieces of bone from her hair as she peered into every shadowy corner. Sharp rays of daylight sliced through arrow slits on the staircase, creating a grid of light and dark that resembled prison bars.

A dull thump sounded from behind heavy wooden doors. We glanced at each other.

"What's that?" she whispered.

My *Perception* oscillated in an erratic manner.

"Feel the tempo of that? Something incorporeal." This teaching business wasn't so difficult.

I pushed open the door to the great hall. The room appeared much as it had when I'd spied on the Covenant meeting, except the fireplace was dark and cold. Daylight streamed in from above.

A flash of green caught our eyes, and a beer keg rattled in the corner. We both jumped. A rat would never budge one of the large barrels. Ayla headed toward it, but I hesitated before following. I couldn't stop the sickening feeling that expected lochtars or revenants to materialize en masse.

"Nothing here." She frowned.

Nothing we could see, anyway.

Something else jabbed at my *Perception*. A tall man dressed in a black robe appeared in front of us. I sucked in a sharp breath. I knew what came next. He erupted in white fire that flickered across his body and ignited his hair. His mouth opened wide in a scream but he made no sound. Flesh peeled from his body and his face melted. Ayla gasped and took a step back. The man thrashed and panicked. Finally, he pitched to the floor, kicked some more, and then faded out of existence.

Ayla circled the spot where he had fallen, picking at her lip.

"What happened?" she said.

Lightning flashed through arrow slits high on the walls, followed by the boom of thunder. I shot a glance outside. The sky was bright and cloudless. I shook my head to clear it. Ghosts loved to torment the living.

"An apparition," I said and laid a hand on her shoulder. "It's not real."

Her eyes were wide and her breathing rapid. Then she cried out, a deafening sound in the tomblike tower. A bodiless arm had grabbed her leg. She tried futilely to shake it off. The skin of her leg turned black and sloughed off in shreds.

"Oh, Gods. Get it off. Get it off me!"

She kicked and kicked but the blackness continued to spread upward, until her leg crumbled like a pile of dust caught in the wind. She toppled and screamed.

I whipped up a hasty *Dispel* and smothered her with it. Her leg returned to normal, but she grabbed it and touched it all over to make sure, panting and whimpering.

Mocking laughter echoed through the tower.

"Damn it, Caradan," I muttered and helped her up. I squeezed her trembling hands. "Don't believe your eyes."

She gritted her teeth, pulled her hands from mine, and balled them into fists. Her glare challenged me to dare comment on her moment of weakness.

"Enough of this tristak nonsense," she said. "Ghosts can't

hurt us, right? Let's get on with it."

We hurried back out into the hallway. It faded and I stared down at Phyxia's blood-soaked, stiff, and bloated corpse on the bed. I shook my head again and stamped my feet. I wasn't in the mood for games anymore.

I led the way up to the gallery where Kolta and I had lurked as skeletons. The stairs beyond were still bricked up, as was the exit on the opposite side of the gallery. Who had done so and why? Even as I pondered the next move, everything shimmered. My *Perception* bucked like waves in a storm. Ayla clutched her belly.

"What now?" she snapped.

I tensed. Caradan had started a new game.

Color leeched from the world. Her dress turned gray, as did her hair and the daylight. The walls became indeterminate and hazy, as if unsure whether they wanted to exist or not. Waves rippled through the floor, yet it remained solid underfoot. Ayla blinked repeatedly, her face determined, but I knew she couldn't disbelieve this. This was no apparition, no ghost in our world. The situation had reversed. Now we were impostors in the spirit world.

Caradan had sucked us into The Gray. Kristach. Here, everything could hurt us. Worse, I didn't know the spell to get back.

Ayla studied the condensation on the walls as it dribbled steadily upward. Fine cracks ran through the stone, and layers crumbled away. Ridges snaked across the surface, as if worms burrowed within the walls. Cobwebs expanded from nowhere to fill the gallery.

"The wall is decaying," she said. "How can it do that so quickly? Another ghostly trick, right?"

"The Gray," I said, assuming that explained everything.

She looked at me quizzically, then glanced behind me. Her hand slipped into mine, the only warmth in this chill place.

I turned to witness black shadows pooling in midair high above the great hall. The darkness circled lazily, deepening, spreading. My heart pounded. Shrieks of pain and cries of mercy echoed in my head, and I remembered from my nightmare how many men this wraith had consumed.

I dragged Ayla back to the stairs. I'd intended to go down, but the way up was no longer blocked. The brick wall had turned transparent, flickering in and out of existence. An invitation. I would regret my next move, but what choice did I have? I stepped through, cringing at the unnatural pressure inside my body as I did. Ayla followed and shivered violently.

"How did we do that?" Her hands probed the insubstantial bricks. "It was solid when we came by, I swear."

"The Gray is a warped version of our world." I studied the stairs curving up and away from us. "Caradan wants us to go up. I don't think we should argue."

I was certain that the wraith would prevent us leaving, anyway.

"Are you going to capture him in your knife?"

"My Ashtar gem won't hold him."

The sky rumbled with repeated booms of thunder, accompanied by an incessant whispering and cackling that shifted location whenever I tried to pin it down.

"Don't leave my side. The creatures here are vicious and even ghosts have power in this place. He's testing our resolve."

"He won't break mine again." She grabbed my hand. "Make him aid us. I'm not taking no for an answer."

I hesitated and rubbed my nose, all too aware that I didn't have a plan, but things usually worked out for the best.

Lines creased her brow. "We can't do this if you're scared."

I snorted. "I'm never scared. This is my job. Let's go."

The stairs curved around the inside of the tower wall. I paused on the next landing, peering into a gloomy hallway full of closed doors. A gust of wind blew from nowhere, passed me, and rushed up the stairs. I took that as a hint and ascended once more. Opaque, gray water dribbled down the steps and walls, which rippled and flaked as we passed. Two floors higher, the walls leaned in over our heads as if hastening to catch our every whisper.

Thick webs choked the hallway. The chill wind blew along

it, rustling them, giving the appearance that they breathed. Light shone through them, and when they moved I realized they belonged to hairy spiders as large as my hand. Ayla grunted her disgust.

No sooner had she done so, than she was dragged from my side and thrown to the ground by some invisible force. I reached for her but she shot off along the damp tiles, kicking and trying to grab a hold of the walls, her hands coming away with nothing but slimy mortar and sticky strands.

"Maldren," she yelled.

Then she was gone.

Utter silence fell over the tower. Kristach! He had Ayla. Why her? In my mind's eye, his dagger stabbed into the heart of his wife, Yolanda. *Gods, no!*

I hurtled down the hallway, clawing aside the webs and sweeping the spiders from my robe. Double doors stood wide at the end. Warding symbols had been branded into the wood and later scratched out. Whatever. I burst through and skidded to a halt just inside, scanning for, but failing to see her.

"Ayla? Where are you?"

The rotted remains of a bed dominated the room. Its legs had decayed, allowing the frame to sink to the floor. The bedcovers lay shredded and blotched with darker shades of gray. Thank the Gods Phyxia wasn't lying there. Or Ayla. The other furniture lay in heaps of timber. My skin tingled in the magical residue that permeated the place.

"Ayla!" My voice broke. I coughed and swallowed hard.

Shadows gathered in the far corner, forming a black smear that consumed the daylight oozing through the shimmering, bricked-up window. The walls cracked and splintered at the shadow's touch. They physically cringed. Warts and pustules formed on every surface, bursting and dribbling a gray pus. Teeth set, I stared into the corner. I was immune to such foolish haunts now. Show me something to fight.

The boiling shadows grew to resemble the thing in the great hall, a stark reminder that Caradan was no innocent ghost but a wretched, depraved wraith.

Never had I sensed such malevolence—not the grak, nor the soul wraith. The elemental had projected a chaotic, primeval power. This entity overwhelmed me with a focused rage. I stumbled backward. The shadows coalesced into a middle-aged man, hair below his shoulders. Runes writhed across his black robe. He drew himself up to his full height of seven feet. Fierce, unblinking eyes bore into me.

Lak and all his demons!

I stood tall, fists clenched. "Where is she?"

"Manners. Is this how you address all your elders?"

My shoulders drooped. My resolve wilted. "Please, Lord Caradan, don't harm her. We came—"

"Why did you bring that traitor here?"

"I…I don't understand. She's my apprentice."

"Lies. You brought this…monster into my house."

He gestured toward the window and Ayla materialized, feet together, hands at her side. I started toward her, and then slammed into a force wall that knocked me crashing back against the doorjamb. It splintered under my weight. I stepped forward again, then hesitated.

"Ayla, look at me." I turned on Caradan. "What have you done to her?"

Magic flared from his fingers. It burned through my body and I cried out. It was like a thug had me in a bear hug. I gasped for breath and wheezed, desperately trying to tell him to stop. Still, his spell constricted me. Ribs cracked. Searing pain narrowed my vision to a shrinking, dark tunnel. The force let up and I crumpled into a heap. Each time I sucked in air, hot fire lanced through my chest.

"How dare you break into my home and make demands of me in such an insolent tone? Such arrogance. It was my will that you came here. Did you have sweet dreams?" He gave a crooked grin. "You've seen my history firsthand. I wanted to show you the choices that I made. For a hundred solars I have relived them. I regret the corrupted path I set the Guild upon, and regret more that Fortak perpetuated my mistakes. I can see into your soul, do you know that?"

Kristach. I didn't dare move, wincing at the pain in my chest. My mind tumbled over everything I had done, every decision, every action. I bet it didn't look good, but I was no Fortak.

"I see no evidence of our nihilism in you," he said.

Blowing out my breath made an unnatural wheezing sound. I glanced at Ayla but she remained statuesque, her gaze fixated on Caradan across the room.

"Phyxia told me about you," he said. "But I needed to see for myself."

The room fell silent. One agonizing breath. Two. Three. I knew that I played into his hands but couldn't help myself. "See what?"

"If Fortak had tainted you."

I hoped he liked what he'd seen. I was still alive. For now. I was walking a treacherous line here.

"My choices brought me damnation," Caradan said. "I hope that yours bring salvation."

His expression turned wistful and I seized my chance.

"Lord Caradan, long ago you served Malkandrah."

No need to expand on that. He *had* served, just incurred the wrath of the people.

"Our city needs you once again. Will you help us against Fortak and the elemental? Perhaps such an act would lift your curse."

His eyes flared. "You can speak for the Gods now? I have conditions, one of which is that Fortak must die."

I blinked. I hadn't considered going that far, but Fortak had tried to kill me. It seemed just for the hundreds he had murdered. Besides, who was I to prevent Caradan from killing him?

"Agreed. The other conditions?"

His gaze turned steely. "She is mine."

With a wave of his hand, Ayla's body jerked into action and she took a labored step toward him. I caught the glint of a knife blade as it appeared in the hand behind his back.

Oh Gods, no.

"Stop!" I reached for her.

"Yolanda, come to me, my darling," Caradan murmured with a sneer.

She took slow, deliberate steps toward him, head high, her body rigid, each step reluctant, forced.

I crawled across the damp, unnaturally spongy floor.

"Ayla, it's Maldren. Turn around. Fight it. Caradan, don't do this."

"Let me help you, my love," she said to him. Her voice had changed, taken on a southern accent.

She raised her arms and he stepped forward into her embrace. Mechanically, her arms closed around his neck and she stroked his back. Head pitched down, he nuzzled her hair and nibbled her ears.

"Ayla, no," I said. "It's a trick. Run to me. Run…"

One hand clutched to my chest, I pulled myself to my feet. Needles of agony stabbed my torso. I cried out, fighting the heaviness in my head, blinking against the sparks in my vision. If I breathed softly, the pain reduced to a jaw-clenching throbbing.

Caradan brought the knife to within an inch of her body. Her eyes fluttered shut, and she mewed at each caress of his lips on her neck.

I took a step forward, my empty hands palm up and trembling.

"Lord Caradan, I beg you. She's not your wife. She isn't Yolanda. I can free you from your curse, but you have to stop. She's innocent. You spoke of choices. Don't fail another. Please."

He pulled back and his gaze wandered up and down her body. Then he turned to me, eyes narrowed. I had a chance. I had to have a chance.

My pulse raced and my legs shook. I couldn't hold on to consciousness much longer. I gasped for air. Pain lanced through my chest and I bit down on a moan. A whisper was the most I could manage.

"The city, my lord. You can escape your curse."

"If I help you?" he asked, deep furrows on his forehead. The knife wavered.

"Yes, yes." I stepped forward, regretted it, and doubled over in agony. "Don't...harm her... We can talk...you and I."

He took long, deep breaths while mine were short and ragged.

"She isn't my bitch wife?"

I shook my head, not trusting myself to speak.

He glanced down at Ayla, who hadn't moved or reacted to anything we had said, then back at me. The knife hand lowered and he reached out with his other hand. It was gigantic compared to Ayla's head, but very gentle as he stroked her cheek, trickled his fingers through her hair. She gazed lovingly up at him and he smiled.

Thank the Gods.

"I send you to The Deep, Yolanda. We'll be together again."

He thrust the blade into Ayla's chest.

 TWENTY

Caradan and the knife vanished. No theatricals, no blast of shadow magic.

Ayla crumpled into a heap, blood gushing from her body. I stumbled across the room and dropped to my knees at her side.

Blood soaked her dress, spreading outward like necrosis. *So much blood.* Why was there so much blood? My hands flew to her wound, pushing down hard, not caring how much I might bruise her. Her life trickled between my fingers, warm and slippery. While I maintained pressure with one hand, I ripped free a section of her dress below her waist. Then I rolled her limp form over and back until I had the makeshift bandage wrapped around her chest and pulled as tight as I could manage. Pain seared through my gut but I didn't dare stop. My breath came in wheezing pants.

She whimpered, a noise so quiet that I nearly missed it.

Thank the Gods. She still lived.

I steeled myself for excruciating pain, scooped her into my arms, and tried to stand. My cries echoed through the empty tower. My vision tunneled and I dropped her. I wiped my sweat-drenched face and tried again, pushing myself to the brink. Just a bit more. Give me strength. One of my ribs snapped. I bit down hard against the agony and caught my tongue. A slimy, metallic taste made me want to puke. I stumbled against the wall, turning to protect Ayla's head. I didn't care about myself, but only while I lived did I have a chance to save her.

"I won't give up on you," I murmured into her hair.

I set my sights on the door. *Just get to the door.* Prayers to every God I could name rattled through my mind in an endless chant, while I willed myself to take one step after another. The walls oozed and pulsed as if mocking the life seeping from Ayla.

Step. Step.

I staggered into the hallway, which seemed to stretch away into the distance. The spiders had gathered in a vigil, hovering like vultures for our deaths. The stairs looked a lifetime away. That was my new goal—reach the stairs.

Step. Step.

Stay with me, Ayla. Stay with me.

Somehow I got there and sagged against the curving wall, sliding my back along it as I inched down, grimacing at every jarring step. Sweat poured off me. My knees threatened to give out but I made it to the floor below. I looked down the winding staircase, fighting to focus my blurred vision. How long had it taken to get this far? Was this my purgatory for disturbing Caradan?

With my ear to Ayla's mouth, I could barely make out her tiniest breath. My throbbing muscles implored me to rest. Pain from my broken ribs stabbed me breath after breath, making me relive the sight of the dagger entering her breast.

I wanted to give up. I couldn't give up.

The next goal—two more flights.

Step. Step.

I longed to talk to her, whisper in her ear, anything to keep her with me, let her know that she wasn't alone. I didn't dare expend the energy. My rapid breathing would have to serve.

Step. Step.

Daylight lanced into the hallway before me. Something was different. Solas beckoned me with a beacon of light, and I couldn't wait to escape this cursed place. One foot after the other until, finally, fresh air chilled me. My vision sharpened. Only then did I realize that at some point in my agonizing journey I'd departed The Gray. I retraced each painful step in my mind, and then shook my head. It didn't matter. It was enough to know that Caradan had let us go.

I toppled from the springy plank, plunging into the swamp. Ayla flew from my arms as if in slow motion, making an almighty splash as she entered the bracken water with her back first. I grabbed a clump of reeds for support, waded after her, and used her natural buoyancy to my favor in bringing her back into my arms. Her face had turned blue and her eyes hollow. I scraped muck from her nose and mouth. She didn't stir.

"Stay with me," I said. "Don't leave me."

The gleaming temple spires in the distance reminded me of my mission. My life had one purpose, and if necessary I would die doing it. I waded in a direct line toward the hole in the wall, weaving only to avoid the ancient, sunken tombs. Ayla's head lolled and bounced.

How long could she hold on—or had she already passed on? My vision blurred again, this time with tears. What would I do if she died? Would she return as a ghost? Could I *Séance* with her as I had my mother? What if she fled and refused all contact with the physical world? I couldn't bear to be so alone. Not now. Not after everything we had shared. I relived the touch of her lips on mine.

I lost count of how many ever-decreasing goals I set and miraculously achieved. After what seemed like days after I had left the tower, I blundered into Temple Plaza. I shuffled her weight in my arms, shocked at the quantities of blood covering us both. This couldn't be real. Any moment I'd wake from another of Caradan's nightmares.

"Please help," I said, my throat parched, sweat stinging my eyes.

Passersby recoiled and hurried past. Why wouldn't they help? Ayla was likely dead because two people chose to stand up for their city. *Damn every one of you trying hard to ignore us, too busy, too scared to help.*

"You ungrateful tristak," I muttered. "Look what this girl gave up for you."

Anger revitalized me. I blinked back tears and staggered to the closest temple. I didn't recognize the deity it served, and didn't care. I would worship them later. When I moved between the ornate entrance pillars, two brown-cloaked guards intercepted me.

"Let me in. She needs healing."

"Your kind isn't welcome." The man shoved me.

Pain lanced through me, but all I cared about was not dropping Ayla.

I moved forward again, and both guards reached for their swords.

Damn my profession.

My arms cramped and buckled. I couldn't carry her much further. I couldn't remain conscious much longer. The towering temple buildings blurred into a single fuzzy blob. I shook my head to clear it and my gaze settled on an impressive edifice constructed from white stone.

It called to me like a beacon. I stumbled forward, knowing in my heart I would never reach its distant entrance. I put one foot stubbornly after the other, and made it to a sprawling garden filled with emerald-leafed trees and flowers of every hue. I'd forgotten that colors existed other than blood red.

Ayla's face was serene, her lips parted but lifeless. I willed her chest to make the barest motion, but it didn't. Tears streamed down my face as I lay her gently on a bench in the garden. A pair of blurry white shapes moved toward me through the bushes.

"Save her," I muttered.

They looked up and hurried toward me, resolving into white-robed priests. I considered my Guild robe, then slipped out of it, balled it up, and cast it into the undergrowth. I knelt beside Ayla in plain clothing. At that moment we were equals, not master and apprentice.

I stroked her forehead with one hand, accidentally smearing blood into her hair. I wanted to say something profound and encouraging, but no words came. All I could do was stare into her still face. The priest said something, but his voice seemed to disappear down a long tunnel. Everything on my body hurt. I was spent. My vision darkened.

I fumbled with her hand, fingering the Duke's signet ring that she wore.

"Duke Imarian," I mumbled. "Whatever...cost..."

I crashed to the ground and into darkness.

I dreamed of flowers and a manicured garden, through which a young woman ran, her hands trailing through hanging tree fronds before she stopped to breathe deep from immaculately arranged flower beds. She giggled when I gave chase, teasing me, allowing me to catch her. I swept her into my arms and we gazed into each other's eyes, grinning like fools in love. From behind her, my mother appeared, scowling.

"Stop playing childish games, Maldren." She waggled a finger. "There is study to be done. Where is your robe?"

I eased the girl away guiltily and glanced down at my gray shirt and brown pants.

Mother stepped forward. "Go and find your robe at once."

"I found your robe," a man's voice said.

I spun but no one was there.

"Your robe," the man repeated. "I found it."

My eyes fluttered open and focused on an elderly man. He walked around the bed in which I lay.

"I understand why you discarded it."

He placed a neatly folded black bundle on a chair, on top of what looked like my clothes. Then he crossed to the open window and inhaled deeply. Birds chirped in a bush speckled with snow-white flowers that waved in the breeze, wafting a fresh scent into the room. He turned back to face me and smoothed his white eyebrows with one finger.

"You need not be ashamed. Solas welcomes anyone in need. We cleaned and repaired your robe."

"Ayla?" My stomach quivered. I needed to know right then.

"She sleeps in the next room."

My heart pounded. She was alive. I choked on a cry of joy, coughed, and tried again.

"Thank Belaya for all her mercy."

He smiled back. "You mumbled her name continuously."

I sat up, stiff, but breathing wasn't difficult. My body barely ached. I probed my ribs tenderly but there was no pain.

"You were in dire need of healing yourself."

He poured juice from a pitcher and handed me a goblet.

"Your qe was severely depressed in many places. So much pain for one so young."

I sipped the wazh, savoring its tart, refreshing taste.

I threw back the bedcovers. "I must see her."

"From the doorway only. She is still in qe-afreet and must not be disturbed."

I could only assume that was some kind of ritual. I took a long gulp of cool juice and then swung my legs out of bed. I wore a simple white robe and my feet were bare.

"How long will she—?"

"She will awake tomorrow."

I peered out the window, trying to see around the large bush. "What time is it? What day is it?"

"You arrived five hours ago. Healing you was a simple matter. Her wounds were substantial. Twice she nearly died."

My hands trembled and I gripped the goblet tightly.

"I don't know what happened," he said, then raised one hand to quell my interruption, "and I don't care to know, but had you been five minutes later..."

I stood, surprised by how rested I felt. I hadn't felt so good in ages. Maybe I should move in here. I might get a decent sleep for once. Too many days straining my back in the sewers and undercity.

"Dress and then you can see her. My name is Perris."

He stepped out of the room, untied a cord, and a drape fell across the entrance to the room to serve as a door.

I wasted no time in dressing in my shirt and pants. I admired the neat repairs they had made to my Guild robe, but chose to carry it out of respect for the old priest and his order. I slipped past the drape and into a long hallway that shone as bright as day. It was airy and carried a delicate aroma of feresen flowers. Holes in the roof funneled in daylight somehow. Why didn't the Guild have such things?

"Stay in the hallway," Perris whispered. "You must not go in, however much you wish to."

When he pushed aside the drape to her room, I stepped up to the threshold. His hand hovered near my arm.

The room was identical to mine except that Ayla lay upon the bed, or at least I thought it was her. Undulating waves of magic orbited the bed, moving between metallic spiked pillars that stood in each corner. The magical field blazed blue and white and purple, barely transparent enough for me to make out a body clothed in a white robe. The air thrummed as the magic whipped around.

I wanted to rush over, lie beside her, and stroke her hair, kiss her lips. Maybe I had moved, because Perris gently pulled me back into the hallway and the drape fell. I had no idea that temples possessed such healing magic. They must have recovered her from the very brink of death. Or had she died and the bizarre contraption in the room had resparked life into her? I shivered.

Perris placed a hand on my shoulder and squeezed it gently. The desire to remain in the temple tugged at my heart. Ayla and I could stay here, walk the peaceful gardens, forget the city, and forget the evil outside. I could forsake necromancy and become a priest, paying forward the healing that had saved her. Saved us both.

My idyllic bubble popped. The coronation was three days away. No time for such silly dreams.

"I need to leave for a while," I told Perris.

He nodded and led me along the hallway. I glanced over my

shoulder. I wanted to stand outside her room until she awoke, but there was something I had to do.

"Thank you for saving her. I can't... She's everything to me. I love her."

I halted and he looked at me, puzzled. I couldn't believe it had been that easy to say, but it was true, and I wasn't afraid of that truth anymore.

"I can see." His eyes smiled.

"I never expected the temple...anyone, in fact...to help me. I—"

I'd imagined waking in the street, clutching her cold corpse. I shuddered.

He frowned and waggled a finger at me. "Being judgmental clouds the qe, the spirit."

"Her father's estate will make a generous donation to your cause, I promise, if you can wait until after the coronation."

"Of course. You can find your way from here."

We emerged into the public temple, a gargantuan hall whose towering pillars appeared to have been carved from single pieces of marble. I gawked in wonder at the inside of a cone that stretched above the ceiling and into the late-afternoon sky. The hollow spire had been manufactured entirely from crystal panels, and I couldn't fathom how such a thing could have been built.

Three enormous arches on the far side of the hall exited to Temple Plaza. On the right wall stood a forty-feet-tall statue of Solas. I veered toward it, my heart telling me it was the right place to go. My heart had been saying a lot lately, probably glad it could get a word in between the endless chattering of my mind. As I arrived at benches set at the base of the statue, I glanced back. Perris had been watching me. He dipped his head and turned into the hallway. I took that as approval.

Solas was dressed in a toga, cinched at the waist with a belt fashioned like a sunbeam traced in a circle. His hands were crossed over his chest as if in peaceful repose, yet clutched a serrated-edged greatsword. I perched on the end of an empty bench.

If you can hear me, Solas, if you bother—no, that sounds rude. If you choose to grace me with your attention, I apologize for my poor articulation. I don't worship much. Well, at all, really, at least not in temple. Anyway, thank you. Thank you for your kind priests, thank you for taking me in, and thank you for Ayla's life. As a God, I know you can see below the surface, to see that she and I are trying hard to save lives. Necromancers aren't bad people. Well, most of us. Ayla is a good soul. Thank you.

I stood, crossed to a copper bowl set near his feet, and threw in five gold coins.

The long delve underground to my mother's grave gave me time to think of what I wanted to say. Needed to say. I wished I had Ayla as moral support, but it was better this way. I didn't trust Mother's games. What *had* she said to Ayla last time?

I strode boldly into the catacombs. Unseen ghouls tingled on my *Perception*, skulking in holes or dark coffin niches. They'd regret messing with me. Magic surged in my veins and I itched for an excuse to release it as I stepped over crumbling skeletons and loose rubble. The contented hum of the glow beetle in its cage relaxed me.

At my mother's grave, I laid the bunch of yellow flowers I had carried all the way from street level. Then I trickled magic through my palms and let my *Séance* spell seep into the ground.

Hello, Mother.

Nothing.

I've come to beg your forgiveness.

I really, genuinely meant it, and hoped that she could sense that.

I was rude and selfish. I—

She appeared in the air before me, transparent yet real enough to let me see her every movement. She looked down at me and smiled.

You remembered my favorite flowers. I can't smell them but it's a lovely gesture. Thank you. I didn't expect to see you again so soon.

I lowered my head and warmth flooded my cheeks.

Everything you said was true. I'm sorry it took me so long to realize it. Ever since you... No, that's not fair. This isn't about you. I spent so many solars trying to be a man everyone would respect, that I...well, I wrapped myself into my own world. I wanted to prove myself. I needed to do it all. Be it all. The masters lectured me about your talents, your prowess. It was like you were a legend. I didn't know how to live up to that.

Maldren—

I didn't want to mess up. Alone, I thought no one could get hurt, but they did. People are still getting hurt, because I'm still messing up.

Maldren—

And all the while I hated that the Guild had lost its way. Why was I the only one who cared, the only one with no lust for power? I slapped my palm on her gravestone. *They're perpetuating a culture of fear. They've forgotten whom we serve. What good is the might of the Guild if they're on the wrong path?*

Maldren!

She extended her arm and a wave of soothing warmth washed over me, from the top of my head to my toes. I snapped my head up to look into her smiling face. The delicious heat faded, leaving me tingling all over.

I'm proud to have you as my son. More than you know. It's been rough for you. I wanted so much to nudge you, to reassure or comfort you.

I uttered a short laugh that echoed through the catacombs, alien and startling.

I wish I could have done the same for Ayla, I said. *I think I've learned more from her than she from me.*

A wide grin spread across her face, revealing perfect spectral teeth.

Even though I almost got her killed...

But you saved her. That's all that matters. I'm glad you're confiding in Kolta. I never had a better apprentice.

That was how they knew each other! It also explained Kolta's remarks in Boattown, but why hadn't he told me he studied under my mother? I sank back on my heels.

I followed your advice and did some reading. Caradan's been in the background since day one. He's the missing piece, I'm sure of it.

I stared through her to the next mausoleum, its walls cracked and pitted. Fortak was still trying to impress Caradan. Wasn't the elemental enough for him?

Good question, she said.

I'd forgotten she could read my surface thoughts.

Her eyes flashed dark. *Fortak's a fool. He failed before because Phyxia and I put a stop to his plans, though the cost was high.*

One hand flew to my nose and rubbed it. Gods, it had been the two of them that had prevented Fortak resurrecting Caradan. Why hadn't I known that? Why had Phyxia never spoken about her friendship with my mother? She'd been fond of reminding me of her inability to get involved, but I'd call stopping Fortak being completely involved. She'd stopped him then, but now she was helping him with the elemental. That made no sense. I knew next to nothing about the woman.

I blew out my held breath. *Caradan is no friend of Fortak. He told me so.*

Had the events in the tower soured attempts for me to gain his help, his trust? I believed we could still be allies.

I can win over Caradan if I knew how to reach him. He's the most powerful, evil force in recent history. I know he can help.

She smirked. *You're lucky that train of thought makes sense to me. Don't underestimate him, Maldren. I can protect you, but be careful.*

I can't go back to the tower. Not that place. Never again.

I can summon him if you truly believe you can win him over. She sat cross-legged on her grave—actually, about a foot above it.

I didn't, but I had to try. I'd promised Ayla that much.

This is going to be fun. Her outstretched hand passed through mine. I savored the delicious tingling. *Mother and son working together.*

Dead mother, which was a little weird, but I was game. I shifted into a more comfortable sitting position.

Magic washed out from her, shaping a spell that resembled a *Ward*, with something else thrown in that I'd never seen. Green sparks traced a circle on the ground around us. She twirled a single finger and the sparkles grew vertically until a shimmering cylinder encased us. With a final flourish, she drew the magic above her head. It was like sitting in a giant glow beetle cage.

Bell Ward, she said. *As long as it holds, don't attempt protections of your own. They'll interfere.*

I nodded and canceled my *Perception*. She hadn't mentioned it specifically but if this green cylinder could keep us safe from Caradan, I wasn't worried about any ghouls that decided to investigate.

Ready?

Not really.

"Yes."

TWENTY-ONE

The magic of Mother's *Summoning* was familiar as it rippled through my body, but her finesse in shaping it was incredible. She stepped up the power beyond my entire reserves, maintained, and then ramped it up further. Being dead had its benefits, or had she wielded this much power when alive? I'd heard my mother's name spoken reverently among the Guild, but I hadn't really thought it through to the operational level. The surge of family pride surprised me. I started to think I should be asking her to defeat the elemental, when her power reached a crescendo and then faded.

A sensation of malice overwhelmed me. The air turned chill and stung my throat. I studied my trembling hands, and my heart fluttered. The brooding menace took form as a dark blotch in the air beyond the shimmering cylinder. It coalesced into a gray, spectral form and then resolved further until Caradan hovered before us, tall and defiant. His robe billowed out in an unfelt wind, and silver symbols rippled along its hems.

Lassira, he boomed in my mind, lips unmoving. He glared at my mother. *I'd hoped never to see you again. How dare you bring me here?*

They knew each other on a first-name basis? Caradan had lived and died way before her time. There was clearly a juicy story in how she'd prevented Fortak resurrecting Caradan.

I do as I please, she said, and I was glad I could hear their conversation. *Your feelings for me are mutual. I have little to say, but my son may possess greater wisdom than us both.*

She turned her attention to me, and he followed her gaze, his brow furrowing deeper. My heart raced under such scrutiny.

Don't try to trick me again, boy. I'm not the fool you think. Your woman had more in common with Yolanda than you know.

What did that mean? If he'd had his way they would have been united in death. I erected a barrier over my thoughts, hopefully not too late.

Fortak must die and you will do it. That is the price of my help. You want a better Guild? Actions, boy. Words are cheap.

A cloying miasma of evil flowed from his spirit into me, and my stomach flipped. I swallowed hard. Yakking on my mother's grave wouldn't do. I had no doubt he would tear me apart were he to catch me outside the *Bell Ward*. I stood, trying to meet him face-to-face, yet falling at least a foot short.

You'll help for revenge but not to save the city? I asked.

His mental guffaw rattled in my skull. *It's all I have left, boy. The laugh is on me. I corrupted the Guild long before Fortak's birth. I'm saving the city from the choices I made. Make your own. If they are right, I will help.*

His form faded.

Wait. You'll defeat the elemental? Let the people see you fight for them and they will fear you no more.

I stepped to the edge of the shimmering wall. His will commanded me to step through. I clenched my fists and resisted.

What do you know of fear? he asked. *Maybe fear is good for people. They aren't afraid enough of what lurks beyond their fragile world. Perhaps Fortak acts with the blessing of the Gods, to teach them a lesson with his pet elemental.*

His eyes bore into mine, but I refused to look away. Damn

it, I was losing him.

Like my mother, like you, I'm not afraid of the ultimate sacrifice. I will not stop. If I fail, Fortak wins. You want him to lead the Guild down the path you did? The path you regret?

Caradan's face turned cold and expressionless. He looked to my mother.

He is without doubt your son, Lassira. And then to me, *You trust me to help? You won't have your mummy's spells to protect you.*

I do. Kristach, I needed him.

I'll consider your plea. Lassira, send me back.

They locked eyes for such a long time that I wondered if a private conversation occurred between them. She nodded, waved her hand, and he vanished. A sense of lightness replaced the menace that had hung heavy in the air. The glow from my beetle seemed to fill the catacombs with light.

You could not have done more, she said to me.

Are you going to fight with us?

It is your time, your destiny, not mine. Thank you for the lilies. It means a lot that you no longer resent me. Her eyes sought confirmation in mine.

I promise to visit more often.

If I'm alive three days from now.

Go and look after your woman. She's what you need right now.

I smiled, retrieved the beetle cage, and headed out of the catacombs. Before turning the corner, I glanced back. She was watching me—a pale glow in the shadows. I waved once and hurried away. *Would I ever see her again?*

I took my time in walking back from Eastside to Temple Plaza as I measured the pulse of the city. A chill wind gusted through the narrow streets and I wrapped my robe tighter. When I reached the river, I looked up Kand Hill. The black scar of my old neighborhood still blighted the skyline.

I sensed a mixed mood among the people. Families labored together to hang decorations and bunches of purple feresens from their houses. The merriment was muted, devoid of the raucous laughter, pranks, and singing of previous celebrations. I perceived a collective feeling of impending doom, of not knowing when disaster might strike, not knowing if their house or street would burn before the next dawn. People jumped at every fall of a hammer or clattering cart wheel. In every street I walked, they scowled at me, muttering prayers and shooing their children in the other direction. My presence wasn't helping their mood.

A light fog had rolled in as Solas dipped below the horizon, the mist flowing upriver and spreading into the maze of streets. Atop the southern bridge, I paused to study the eerie patterns in the slow-flowing river. They reminded me of the inky smoke let loose by the elemental. I shivered and hurried down the other side.

The uncertainty was killing me. What if I was wrong about coronation day? Maybe the elemental would strike tonight. Had I convinced Caradan or had he outsmarted me? What had I expected? With Ayla out of the fight, I had no chance alone against the elemental. According to Phyxia, Fortak lacked full control over the creature. Damn the woman. Why was she involved at all? If only I'd heard the rest of her words at the Covenant meeting.

A dark figure stood at the far end of the bridge, partly obscured by the drifting fog. Something told me I should turn back. He stepped out of the shadows and proceeded toward me. He wore no Guild robe, nor was he dressed like the Duke's spies. His right hand was tucked inside his jacket. My own hand dropped to my dagger.

We closed rapidly, the only people on the bridge. The clamor of the city sounded from both sides of the river, but it was like the two of us were in our own silent world. Only twenty feet from me, his hand slid from his jacket. I tensed. My fingers clutched the familiar grooves of my dagger hilt.

Ten feet. He withdrew a slip of paper. His head was lowered, hidden beneath long, wayward hair. He passed on the left side of me, holding the piece of paper toward me. I took it and he continued without missing a step. I exhaled violently. The note bore no seal, so I fumbled to unfold it and immediately recognized Kolta's scrawl.

Noon tomorrow. Pudge Street Cistern. I'll have Semplis and hopefully others.

So Semplis had come around and learned the truth. To have the support of the other masters was more than I'd hoped for. With new plans careening through my head, it seemed to take no time at all to reach Temple Square.

My robe garnered little attention as I marched through the main temple and into the back hallway. A couple of the priests greeted me warmly. On the way here, the whole city had judged and cursed me, and the lack of accusation in this place refreshed me as much as the delicious floral scent. Perris intercepted me and with a firm grip on my arm, steered me away from Ayla's room.

"This is a critical time for her. Dine with me."

"Another time?" I asked. "I'm very tired."

In reality, my brain was fizzing like a lightstick, but I needed the void of sleep. My head hurt going over the options, the what-ifs and contingency plans. Enough of this whole Lak-be-damned crisis. Perris knew none of what I knew and I certainly wasn't going to weigh down his—what had he called it?—qe with all my worries. All I wanted was to see Ayla again, to see her smile and to touch her. The faster I went to sleep, the sooner that moment would arrive.

"As you wish. The same room is yours." He clapped me on the shoulder and left.

I sighed. The Guild could learn from how these men selflessly gave of themselves to those in need.

I woke long before dawn to the soothing sound of chanting drifting from the depths of the temple. Part of me wanted to leap up, dress, and run next door, but I practiced restraint. Perris knew my anxiety. He wouldn't make me wait a moment longer than necessary. Slowly, as the black turned to gray outside my window, I tuned in to more and more sounds: birds in the bush outside, people walking and laughing, and eventually, voices in the room behind my head—Ayla's room.

It seemed like forever since I had last seen her.

I slipped out of bed, washed in a basin of cold water, and dressed. A tray of food sat invitingly on a side table but I still didn't feel like eating. The drape across the door swished, and Perris bade me good morning as he tied it open. He stepped back, gesturing to the hallway.

It was time.

I hesitated at first, my mind reeling with everything that I wanted to tell her: how sorry I was for letting her down, for nearly killing her, that I loved her? I'd never genuinely loved a woman before. The words were important. I blew out my breath and strode into her room. The contraption with the metallic pillars had been removed. She sat upright on the bed, back against the wall. A smile spread across her face and she raised her hands to embrace me.

Her eyes were colored a violet so bright that they almost shone. Gone was the chestnut with tiny green flecks. Her hair had been washed and neatly tied back, but was now albino white. Her entire body was deathly pale.

I faltered halfway to the bed.

"Oh, dear Gods," I muttered.

Her beaming smile collapsed and her wide eyes searched my face.

"What?" she asked, voice wavering.

I scrutinized every inch of her, expecting her to shimmer and fade like a ghost. It was like staring at the picture of Caradan's wife, Yolanda, in the book. What had he done to her? Was it even Ayla?

"Who are you?" I asked. "What are you?"

She recoiled and brought her knees up to her stomach.

"What do you mean?" She whimpered. "You know who I am. You're scaring me. What's wrong?"

She didn't know. Why hadn't those tristak priests told her? I looked for Perris but he had gone.

"You...you look different." What else could I say?

She inspected her legs, turned her arms, and studied both sides of her hands. Then she touched her right breast that had been pierced by Caradan's dagger.

"No I don't."

I couldn't stop staring at her eyes.

She trembled and drew her knees tighter. "Stop it. Tell me what's wrong."

"Your hair…"

She grabbed behind her head and tugged her hair free of the clip. She'd cut it too short to cascade over her shoulders, so she pulled at it, desperate to see it.

"It's white," she said shrilly. "Who bleached it?"

Those violet eyes flashed and I took a step back.

We spotted the hand mirror on the side table at the same time. I leaped to intercept, but she snatched it. After a single glance in the mirror, she yelped and dropped it on the bed as if it had burned her.

I extended a hand toward her. "It's all right…"

She jerked away. "No, it's not. What did they do to me?"

She yanked at her hair, trying to get a better look. Some of it tore loose in her hand.

"Don't," I said softly. "Stop that."

She brought the mirror to her face again. Then she flung it against the wall, where it smashed into a thousand shards that rained down on the floor.

"My eyes. I'm a monster."

"Calm down. Let me help…" I couldn't say her name. Shame filled me.

"You can't help," she said. "I'm horrible. Leave me alone."

"I want to be with you. I…I…"

I couldn't say that I loved her? But I did. Why couldn't I say it?

"Go away."

Her demonic eyes bore into me and I averted my gaze. I didn't know how to make her feel better. Every part of her was tensed, and her raised legs formed a barrier between us. I reached for her but all she did was stare at my hand. My gut turned upside down. She didn't love me anymore.

Perris appeared in the doorway, surveyed the broken glass,

and then looked at Ayla as if for the first time.

"Why didn't you warn me?" Ayla snapped at him. "Break it to me gently?"

"I—"

"Get out," she said. "Both of you. I'm hideous and I want to be alone."

She snatched up a full pitcher of juice, ready to hurl it. Perris pulled me from the room.

He rushed me down the hallway to a small refectory that looked far too small to serve the number of priests I had seen. He pushed me gently onto a bench.

"When was the last time you ate?" he asked. "Eat and then we'll talk."

He filled two plates and goblets from a side table. I stared vacantly at the plate he set before me, stacked with bread, cheeses, and meats. Food was the last thing I wanted.

"Tell me now. What did you do to her?" I asked.

"I'm sorry. I hadn't been informed of her physical changes."

"What did you do to her?"

"Qe-afreet never causes harm. The ritual cannot alter someone like that."

"Clearly you're wrong."

He sighed. "I would not challenge your profession. Please trust mine. In rare cases the ritual reveals the inner person, but in a spiritual way, never a physical one. Please eat something."

As if to set an example, he bit into cheese on bread.

"Did she die?" I had to know. "Is it possible she's someone else? Possessed?"

I couldn't tell if his smile was sympathetic or humoring. Kristach, Yolanda had possessed her.

"She came close to death more than once. Only you can answer your other questions."

"Because I'm a necromancer?" I growled.

"Because you're her friend. You saved her life. Give her time." He continued eating.

Time was one thing we didn't have.

I picked at the pungent cheese and washed it down with wazh. Did the ghost of Yolanda look through her eyes? Was she still my Ayla? That sounded so selfish. The poor girl must be tormented out of her mind.

"The internal demons are harder to battle, aren't they?" he asked a while later. His gaze fixed on something behind me, and his brow furrowed. He stood. "I have things to attend to. Stay as long as you wish."

I swiveled on the bench. Ayla had entered the room. My whole body tensed. I wanted to run to her, to hold her. I didn't dare.

She approached cautiously. A line of stitching scarred the material of her blue dress below her right breast. The hem rode higher on her legs, where someone had removed the section I had torn to bind her wounds. A faded green headscarf hid her hair.

I didn't know what to say. Instead, I pushed my plate toward her. She took it and sat at the opposite end of the table. I searched her face. If only I could read minds like my mother.

"Don't stare at me," she said.

I mumbled an apology and studied her hands instead, as she ate swiftly but with manners. I could chew the tension in the air as easily as the cheese.

"What now?" she asked. "Caradan's clearly out of the picture."

I think my mouth made an O with astonishment that she could even speak of him.

"Actually, he's not."

While she ate, I summarized the meeting with my mother and Caradan.

Her violet eyes flashed. "I don't trust the tristak murderer. Don't let him anywhere near me."

"I'm still holding out hope he will aid us," I said. "I think he considers you dead."

She snorted.

"I managed to sway Master Semplis. We're going to meet." I couldn't put off the question any longer. "Are you still...? I mean...I understand if you just want to go home, now that..."

This rift was killing me. I ached to have her back. I just hoped it was still Ayla.

"Do you think that little of me?" she asked. "We finish this together."

"And then?"

She scowled and flung the remains of her bread onto her plate.

"There is no 'then' until this is over."

Before she changed her mind, I led her through the huge hall with the immense statues, and out into Temple Plaza. It seemed fitting that Solas was the first thing we saw, blazing through a gap in the growing black clouds. Which was the omen, the gathering storm or the light of Solas? I tipped my head to feel his warmth, but Ayla squirmed, trying to hide from everyone around us. She ducked her head and looked at her feet. My hand sought hers and the connection between us made me tingle. A moment later, she gently pulled hers free.

We walked back to the inn in silence. She was close enough to touch, but we might as well have been on opposite sides of the river. I steered us away from the crowds, hoping she'd regain her confidence, but not once did she look up.

When we left our rooms at the inn, Ayla had swapped the headscarf for one that matched her dress, and had draped a cloak around her shoulders. She'd rouged her face and lips, and darkened her eyes with heavy black liner, but her wrists and hands betrayed how pale she'd become. Like a ghost. She stumbled on a loose cobble and I seized the opportunity to take her arm, but she shook away my assistance.

Talk to me, accuse me, scream at me. Anything besides the tense silence.

I attempted to break the ice by telling her stories of my misadventures as an apprentice, and how poor Kolta had tried to drum some sense and maturity into me. I didn't know if she cared, but she didn't tell me to shut up. That was enough for now. I played up my encounter with the mysterious man on the bridge, explaining how I'd wished to have her at my side, hefting a thighbone club to defend me.

Come on, woman. Laugh.

I gave up and we finished the journey entertaining our own thoughts.

Halfway along Pudge Street, before it turns a sharp right toward the waterfront, there stood a pair of grim, windowless buildings. One was a textile mill. I'd never bothered to find out what hid behind the smoke-blackened walls of the other. This morning, a strong breeze blew off the harbor, chasing the smoke away, but when it didn't, smoke poured out of the rooftop chimneystacks and settled down to fill the street, giving it the nickname Smudge Street. A narrow, dark alley ran between the buildings.

After taking a final look around, I led us along it, past heaps of refuse to a narrow staircase descending into the ground. The city was full of such sewer entrances. At the bottom, we emerged into a dark chamber, its size evident from the distant echo of dripping water. The glow beetle alcove was empty, so I struck a lightstick against the wall and it spluttered to life.

The red-orange glare revealed a long, low-ceilinged hall, about eighty feet across and longer than the light could penetrate. A dark pool of water filled most of the chamber, except for the rotting loading dock upon which we stood. Pillars held up the arched ceiling, their two lines marching into the darkness. Two moss-covered steps descended into the still water, and I could make out another below the surface.

Ayla studied a pair of skeletons chained to the dock but half submerged, green with mold from the waist down.

"We're meeting the masters here?" The echo mocked her.

She speaks!

"Didn't you try that?" Her voice dropped to a whisper.

"Yes," I said. "But Semplis is with us now. He and Kolta will bring as many others as they can."

She pointed out a boat tied to a far pillar. The angle of the rope betrayed a left-to-right current, though the surface showed no sign of movement. The knot resembled the quick-release ties that the bargees used. I moved along the dock to a cluster of damp and moldering crates. Slats lay strewn about and the lids had been discarded.

Voices echoed on the stairs and the light from multiple sources bounced off the walls. Three men emerged, dressed in Guild robes emblazoned with the runes of a master. Kolta led, carrying a lantern with a handle that creaked at every step. Master Wampor limped behind him, resting on a cane that had seen better days, and Master Semplis followed at the rear. Kolta shot me a warning glance.

"You didn't tell me the full story, lad," Semplis said.

Not an auspicious start. "What do you mean?"

"You think that the Prime Guildmaster consorts with evil to destroy the city?" The chamber echoed his words, distorting them into a demonic language.

The ghoul was out of the grave now. *Ah well, go big or go home.*

"I have evidence he murdered Duke Imarian." My hand itched to seek Ayla's.

"He was a fool to frequent such a dangerous place," Semplis said.

Ayla sucked in her breath and my heart jumped, but she said nothing. The masters glanced her way and I pushed her behind me. I didn't want them asking questions.

I glowered at Semplis. Was he being disrespectful on purpose or did he not know whom Ayla was?

"The Duke was supplying me with information," I said. "He wanted to stop the elemental."

Keep the focus on the creature.

"Which, according to you, our beloved Prime Guildmaster is in league with?"

"I…I don't know the truth of it. All I ask is that you help us stop the elemental."

"I can see through your lies, lad. Always have done."

Semplis leaned right into my face.

"Listen to yourself with such conspiracies. This is why the Prime Guildmaster seeks to apprehend you." His finger stabbed my chest. "You are dragging his name and the Guild through the sewer muck. Stop this nonsense right now and save your career."

He turned on Kolta. "You might want to look after your own too."

"Hear him out," Kolta said in an even tone.

"Only if I'll hear something other than childish fantasies."

I handed Semplis the note that had accompanied the dead Duke. He held it to the lantern and scrutinized it.

"This is the basis for your elaborate theory? I'm sure it's a fake." He slipped it inside his robe.

I took a deep breath and looked at each of them in turn.

"I'm asking you to trust me, Masters. That's all. The coronation is in two days. I beg you not to wait until the last moment."

"Trust you? You repeatedly ignore orders and act unilaterally. You've been passed over for master because we *don't* trust you."

"But that's why we're here," I said. Echoes ran the length of the chamber.

I turned to Wampor, who leaned on his cane and had been scowling at me all the while.

"Master, you taught me Guild order, to consult my seniors. Here I am. I need your help. I'm bringing this before the officers of the Guild. What more do I have to do?" I slammed my hand onto the crate and it splintered.

"Have some respect, son," Wampor said.

"I'm tired of trying to do this alone. Please believe me."

"Kolta wouldn't waste our time," Wampor said to Semplis, then swept back his wayward hair.

"In my mind, this ain't about Fortak or some mischief that may or may not be happening…" He held a hand up to silence me. "…but about stopping this elemental. If the boy has information 'bout that then it'd behoove us to pay attention."

"So be it," Semplis said, "if this were solely about the creature, but why is he so determined to smear the Prime Guildmaster's name?"

"Can't you drop it, you old curmudgeon?" Kolta asked,

taking the sting out of his words with a wink.

"Tell us what you know, son." Wampor pulled an iskat from his pocket, peeled it, and tossed the rind behind him.

"I'm certain the creature will attack during the ceremony," I said, damping my temper. "Thousands will die. We think…"

The truth about Caradan wouldn't sound plausible. I scratched my nose and flashed my eyes at Kolta.

"It's not up to us," Semplis said. "The Council has agents searching for any lone Elik Magi in the North. Negotiations are under way with the Sylarians to send sorcerers."

The idiot! Now I knew why no one had taken action.

"The Elik Magi are dead," I said. "We have to act now. Speak with the Guildmaster. Persuade him to stop, or ask the Council to speak with him and give…"

It wouldn't do to reveal I'd overheard Fortak's conversations about the Council.

Semplis glanced at me and took a long, deep breath. His shoulders drooped. I nodded rapidly. I only had to keep my mouth shut and let him reach the same conclusion.

He took two steps back. "I've heard enough of this personal vendetta of yours. Guards!"

A clamor of boots, chinking of metal, and scraping of leather echoed down the stairwell, and a moment later a dozen Black and Reds jogged into the chamber. They wore chain mail over red leather tunics with black undershirts and pants. Swords and axes were already in their hands. Wampor stepped behind Semplis.

I threw the lightstick at the nearest guard, grabbed Ayla, and dragged her behind the crates.

"Arrest them all," Semplis barked, moving out of harm's way.

"What is this?" Kolta asked.

While a half dozen guards blocked the stairs, the others surged forward, grabbing Kolta by the arms and smashing him against the wall.

TWENTY-TWO

Two Black and Reds rushed us and I shoved a crate in their path, cracking them in the knees. I peered into the darkness. There had to be a walkway, tunnel, or some other exit. Damn Semplis. I wouldn't go back to the Guild without a fight. The two men recovered and advanced, their axes glinting in the lantern light. I dragged Ayla toward the edge of the dock, glad that she didn't resist.

"Can you swim?" I asked.

When she didn't answer, I shoved her from the dock and leaped after her. We plunged into the frigid water, yelping in shock. Our double splash echoed around the chamber.

"After them," the sergeant bellowed from the dock.

"Take that cloak off," I told her, my teeth chattering.

After she had squirmed out of it, I balled it up and flung it at a guard cautiously descending the slime-covered steps. He swung his axe, ripping it in two.

"Take a deep breath." I attempted to swim for the sidewall, but my saturated robe dragged me down. No time to remove it now. "Another, and hold it for dear life."

Her strong strokes carried her ahead of me. "But there's nowhere—"

An arrow swished by her ear and plopped into the water. She gulped air and dived beneath the surface. I was right behind her, swimming underwater toward the wall, looking for the outflow pipe I knew was there somewhere. Her feet kicked in front of my face, sending rapid vibrations through the water.

We were in a world of our own. The men's shouts reduced to a muted drone. Visibility in the dark, freezing water was about a foot. Another arrow whizzed into the water a few inches from my head, and then another on my other side.

I kicked frantically. My hands touched the algae-covered wall and I probed along the slimy surface. If the outflow had a grating or was too narrow then we were done for. Since I'd added a new deity to my pantheon, I prayed to Solas, Belaya, and Lak. Surely one of them would help? My hand plunged into a gap, and I kicked into a pipe easily wide enough for both of us. My waterlogged robe dragged me down, and I could no longer feel my legs in the icy temperature. I pawed at the pipe walls for extra leverage. My lungs seared with the urge to breathe. I fought the impulse and kicked harder, but barely seemed to be moving.

The darkness was total. I had no idea if Ayla was still with me. There had to be an opening, steps, another chamber…something. What if the pipe remained flooded? Another five strokes. My legs cramped and screamed at me. My chest was ready to burst. This had been a mistake. *Turn around.* Capture had to be better than drowning, but which way was back?

My throat spasmed. I flailed my limbs but they couldn't find the walls, or Ayla. I was alone in a black void. *Must breathe.*

I opened my mouth and water flooded my throat.

My jaw scraped on cold stone. Something heavy pressed down on my back, preventing me from catching a breath. I tried to complain but could make only a gurgling sound. The weight lifted and I raised my head. My stomach heaved and I puked water.

With effort, I opened my eyes, blinking against ice that coated my lashes. Frigid water rushed along a storm drain a few inches below my nose, lit by the barest scrap of daylight filtering from somewhere above. I rolled onto my back on the hard surface, groaning and shivering. Ayla squatted on her haunches watching me, likewise shivering. Her violet eyes seemed to glow in the gloom, giving her the appearance of a demonic bikka.

"I thought you were dead," she said.

It was impossible to read her expression. Her soaked clothes clung to her figure, especially tight across her breasts, while her white hair lay plastered against her scalp, its ends stuck to her cheeks.

Torrents of water poured down the walls and gushed from a grate in the ceiling, the source of the distant daylight. Rain hammered far above us.

"Thank you." I sat, an awkward movement in my heavy robe. "For saving me."

"You think I'd let you drown?" She scowled. "You should have taken your robe off."

We stared at each other, both rubbing our blue arms and clenching our chattering teeth. I risked a weak grin but she didn't return it. Her lips had a purple tinge and her skin was even paler than before. I edited my impression of her—not a bikka but a ghost. I probably looked worse.

"They didn't follow." Her gaze darted to the tunnel we had swam along.

"We can't stay here. We need to get somewhere warm."

A third storm drain ran from the rear of the stone landing. We sidestepped the waterfall plunging from the grate and entered the circular tunnel. I set a fast pace to warm us up, and wrung the water from my robe as we went.

"What about Kolta?" she asked as we approached a ladder leading up to a manhole.

A shaft of daylight stabbed from above, illuminating every droplet of rain that splashed at our feet. I thought back to the first time we'd walked the sewers together and I'd played tricks to frighten her. She'd shown such childlike delight at the cling spirits. So much had changed in ten days.

"You 'ear that?" a gravelly voice spoke from the street above. "They're on foot down there."

Kristach! I snatched Ayla's hand and ran as fast as I could with my shoulders ducked in the cramped space, heading toward the next shaft of light. The sound of boots descending the metal ladder rang loud behind us. She tripped several times, and I yanked her up before she hit the brick floor. Our pursuers yelled something about a lantern.

We thudded under the next manhole, getting momentarily drenched by the cascading water. Ayla tried to grab the ladder, but I dragged her on into the black tunnel. The pursuit was gaining. When we came to the first side tunnel, I dived into it without slowing. The next shaft of light seemed an impossible distance ahead.

We blundered and slipped along the narrow storm drain, and it saddened me that she hadn't asked why I had taken the detour. I missed her incessant curiosity. Her conversation had become little more than functional. The old, gutsy Ayla would have relished in the challenge of escaping the guards. Now she followed like a trained dog. That reminded me of her actions in Caradan's bedchamber, and I couldn't dwell on that right then.

I wanted to be a long way from the corner before our pursuers arrived, and with luck they wouldn't know that we had deviated. The echoing voices made it impossible to comprehend what they were doing back there. I didn't dare look.

A deluge of water poured from a side pipe and soaked us again, but at least it was clean, wholesome rainwater, not sewage. The stream in the bottom of the tunnel had deepened, forcing us to wade through up to our waists. Eventually, we emerged into the drain running beneath the adjacent street.

Ayla was tiring, but we made it to the next manhole. She doubled over, panting and coughing. I put her hands on the rungs of the ladder and urged her to climb. Her face carried a healthy flush from our exertions and I'd begun to sweat too.

My clammy clothes pinched my skin. She heaved the manhole cover aside before I had a chance to urge caution, and by the time I had reached the surface, she was skulking in a doorway out of the pelting rain.

The street was empty. Unusually empty.

The buildings on the corner were nothing more than a pile of blackened rubble with burned timbers sticking up like grave markers. The adjoining street was similarly burned out—mounds of broken brick and charcoal on either side of the charred cobbled road.

I joined Ayla in the doorway and surveyed the intact tenements where we stood. No decorations had been hung. Every door and window was shut with drapes pulled closed. We wouldn't find sanctuary here.

"We need to find a hiding place out of the rain." I started walking toward the destruction, clutching at the stitch in my side.

Then I recognized where we were and memories flooded back. The men had fought the tomb wight over there. The elemental had exploded from a building on the right. Only a wasteland remained. The rear of the buildings on the parallel street had burned too, clear across a space that had once held thriving kitchen gardens. The woman had jumped from somewhere on the left, though it was impossible to determine where each building had once stood. A blackened ax lay half-buried under a heap of charcoal. I remembered its owner and shuddered. An ashy sludge coated every surface.

A whole neighborhood gone. A grievous wound in my city. I'd been there as each person had died. But I had lived. I shook my head against the grim memories.

The normal sounds of the city seemed so far away. Shouts behind me shattered the peace. The guards were still on our trail. I sucked in a deep breath, grabbed Ayla's hand, and ran toward the first intact building in sight. It was badly burned but still standing. A hole in the side provided a way in, and I pushed an unhinged door across it to hide our trail.

Out of the rain and wind at last. We stepped over broken

furniture to the kitchen at the back. Part of the ceiling had collapsed, but what remained looked secure. Water dribbled down the walls to form puddles, but most of the furniture had escaped water damage. Frozen and soaked, we stood dejected in the abandoned room, dripping and shivering violently.

"Start that fire while I hunt for blankets," Ayla said.

"Quietly. They're still searching for us."

She left and I turned my attention to the hearth. A cauldron of congealed stew smelled awful, so I moved it into the next room. The fireplace held a heap of dry logs, ready to light. It seemed vindictive to bring fire back to this place, but we had to get warm. I hoped that the darkness outside would mask the chimney smoke. I found firestarters in a cupboard and lit the fire. It crackled and spluttered to life. My stomach growled but all I found were stale oatcakes.

The stairs creaked and I spun, hand dropping to the hilt of my dagger. Ayla descended, wrapped in a large blanket and carrying a stack of dry clothes under one arm and her folded, wet dress under the other. Her expression was one of resolve. She'd come a long way from being a looked-after aristo's daughter.

"You'll catch damp fever." She dumped the clothes on a couch and approached the hearth. Her teeth chattered. "Take those wet clothes off."

The flickering fire cast shadows that danced eerily around the room. Naked flame had once soothed and mesmerized me, but no longer. Now I understood its raw power, seething and sparking, waiting for a chance to spread and destroy. I blinked and glanced around the simply furnished room. Outside, the rain had lessened to a barely audible patter.

"Give me your knife," she said. "I want to get rid of this horrible hair."

"Ayla, I don't want to do this anymore."

"What?" She folded her arms across her chest.

"Fight."

"I'm not fighting."

I sighed and took a step forward. Her eyes narrowed.

"I can't stand this awkwardness," I said. "You've changed since the temple. You—"

"Don't feed me tristak! I know I've damn well changed. I'm a monster now."

"That's not what I meant. I… You've every right to be angry but I don't want you to hate me. I know it's all my fault—"

"Why do you think it's your fault? It's not always about you."

"I did this to you. I didn't mean to. I had no idea—"

"Stop whining. What do you want from me?" She flicked her bangs from her face.

I looked into her fiery, violet eyes. "I want you to see how much I care for you. I…want to be with you."

Her gaze flicked rapidly between my eyes and mouth.

"I saw the horror on your face," she whispered.

"I wasn't prepared. They didn't warn me, either. My feelings for you haven't changed." I reached out to smooth her bangs but she stepped away.

"Don't."

"I don't care about the color of your hair or eyes. I care about *you*. Kristach. Are you going to make me keep going like this? Stop me before I turn into one of those simpering fools you hated dancing with."

The barest smile twitched on her lips, and the furrows in her forehead vanished. She inched forward.

My pulse quickened and a jittery sensation gripped my stomach. After all that had happened, and the threat of disaster the day after tomorrow, all that mattered was how close she stood. We leaned forward at the same time and our lips met, no gentle kiss but one full of pent-up passion. Her hot lips moved across mine, and she held nothing back. Neither did I. My tongue slipped between her teeth to find hers just as playful. Warmth spread through my body, pushing out the cold and damp. I cupped my hand at the back of her head and threaded my fingers in and out of her wet hair. Her hands clasped around my neck and she pulled me tighter into our kiss.

She pulled back. "I told you to get out of those clothes."

Ayla unbuttoned my shirt. My skin tingled deliciously as her fingers brushed across my chest. She peeled the shirt from my body and threw it behind us, picking up a folded blanket from the stack of clothing. She dabbed my chest dry, and a fuzzy numbness claimed me. I savored every movement, every time her fingers touched flesh. I studied how the firelight flickered across her face and the curves of her neck, emphasizing her beauty.

When she reached for the button on my trousers, my breathing turned to rapid pants and I stiffened within my shorts. I took over from her fumbling hands and my trousers fell to my knees. I sat on the floor, yanked off my boots, and wrestled with the clammy trousers sticking to my wet legs. Then I was free.

She sat beside me, studying my body while her fingers gently traced scars across my legs and belly. I wanted to reach out and pull her to me, but instead enjoyed the sensual, thoughtful way that she dried my legs. She paused now and then, glanced sidelong at me, and then looked away, and I had a sense that she was mulling over something.

She very deliberately put down the blanket, shuffled closer, and wrapped her arms around me in a tight embrace, cheek to cheek. This was more than I had dared hope for. I massaged and stroked the nape of her neck, her skin soft and warm. Her body quivered with my every movement. And so we sat, clinging to each other in the dim room, the only sounds the crackling of the fire and her occasional high-pitched murmurs of contentment.

I took a gentle hold of her shoulders and pushed her away enough to study her face. Her white hair and violet eyes lent her an exotic, even dangerous look. The haunted, desperate yearning in her eyes confirmed that her longing matched my own. I leaned forward and kissed her in the hollow at the base of her neck. My fingers threaded through her hair and gently rubbed the top of her ears. I planted kiss after kiss along her neck. Her breath became quick and uneven.

My fingers moved lower to stroke her perfect neck, and then I traced them down, making tiny S shapes across her skin.

"Damn this thing." I tugged at the blanket wrapped around her.

She shrugged out of it and flung it aside. My thumping heart stuttered to see her naked, a bronze goddess in the firelight. I lay down and pulled her gently on top of me, trembling as her hot skin touched mine and her hardened nipples pressed into my chest.

"I was so scared you didn't want me anymore." She kissed me.

"I love you so much," she murmured, nibbling my lips.

"I love you too."

It didn't sound soppy or melodramatic, and that surprised me. A sixday ago it would have. A single tear spilled from her left eye. I kissed it dry, tasting the saltiness. She rolled over, dragging me on top of her.

"Prove it," she whispered in my ear, one hand reaching for my shorts.

TWENTY-THREE

I woke to stiff, aching muscles and Ayla's warm, naked body against mine. Her right arm was draped across me, while her head rested on my chest, rising and falling with my shallow breathing. I didn't remember us moving to the couch last night, but it was certainly more comfortable than the floor.

Glowing embers flickered in the fireplace, and a predawn gray permeated the room through soot-smeared windows. If only we could lie here all day in each other's arms, alternating sleep and making love, but the tightness in my stomach and dryness in my throat demanded attention.

Careful to cradle her head, I squirmed out from under her, lowered her gently back onto the couch, and draped a blanket over her naked body. She stirred but did not wake. When I kissed her softly on the cheek she mewed and a smile spread across her face, but she remained asleep.

I had to pee, so I dressed hurriedly in the dry workers' clothes she had found the night before. The outside air was chill and damp but the rain had long stopped. There was no one in sight, but the sounds of the city coming to life in the next street over were welcoming. The aroma of freshly baked pastries made my stomach cramp and rumble. I rounded the corner into an alley that ran alongside the tenement building. An upper wall had collapsed and rubble lay strewn about. There I did my business.

When I hurried back inside, Ayla lay on the couch, propped up on one elbow with a blanket pulled up to her neck.

"Sneaking out now you've had your wicked way with me?"

I grinned and tossed her another set of clothes. "Let's get back to the inn. I'm starved."

"Won't the Black and Reds be waiting for us there?"

I rubbed my nose and remembered the man on the bridge.

"Semplis and the others don't know we're staying there."

She slid out from beneath the blanket. I could get used to seeing her naked. Her shocking white hair barely kissed her shoulders, almost transparent against her pale skin. She looked as beautiful in the stark morning light as she had at the height of our passion. To think I'd nearly ditched her as a stupid girl, or one possessed by some long-dead witch.

She glanced, scowling, around the room.

"Sorry," I said. "I know it's not the romantic nest you'd hoped for, for our first time. Nothing a hot bath won't solve."

"The magic words to my heart." She melted in my arms, pulling my head down for a kiss.

"Get dressed before I ravish you again." I pushed her away.

"Promise?"

While she did so, I bundled up my robe and her blue dress and stuffed them under the couch. When I looked up, she resembled a peasant woman in a dirty brown skirt and gray shirt. Her blue headscarf provided a dash of color. I wasn't much better off with dark blue trousers and a torn, stained white shirt and brown jacket. Good enough disguises.

Jade Road wound around the base of Kand Hill, serving as a cross street linking Canal Street to the Heroes Bridge. I chose it as the fastest route back to The Pumphouse, except that I hadn't expected the hordes of citizens meandering from store to store, heading east in preparation for the Crown Prince's coronation tomorrow.

Tomorrow. We'd run out of time.

Whole families had turned out: parents trying to rein in excited children who chased each other through the crowd; grandparents leaning on each other, their faces set and determined to witness another moment of history in their long lives; babies wailing and crying in mothers' arms. Numerous Black and Reds stood along the route, scanning the crowd for pickpockets. As we merged with the flow, I accidentally caught the eye of a pair of them, and they headed toward us through the crowd. I took Ayla's hand and pulled her into the throng as we weaved through the people.

She caught me glancing back. "Are they following us?"

I nodded. Quickening our pace would arouse suspicion. I scanned the side alleys. Our best course was to continue and hope to lose them. Something crashed into my legs and a little boy flopped onto his butt and began to cry. Kristach. I stepped around him but Ayla pulled me back. She lifted him up, cooing and crooning, and sat him against her hip, wiping his tears with her free hand.

"What are you doing?" I asked, imagining that the boy's father would be a hulking brawler and none too happy with us interfering.

"You there. Turn around."

A hand clamped on to my shoulder and spun me around. My abused muscles ached in anticipation of his attack, but instead I stared at a Black and Red. The fat guard studied me but didn't relax his grip.

"You came from that burned-out street," he said. "What were you doing there?"

Ayla turned, staring at the man's feet as she continued to jostle the child, humming to him.

"He ran over there," she said, affecting a strong slum accent and patting the boy's head. "Sorry, sir."

"Do I know you?" he asked and leaned closer.

"We lives on Moor Street." I tried to step in front of her.

"Do you know a necromancer?"

"Aye, but we keeps away." I think my eyes had widened, but too late now.

"Yer scaring 'im," Ayla said, kissed the boy on his forehead, and turned away.

A cry rang out from across the street. "Oy, thief! He took me bag."

The Black and Red glared at me, snorted, and pushed his way into the crowd toward the cry. I glanced after him, spotting the man calling for help. What was Targ doing here?

"You found him, thank Belaya," a soft-spoken woman said, scanning the little boy for harm.

A young couple stood before us. Ayla handed over the boy into the woman's eager arms. The man gave me a single nod.

"I'm so glad he isn't lost," Ayla said.

She wanted to remain and talk, but I caught the husband trying to get a better look at her eyes, even though she kept her head lowered. I bid the couple good luck and pulled Ayla back into the tide of people. I wanted to be far from here.

We'd crossed Broad Street and were in sight of the river, when I asked, "Do you have siblings?"

"No. Why?"

"You handled that baby like you'd cared for little ones." I chuckled. "Maybe you're a natural parent. Baby Aylas would be too much to handle, though."

She punched my arm and her tongue poked from the corner of her mouth. "For you, maybe."

The old Ayla was definitely back. Her ordeal in the tower had brought us closer. Last night had been special and not just because of the sex.

"Are you going to move in to your father's mansion now?"

She sucked in a sharp breath.

"Sorry, I was thinking about family. I shouldn't have said that."

"It's all right." Her shoulders drooped. "I have no idea what to do with his estate and mining assets. Or the Duchy."

"Duchy?"

"Father owns about a hundred square leagues. We've a huge house butted up against the southern mountains."

I whistled. "You must be stinking rich."

Ouch, I hadn't meant that to sound harsh.

She halted and took my hands in hers. The crowd flowed around us, jostling us with their shoulders.

"You really hate the aristocracy, don't you?" she asked. "I don't care about it, either. I'd much prefer to share a home with you."

I stared into her violet eyes. They seemed to glow in the bright daylight.

"We could move in to the Duchy, my lady."

Her eyes narrowed.

"Kidding," I said. "Seriously, can you see me as an aristo?"

I'd grown up in rooms barely large enough to turn around in. What would I do with a damn mansion? Besides, I couldn't live outside the city.

"We'll sell the houses," she said. "I only need a small place. Cozy."

"As long as you're there." I tucked her loose hair back under her headscarf. "Beautiful."

"Looking like I do?"

"Dye your hair if you'd feel happier, but I love you just the way you are."

She pulled my head down and kissed me deeply.

The crowd complained about us standing in the middle of the road, so I squeezed her hand and we continued to the inn.

Lupan was nowhere to be seen, thank the Gods. I didn't need his questions. His inn had filled considerably and his taproom was teeming with guests. I bribed a serving wench with way too many coins to bring lunch to my room, and then we slipped up the stairs. At least he hadn't leased our rooms. I owed him that much. We collapsed on my bed and lay there, loosely draping our arms across the other. It felt as natural as if we'd been together for several solars. I reveled in the dry bed linens and sun streaming in the window.

"We should be planning for tomorrow." She sat up. "Without the masters we have nothing, do we?"

"We know negative energy will hurt that thing. What we don't know is what the Covenant is going to do and when."

I drummed my fingers against my lips.

"Every time that tristak elemental appears, I've been late to the party and people have died. This time we strike the moment it shows up. I'll need Kolta to protect me while I summon Caradan. Can you do something with your cling spirits?"

"I can't exactly control them."

"Do your best. If you can channel their power, that'll give me an edge, but my spells aren't going to cut it. Caradan's the secret weapon. I hope I'm right about him."

The ghost's assistance was far from guaranteed. I pondered the irony of fighting evil with evil. I could live with that if it saved the city. Choices, Phyxia had said. Most of the time I felt like I had none, but she was right—everything was a choice. Doing nothing was a choice. Fighting against all odds was a choice.

"I'm not scared anymore," Ayla said.

"I want to be glad about that, but you should be."

"I know. I meant I'm not scared that you're going to abandon me."

I planted the gentlest of kisses on her nose. One thing scared me more than the elemental—that Fortak would make good his threat and take her from me forever.

Coronation day.

White clouds raced across a green sky. Market Plaza was so packed with the citizens of Malkandrah that I couldn't figure out how they could breathe, let alone move. The horrific fires had not kept them away. I was proud of my city.

Market Plaza ran a quarter league from the imposing clock tower at the eastern end, to the forbidding edifice of the tax office at the other. A hundred wooden buildings were squeezed together around the perimeter—stores below and apartments above. It was normally home to hundreds of market carts, stalls, and tents, whose owners traded many kinds of goods or services. Today, the only structure in the plaza was an ornate raised dais dominating the center, visible from everywhere.

Black and Reds maintained a definitive gap between the jostling crowds and the stage, upon which stood rows of soldiers of the High Guard, and between them a pair of padded thrones. The aging steward sat in one, grasping his bronze-tipped cane and talking to a diminutive figure in the other. The boy was mostly hidden from me, but I recognized him as the Crown Prince.

I shifted my backside on the window ledge and scanned the crowds for Fortak. Kolta and Ayla sat on the bed in the room behind me, and I was glad Kolta had found us such a superb vantage point. He'd had the gall to compliment her on the dazzling nature of her appearance. They'd been chatting ever since. Even now I was learning from my tutor.

I yawned from little sleep. The chatter of blackwings outside the window had woken us before dawn. As tempted as we had been to stay in bed, we had dressed quickly and silently, I in the last clean robe I had. During our hurried breakfast we'd been harassed by endless revelers trying to drag us out of our chairs to dance, or hold hands in a huge line leading out into the street. Upon seeing our grim faces, they shook their heads and left us alone, breaking into impromptu songs about the sourpusses.

They had no clue of what awaited them. I pressed my trembling hands onto the table and wished I hadn't, either.

We'd walked the short distance from the inn to the plaza, washed along in the tide of people. My Guild robe spared us the worst of the shoving as people tried hard to avoid me. It hadn't upset me, just increased my protectiveness. I peered closely at individual faces. Would he survive this day? Would that couple get to enjoy a long life together? Such cute children dancing around their parents. Gods, spare them at least.

Ayla had argued with me about wearing my robe, but I refused to practice my art this day without its familiar presence. Ayla had dressed in common clothes of muted colors. I was thrilled that she no longer wore her headscarf, but she still lowered her gaze and avoided eye contact. I could accept that it could take time for her to accept that change. Deep down I hoped that, over time, the violet hue would fade. Did I wish that for her benefit or mine?

A couple of streets before the plaza, forward progress had ground to a halt, everyone pushing against the backs of the people in front. It was there that Kolta had found us, dragged us into a narrow alley and up and over the rooftops, until we had climbed down into the building in which we now sat.

Once more I scanned the endless sea of people in the plaza below. *Where are you, Fortak?* I itched to use *Perception* to warn me of the elemental's approach, but knew that Fortak would use my spell to find me. Every movement in the crowd, every turned head, put me on edge.

The roar of singing, laughing, and music seemed to fill the entire city. Streamers tumbled from windows, zinging between banners and flags. Kites leaned in the stiff wind overhead, pulling at their taut ties. A huge banner strung beneath the adjacent window bore images of the city's favorite flower, the feresens. Despite the wind, the air was heavy with its sweet perfume. Very few families had turned out without a bouquet, and they were draped from every window ledge and archway.

The whole scene lifted my spirits. We would win today. Malkandrah had always been a resilient city. It took more than a traitorous Covenant to destroy what had stood for millennia. My mother's blood flowed in my veins. I was willing to spill every drop of it to save these people.

The steward moved to the edge of the dais.

"Citizens of our eternal city."

His voice boomed, reverberating off buildings. A myriad of conversations decayed into shushing noises and then near silence, just stifled coughs and the shuffling of feet as people jostled to see. I scanned the crowd, my breath catching every time someone fidgeted. I saw an outbreak of fire or jet of steam in every movement.

"Today we have gathered for a monumental occasion. Today our beloved Crown Prince becomes our new King."

He flung his arms into the air and the crowd went wild, clapping and cheering.

Ayla squeezed beside me at the open window and wrapped her arm around my waist. Kolta placed a hand on my shoulder.

The steward droned on about the virtues of our young prince, about how he had been nurtured and groomed from birth to assume the lofty title of absolute ruler of our small kingdom. The crowd hung on his every word, but my gaze drifted from window to window in the buildings opposite. Perhaps Fortak and his cronies had sought a high vantage point as we had, but all I saw were normal folk hanging out, three to a window, waving flags on sticks to punctuate the steward's speech.

"I can't bear the wait," Ayla said. "I want this over with."

I nodded and loosened my tight grip on the window frame. Any moment now. Even the air had stilled, expectant. Fleeing would be impossible in the ocean of people. It would be a slaughter. I wanted to cry out, order everyone to leave, to go home, but the resulting stampede would be as lethal.

I thought desperately of anything I could do if I spotted Fortak before the elemental, but came up with nothing. I'd failed to convince Semplis. Fortak probably had every master on his side now, and the entire force of Black and Reds. I should have recruited my own army. My stomach lurched. I'd been a fool to go toe to toe with the Prime Guildmaster himself. Had I damned the city with my naïveté? My only hope was to force him to make a mistake, stall the elemental until Caradan showed up.

A dark shape drew my attention to the Mercantile Guild building across the plaza. There, in a third-floor window, I spotted a Guild robe. My heart raced. The man leaned out. Semplis. If only I knew who was with him, but the room was in shadow.

"What?" Ayla murmured. "I know when you're thinking—you rub your nose."

I lowered my hand and showed her and Kolta what I'd seen.

"He may yet come around, my boy. You gave him plenty to mull over."

Ayla cupped my head and kissed me. "For luck."

She hesitated and then kissed Kolta full on the lips. His eyes bugged out and he grinned.

I smoothed her bangs behind her ears and my hand lingered on her cheek.

No matter what you believe, always believe in her.

I blinked. What had Phyxia meant by that? Of course I believed in her.

Kolta leaned between us and out the window.

"Smoke."

 TWENTY-FOUR

Ayla's smile drooped. My heart skipped. All three of us squeezed into the window frame.

Wisps of smoke drifted above the tax office, and then a larger cloud billowed across the rooftops opposite us, like a sea fog rolling ashore.

"There's fire in the next street over." Kolta pointed to the flickering orange reflections in the windows of a side street.

A few individuals in the crowd below gesticulated wildly at the smoke above them. Boots shuffled. A towering wall of blackness gathered behind the clock tower. Heads turned. As more and more cries alerted the crowd, the singing and music faltered to a strangled stop. Confusion rippled across the plaza. Flags and bouquets slipped from hands to become trampled underfoot. Freed kites spiraled up and away from the advancing menace. The smoke gobbled up Solas, plunging us into shade. I craned my neck out of the window. More thick smoke flowed against the prevailing wind over our own building.

"Fortak means to surround the plaza," I said.

The crowd came alive like a lumbering beast. People surged toward every exit from the plaza, pushing, shoving, knocking each other to the ground. Shouts turned to screams. With every punch and kick, the smoke drew closer like a tightening noose. Arms and ropes were dangled from second-floor windows, and fights broke out in an effort to climb free of the seething melee. A wall of fire erupted in an adjacent street, and flames reached for the sky. The acrid stench of burning was all too familiar.

"There," Ayla said.

Fortak hurried down the steps of the tax office, his robe swirling about him. Master Begara scampered at his heels, while the Wynarian and the battle-scarred general followed, their armor and weapons clearly visible. No sign of Phyxia. Good. I didn't want to see her at Fortak's side any longer. A contingent of Black and Reds met them at the bottom of the steps, and preceded them into the crowd, pushing citizens aside with shields and drawn swords. Their destination was obvious.

On the stage, the royal soldiers shuffled into a tight circle surrounding the steward and Crown Prince. They stood stalwart as crowds surged through the plaza.

"I have to get down there." I swung my legs out the window.

Ayla grabbed my arm. "Two stories? You'll break your neck."

Blazing rooftops formed a ring of fire that flickered orange and red against the smoke. How much closer would Fortak bring the elemental? *For Lak's sake, man, play the hero card and end this thing. Take your glory. Stop before the slaughter.*

A banner fluttered before my face, tied to a railing on the next window over. I jerked free of Ayla's grasp and leaped for it. She cried out. The crude material burned my hands as I rode it down. It ripped and I plummeted, crashing atop a pair of men's shoulders before tumbling to the ground at their feet. Boots kicked me in the legs and side. I scrambled against the wall and stood.

People jostled and elbowed, trying to squirm through the chaos, dragging loved ones behind them. Parents carried children on their shoulders, the eldest of which swung sticks indiscriminately at passing heads. Neighbor fighting neighbor.

An elderly woman crawled toward me, her clothes torn and speckled with blood. I dragged her to the safety of the wall beside me. She sobbed quietly but her eyes were fixed on the crowd, not her cuts and scratches.

How could my city devolve so fast?

The smoke descended like a blanket, thankfully showing no evidence—yet—of the brooding intelligence I'd witnessed before. Thank Belaya! That was a level of insanity that would turn the plaza into a bloodbath.

I sucked in a deep breath, took aim on the stage, and plunged into the mob. If I could alert the steward of Fortak's intentions, I might be able to stop this disaster without summoning Caradan. I still didn't trust him.

I'd hoped that sight of my Guild robe would part the crowd. No one noticed, so I resorted to shoving with the rest of them. Elbows thumped me and I took a vicious blow to the face. Warm blood oozed from my nostrils. I jumped and strained to peer over the seething tide of people as they surged this way and that, looking for an escape. Semplis was no longer at the window, or had I become turned around?

Fire raced through every wooden building on the plaza perimeter, its dull roar competing with the screaming and wailing. I spun. It was all around me. I was trapped, as I had been in the barrow of the soul wraith. My heart thumped, and I fought the urge to join the fleeing masses. In an effort to escape their burning homes, people jumped or were pushed from windows. At the sound of splintering timber, I whirled to see an entire building tilt and slide into the plaza. Dozens of families huddled and clutched one another until the rubble crushed out their life. Dust billowed outward, mixing with the smoke. None of my nightmares had prepared me for such wholesale slaughter. It was all happening too fast.

Heat blistered my back. Fire erupted in the building I had just left. The roof sagged and ruptured. Tiles and broken rafters crashed down into the top floor, which pancaked into the one below. A lump caught in my throat.

Ayla! Why had I left her? What had I done?

I pushed and shouldered my way back to find her, but made no headway. The crowd dragged me further into the plaza. I should have stayed with her. I had to trust that Kolta had saved her, done the job I had failed to do. Reluctantly, I turned once more toward the central stage. I gritted my teeth until they ached. It was time to stop this madness. I had to get to the steward before Fortak.

Two men fell at my feet and I leaped their bodies into an open space. A sword stabbed inches from my torso, thrust by a heavyset man dressed in black leather adorned with red trim. I leaped aside, sweat stinging my eyes. By fortune or otherwise, I'd stumbled upon Fortak's armed guard.

Others retreated before their slashing blades and bludgeoning shields. They gave no warning and no mercy. A dozen bodies lay in their wake, writhing and clutching at grievous wounds. Fortak came into view, his disdainful gaze sweeping the crowd until it settled upon me.

"Bring that one," he said.

I heaved against the flow of the horde, which surged toward the stage as if the platoon of soldiers could hold back the raging inferno. The crash of shields against bodies gained on me.

"You in the black. Halt!"

Not a chance. People turned to stare, perhaps noticing my robe for the first time. They inched away, making room for the Black and Reds at my heels.

Someone yanked me sideways. A kick swept me off my feet and I toppled to the cobbles. Pain lanced up my left side. Bleak outcomes flashed through my mind: trampled to death; stabbed and left to bleed out; or tortured and certain death at the hands of Fortak.

None of them appealed to me, so I grabbed hold of the nearest leg to haul myself up, my other hand reaching for the knife in my boot.

"Stay down, you bloody fool," Kolta said, and stamped on

my arm. Did he have to do that so damned hard?

I almost failed to recognize him without his Guild robe and a hat pulled over his eyes. He rolled a corpse on top of me. The stench of body odor made me gag but I lay still. Not the first time I'd been buried with the dead.

"Where is he?" a growling voice asked.

"Who are you looking for, Sergeant?" Kolta asked.

"A criminal in a black robe. Necromancer."

"He ran that way. Hurry, he had a knife."

I held my breath, resisting the urge to shove the sweaty, urine-soaked body aside. I listened to the cacophony of coughs and screams, and tensed at every crushing blow as people trampled the corpse on top of me. I was ready to retch when Kolta heaved me free and yanked me to my feet.

"Where's Ayla?" I scanned the crowd.

"The whole place is alight," he said. "I think I see a way out."

"We're not here to escape. Where is she?"

"Over here. There's no time, my boy. We can't save all these people. It's over."

"It hasn't even started yet. Take me to her."

I saw the terror in the people's eyes, their exhaustion at watching loved ones trampled underfoot. They were on the verge of despair, ambling erratically, gawking at the building-high flames bearing down on them. The adamantine fortitude of my great city had cracked. These were the citizens I'd taken under my wing. My heart sank, but I was still determined to save them.

The stage was only forty feet away. The royal soldiers had descended to ground level and formed a barrier around it, using their tall shields to deflect the crowd. A handful remained on the stage above, gathered tight around the Crown Prince. They glanced around nervously but their resolve was plain. The steward leaned on his cane, shouting to someone below. Between the weaving and bobbing heads I caught glimpses of Fortak below him.

He'd beaten me to it. Damn the man.

A figure charged out of the smoke in my peripheral vision. Before I could react, arms snaked around me. The scent of lavender momentarily masked the stench of smoke and burned flesh. Ayla squeezed me so tight that I grunted, black and blue from my struggles. She pulled back but her hand slipped into mine and gripped it tight. Thank the Gods she was safe. I owed Kolta for saving us both.

A gust of stifling-hot air whooshed through the plaza, swirling the smoke upward in vortices and spirals, lifting the haze. Only now could I witness the true devastation of the inferno. Flames tore hungrily at every building surrounding the plaza and in the adjacent streets. The scene resembled a painting of The Deep. A thunderous roar rolled overhead like the chariots of the Gods. I didn't need *Perception* to sense the primeval power of the elemental as it boiled in the sky, surveying its prey like a raptor did mice.

Bathed in a demonic orange glow, Fortak argued with the steward that he alone could save the city. How great a reward would his megalomania demand? He'd dealt himself a strong hand. Time to improve my own. Time to make him pay.

"Let's steal his bargaining chits," I said.

Kolta and Ayla glanced at me quizzically.

"We came here to fight," I said, and he nodded.

Kolta and I stood back to back with Ayla sandwiched between us.

I wanted Caradan to come to our aid willingly. *Summoning* was an expensive spell.

Fulfill your promise, Caradan. This is no time to sit on the battle's flank waiting for a tactical advantage. We have no advantage, only the guiding hands of justice and righteousness. Kristach. I'd spent too long in the company of priests! Are you waiting for me to start, is that it, Caradan? So be it. I'm not afraid.

It was second nature now to suck enormous power from my core. It no longer burned me. Focused power raced up my arms and out my fingers, crackling loudly as I unleashed a massive *Dispel*. Purple flashed across the closest building, dousing the flames. I sustained the spell, sweeping it the length of the plaza.

Shouts and cheers competed against screams of terror. *Yes, let them see hope.* People hopped up and down, gesturing toward the smoldering ruins no longer alight. Those closest to me backed away. Out of respect or fear? Either worked for me right then.

Rattling armor drew my attention back to the stage. The royal party was on the move, heading for the stairs. Inside the protective ring of soldiers, the steward retained a disrespectful grip on the Crown Prince's arm.

"A city of fools, led by fools," Fortak called after them.

Looks like his negotiations have failed.

He stamped his foot like a child and raised his hands to the sky. Lightning crackled through the firestorm, and a tornado of superheated gas dropped on top of the fleeing dignitaries. The soldiers of the High Guard cowered beneath their shields.

"Now it's started," I mumbled.

Witnessing the primordial chaos overhead sharpened my resolve. I was so sick of this elemental. I would destroy it or die trying.

Master Begara stumbled forward to deflect Fortak's arm. A sharp burst of purple shot from Begara's hands, ripping the tornado to shreds. Fortak spun and backhanded Begara, flinging him to the ground.

"Help that man," I said. "He's trying to save us."

I straightened my shoulders with newfound pride that my Guild had not entirely deserted me.

Though I'd directed my plea to the mob, Kolta rushed forward. I covered him by sending a twin blast of *Death's Spark* into the heart of the elemental. The lightning from my spell stabbed and flickered through the boiling clouds. The pitch of the creature's roar rose to a screech.

Fortak's narrowed gaze sought me out through the throng of fleeing people. Barely twenty feet of empty space separated us. His fingers sparked with readied magic as he extended one arm in my direction.

"Maldren, watch out," Ayla screamed.

I stared into Fortak's cold eyes and the entire plaza faded into the background. The world shrunk to only us. I understood the ethical dilemma that betrayed itself in his face. I had no protection against his spells. A single thought and I was dead, and his soul damned for eternity. If it wasn't already. I shivered. Ayla tugged at me. I resisted.

His expression softened and his arm drooped. He still paid obedience to Guild law. He turned away and barked at his men to intercept Kolta.

My tiny victory was short-lived. Repeated bursts of power radiated from Fortak's body, absorbed greedily by the elemental. The ground shook under the force of his magic. I stumbled. The extent of the man's power was insane.

The dark, gutted remnants of buildings erupted into flames once more. Timber frames buckled and cascaded into the scattering crowd, littering the plaza with bricks and burning timber. The faces of the clock tower shattered into a million shards, and fire erupted inside.

A motion to my left seized my attention. The Wynarian stepped from the crowd just six feet away, a vicious blade in each hand. He crouched like a predator about to pounce. He said nothing but his expression spoke of murder.

I gasped and froze.

Two men tackled him from behind. He ducked out of their grasp, pivoted on one foot, and drove a blade into each of their hearts. Blood sprayed in all directions. People edged away, wobbling with conflicting urges to flee or stay and watch like ghouls.

Move, Maldren, move!

A snarl deformed the Wynarian's thick lips. He closed the gap between us in a single stride, and I had no time to reach my knife.

It couldn't end like this, not at the blade of an assassin. I sidestepped to shield Ayla, pushing her behind me. My breath stuck in my throat, my stomach lurched, and I fought to picture her face, to hold it in my mind's eye. We'd had so little time together.

Loss stabbed my heart. I waited for the two blades to do the same.

 TWENTY-FIVE

A metal pipe smashed into the Wynarian assassin's shoulder, making him stumble. I shuddered at the horrific crunching of bones. His arm flopped limply to his side and the knife fell from his hand. I stared in disbelief as Targ hefted the pipe for another attack, but the Wynarian was faster. Without turning, he thrust backward and pierced his remaining blade right through Targ's throat.

"Damn it, no!" I leaped forward.

Targ gurgled, coughing up a fountain of blood before crumpling to his knees. The Wynarian tugged at his blade, which had lodged in Targ's spine. *You bastard!* I grabbed the assassin and yanked his dislocated arm. He cried out, let go of the knife in Targ's throat, and dived for the one he had dropped, barging me aside.

I tumbled next to Targ. His eyes bulged while blood spurted from his throat with every strangled, desperate breath. My hands shook. *What do I do?* One of his trembling hands reached up, gripped the knife stuck in his own neck, and wrenched it free. Hot blood gushed over me. I jerked my head aside and hated myself for flinching. He uttered a drawn-out wheeze and toppled over, dead. Something slippery lay in my hand—he had placed the knife there.

The crowd's movement gave warning of the assassin's next attack. I rolled aside and he pounced into the empty space I had occupied, grunting as he jarred his arm. He swung wildly at me. I dodged him, climbed onto his back, and jammed his knife up to its hilt between his shoulder blades. Ugh, it felt like cutting a steak. I hadn't expected that. He flopped to the ground and moaned, his limbs twitching uncontrollably.

I'd knifed a man in the back. I'd killed a living person. My stomach seized control and I puked all over him, retching and coughing. After making the mistake of looking at the blood-drenched Targ, I threw up again.

Another plume of fire erupted from the burning sky, aimed directly for the royal party. The steward knocked the Crown Prince to the ground and threw his body on top. The fiery lick of the elemental ignited several soldiers into human candles. They screamed and flailed before collapsing to the ground.

"Ayla," I yelled, spinning about, peering into the thick smoke drifting across the plaza.

To my right, another building caved in, four floors pancaking atop each other. It tilted precariously for a long moment before crashing down, burying a couple dozen people. Their cries ended abruptly, replaced by an ominous keening. Hordes of pale spirits spiraled up from the rubble toward the beast above.

Help us. Save us.

My eyes teared. Probably from the soot.

Hands grabbed me from behind. I spun and lashed out. My fist crashed into Ayla's cheek, knocking her down atop a smoldering corpse.

"I'm sorry." I sank beside her and cradled her head. "Stop creeping up on me like that."

She sat up, nursing her inflamed cheek. Ash dappled her hair. Her wide, violet eyes stared past me.

The devastation had removed all traces of Market Plaza, leveling it and the surrounding streets to heaps of smoking rubble. Ink-black tendrils of smoke prowled the wasteland, weaving left and right, hugging the ground, splitting and hunting survivors. Above, the elemental's roar changed pitch defiantly.

Fortak had gone too far. Hadn't he made his point? *Belaya, is it your will that Lak claim so many innocents this day?*

Ayla and I stood. She gripped my hand but I shook mine free and turned my attention to the elemental. I was so done with this thing.

I drew power from my core and launched *Dispel* after *Dispel* into the creature. Purple flares flickered across the sky. I gritted my teeth, dug deep, and sent the biggest *Deathwall* I could muster to rip a hole in the elemental's underside. We cried out in unison, it in rage and I at the magic melting my veins. More magic than my body could handle. I needed to rest.

Caradan! Have I not earned your respect yet? I can't keep this up. You've made me suffer by waiting, now show yourself.

I stumbled and Ayla caught me.

"Stop it. You're killing yourself." Her sweaty hands touched the blisters bubbling on my arms.

I doubled over, panting. Kolta had dragged Master Begara to safety. The crowd had thinned and I caught sight of Fortak again, less than fifty feet away. He stooped low, clutching his stomach. With his withered, strained face he looked as bad as I felt. I gave a grim laugh.

A petite figure in an emerald-green cloak stepped forward to help him.

"Phyxia!"

I hadn't meant to call her name.

She turned. Her ears stood erect from her silver hair, twitching erratically. Orange and yellow flecks whirled in her eyes. I'd expected anger or at least surprise, but her face sagged with sadness. What did that mean?

Fortak dropped to his knees. Though he hung his head, his hands stretched high, sparking and glowing with magic. Phyxia remained standing, and when she looked skyward I swore that the elemental shied away from her. I perceived an invisible, but incredible mesh of power stretching from her petite body up and around the creature. It resembled a magical net.

Scattered groups of survivors fled from the smoke that darted after them, overrunning the stragglers and coiling tightly around their bodies. I'd dared to hope it wouldn't come to this. The victims spasmed and turned on each other, snatching up rubble or scratching with fingernails. Fireballs rained down, exploding on impact and splashing fire across a wide area. A never-ending rain of ash washed out the whole macabre scene.

"Summon Caradan," Ayla said. "Before it's too late."

Kolta appeared beside us and I shivered with an intense cold. Our breath froze in the air. I'd forgotten to raise my own *Cleansing Shield*. Stupid. I was letting my obsession blind my sensibilities.

"Caradan and I are going to end this," I said. "Neither of you have to stay."

They remained at my side. My heart thumped and I felt renewed. I was tired of working alone. I needed help.

"Hold it off," I said to Kolta.

He nodded grimly and his face scrunched with intense concentration. I felt the pulse of power within him.

Since my legs insisted on trembling, I knelt on the ground. The irony of Fortak and I dueling from such a position hadn't escaped me.

I pulled every last flicker of energy from my core, stretching inside until my gut ached, then reached some more. Satisfied with the intensity of my *Summoning* spell, I fought to ignore the screaming around me, the wails of pain, the ragged panting of our breaths.

My spell faltered. *Kristach!* Why had I left it so late? Everything hinged on this spell. I should have cast it straight away. I shook my head. *Concentrate, damn it!*

I renewed my efforts. Thunderous pain trampled through my skull. My limbs turned to jelly. I fought to breathe.

"Stop," Ayla yelled. "Maldren, please. You can't take any more."

I couldn't stop. Not now.

Something incorporeal touched my legs. Cling spirits

poured from the ground, enveloping Ayla, cocooning her body. Pulsing blue threads crawled over me and my skin tingled. I felt the familiar rush of cool power filling my gut.

Kolta dropped beside me, but the luminescent tendrils avoided him. "What in Lak's name is she doing?"

Every corpse within a hundred-foot radius glowed, brighter and brighter until trickles of energy rushed out of them, arrowing across the ground to merge with her blinding, pulsating web.

A whooshing sound drowned out everything. A fireball the size of a tenement building ejected from the elemental, aimed right at us. Ayla transformed into a beacon of blinding white light. Its blaze moved outward from her, enveloping Kolta and me, crushing our shields. My every nerve ending jangled with the raw power.

Lak and all his demons!

The fireball impacted her white halo, splashing flames in all directions and turning the air to steam. Our bodies went from shivering to sweating, and we cowered under the might of a primeval force that would have incinerated us.

"Finish the *Summoning*," Ayla said.

"How are you doing that?" Fortak asked.

He got to his feet and shambled awkwardly toward us, leaving Phyxia staring after him.

"The last of you died decades ago." He stabbed a finger at Ayla, squinting against her blazing light. "Not you. That's impossible."

What was he talking about? What did he know about the cling spirits?

"Fool of a child," he said to me. "You can't control this...abomination of a woman. Their line was destroyed."

He straightened and the air quivered under the might of his magic. I stiffened. I'd thought he was spent.

"Enough from you," Ayla said.

Though her blazing light dimmed, she seemed to grow in stature. Her hair fluttered in the breeze like blue flames. Her robe of luminescent threads pulsed angrily. The entire plaza glowed blue and green, dulling the color of the fires. Lines of energy zipped across the ground toward her from the distant buildings and from the piles of rubble. Street lantern poles bent effortlessly toward her, melting, radiating power that she harvested.

Kolta cried in pain. I fell beside him, clutching my head. How did she command such power?

Then I understood what Fortak had already.

Ayla was an Elik Magi.

My mind raced, desperate to understand the reality of that.

Behind Fortak, Phyxia stumbled. Her ears were bent over, her fists clenched. I remembered her prediction. Fortak had lost control of the elemental and even Phyxia was struggling with it. The strands of her magical net was unraveling. My gaze flicked between her and the flaming blue torch that was Ayla. Both women weaved tremendous power, and in that moment I felt insignificant. I wondered fleetingly if Fortak did too. Despite Ayla's power flooding through me, I realized that our fate was bound to Phyxia's now. Why had she broken her immortal oath not to intervene? Where did her loyalties lie now? If the elemental wrestled free of her tenuous grip then the city was doomed.

Phyxia knelt, draped in ash, head doubled over. I'd never seen her like this, disheveled and beaten down. Despite everything, I pitied her.

Fortak groaned, clapped his hands, and yellow magic oozed from every pore, coating him in a sickly sheen. He spun a single finger in the air and the oily surface transformed into a garish fog that whirled around him. The faster his finger moved, the quicker it whipped about and spread outward like a hurricane.

I relived my nightmare. Visions of Guild fighting Elik Magi played in my head.

"Stop this madness, Fortak. This isn't some age-old battle. Ayla isn't the Guild's enemy."

His spell moved through me and the hairs on my skin stood erect. Static crackled across my scalp. I had expected a blast of air but its resemblance to a storm was purely visual.

The instant the yellow fog touched Ayla, it neutralized her web of power. Her light extinguished and she crumpled to the ground. I tried to go to her but my weary legs gave way.

"What do you know, boy?" Fortak asked. "You always lacked the imagination to become a true master."

"No, you kept me down because I threatened your petty reign of tyranny."

He laughed, which turned into a bout of coughing. His maelstrom spread across the plaza, blighting everything yellow like a fungus.

"You're no threat to anything except yourself," he said.

"Speaking of threats, you're losing control of yours." I pointed to the elemental expanding outward into the city. "But then you never did have control. Only she did."

I glanced at Phyxia and saw a glimmer of hope—a twitch of her ears, the way the flecks in her eyes changed from blue to green, a tiny rise in one corner of her mouth.

"I have full control." Blood splattered his lips and chin and he coughed into a handkerchief.

He waved his hands and the maelstrom picked up speed. The sound of crashing buildings and wailing people dulled to a hiss. Colors faded to gray. Everything around me shimmered and turned hazy. A thick mist formed out of the very air itself.

Phyxia stared directly at me. "All that remains are your choices."

What did that mean? Life is full of choices.

"Let go of what cannot be."

Kristach! This is no time for cryptic mumbo-jumbo, woman.

"I don't understand," I said.

The mist enveloped me.

At first, I thought myself alone in the void. A diffuse light emanated from everywhere at once, and slowly the gray shroud rolled back. Hazy forms wavered in and out of view. Spirits lurked, whimpering and agitated, but keeping their distance. Their hair had been burned to the roots. Blisters speckled their skin, which peeled and flaked away as they shambled back and forth.

Ghostlike structures materialized—crumbling buildings with gaping maws for windows and doors. The walls oozed a viscous, gray fluid, and they throbbed in and out as if sobbing. The decapitated stump of the clock tower cowered beneath a seething, bubbling overcast. Even in monochrome, I recognized the amorphous elemental smothering the plaza.

My second time in The Gray.

As the mists and spirits retreated, I realized I was not alone. Kolta limped to my side, his bug eyes darting back and forth. We clung to each other. Where was Ayla?

At the sound of a half laugh, half cough, I whirled about. Fortak stood thirty feet away, his legs apart and back straight, the strongest I had seen him since the battle for the plaza began.

The spirits retreated further, revealing Phyxia several steps behind him. She was on her knees, head in her hands. Her ears spasmed repeatedly and her chest heaved with her labored breathing. She resembled a beaten dog cringing before its master. Her magic net hung overhead, crumpled and torn, barely holding the bloated elemental.

I hung my head. I'd doubted her intentions. She never had been my enemy.

"Ayla?" My voice sounded flat and dead.

"Her kind has no power in this place," Fortak said. "I have the upper hand once more."

Of course. That was why he'd brought us here. But I still didn't understand. Caradan wasn't the Elik Magi, his wife was. Had he woven a curse upon Ayla in the tower, or simply awoken her true nature? I shook my head. It was too much to piece together. Where was he, anyway? It was time he made an appearance and owned up to his part of this mess.

"Looking for this?" Fortak dispelled the mist swimming around his legs.

Pale spirits encircled Ayla where she lay at his feet. Their long dresses and hair billowed in an unfelt breeze and their hands pawed at the air, seemingly unable to reach her. One of them turned and hissed. Worms devoured its face until a fleshless, cackling skull remained.

I flinched, then gritted my teeth and started toward Ayla.

Fortak raised his hand. "Don't. I need only release the protection circle..."

The lochtars keened loudly and their talons inched toward Ayla.

I halted. Was this what Phyxia meant by letting go? I'd never let go of Ayla.

A standoff. Only the five of us, segregated from the havoc and destruction still being wrought by the elemental in the real world.

"What happened to your oath to protect the city?" I asked. "*'Bring no harm to the living.'* Are your teachings of no consequence now?" I growled. "Leave her alone. Punish me."

He laughed. "Such misguided chivalry. Her father double-crossed me. She will not do likewise."

"The Duke wasn't a coward like you. He didn't hold hostages. Let her go. Your feud is with me. You've always hated me, as you despised my mother. She was the better necromancer. You fear me because I will become as powerful as her."

"Don't taunt him," Kolta said.

I blew out my anger and glanced at Ayla. For such a strong-willed woman to cower before him was totally unacceptable to me. I had to free her.

Fortak watched me warily. He *was* afraid of me, and that was the only thing keeping my precious Ayla alive.

Ghostly husks of buildings stretched as far as I could see, distorted, perverted versions of the ones in the real world. How much of the city's heart had the creature torn out? How much burned while I stood here uselessly? I molded a ball of energy, determined to strike back.

"Give me an excuse to harm the girl," Fortak said. "Make that foolish act and watch her suffer because of it. Because of you."

Kolta laid a hand on my arm and squeezed. My eyes

narrowed, challenging my mentor, but I let my hand drop.

With a satisfied sneer, Fortak turned and dragged Phyxia to her feet.

"Release the elemental," he told her. "Let this pathetic, simpering city burn to the ground. Unbind it, woman."

Phyxia met his wild gaze with calm and dignity, and then shook her head once.

"You should have heeded my warning. I bound it because you were incapable."

I remembered her words to me in her home:

I'm sorry, sishka. I can only help those who cannot help themselves.

"Do as I command," he said, "or witness the girl ripped apart. Then your pet, the boy, dies next. Do you want their blood on your hands?"

"It stays bound."

I whispered in Kolta's ear. "If you distract him, I can save Ayla. We can do this. We can end this."

He shook his head. "No, my boy. Fortak is master of The Gray. Always has been. In this place his power is amplified. For every lochtar you kill, three more will replace it. Follow your plan."

My gaze flicked between him, Fortak, and Ayla cringing among the hissing, clawing lochtars.

I'd underestimated Fortak. He had no intention of letting her live. Why hadn't he killed both of us already?

Then it made sense. He was stalling. Despite Phyxia's hold on the elemental, gobbets of fire still rained down into our city. Phyxia sagged in his grasp. He was waiting for her to fail, for the elemental to break free.

Kolta was right. Knee-jerk reactions weren't getting me anywhere except into deeper trouble. Time to bring in my secret weapon.

I planted my feet firmly and restarted the long and complex *Summoning* spell.

Fortak snorted. "So it's Caradan you seek? You've no chance of influencing that one."

Not so much a secret then. I had no doubt he could sense

and identify every shred of magic within sight, but it would take more than that to distract me.

He began his own spell. The mists shimmered. Insubstantial phantoms emerged from the gray haze, uttering guttural, rasping noises as if fighting for breath. Most had throats ripped out or skulls caved in, while others had holes torn through their torsos, their flesh and muscle hanging loose, revealing broken rib cages or punctured ghost organs. Their eyes pulsed a lurid green.

Revenants.

I flinched and ducked as they fell upon us, flitting in tight loops around Kolta and me. Where they touched me, my already-blistered skin broke out in lesions that oozed a pus. The stench of decay filled my nostrils. My spell faltered. Damn. Fortak had found the right distraction.

Together, Kolta and I whipped up a *Repulsion*. The loathsome creatures bounced off the energy field, repeatedly charging and clawing. It wouldn't hold them for long.

"This is my domain," Fortak said. "If you're so determined to die before the girl, so be it, but your death won't spare her."

Insanity had finally taken him. He seemed more intent on punishing Ayla and me than carrying out the Covenant's plan. His plan.

My stomach turned. *To The Deep with the Guild oath!* I faced him standing tall, and my veins burned with power.

Kolta slapped me hard, jerking my head back.

"That's what he wants you to do," he said, his face an inch from mine. "Cast that bloody *Summoning*, or I will. Stay focused, Maldren. Can't you see what he's doing?"

"Oh, Kolta," Fortak said. "Always the voice of reason. Rationalize this."

He waved a hand and hundreds of revenants surged against our *Repulsion*. We were done for.

TWENTY-SIX

Fortak chuckled in a gravelly voice as the revenants careened against our *Repulsion*, desperate to rip us apart.

"Resourceful," he said. "But it would be more entertaining if you fought each other too."

The gray mists darkened and clumped into thick, black tendrils that spread out along the ground and meandered like snakes toward us.

"Master." I reached for Kolta. "The smoke..."

"I know, I know. Finish the *Summoning*." He zapped *Dispel* after *Dispel* against the horde of revenants.

Our shield was already buckling. A revenant bit Kolta's leg and he stumbled. Boils bubbled beneath his skin, spreading to his foot. His clenched jaw and grimace said it all.

How could I abandon him for the sake of the spell? What use had Caradan been? Kolta had stood by my side while none in the Guild had. I stepped closer and thrust my shoulder under his armpit. He returned a weak smile. I couldn't hold the *Repulsion* anymore. The smoke poured in through invisible cracks in our magic. I cast a *Cleansing Shield* tight about us.

Damn Fortak! He had all the cards, driving us on the defensive. There had to be a way to fight back.

"That isn't smoke from the elemental," a voice, crisp and clear, said across the guttural cries of the revenants.

Kolta and I spun around. I had to blink to believe my own eyes, certain this was more of Fortak's treachery.

Masters Semplis and Wampor strode out of the smoke, ushering black wraiths before them. At their signal, the dark creatures ripped into the revenants, tearing them into gobbets of tissue that piled high on the ground.

Semplis acknowledged me with a nod. I'd never been so pleased to see him.

"Neither it nor its smoke can exist in The Gray. It's a trick. We have little time. Do what you have to do."

I had the backup of three masters. Anything was possible. Tension fled my body like a cast spell. My gaze drifted toward Ayla but Kolta stood pointedly in the way. His softened eyes met mine. He was proud of me. I felt strong.

I nodded. No more distractions. I restarted the *Summoning*, tuning out the ruckus of the spirits battling around us.

"Don't be a fool," Fortak said. "I warned you that I'd take from you everyone you love."

He gestured with one hand and the lochtars surged upon Ayla, screeching with delight. I lost sight of her beneath the tangle of spirit limbs, flowing dresses and billowing hair.

She screamed and screamed and wouldn't stop.

The thumping, rapid pace of my pulse threatened to tear me apart. My stomach seized and my vision blurred, filled with tears. I wanted to run to her but I'd committed myself to the spell. This was my last chance to save the city. My fists clenched and I punched the air. *Hold on, Ayla, just hold on.* If only she could summon the cling spirits, but Fortak had taken away her only protection by bringing us here.

"Unbind my elemental," Fortak screamed at Phyxia. "You can save them all. Submit to my will and they can live. Damn it, woman."

He broke down in a fit of coughing.

Ayla's endless shrieking ripped a hole in my heart. I fell to the ground, oblivious of the masters, wraiths, and revenants around me. Why weren't they helping? *Send the wraiths against the lochtars.*

Save Ayla! I can't lose her. Not now.

Caradan was the key. I was the key.

I uttered the final words of the *Summoning* ritual. Binding magic tugged at my life force. A brooding menace hung at the end of that bond, intent on devouring me.

You promised the end of my curse. Caradan's words echoed loud in my mind.

Aid us, I thought back. *If my promise proves false I submit to your wrath. But first you serve me.*

Thunder boomed in my head. *I serve no mortal.*

A necromancer can never show weakness. I pinched the bond, threatening to sever it.

Serve me now or Fortak wins and you are damned for eternity.

No answer.

I looked around me. Kolta and the others huddled inside a protective ring of wraiths that tore and shredded endless waves of revenants pouring out of the mist. Phyxia stood beside Fortak, doubled over, her ears crumpled back against her disheveled silver hair. Arms folded, his eyes sparkled as he watched every jab, every strike of the lochtars against Ayla's spasming body.

"Ayla. I'm coming. Hold on."

I stumbled toward her, sucking magic from my core and flinging it carelessly at the lochtars—raw power, no cohesive spell, over and over. Still, she screamed.

"Leave her alone. Don't do this. Phyxia, please help."

She met my gaze but did nothing. Damn her and her kind.

One of the lochtars swam toward me. *Yes, take me, not Ayla.* Its petite but arthritic hand slid effortlessly into my chest, tightening around my organs. It was as if a thousand pins pierced my heart. It beat erratically and then stopped. My legs buckled. I couldn't breathe, but I vowed not to die, not while Ayla needed me. I cast *Dispel* right into the lochtar's face and she exploded into a cloud of gray particles.

I fell prone, gasping for air. My heart restarted with a

violent shock.

Twenty feet separated me from Ayla. I crawled toward her. Her body arched and flailed as the lochtars swarmed over her. Her screams had turned to an inhuman wail.

"Look at her," Fortak said. "Daughter of a Duke? All I see is a traitorous scum getting what she deserves."

I tried to throw more magic at the lochtars, but only a dull ache remained in my gut. I crawled with no idea what I could do if I reached her. I just didn't want her to die alone. "Hold on," I wanted to tell her, but no words came out.

"Yolanda!" Caradan yelled.

A seething cloud, black as the darkest crypt, materialized between Fortak and me. It expanded from nothing, coalescing into a vague human form forty feet tall, towering above us all.

"What have they done to you?"

It stamped one foot and a blast wave raced outward, pushing back the gray mist for a hundred feet in all directions. Its impact obliterated every lochtar, revenant, and wraith, grinding them into ash that fell like snow. Ayla slumped to the ground, unmoving. The total silence was unnerving.

Fortak stumbled backward, mouth agape. His dilated pupils and hoarse, raspy breathing betrayed him. If I lost everything now it would have almost been worth it to see his disbelief.

"How did you do this? I…"

I scrambled to my feet and smoothed my Guild robe, brushing off the ash. "You're finished Prime Guildmaster."

Freed from the revenants, Semplis and Wampor sprinted forward, hurling spells against Caradan. Their magic fizzled against his hazy, undulating form.

"No," I said, reaching for them, trying to swat away their raised arms. "It was he that I summoned. He fights with us."

I hoped that was still the case.

"I am the greatest Prime Guildmaster that ever lived," Caradan said. "How dare you."

He stamped his foot once more and a second wall of energy pulsed through me, almost sweeping me off my feet. Energy sparked between the masters as they hastened to erect a shield, but too late. Caradan's own spell tore into them, lifting them high into the air and carrying all three of them, Kolta too, away into the darkness. The mist swallowed them and their wailing cries diminished, giving an indication of the distance he had hurled them.

Fortak, Phyxia, Ayla, and I remained. I peered at the gigantic Caradan. Thankfully the binding magic still burned within me, but I didn't feel like testing the control that I had over him.

"Yolanda, I'm sorry for what I did to you." He crossed to Ayla in two ten-feet strides. His night-black form writhed and morphed between human and wraith. "I can't bear this torment inside me. I miss you. Tell me you forgive me."

"Caradan," I said. "The elemental. Save the city."

"She's mine. I stay."

"No," I said, trying to appear strong while inside I wanted to pee myself. "Our bond demands you obey me. Destroy that creature."

He raised his maul-like arms above me. A powerful suction tugged me toward his seething cloud of a body—a promise of eternal blackness.

"Do not test your fragile bond," he said.

"Kill it for me...my lord," Ayla whispered.

My heart skipped and I choked for breath. Thank the Gods. She still lived.

Caradan said nothing, simply tapered into an arrow and arced high into the sky. He penetrated the firestorm of the elemental and vanished within its bulk. No sound from the real world reached us here in The Gray, but I imagined the elemental roaring with pain. It drew in on itself, twisting, contorting, desperate to evade the wraith that burrowed within.

I rushed to Ayla, fell beside her, and gathered her into my arms. Wicked purple welts covered her body and she twitched uncontrollably. I kissed her repeatedly. Her lack of response stabbed me like a dagger. A tear dripped from my face onto her lips.

Fortak watched me, his expression masked. I wanted to

damn him, curse him but no words could do my anger justice.

She stopped twitching. I gave her a gentle shake but she hung limp like a child's doll. I put my cheek to her mouth. Did she breathe? I couldn't tell past my own trembling. I held her tight, stroked her hair, and freed the strands stuck to her blood-streaked face. I prayed that she knew I was there.

Hold on, I beg you. Don't leave me.

The sky brightened as Caradan rapidly shredded the elemental. The fires in the city had diminished, but I had no cause to celebrate, not at the cost of Ayla.

Fortak whirled and grabbed Phyxia by her wrist, so hard I expected to hear her dainty bones break. She didn't flinch.

"This is your fault," he said. "You had this planned all along. Your kind disgusts me."

He withdrew a serpentlike blade from his robe, seized her from behind, and brought the blade to her throat. A thin bead of blood trickled down her flawless neck. Even then, she offered no resistance.

"Last chance," he whispered into one of her tall ears. "Unbind my elemental or I will slice off your head, inch by inch."

He panted rapid breaths and his nostrils flared, yet his blade on her throat was rock steady. She raised her head to look him in the eye. Gray flecks drifted calmly around her irises. Then her skin shimmered like a heat haze. It turned darker and then erupted into flame. I held my ground, but Fortak cried out and leaped back. His knife tumbled from his hand and he nursed his blistered arm. Her whole body blazed but she remained unharmed by the heat. Her long hair had transformed into a flaming torch, yet did not burn. Scorching heat radiated from the inferno of her body.

"What are you doing?" Fortak asked.

I jerked my gaze upward. The tattered remnants of the elemental spiraled down in a tight vortex around her and into her.

Fortak fell to his knees, his unburned hand reaching for her, his eyes wide and feral.

"You fool," he said. "You think you can consume that thing? I dare you. It will devour you from within and your death shall free it."

The man was completely delusional. If she lost that battle of wills then we all lost. His control had failed long ago and it was all too obvious that hers was failing too. Visions of Malkandrah gutted to rubble flashed before my eyes, its people incinerated and flocking to The Gray as angry revenants, forever haunting the ghostly ruins. I imagined the pitiful wailing of women and children in my head.

"And now I'll deal with you." Fortak had regained his footing and took a stride toward me, arm raised, fingers splayed. Incredible magic tore from his fingers and enveloped Ayla and me.

A low, rumbling moan sounded from everywhere at once. Something shoved me from her and I winced as her head thudded against the oozing, brackish ground that mirrored the plaza cobbles in the real world. I came up onto all fours, staring into the face of a demonic creature as it materialized above her still body, lying atop her like some perverted tantric ritual. It bellowed at me, drenching me in hot, slimy drool.

Kristach! An Incuba.

Then it drank from her life force, breathing deep and sucking it from pustules that formed all over her skin before bursting with sprays of gunk. The sparkling, purple substance spiraled up into the thing's mouth. The slurping, smacking noises made my stomach lurch.

I tried futilely to shove it aside, but even incorporeal, it remained as firm as a rock. My *Dispels* had no effect. More potent spells were impossible—my gut growled, empty of magic. I pummeled it with my fists. It paid me no attention.

No more. It ended now.

I snatched my dagger from its sheath and advanced on Fortak.

"Stay back," he said.

Not a chance. I marched up to him and glanced at Phyxia one step behind him.

The last of the elemental disappeared into her. Her gaze met mine and the streaks in her irises whirled faster than I had ever seen. Pain tortured her face, distorting her timeless beauty. Blisters etched along her arms. What had she done?

"All that is left is your choice," she whimpered.

Time slowed to a crawl. She'd used the same phrase in the plaza earlier. No, then she had said "choices." My heart thumped in my chest and blood surged into my brain, delivering clarity. My gaze dropped to the Ashtar dagger in my hand.

Choose.

Kill Phyxia and with her the elemental: the city is saved but Fortak lives and my darling Ayla dies.

Kill Fortak: Ayla lives but the elemental breaks free and the city is consumed.

Choose.

Phyxia: I had doubted her, let her down. She'd tried to tell me all along. I'd been too dim to understand. Grief stabbed at me. Tears poured down my cheeks. My mentor, my first love, how could I live without her enigmatic ways and heart-stopping beauty?

Ayla: brave, fearless, special in a way it had taken me ages to realize. So giving yet demanding of little in return.

The city—my city: the lives, hopes, and dreams of tens of thousands. Their right to live superseded any individual. I had sworn an oath to protect them. Everything I stood for demanded I save them.

Choose.

Still locked in an unreal slow motion, I took a single stride forward, my trembling hand gripping the dagger. I brought my other hand to bear, to hold it still.

I looked for the last time into Phyxia's incredible eyes. I sought wisdom in her words, certain that her augury had foreseen all that had happened.

Could you harm a friend? If much depended on it?
Let go of what cannot be.

Did that mean her or Ayla? It meant both. Killing Phyxia

condemned Ayla to death. Kill Fortak and neither friend are harmed, but the city is destroyed.

There was no choice.

I had a vision of being in this dilemma once before in Caradan's bedchamber. I blinked away tears and plunged the dagger up to the hilt into Phyxia's heart.

I'd killed the two women I loved most in this world.

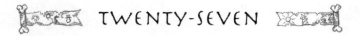 TWENTY-SEVEN

There'd been a flicker of a smile on Phyxia's face right before she and the elemental were vaporized in a single blast of hot air. My hands flew up to protect my head, but there was no fire.

Sobs shook me and I ached to my bones with loss. I'd killed Phyxia. I'd actually done it. There was so much that I had wanted to know about her. I'd lost that chance forever. For all her talk of choices, I really hadn't had one. I'd done what had to be done.

Damn everything. I didn't care. All I wanted was to hold Ayla's body for the final time, etch her features into my mind so that I would never forget her.

She was gone. I lurched about in the mists that had swirled back into the empty space. She'd been right here. To my left, Caradan returned, this time as a man. I ignored him, Fortak too. Ayla was nowhere to be found. Had the Incuba consumed her? Had she been taken to The Deep with Phyxia?

I threw my head back and howled.

"Lak, must you claim everything I hold dear?"

I stormed back to Fortak, finding him cowering before a pack of shadowy wraiths. Caradan looked on, the curl of a grin on his face, and he smoothed his already-immaculate Guild robe. It was like their roles had become reversed.

The ethereal forms of the wraiths streamed behind them like cloaks, while their eyes burned like fire. I knew their color would be red, except there was no color in this forsaken place, just endless shades of gray. At times they edged closer, and Fortak groaned and writhed. I wished I could get pleasure from that, but all feeling had gone.

"Damn you both," I said. "What have you done with her body?"

Caradan crossed his arms. "I have done your bidding and the elemental is gone. Now fulfill your end of our bargain."

"I release you from the bond. Send me back. This place depresses me. It's over. It's all over."

"Not yet. We agreed to Fortak's death. Take up your blade and finish him."

I studied my dagger that lay on the ground, dripping with Phyxia's blood. I never wanted to see that thing again, and turned my back on it.

"You do it, Caradan. I choose to kill no more."

"*You* must take his life as a symbol of the new generation casting out the old," he said. "Let the Guild choose a new path."

"Kill him yourself and the symbolism runs deeper. You inspired him. Rectify your own failure."

"He killed your mother," Caradan said.

I whirled to face Fortak. No, that couldn't be true. Why hadn't she told me? The dagger gleamed in my peripheral vision. I took a step toward it.

"Why?" I screamed at him. "She was a staunch defender of the Guild. She...she was the only family I had left."

The wraiths tightened around him and he paled. I expected him to argue, but his face softened and his eyes pleaded with Caradan.

"Why did you have to tell him?" He reached for me. "Yes, yes, I killed your mother but she forced my hand. That was her big sacrifice, to keep me from claiming Caradan's power."

Caradan hissed.

I spat at Fortak. "She was superior to you in every way, and you knew it. Her noble act saved the city we all swore to protect, the city you betrayed."

"She was soft and full of ideals. She shouldn't have disobeyed me."

Caradan laid a hand on my shoulder and I jumped.

"Kill him for all that he has taken from you," he said.

I looked up at his determined expression, then at Fortak's clenched face and narrowed eyes.

"I deal with the dead to protect the living," I said. "I will not kill even him."

Caradan nodded and approached Fortak, looming over him.

"We're kindred spirits," Caradan said. "I killed my wife and you your daughter…"

Wait. What?

"Rather touching that the boy won't put you out of your misery. He should have, because I won't. It's time you shared my endless suffering."

He snapped his fingers and the wraiths dived upon Fortak. They made no sound. His skin shriveled and flaked at their touch.

"I'm sorry." Fortak wheezed between his wailing, shrieks so primal that blood sprayed from his nose and throat. "I tried…to keep you…safe."

Flesh and muscle sloughed from his bones. I forced myself to watch the horrific sight though I wanted to turn away. His legs gave way and he fell onto his side. In seconds, his hair frizzled and crumbled. His eyeballs shriveled and turned to dust in their sockets. Finally, his desiccated body imploded and toppled into a heap.

Gods, I was descended from this man? He murdered my mother. I glanced once more at the heap of dust and bones licked clean by the wraiths, then pitched forward into blackness.

I choked, my mouth full of ash and blood. I attempted to roll over but something heavy pinned my legs. Pain lanced through them. Unable to breathe, I gasped and hacked. When I opened my eyes, the light from Solas above was blinding after the gloom of The Gray, and the sky an incredible, clear green.

So I wasn't dead.

"He's over here," Kolta said from somewhere to my right. "Hurry."

I tried to call out but could only cough up ash and phlegm.

Hands grabbed my body and something soft slid under my head. The heavy weight scraped across my right leg. I yelped.

"Careful." Kolta stared down at me with his bug eyes, his face black and marred by oozing scratches.

The crushing weight eased. Several hands pushed and pulled me to my feet, and I found myself standing with Kolta and Semplis in the ruins of a building. It leaned precariously and wide cracks snaked across its charred walls.

"I thought Caradan had killed you both. It's as good to see you now as it was in The Gray." I shook Master Semplis's hand. "Thank you."

He nodded and started to speak several times before settling on "Sorry."

Kolta slapped me on the back. "I knew you'd do it, my boy."

I hung my head. "Ayla's dead. It's over. The elemental, Phyxia, Fortak, Caradan, all gone."

The bones of the building groaned and it settled a few inches.

"We have to move," Semplis said. "Before it collapses on us."

My right leg gave way under pressure and I stifled a cry, putting all my weight on my left. Both men leaned in to support my arms on their shoulders. We limped away from the ruins.

Little remained of Market Plaza. Rubble marked its original perimeter, and streets in all directions had been incinerated. Wisps of smoke spiraled into the sky. The clock tower had completely collapsed and only a single wall remained from the once-formidable tax building. Corpses littered every free space, burned to a crisp.

A sorrowful keening came from all around as people wandered aimlessly through the carnage, their shoulders drooped, clothes torn and burned. At intervals they paused to study a body at their feet. They either shook their head and moved on or fell to their knees to clutch a dead loved one. Some did so in silence, while others rocked it in their arms and wailed or sobbed.

My city had reached its lowest point. I had given up everything for this. Ayla and Phyxia were gone, and all around me had been laid waste.

A mother clutched a charred child to her bosom. Tears poured down her face like rain on a window. She said nothing, did nothing, simply held it, stroking its head, seeming not to notice that hair came away with every movement of her hand. What could I say to her? Sorry for your loss but at least we won the war?

I shuffled away through the rubble. The last thing she needed to see was a necromancer. In time she might seek us out to aid the spirits of her dead loved ones, but not yet. Too soon.

Kolta lay a hand on my shoulder. "We should return to the Guild."

"You go. I want to be alone."

"There's nothing you can do here. Come with us."

I pulled free. "No, I don't want to hide. I want to see everything that happened here today. I want to revel in the sorrow. I want to remember."

"Don't be a fool," Master Semplis said, but his words carried no sting. He looked old and frail. He and Kolta exchanged a glance and then he nodded once.

"Don't linger too long," Kolta said, and the two masters left.

Dogs chased each other through the carnage. One stopped nearby to chew on a still-smoking corpse. I hurled a stone at it. It growled and bared its teeth but moved on. The stench of burned flesh made me want to puke. At the sound of splintering timber and crashing bricks, I turned to see one of the last plaza buildings collapse into a heap, kicking up dust to merge with the smoke.

A tiny girl came out of nowhere, her face and dress black with soot, but she looked unharmed. She approached and craned her neck to peer up at me. Her face was sticky with tears. The poor thing couldn't be more than five solars old. She wrapped her arms around my lower body, holding me tight.

She seemed naive as to who I was. Had her parents never told her to fear the Guild, or was I simply less of a threat than all that had happened? I chose to hope for the former. With Fortak gone, I was determined to make sure that everyone learned of what the Guild had done to save the city. I never wanted people to fear and hate us again. This event should unite us, make us stronger.

I peeled the girl from my legs. Her tiny hand reached up and wriggled into mine. How could I refuse such an innocent face? I took her with me while I stumbled through the plaza.

A heap of smoldering timber marked where the stage had stood. I came across an old woman and was convinced it was she that I had pulled from the jostling crowds earlier that day. It seemed so long ago. What were the odds of meeting the same person from the thousands that had filled the plaza? She smiled and raised an unsteady hand, her trembling fingers pointing to the north. The devastation looked the same there as everywhere, and I didn't understand her gesture. She nodded and pointed again.

I shrugged and limped off in that direction, still leading the girl who kept close to my side. We caught up with a man wearing a scuffed, red leather tunic and black pants, though he had lost his chain mail and weapon. I hesitated, peering at him through the smoky haze. He slouched wearily and didn't appear a threat, and when I advanced, he raised his left arm straight out from his side and pointed to my right. His gaze never left mine.

What did these people want me to see?

I turned to the right and shuffled around a gruesome heap of bodies that a handful of men had created. I tried to give them a wide berth but one of them stepped in front of me. I pulled the girl close, ready to push her behind me if the man started anything.

"Thank you," he said.

"What?"

"We saw what you did."

I stared at his back for a long moment, interrupted by a woman who appeared silently at my side. I jumped. Her hair was badly burned, her arms covered in scratches and burns. Little of her clothing remained and she had wrapped a blanket around herself.

"Is this child yours?" I said.

She smiled at the girl but shook her head. Then she opened her closed fist to reveal crushed feresens petals. In a swift motion she sprinkled the purple flowers over my head and they cascaded over my robes.

"Go," she whispered and pushed me onward. "Belaya bless you."

The girl and I continued past the growing pile of corpses. Others had returned to the plaza with shovels and barrows, and that made me proud of my people.

Then I faltered. What cruel trick made me think Ayla sat on the brick pile ahead? I blinked furiously and my pulse raced. The young woman had shocking white hair, and she chatted to a couple of men as if today were any ordinary day. *Damn you, Lak, don't make me hope.*

No matter what you believe, always believe in her.

What did that mean, Phyxia? Since accusing Ayla of spying I had always believed in her.

The seated woman turned. Her violet eyes flashed in the sunlight. Oh Gods!

I lurched forward onto my bad leg and pain tore through it. I cried out and stumbled to the cobbles, grazing my knee.

"Ayla!"

Unable to get back up, I dragged my broken body across

the ground, the little girl at my side. Ayla leaped up and ran toward me, throwing herself to the ground so that we met on our knees in a crushing embrace. She still smelled of lavender, whereas I smelled of death with a hint of feresens. I put my hands on her cheeks and wanted to look into those exotic eyes that I had grown to love, but she had other plans. She slid her arms from my back to my neck, leaned in, and pressed her lips to mine, kissing me over and over, squealing between each wonderful touch. Then she settled down into a lingering kiss and the world faded. All that existed were our hot lips and tongues, and our hands stroking each other's skin and hair. Finally, reluctantly, we pulled apart.

I dabbed at a tear trickling down her face. "You're alive. The lochtars…"

"I don't know. I don't remember. I woke covered in cling spirits. And…something else."

"What do you mean?"

She touched her belly. "The ball of magic you taught me? I feel it growing, but there's a different energy alongside it. It's not the same. I can't describe it."

"Don't worry. I can explain it to you, but not now."

A crowd had gathered around us. Men and women clung to each other and smiled. Hope flashed in their eyes. Ayla helped me to my feet. The girl's tiny hand slipped into mine once more. Ayla shot me a querying glance, then winked at the girl.

A shudder ran through me. It was if she had been sent to guide me. What an omen for a bright future that a little lost girl had helped a necromancer. I leaned heavily on Ayla and the three of us departed the plaza.

Finally, we left behind the burned and broken streets and moved into the untouched city. It was a relief to return to some semblance of normality among the stores and houses, and I took a deep breath of fresh air.

At the base of the northern river bridge we came across a closed carriage bearing the royal crest. A dozen High Guard soldiers had gathered around it.

"It's him," said one. "He *is* alive."

Three of them stepped forward, blocking the way with their polearms.

"Come with us," a gruff voice said, and the man directed us to the carriage.

What now?

The carriage suspension dipped and the Crown Prince stepped out. His face had been newly washed and someone had scrubbed the worst of the soot from his green, brocaded shirt and leggings. A heavy pendant hung from a chain about his neck outside of his shirt, and several of his fingers bore jeweled rings. The boy looked tired. There was no sign of the steward.

"How can I help...Your Highness?" Disconcerting how one so young could make me nervous.

"You are the necromancer who stood against the Prime Guildmaster?"

My stiff muscles unwound. He wasn't here to arrest me then. I studied him without appearing to stare. He hadn't fled to his palace and I admired that. I dipped my head in respect.

"Yes, Your Highness. He is dead."

He nodded. "Will that fire elemental return?"

"No, Your Highness. Caradan is likely gone too."

"Then we and the city hold you and your allies as our saviors."

He removed a sprig of feresens from his buttonhole and handed me the purple flowers. I accepted them, noting their wilted, singed state, even now symbolic of the great city of Malkandrah.

"Your deeds will not go unrewarded," he said, as if reciting a rehearsed speech. "We think the Prime Guildmaster ruined the reputation of your Guild."

His deep blue eyes looked to me for a reply. I had nothing intelligent. "Yes, Your Highness."

"We hope it can be set to rights. The city will hear of your acts today. Your young age inspires us for the future."

I bowed. "Thank you, Your Highness."

"You are hurt," he said as if noticing for the first time.

"You must ride with us."

Was it wise to decline the Crown Prince? Come to think of it, was he now our King? The coronation hadn't actually taken place and yet undoubtedly the steward was dead. I had thought little of this boy, seen only from afar, a mere shadow behind the steward. I too had great hopes for our future.

I squeezed Ayla's hand. "Thank you, but we will walk. I want to remind myself how wonderful our city is."

He dipped his head toward me—the Crown Prince to a necromancer. I returned the gesture and he stepped back into the carriage. The guards let the three of us pass onto the bridge.

I'd never faced all twelve masters alone. Alone in the dim hallway of the Guild, I patted my hair to make sure nothing stood on end. My skin most likely glowed pink after the hours I'd spent scrubbing away the sweat, blood, and soot, and shaving every blade of stubble from my face. I knocked loudly and smoothed my new robe for the tenth time.

At the instruction to enter, I limped into the masters' sitting room, trying hard not to gawk like a nervous apprentice or stare at the rare book collection stretching along one wall. Couches and armchairs clustered cozily around a sunken fire pit, in which burning logs crackled and spat. I'd hoped never to see open flames for a long time.

All eyes were upon me.

Kolta grinned, then swigged on his bottle of beer. Wampor appeared almost crazy, his wayward hair sticking out in all directions, and his narrow eyes scanned me up and down. Begara hastily drained the liquor from his goblet and would not meet my gaze. I turned to Master Semplis as the eldest, but his expression was impossible to read, his mouth askew. The others I knew little about, some of them not even their names, but I saw respect, weariness, and excitement in their faces.

Semplis gestured to the armchair opposite him, and I sat, thankful of the chair arms on which to lay my fidgeting hands.

"As a group," Semplis said, "we thought it important to meet with you in all haste. Though only a day has passed, it is important that we make our considerations known in an expedient—"

Petay growled. "This isn't a time for speeches."

Semplis shot him a glare. "The Guild is, of course, extremely grateful for your brave, expedient actions in this terrible matter, and—"

"If only someone had listened to you, lad," Petay said. "We had no inkling what the Prime Guildmaster was up to."

"Why would we?" one of the younger masters asked. "Our leader, of all people—"

"Let's leave Fortak out of this," Semplis raised his voice.

Begara sat on the edge of the group, his head bowed. I had no sympathy for his awkwardness, after nearly sending me to my death with Babbas. I had since found out that he had been the only master to join Fortak and the Covenant. Frankly, I was surprised he had retained his rank. I guess he had attempted to redeem himself in the plaza.

"It's true," Semplis said, addressing me once more. "We should have paid heed to your warnings, and we are eternally thankful that you chose to continue your investigations without our assistance. Your tenacity is admirable, and we wish to make amends for something that should have taken its course a long—"

"Lak, take us now and save our tortured ears from your speeches." Kolta slammed his beer bottle onto a side table. "Reward the boy already."

I looked from one master to another. This wasn't at all what I'd expected. It all seemed so informal and argumentative for a Masters' Council. Is this how they always made Guild decisions? I couldn't imagine Fortak allowing such banter.

Semplis reached down and retrieved a neatly folded stack of material. My heart skipped as I stared at the robe marked with runes and flecked with silver and purple. He stood and I leaped to my feet.

"From here on you are Maldren, Master Necromancer of

our Guild." He offered them ceremoniously across the fire to me.

I accepted them with the care I would a rare tome or an Iathic antique.

"I… Thank you, Master. I am deeply honored."

Kolta chuckled. "Try them on then."

I slipped out of my plain black robe. My hands trembled as I put on the new master's robe over my shirt and trousers, very conscious of everyone's stares. I studied the ancient runes decorating the collar, waist, and hem.

This had been a very long time coming. Semplis was right about that. Fortak had single-handedly kept me from my promotion all these solars, but with good reason. I'd been cocky and foolish. Now I truly felt worthy of the rank.

I still didn't know what to make of him being my grandfather. Had he been so unforgiving, so hard on me because of that? He'd told me that he'd been trying to keep me safe. Like he had my mother before he killed her? I rubbed my nose. He *had* tried to keep me innocent of his depraved plans, that much was true, but beyond that he'd failed me as family. I scanned the circle of men before me, every one of them smiling. Even Begara looked happy.

This was where I belonged. This was my family.

"Please sit," Semplis said.

Kolta thrust a goblet of Akra into my hand. I took a long swallow and savored the burn in my throat.

"Our apologies that this important ceremony did not take place in the more traditional environment of the dome, before all of your peers, but there is another matter of which we must speak. We have deliberated long into the night on this matter only—"

"More brevity," Petay said.

Semplis sighed. "We find ourselves without a Guildmaster for the first time in thirty-three solars. As the charter dictates, we took a vote upon the successor."

And he had won, I had no doubt. Gods help the poor apprentices. They'd have had more fun under Kolta's leadership.

"We chose you," Semplis said.

Lak and all his demons!

Goblet to my lips, I spat the Akra back out. My attempt to speak ended up with me coughing and choking on the strong liquor. I sounded like Fortak.

"Did you have to do that while he was drinking?" Kolta scolded Semplis.

After spluttering and wheezing, I finally managed to talk.

"Me?" Now I sounded like a mouse.

"We forgot what the people really need from us," Kolta said. "Fortak wanted to rule by awe and fear and none of us stood against him. Except you, my boy."

"We forgot how to serve," Wampor said, "and we cared more about prestige and weaving a mysterious cloak around us. Lassira tried to break us out of it."

It was strange to think that most of these men had known my mother well. I had a burning urge to learn more about her tenure at the Guild. In truth, more about her as a person. Kolta looked deep in his memories.

"We've had this argument all night," Semplis said. "Maldren, you represent a return to our old values: befriending the people, living among them, letting them see the Guild's human side. We could do no better than following your example."

"Hear, hear."

"Most of us are old, boy," Semplis said. "We need a fresh perspective. You won the vote. We ask that you accept the title of Prime Guildmaster."

I slumped back in the chair. All I wanted was to properly train Ayla. The old me would have said yes in an instant.

"No."

Eleven faces dropped. Kolta grinned.

"It is the greatest honor you could present," I said, "but I have much to learn. In this room are lifetimes of knowledge. It just needs to trickle down to the apprentices. No retaining secret lore for personal prestige."

Fancy that, me lecturing the masters.

"I've grown considerably these last fifteen days, but not enough. I deserve no more than the master rank. But one among us is a more tempered version of me, someone who taught me all I know."

I stared at Kolta, and everyone else did too. His grin faded and he shifted uneasily on the couch.

"Someone who takes equal credit in saving the city. Earlier you spoke reverently of my mother, so who better than her apprentice."

Semplis searched my face, then his frown eased and he nodded.

"Master Kolta shared second place in the vote. Do we have any naysayers to electing him as Prime Guildmaster?"

None spoke, and then Wampor let out a hoot.

"I accept," said Kolta, grinning once more.

The masters surged around him, giving congratulatory pats on the shoulder, shaking his hand, and passing around drinks.

I fingered the superior quality of my Guild robe and traced a finger along the runes.

Semplis stepped up behind my chair and leaned forward to whisper in my ear. "I cannot promise that others won't learn Ayla's secret. It is rather obvious. Only three of us know, and I'll do all I can to discourage speculation."

"I appreciate that. I don't want her labeled a monster." Her words, not mine.

"If she truly bridges both disciplines as the Lady Yolanda did, then we're going to have to face the truth of her training. Have you given any thought to that?"

"One thing at a time, please. We have no knowledge of…" I glanced at the others who were paying us no attention. "…their rituals. Let her become a necromancer first, and then it should be her choice."

He patted my shoulder and returned to the other masters drinking by the fire.

I reclined in my chair by the window, except this time I looked inward, surveying my new Guild room. Several sets of master's robes hung neatly in a tiny closet by the door. The desk looked bare with my meager belongings. A handful of dusty volumes huddled on one end of the bookshelf, left over from the previous occupant.

I stared at the empty dagger sheath lying on the desk. Last night, I dreamed of the gem in its hilt and woke convinced that it held her, that Phyxia's soul remained. I smiled to think of it now. As an immortal, surely she didn't need a gem. Did she live still?

Someone knocked on the door.

"A moment." I kicked dirty clothes under the bed. "Enter."

The door opened a crack and Ayla slipped inside, shutting it behind her. She breezed past me to perch on the bed, and the scent of lavender washed over me. She wore a green dress with a shawl draped across her shoulders. Her violet eyes twinkled along with her smile, and her pale hair cascaded over her shoulders. How had the other apprentices dealt with her, the only woman in the building and so startling to gaze upon?

"You shouldn't be found here after hours." I scowled and gestured to the door.

She rolled her eyes and stuck her tongue out the corner of her mouth. So much for the extent of my authority.

I shrugged. "How were classes your first sixday?"

"I'm settling in. The first day was tough. People wouldn't stop staring, even the masters."

"They'll get over it. Let me know if the boys give you grief."

"Are you kidding me?" She giggled. "They're scared witless. They think I'm your mother's ghost returned."

I rubbed my nose. "What makes them think that?"

Yolanda's ghost I could understand.

"Actually I'm honored," she said. "Know what Master Kolta said in class?"

She performed a great imitation. "Mistress Lassira was the most bloody powerful necromancer we ever had. You boys do as your told and do your homework, else you'll have her son and her bloody ghost visiting you in the dead of night."

We laughed. It was wonderful to have my old Ayla back, so confident and full of life.

Ayla caught me staring at her. "What?"

"You're beautiful."

Her cheeks flushed but a wicked gleam flared in her eyes.

"I've come to finish your lesson." She stood and sauntered toward me, fingers twirling her hair. "The one you began in the plaza."

"I'm afraid I don't recall." I hated that I grinned ear to ear.

"I understand how age dulls the memory, Master."

"Don't get flippant with me, apprentice."

She stopped inches from me, her eyes flicking rapidly between mine. Her breasts heaved under her dress, and my own breathing fell into the same rhythm, seemingly competing with my thumping heart to turn my insides numb. Her hands settled around my neck. I slipped my own around her waist and made room for her in the oversize armchair. This would never do—the apprentice leading the master.

My lips fell upon hers, finding them moist and welcoming. I pulled her closer, her body like fire even through our clothing. We explored each other's lips and mouths until we could breathe no more and broke apart.

She stroked my smooth jaw, traced a scar up my cheek.

"Being a necromancer will be fun. I hope we can find time to explore the undercity together." She grinned. "Smash up some more skeletons?"

"There'll be plenty more adventures. Don't worry."

I planted a light kiss on her nose and then turned to her luscious neck, making sure I left no spot unkissed. She arched her head back and uttered tiny murmurs at each touch.

Had Fortak known that day had been my birthday, the day at the dome when he'd given his grandson the most wonderful gift I could have dreamed of?

Ayla.

ACKNOWLEDGMENTS

Thank you to my editors, Lynnette Labelle (developmental editor), Michael (copyeditor), and Rich "The Wandering Editor" McDowell. Each of you made a substantial contribution to improving and polishing this book.

To Erin at EDHGraphics: Once again you have delivered a stunning cover that made my jaw drop. Bradley Cavin is the genius behind the creepy interior art, which makes me smile every time I see it. Your skulls and scrolls give the book that extra pizazz.

My eternal gratitude to my writer's group, beta readers and friends whose no-holds-barred critiques, comments and insight helped me deliver a deeper, richer story: Dan Jeffries, Deborah Reed, Lisa Shapiro, Leo Dufresne, Adrianna Lewis, Linda Mitchell, Kerry-ann Daniels, Kim Hicks, Lynn Nevala, Jeannie Holbrook and Cristie Poole. I'm sure I'm forgetting someone, and if so, feel free to set the soul wraiths on me!

Thank you to my wonderful wife, Tamara, for continuing to support my writing addiction. I think I owe you a trip to Paris.

Finally, thank you, dear reader, for spending your precious time reading my book. I hope I made you tremble and shudder, but also smile and laugh somewhere along this grim journey. Please forgive me for any nightmares you may have regarding skeletons and ghouls!

OTHER BOOKS BY GRAEME ING

OCEAN OF DUST

Can Lissa unravel the secret of the dust before it's too late?

Fourteen-year old Lissa is snatched from her home and finds herself a slave on a trading ship traveling on a waterless ocean of nothing but gray dust. A feisty, curious and intelligent girl, her desire to explore the ship earns her the hatred of the cruel first officer, Farq.

Fascinated by the ocean of dust, Lissa becomes embroiled in its mysteries, sensing things that the crew cannot, while cryptic whispers in her head are leading her toward a destiny linked to the dust itself. Only one man aboard can help her make sense of her new talent, but can she trust him? All is not as it seems, and she must unravel the clues before it's too late.

When a sinister plot casts her adrift on the barren ocean, her best friend is left in the hands of the treacherous crew. Everything hinges upon her courage, quick wits, and her ability to master her new talent.

ABOUT THE AUTHOR

Graeme Ing engineers original fantasy worlds, both YA and adult, but hang around, and you'll likely read tales of romance, sci-fi, paranormal, cyberpunk, steampunk or any blend of the above.

Born in England in 1965, Graeme moved to San Diego, California in 1996 and lives there still. His career as a software engineer and development manager spans 30 years, mostly in the computer games industry. He is also an armchair mountaineer, astronomer, mapmaker, pilot and general geek. He and his wife, Tamara, share their house with more cats than he can count.

Graeme loves to hear from readers:

Website: http://www.graemeing.com
Twitter: @GraemeIng
Facebook: https://www.facebook.com/GraemeIngAuthor

Subscribe to Graeme's newsletter to be informed of new releases: http://bit.ly/subscribe-graemeing-newsletter

If you enjoyed this book, please leave a review to help other readers. Thank you.

Made in the USA
San Bernardino, CA
28 June 2015